RAPTOR BLOOM

RAPTOR BLOOM

A NOVEL

Thomas Belisle

LUMINARE PRESS

WWW.LUMINAREPRESS.COM

Luminare Press
442 Charnelton St.
Eugene, OR 97401
www.luminarepress.com

LCCN: 2020902162
ISBN: 978-1-64388-323-6

Dedicated to my family

Definitions

Raptor: A beast of prey that hunts and kills
Bloom: Appearing unexpectedly, without warning

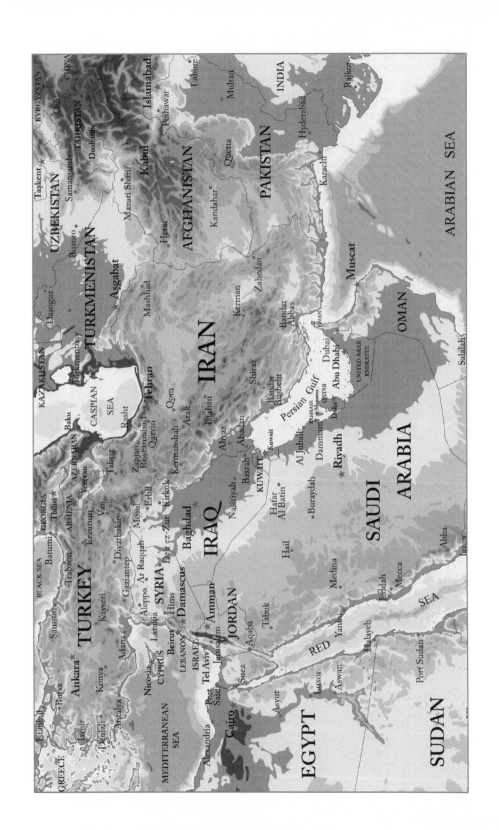

The Middle East

Chapter 1

t was the darkest part of the night, still a few hours away from astronomical twilight in the airspace over Turkey. The stark beauty of the environment that enveloped him always amazed the seasoned fighter pilot. His jet took him above the dirty surface layers of air, the brown haze, the gray-and-white clouds. There was only a sliver of moon visible to him, and a hundred thousand pinpricks of light from stars billions of miles away. The view calmed him somewhat. It relaxed him, gave him some inner peace. He knew that the calm would not last.

The jets streaked along at thirty thousand feet, racing through the thin, frigid air at a little over 550 miles per hour. The flight of four dark gray fighter bombers blended into the night's blackness, amorphous shapes against the starlit sky. Slightly behind and to the left of the lead aircraft, the soft glow of the red and green wingtip lights gave a visual reminder of the other jets accompanying him. The lights were only a slight contrast to the white stars.

Inside the cockpit of his twin-engined swept-wing jet, the muted green glow of the instruments cast eerie reflections off the canopy glass. The combat pilot looked over his shoulder and could just barely see his teammates in the distance, a mile away in their finger-four formation. He knew they were doing the same thing he was doing. They were watching him visually, and on their radar screen. They also used their jet's powerful radar to watch for other things, some not so friendly.

The positive-pressure flow of nearly pure oxygen coursed through the specially designed life support tube from his jet's oxygen-generating system. The air was dry and carried a distinctive after-taste into his mouth and throat. He was used to it after several thousands of hours in fighter aircraft. The low hum of the engines could be heard even with his helmet on—almost like the white-noise he liked to use in his bedroom to help him sleep. No sleeping today.

He constantly scanned the array of his glass multifunction displays for assurance of the beast's health—its readiness to inflict pain where it was needed most. He smiled inside his oxygen mask. All was as it should be. The beast was, at least at this point, ready to follow the commands of the master who was piloting it. For now, there was no apparent threat, nothing that would get in his way, nothing to try and stop him from doing what he intended to do.

The pilot was not alone in the relative silence of his warbird. In the rear cockpit, his weapons systems officer was also busy, checking fuel consumption, weapons status and the aircraft's electronic warfare and infrared sensors, and closely tracking the flight path. He was thinking about the target—and his responsibility to ensure the target coordinates were updated with the latest data from his source on the ground. Once that was done, the GPS system in the tail kits attached to the bombs would do the rest, guiding them with pinpoint accuracy to their ultimate destination.

The circuitous route to their target was carefully planned. The aircraft remained in the safety of Turkish skies for most of the flight, flying close to the southern border to mask their true mission from the country whose airspace they were about to violate. Syrian air defense monitors were always searching for intruders crossing into their sovereign territory. If they picked up the movement of the strike force near their border, it would hopefully look routine to them, like just another group of aircraft heading toward the big Turkish air base a few miles inland from the Mediterranean Sea, near Adana.

Their safety would not be assured for long once they entered Syria and began the most critical part of their mission. Find the target—kill the target. But they had some insurance they all hoped they wouldn't need. Two electronic warfare aircraft were teamed with the Air Force fighters, each carrying powerful jamming pods and anti-radiation missiles to eliminate any threatening Syrian surface-to-air missiles. Even *with* that insurance, the combat-hardened pilots didn't expect this mission to be a cakewalk. Lieutenant Colonel Alec "Ace" Black knew that combat always carried a risk that things might not go exactly as planned. Most of the time, things didn't.

Chapter 2

One Month Earlier

The screams coming from the small village outside the Syrian town of Idlib were a clear indication that something was terribly wrong. Most of the small stone-and-wood-framed homes there appeared almost deserted, their occupants corralled into the central market area. The huddled group of terrified young women had been separated from their families. Across from them in the formerly peaceful outpost, the men stood shoulder to shoulder as well-armed groups of Black Dawn warriors methodically pulled the fittest young men, one by one, away from the rest. The process was always the same.

Abdul al-Salaam had repeated his violent recruitment campaign again and again. He knew that healthy young men were the lifeblood of his small army of twelve hundred warriors. They were split into fighting-sized subcells, each occupying strategic locations to control the territory that they had at least temporarily conquered. That territory was subsequently subjected to the harshest interpretation of Sharia law, per Abdul's direction. It was fundamental to his desire to unite the population under his radical brand of Islam. But occupation had a price, always paid in blood. Brutal combat between radical rebel groups resulted in horrific wounds that few survived. As a result, Abdul was in constant need of men to fill his ranks after battlefield attrition took its heavy toll.

The culling process was well underway in Idlib. The black-bearded jihadi leader knew the secret to gaining total cooperation from new subjects. His approach was practiced hundreds of times, refined in its cruelty. When it came to replacing men lost in battle, resistance to Abdul was futile—and the consequences tragic. Entire families were butchered by Black Dawn warriors for refusing to relinquish their sons to the jihadi leader. Over the course of the day, sixteen new recruits were brought into Black Dawn's army.

The Black Dawn leader had been consistently successful in moving his radical cause forward—and in staying alive. His longevity relied upon a faithful following who were ready to give their lives to protect him, and secrecy to keep his location hidden. Loyalty among his followers was most important. If he suspected any of them were wavering in his holy cause, he eliminated them.

Abdul al-Salaam didn't believe in luck. He trusted Allah to protect him. Nonetheless, he was an extremely careful man, almost to the point of paranoia. He knew that he was near the top of the lengthy American terrorist kill list—high-value targets, as they were known. He also knew full well that even a very clever man could not survive for long without being targeted and vaporized by the most powerful military force on earth. Consequently, he moved constantly, never spending more than a day at one location, never repeating a visit to a home he invaded for the night. He trusted no one but his younger brother, Basim. After all, blood was a bond that couldn't be broken. Blood was everything.

Inside the confiscated home of the local village leader, Abdul finished the meager meal that had been prepared for him—hummus and flatbread, some fruit, and of course, shai, the ubiquitous sweet hot tea. It was the best food the village had to offer.

"Basim," he called out. "I need to speak with you about our upcoming plans." He sipped from the small copper cup of steaming herbal tea as he looked across the crude wooden table toward his brother, who had just entered the room.

"Yes, my brother, I have them here," he responded, reaching into his weathered leather satchel. He produced a faded blue-and-white hardcover book, similar in size to his leather-bound Quran. The small book's sun-bleached pages were in Basim's own handwriting and foretold the upcoming plans.

Basim al-Salaam had an immense responsibility to keep the jihad alive, which meant keeping Abdul alive. He planned the overnight stops very carefully, up to a week in advance. Future locations were known only to himself and never electronically transmitted. They were documented *only* in his sacred notebook. Abdul knew that electronic eavesdropping was rampant by those who spent most of their day looking for any shred of information needed to plot his demise. It was only at the last minute that the following day's stop was made known. Even then, only small shreds of information were revealed, making it difficult, if not impossible, for any single person besides Abdul and Basim to know where they would be next.

"I know that the Americans are hunting for me. I believe they have been trying to track me. Their drones are everywhere."

"They will never find us, Abdul. We have the advantages of our secrecy and constant movement. By the time the infidels learn anything useful and try to act on it, we are far from where they believe us to be."

"Regardless of that, we must be extremely careful. Nothing must get in the way of our holy promise to unite Syria under our true cause. Islam demands it!"

Basim nodded.

Abdul looked intently at his brother and gently rested his scarred hand on his shoulder. "You are my rock, and I know that Allah guides your hand. I trust you with my life. We will do great things in the name of our holy cause."

"*Inshallah*—if Allah wills it. Our prayers will be answered."

———————•———————

As dawn broke in the village outside Idlib, it was time to move on. The terrorist leader moved his forces to the outskirts of Azaz, a large town that was sure to provide plenty of expendable men for their upcoming battles. As his jihadi warriors infiltrated the town, their eyes scanned the streets, searching for new recruits. For some young men, serving Abdul actually offered a better life than living in poverty. In spite of the battlefield risk, at least they knew they would be able to fill their stomachs. A few actually saw it as their religious duty to support Black Dawn's holy cause. By early evening, ten new members were conscripted.

The celebration began for Abdul's men. Their allegiance to him on the Syrian battlefields was generously rewarded with an opportunity to satisfy their insatiable lust and let off some steam. In the town's central market square, young women were gathered for entertainment. The frightened group was rushed by the battle-hardened combatants in a free-for-all. They were roughly pulled from their families, screaming as they were dragged away—some to the limited privacy of a small home, and others simply around a wall, a fence, or out in the open. The savages were especially brutal in their desire for sexual fulfillment. Any resistance resulted in an often-fatal beating. None of the village men attempted to interfere, afraid of the consequences.

As one terrified woman was dragged away, the hijab covering her head was abruptly pulled off, and the thin, veiled niqab fell away. She cried out and looked directly at Basim. He gazed back at her and was quite taken with the beautiful eyes that seemed to pierce his soul like a sharp dagger.

"Stop what you are doing," he abruptly commanded the man who roughly dragged her toward the door of a small house.

The burly warrior whipped around, his face contorted in rage. Who dared to challenge him? "She's mine. Get your own," he snapped back before suddenly recognizing the face of the man who had confronted him. "A thousand pardons, Basim," he said, bowing in absolute submission. He immediately released his grip on the woman. "I didn't know she was yours. A thousand pardons—please, take her."

Basim stepped forward and drew the pretty young Sunni woman aside, away from the offender. He was not sure why he did what he did. Something deep inside had moved him to intervene. It had been two years since his wife's death, and during that time, he had had no relations with a woman. Yet something about her eyes had weakened his willpower. *What am I doing?*

He gently led the young beauty aside. "What is your name, young one?"

"Fatima," she sobbed, not sure what was to come next.

"Do you know who I am?"

She nodded, staying silent. The terrified look in her wide eyes expressed the fear she had about what was likely to happen to her in the next few moments. She expected to be beaten first and then sexually assaulted, as she had been similarly treated before by marauding groups of rebels. She didn't know that this time, things would be a little different.

Basim led her away, finding the privacy of one of the many homes Abdul had commandeered. In the darkness of the dwelling, he tried to calm her. He talked with her softly and assured her that he was not evil and would not harm her. Fatima's racing heartbeat began to slow as she realized that perhaps she wasn't going to be brutalized by this man.

He asked her about her family and then about her life in Syria. He then spoke of what he had been through as a faithful follower of Islam and the tragic loss of his wife. Fatima saw in his eyes the sorrow he felt, the pain he still carried. Yet she knew that in the end, she would still have to submit to this man. But somehow, she saw in him a very different kind of man than any she had been subjected to in the past.

He asked Fatima to clean herself, to make herself presentable for him. She found a copper tub of water in the corner room of the home and did her best to get rid of the grime that had accumulated on her body since her last bath. She covered herself with a clean abaya, a robe-like dress that belonged to one of the women in the home. Walking back into the room, she looked at Basim.

"Go to the bedroom and wait for me," he said softly to her.

After a few minutes, he walked in. He was astounded at the beautiful, silky dark hair that fell across Fatima's shoulders. He gently pulled her to him and slowly began removing the abaya. He paused, awestruck at her naked beauty—her skin, flawless, the color of alabaster.

Fatima still expected the worst, and in the first moments, she believed her fears would be realized. Two years of abstinence was unleashed in a fury, his passion releasing all his pent-up desire and energy. She closed her eyes as he began. Basim was lost in euphoria, his brain spinning from the rush of sensual feelings he thought he had forever lost when his beloved wife had died. *Allah has blessed me again, with this chance meeting of a wonderful Sunni woman.*

As he lay beside her, he was again astonished at her beauty. He had not seen a woman this beautiful in years, at least not since his wife. As he prepared to leave the bed, Fatima cradled her arm around his waist and pulled herself close to him. Basim was touched that this woman would want him after what he had done. She had given all of herself, and somehow, the closeness he now felt to her was a feeling that he hadn't experienced in years. He drifted off to sleep with Fatima snuggled against him.

Before dawn, he awoke. He needed to remove Fatima from the house and safeguard her from any of the Black Dawn warriors who might take her for their own use. He would soon be leaving for the next overnight location, but he had to see her again. He knew he had broken his vow to Allah by sleeping with a woman who was not his wife. But his desire to see her prevailed against his better judgement. He asked her to meet him in a month, fifteen miles away near the town of Shaykh al-Hadid. For the first time, he had broken a sacred trust with Abdul. He had given up a future location where the Black Dawn leader would be.

"The next time I see you, wear some better clothes, clean yourself, use perfume, and make yourself presentable for me."

He handed her a fistful of dinars, knowing that she had no way to pay for the things he requested of her.

"Take this money and get what you need, everything that fits your beauty."

Fatima rushed to dress herself in front of him, putting on her old, ragged abaya. She could not believe what had happened, after what had been a night of sinful pleasure. She smiled and nodded her head in agreement. Did she agree from her desire to be with this powerful man again, or possibly from fear if she did not comply fully with his wishes?

"You are never to mention my name, nor that of my brother, Abdul," he warned as she was about to leave. "And, you must not tell anyone about where we will meet."

Fatima nodded and hastily departed for her home before the sun rose above the horizon.

Under his breath, Basim muttered, "I must see her again. Soon."

The feelings he had for Fatima were unexpected. He struggled a bit in his mind with what he had just done. He had taken a woman, a stranger, and had carnal pleasure. He felt ashamed for a moment. He wondered if what he had done was right in the eyes of Allah. Would he be punished for his actions? After all, he had been faithful to his religion for the two years since his wife had passed. Was it a sin to have fulfilled a need that he so desired, a need to become whole again as a man? He also wondered about giving up the one piece of information that he safeguarded with his life. She knew exactly where he and Abdul would be in a month. What was he thinking? Would she say anything to anyone that mattered?

The path to Shaykh al-Hadid was already plotted in his mind. He found Abdul stirring as the sun was breaking over the horizon. It was time to move again.

Chapter 3

Master Sergeant Joe Decker was growing weary of the dry, dusty landscape. He led his US Army Special Forces team in dispersed patrols across northwest Syria. They had been covertly inserted into the war-torn country three months earlier with very specific objectives. His team was directed to blend in with the rebel factions, adapting their appearance and behavior as much as possible. The United States did not want to call attention to the fact that it had its military forces on the ground in Syria. The organized but ill-equipped group of Syrians courageously battled for their freedom and were appreciative for any help the Americans could provide to counter the violence that Assad and Black Dawn were inflicting on the population. The Special Forces tactics, weapons and technology gave the rebel army at least a fighting chance to combat Assad's much more powerful forces.

Decker had been trying to track Abdul al-Salaam for months, but the jihadi leader's constant movement made setting a trap to eliminate him extremely difficult. Local villagers were very reluctant to provide information on his whereabouts, fearful of the consequences if they were discovered to have collaborated with the Americans. Every time the team got what appeared to be a solid lead, it evaporated in the blowing desert wind.

Almost four weeks had passed since the Black Dawn leader had terrorized the area around Azaz. Sergeant Decker and his team had heard the stories of Abdul's tactics and subsequent cruelty and had personally witnessed the evidence of the atrocities committed on people who never stood a chance to defend themselves.

What kind of animal does these things to another human being? thought Decker. *I'd love to get my hands around his throat, just once, and snuff the life out of this piece of human garbage.*

Decker cringed at the thought of how Black Dawn treated young girls, tearing away their innocence. He had two young daughters, and it made his stomach turn to think of anyone violating them. His rage would be unchecked and would take him to the ends of the earth to make the perpetrators suffer beyond any imagination.

As Decker and his team approached the outskirts of Azaz as part of a sector-by-sector sweep of potential terrorist hideouts, they separated to try to get the most out of their short visit and interact with as many villagers as possible. Luckily, a few of the seasoned soldiers spoke the particular dialect of the region, at least well enough to communicate. Decker's command of the local language was not the greatest, but he managed to get the basics of his message out.

"Has anyone seen Black Dawn? Have they heard of their whereabouts?" Decker had repeated these words again and again. The results were always the same—blank stares or the occasional negative head shake.

But the team knew that brutality only went so far. At some point, people might eventually cooperate if they had any hope at all for a better life, and maybe even peace, in a post-Assad, post–Black Dawn country.

Decker approached what appeared to be the central market area, just outside Azaz. He walked cautiously toward the stalls, littered with a meager sampling of fruits and vegetables. There were some scrawny chickens, and a few skinny goats fenced off from the splintered wooden food stalls. Small children played in the street amongst scattered pieces of garbage and other debris. In this poor area, most people had very little in terms of possessions. It was glaringly evident from their ragged clothes and ramshackle structures that pitifully served as their homes.

A pretty young woman caught his eye. She had removed the niqab, the veil covering her face, in order to smell the fruit she was hoping to purchase. She appeared different from other women perusing the stall contents. This young woman stood out from the rest. She was dressed better than any other woman around the market, her abaya clearly more decorative. Sergeant Decker cautiously approached her, knowing full well the prohibitions in an Islamic society of any public male-to-female contact. She stared at him for several seconds—unusual behavior for any Muslim woman.

As Decker got within a few feet of her, he sensed that he might actually be able to engage in a brief dialogue. He began conversing with her in the local language, a dialect that was commonly used by most of the local population.

"*As-salaamu alaikum*," he said to her.

She dropped her head to avoid further eye contact, looked quickly around, hesitated for a moment, and then responded, "*Wa alaikum assalaam.*"

Decker took his time, walking toward one of the isolated market stalls that had a variety of fruits and produce. He reached for the pomegranate in the basket in front of her. He picked it up and smelled it. "Is this ready to eat?" he said in English, testing her understanding.

She did not look at him but nodded. She understood. As she tried to turn away from Decker, he continued.

"The oranges are very ripe," he said, picking up the mandarin fruit.

She finally turned toward him, her veil now back in place over her face, only her beautiful eyes visible to Decker.

He turned his head, looking around and across the market. He was extremely careful, not wanting to be observed by any of the local village authorities or religious police.

"The children look very hungry. Is there enough food for them to eat in this place?" he asked.

Again, she responded with a shake of her head and told him that this was a poor village. There had been enough food to support the people, but it had been taken by a rebel group only a week prior.

Decker reached in his deep pocket and pulled out a handful of small candies. He enjoyed the wide smiles from children after he had given them treats while his team patrolled the Syrian countryside. After all, kids were kids, and all kids loved candy.

"Would the children like some candy?" he asked. "Will you help me give these to the village children?"

Decker knew from his experience in these poor parts of Syria that most of the time, handing out treats to children helped open up the lines of communication.

Fatima was at first reluctant to speak, but she had seen the kindness previously shown by American military members in other parts of the country. She had seen them try to clean up the contaminated water supply and rebuild other damaged critical infrastructure. The good things these foreigners had done helped make life better and safer for the Syrian people. In a few short minutes, she became slightly more comfortable with the soft-spoken Special Forces team leader.

"I cannot talk to you here," she said quietly. "But I will help make the children happy."

For the next thirty minutes, Decker walked the street, Fatima trailing slightly behind him, sharing the stash of treats with the raucous kids who quickly appeared out of nowhere and excitedly ran toward them. Decker was struck by their torn clothes, their emaciated faces, and the obvious filth that covered them. He was always saddened to see young kids living like this. It tugged at his heart knowing that in the United States, most children had so much more and didn't endure this kind of hardship.

But today, these poor Syrian children would be happy, at least for the moment. Their appearance didn't temper their apparent boundless energy and desire to enjoy a simple pleasure that they rarely got. As the children gained courage and ran up to him, Decker handed them the candy, a large smile on his face while doing so. Some of the youngest screamed with glee, running down the street with their hands full of treats. Fortunately, the supply of candy ran out about the same time as the kids disappeared. Decker headed over to a small goat stall, with Fatima following. When he was sure they were not being observed, he began asking Fatima about herself.

She was not completely sure why this American was so interested in her. What did he really want? She was somewhat fearful that she had already been spotted by other villagers talking with this man, with this American. She knew the penalty in the rigid Islamic culture for open displays of conversation, alone with a man. She glanced around, searching for signs that someone was watching her. No one was in sight. Her fear of being discovered talking alone with Decker subsided. She was calmed by his apparent gentleness. Emboldened by Decker's generosity to the children, she spoke of wanting a better life for the Syrian people. She explained that this was possible if they could ever free themselves from Assad's ruthlessness and utter failure to address the needs of the Syrian people.

"I dream of a day when I may be free from living in constant fear. I have seen so much violence and horror. I wonder if there truly is a God?" she said.

"There is a God," he said softly. "One who helps those who are faithful to their religion. Allah expects true believers to do the right thing—to fight injustice—to seek peace."

Fatima nodded. She smiled, and though it was hidden from Decker under her niqab, he could tell from the change in her eyes. She told him that she was leaving soon for the town of Shaykh al-Hadid to visit friends of her family. Decker was familiar with the western Syrian territory, and knew of the town. As they talked about her visit, the tone of her voice changed a bit as she laughed about American pop music—she loved it—and all the wonderful food that she believed was so plentiful in his country. She dreamed that someday, she would enjoy such a life.

As she became more open in her conversation with Decker, she indicated her dreams might soon be answered. She had met a prominent, wealthy man. Without any prompting from Decker, she indicated this man would see her again very soon, and perhaps her life would improve immensely. He might choose to take her away from her poverty, maybe take her as his wife.

Decker was careful, not wanting to probe too deeply. He wanted to avoid obvious questions that would tip off his real purpose in Syria. As he listened intently, Fatima inadvertently spoke Basim's name. She had forgotten the warning never to speak of him or his whereabouts.

The Special Forces team leader immediately recognized the name as one of the high-interest persons that the United States was desperately looking for—and wherever Basim was, Abdul al-Salaam was assuredly with him. Decker also knew that the town of Shaykh al-Hadid was only a short bus ride for Fatima. He briefly wondered about her safety. Like most Syrians, she would be just another abaya-clad woman moving through the countryside. The Syrian Army checkpoints were seemingly everywhere, and they would question why any Syrian woman was traveling alone. Hopefully, she would make it to her destination.

Decker wished her well, and headed off to rejoin the rest of his team. Later in the evening, he pulled the secure satellite phone from his pack, found a signal to the orbiting NSA communications satellite, and placed a call. Once he had passed his message, he ended his transmission and made immediate plans to move his team toward Shaykh al-Hadid. Once there, he would be on the alert for the Black Dawn leader to show his face. The town had just moved to the top of the US military high-value target locations.

Chapter 4

June 28, 2003
Two Hours Before the Combat Mission

The utter blackness of the night hung over the allied air base in Diyarbakir, Turkey. Lieutenant Colonel Alec "Ace" Black, the strike force leader, had little time to catch his breath since arriving in Turkey.

Once the encrypted message from the Special Forces Team in Syria had flashed forward to its final destination in the Pentagon, the execute order had been given to the Royal Air Force base at Lakenheath, England—and the opportunity to knock off one of the United States most wanted jihadis. The 494th Fighter Squadron was chosen for the honor to reduce the High Value Target list by one name, and they quickly launched toward their forward operating base in Turkey.

After a short rest, Black had begun the preflight checks on his lethal weapon system for his mission. His prep hadn't been much different from any other mission. But he knew the importance of leading the upcoming attack. It was all about sending a strong message to Syria that terrorists really had no place to hide. The United States was pretty good at reaching out and violently touching anyone at any place on the planet if the cause was right.

Alec Black grinned as he turned to his crew chief, Staff Sergeant Ray Davis, who handed him the aircraft forms.

"Thanks, Ray. How does my jet look?"

"I fixed a few minor maintenance items, but nothing to worry about. This baby is ready to fight."

Ace flipped open the sun-faded clear vinyl cover. He paged through the one-inch-thick binder that described the jet's health—its past performance, previous problems and their fixes, and completion of all weapons loading and servicing actions. The forms looked good.

He began his slow, focused walk around the warbird in the dim light of the parking ramp, flashlight in hand. The methodical system he used to check the jet's integrity was chiseled into his brain. He had done the process hundreds of times before. He was thorough, his eyes constantly looking for anything that wasn't as it should be. His fingers glided over the aircraft's cool metal skin—similar to the way he stroked his border collie back home, assuring it that all was good. It was as if his caress of the inanimate fighting machine would help guarantee his safety once he left the bounds of earth.

"Ray, are you sure this bird is going to get me all the way to the target and back?" he chided Davis, a friendly jab to one of the most trusted airmen in his life. His crew chief was the guy that made his mission possible, and potentially his survival.

"Yes, sir," Sergeant Davis responded. "But you'll have to actually put some effort into it. After all, the jet can't do everything," he said with an equally wide grin. The razor-sharp airman took great pride in his job, making sure that his squadron commander's aircraft not only looked better than any of the others but performed better too.

Each F-15E Strike Eagle in tonight's mission carried the same deadly ordnance guaranteed to kill the target—two Tritonal explosive-filled five-hundred-pound bombs. The dark green steel-encased weapons were each configured with bolt-on tail kits that gave the otherwise free-falling "dumb bombs" pinpoint accuracy, enabled by the kit's internal guidance system. Each jet also carried two radar-guided AMRAAMs—advanced medium-range air-to-air missiles, and two Sidewinder infrared homing missiles—powerful insurance in case any Syrian aircraft might be foolish enough to threaten them. A full load of 20 mm high-explosive incendiary ammunition was available to strafe terrorist ground targets, if the opportunity presented itself. There was no room for error—every piece of ordnance had to be ready to do its particular job when the time came.

Sergeant Davis had scrawled a short note with chalk on the sides of each bomb: "With love, from your American friends." He cast the beam of his flashlight across his crude artwork.

"Colonel, check this out. I want to be sure those bastards know where these came from," he said. "Presuming, of course, you actually hit the radical jihadis tonight," he laughed.

Ace smiled and nodded his concurrence. He knew that the message would never be seen by anyone in the target area. When the bombs hit, they would explode into thousands of jagged, unrecognizable fragments. But he appreciated the fact that his ground team was excited about the mission and looked for some payback from those who wreaked unspeakable horror on innocent civilians.

"Ray, these bombs are pretty accurate. All it takes are solid coordinates on where this bad guy is hiding out." He grinned back.

"How confident do you think our intel guys are on the target location?"

"Well, pretty confident, although things can change quickly on the ground. But we're reasonably sure that we'll get him this time."

Darkness was the realm of the Strike Eagles. They were specifically designed for precision night attack using their navigation and targeting pods. The two five-foot-long oblong pods hung opposite each other from pylons under the aircraft's big engine intakes. They gave the deadly jet the ability to attack targets in complete darkness, in any kind of weather, at extremely low altitudes, while closely hugging the contours of the terrain they would be streaking over.

Davis continued, "Sir, your pods are ready to do their job."

"Great, Ray—they'll get us safely into Syria and pinpoint the dude we're after. The bomb's guidance unit will do the rest—and then—boom!"

Ace relished the opportunity to deliver his jet's explosive cocktail through the front door of terrorist hideouts around the world. It seemed that a preponderance of them were in volatile parts of the Middle East, and in recent years Syria in particular. Clearly, in Ace's mind, there was no shortage of radical jihadis that needed killing. He believed that on this particular mission, the individual he was targeting truly deserved to die—along with his top-level leadership, and any warriors in close proximity to him.

Chapter 5

As Sergeant Davis followed Ace in his preflight inspection, he reflected on the upcoming mission.

"Hey, boss. With literally dozens of radical rebel groups in Syria, why are we going after Black Dawn?"

"That particular group is the worst of the bunch. It's led by one of the most dangerous jihadis in the Middle East—Abdul al-Salaam. He views the country's turmoil as a breeding ground to restore the region to what he believes the Quran demands—the return of Sharia law, and the ruthless enforcement of penalties on anyone who violates that law. He's a savage, willing to abuse and even butcher men, women and children to achieve his goals."

"Still, it seems that we're singling out this one terrorist to eliminate when there are plenty of others that appear to be just as bad."

"There's more. Black Dawn didn't really matter *that* much to us until they began emplacing roadside bombs to target other rebel factions. But the unsophisticated bombs were indiscriminate. Beyond killing their intended victims, there had been US casualties as well—Army Special Forces who helped support the anti-government rebels fight Assad's brutality. That pushed Abdul al-Salaam to the top of our list."

As he finished his preflight inspection, he thought about what he had just said to his crew chief. He knew that religious fanatics like Abdul al-Salaam gave Islam and all Muslims some really bad press. He had Muslim friends in England who practiced their faith as it was intended. Like pretty much any part of society, they were predominantly peaceful, law-abiding folks. The extremists represented a tiny fraction of the Islamic faithful population and, unfortunately, gave some the impression that all Muslims were radicals. He hoped he would hit his target tonight and eliminate part of that tiny extremist fraction.

"Okay, time to get going," he remarked to his trusty crew chief.

Ace climbed up the imposing ten-foot aircraft ladder to the cockpit, stepped over the canopy rail, and planted himself gingerly in the front seat of his jet. The weapons system officer, or WSO, Major Michael "Moe" Oden, was already situated in the rear seat after having performed a very detailed check of the Strike Eagle's ordnance.

Sergeant Davis helped Ace position the lap belt and shoulder belts. He leaned over the canopy sill in the back seat. "Sir, you all set?"

"I'm good to go," responded Oden.

After plugging in his oxygen hose and communication cable, Ace checked the cockpit switch settings. His fingers moved quickly across the myriad displays and switches, verifying their correct positions. As he was finishing, Davis pulled additional safety pins and removed the boarding ladder.

Shortly before two o'clock in the morning, Ace looked down the parking ramp at the other three Strike Eagles in his flight. The bright airfield lights illuminated their cockpits. He signaled the other pilots to start their engines.

"Chief, intakes clear, fire bottle ready?" Ace asked his crew chief, linked to him by the long black comm cord attached to his aircraft. Davis stood slightly off to the side of and in front of the jet, ready for engine start and final checks prior to taxi. The assistant crew chief was beside the jet, by the fire bottle, ready to respond to any emergency. Ace got a thumbs-up from Sergeant Davis.

He activated the aircraft's auxiliary power unit, or APU—a small internal jet engine used to provide compressed air and electrical power to start each engine. The stillness of the early morning was ripped apart by the howling whine of the APU, which then engaged the powerful Pratt & Whitney F100-PW-229 turbofan jet engine. Ace watched his engine gauges closely, assuring proper pressure and temperature parameters were met. Once the right engine was running smoothly, he repeated the process on the left engine. He enjoyed the engine rumble, the low-frequency vibration encompassing him. It felt good. The ominous dark gray beast was coming to life.

When all checks were complete, Davis disconnected the comm cord, and on Ace's signal, the large rubber chocks wedged against each of the jet's large black tires were pulled away. He stood in front of the jet, his arms crossed over his head, directing Ace to hold the jet in position. He awaited his pilot's signal.

Ace checked the other aircraft in his flight and called for clearance to taxi.

"Ground Control, Eagle One, flight of four, taxi."

"Roger, Eagle One. Cleared to taxi, Runway Twenty-Four, winds southwest at eight, visibility two miles."

Sergeant Davis signaled his pilot to begin moving the jet out of its parking space. Ace rolled about a foot and then stopped the aircraft for one more tire check. After all, racing down the runway was not the time for a tire failure that could cause a catastrophe.

As the heavy eighty-thousand-pound fighter rolled slowly into the darkness, Davis offered a crisp salute to his boss. Ace smartly returned the courtesy and began the slow trek down the long taxiway, the other three jets right behind him. They eventually reached the arming area for their final checks.

Portable halogen lights strategically placed around the area provided visibility for the arming crews. They scrambled under the jets to verify that the landing gear pins were removed and then removed all ordnance safety pins. Ace checked to ensure the crews were clear of the aircraft and then looked to his left in the darkness at the other three jets. A quick radio check confirmation by each of them verified their readiness to launch.

"Tower, Eagle One flight of four, ready for takeoff."

"Eagle One, cleared onto Runway Twenty-Four, and cleared for takeoff. Contact Departure Control. Godspeed."

Ace's dark gray beast slid out onto the runway. "Okay, Moe, show's on!" The other jets taxied into position and stopped—they all ran up their engines.

He switched to the prescribed frequency, released his brakes, and pushed the F-15E's throttles into the military power setting—the maximum thrust short of afterburner—and then into afterburner. His aircraft smoothly transitioned through the five stages of afterburner ignition, the engine noise now almost deafening outside the jet as twenty-nine thousand pounds of thrust from each powerful turbofan quickly accelerated the aircraft down the darkened concrete runway. Twin yellow-orange daggers of flame leapt from the large engine nozzles. Both crew members were pushed back into their ejection seats by the sheer acceleration of the jet. Ace pulled the stick back at about 170 knots and lifted the jet's nose off the runway, leaving the safety of the dark air base.

Ace retracted the landing gear, aerodynamically cleaning up the jet. He accelerated to 350 knots as he climbed into the clear night sky.

The three aircraft followed Ace, each launching twenty-seconds behind the other. They rapidly joined up with the lead aircraft, sliding gracefully into their planned mission formation. In minutes, the rapidly fading muted glows from their fiery tailpipes were the only visible signs of the departing strike force.

Chapter 6

June 28, 2003
0330 Hours, Local Time

The heavily laden Strike Eagles were thirsty, burning gas at a rapid rate. A midair refueling from a KC-10 Extender tanker would ensure they had plenty of gas to ingress the target, drop their bombs, and then return to the safety of Turkish skies.

"Ace, we've got the tanker on radar, forty miles out off our one o'clock position," Moe remarked.

"Roger, looks like the mission plan is working out just fine so far," said Ace, silently hoping the trip to the target also would be executed as planned.

After they had been airborne for less than an hour, Ace could see the tanker's position lights ahead, the flying gas station waiting to provide their lifeline of jet fuel. He always enjoyed air refueling, a sometimes difficult and always somewhat dangerous task depending on weather, pilot skill level, and tanker boom operator expertise.

As Ace approached, the boom operator transmitted, "Eagle One, you are clear to pre-contact position."

With that call, Ace gracefully slid his jet into the precise refueling position less than fifty feet underneath the behemoth-sized tanker. As he approached, his eyes were focused on the string of lights underneath the big aircraft. The blinking lights were critical to pilots trying to safely hook up for gas. The flashing lights operated by the boom operator directed Ace to maneuver his jet forward, aft, up or down until it was in the precise contact position for refueling. When the lights were blinking green, he was in the perfect position to safely take on gas.

"Eagle One—looking good. Cleared to contact," said the boom operator.

Ace held his jet steady and watched the refueling boom's long metal tube extend toward him. The nozzle on the end looked like a long-nosed bat with its wings spread. As it passed perilously close to their canopy, both crew members watched it intently.

"I hope that boom operator didn't choke down too much coffee this morning. Last thing we need is a fidgety hand maneuvering that nozzle by our head," Moe remarked.

Ace smiled as he heard the familiar clunk of the nozzle connect to his aircraft on top of the inlet, just behind his left shoulder. He concentrated on just holding his position under the tanker. He thought about how new pilots often tensed up the first couple of times they performed the aerial acrobatics. It could be a little nerve-wracking, even ass-puckering, to get within feet of the large flying gas station and try to hold their jet steady. A lapse in concentration, an unexpected blast of turbulence coming off the tanker, could cause a disaster to both aircraft. Fortunately, experience reduced the pucker factor and helped manage the risk.

Another familiar clunk indicated that the nozzle had disconnected and Ace was full of fuel. He slid out of the refueling position, allowing the remaining Strike Eagles in his flight to get their gas. In spite of a minor bit of clear air turbulence, the refueling operation was successful.

Fully fueled, they resumed their flight track to the upcoming turn point near Osmaniye, Turkey. There they would head south along the narrow finger of Turkish territory before entering Syria along the eastern slopes of the An-Nusayriyah Mountain range. Their target was in a small village outside Afrin, east of the mountains and across a shallow valley, about ninety miles beyond the Turkish-Syrian border. Within the darkened cockpit of the strike force aircraft, the only visible light was the soft glow from the multifunction instrument displays.

———•———

"How's it looking?" asked Ace.

"Right on our flight plan, boss. We're good to go," Moe responded with a grunt.

"Sounds good. Sure is pretty this time of morning. Too bad the world can't be as peaceful as it is at this altitude, with the stars twinkling and just the hum of our engines keeping us company."

"Well, it ain't gonna be too peaceful in a bit when we drop our load on these terrorist bastards," Moe replied. "Hopefully the leader of that bunch of Black Dawn jihadis is where we think he is."

Ace missed the last comment. His mind had started to wander, just for a moment. What was going on back at Royal Air Force Base Lakenheath in England, host to his American fighter squadron? His bride and son were still asleep at the sprawling British base. He would have liked to have been there when the alarm clock rang, waking them for the day. He always enjoyed the warm hug from his wife as she woke up. He treasured the interesting conversations he had with his only son, Matt. The young boy was growing so fast. Ace hated to miss even a minute with him.

"Ace, did you copy me?" asked Moe. He had expected some kind of affirmation about kicking some terrorists' butts.

"Roger that, Moe. It won't be long after our strike that we'll know if we got him."

Chapter 7

The strike force was rapidly approaching the southern coast of Turkey, now only about fifty miles off the nose of their aircraft. Ace scanned his powerful radar for any air traffic ahead. It showed some minimal aircraft activity near the big city of Osmaniye, likely commercial traffic arriving from the United States. There was nothing threatening about what he saw on his radar display. He could identify the two Prowler aircraft a few miles away that would shadow them into the target area.

"Moe, it's great to see those Navy boys flying top cover for us. We don't want any flaming candlesticks heading our way," he said, referring to the SAMs.

"Roger that, boss. I ain't ready to cash it in quite yet."

Ace chuckled, looking across his shoulder at the flight of aircraft steadily churning on to complete their deadly mission.

"Turn point Delta in five minutes," Moe noted.

As they approached the turn point near Osmaniye, they could just make out the Mediterranean Sea, its approaching dark boundary identifiable by the city and town lights along the coast. A few miles offshore, dim blinking lights could be seen from the string of freighters waiting for their clearance to enter the Turkish ports.

Ace put his jet in a thirty-degree bank angle to the prescribed heading of 180 degrees—his strike force followed suit. Some high-level cirrus clouds were directly in front of them. As he sliced through them, the white fluff tumbled off his canopy. The turn south would take them along the slopes of the An-Nusayriyah

Mountain range running along the Turkish territory that bordered Syria. While the peaks were not as large as Ace would have liked, they were the only clutter the strike force could use to help hide their presence from prying Syrian radar across the border. The small jagged peaks of the mountain range bordering Syria would also help mask their silhouettes against the sky if any goat herders happened to be up at this early-morning hour. But even in this sparsely populated countryside, pretty much everyone had a cell phone—even goat herders—and reports of the aircraft would immediately be passed to Syrian authorities.

Ace let out a long, slow breath as he noticed the weather along the mountain range—an unexpected bonus. A long stretch of dark clouds had rolled over the peaks from the eastern slopes. While the clouds didn't completely hide them, for now, they were just enough to help with their attempt at concealment.

Gotta get lucky sometime, Ace thought as he and Moe began a shallow descent to get below the top ridgeline and level off at two thousand feet from the base of the mountains.

"Moe, the IP is coming up," Ace remarked, looking at his heads-up display.

"Roger. We'll be at the initial point to make our turn in about one hundred and thirty miles; at this air speed, about sixteen minutes," he replied.

Per the mission plan, the Prowlers pulled away from the Strike Eagles and headed to a higher altitude that would give them the best chance of picking up any Syrian radar activity.

"Good hunting, boys," he remarked to them over his secure comm.

"Roger, Eagle One, we'll do our best to keep you safe."

Ace caught glimpses of the rugged slope of the mountain range in between cloud breaks and through his infrared display.

The rocky crags whizzed by over his right shoulder. *Our nav pod should keep us from having a violent personal introduction with these mountains.* The terrain-hugging system often pitched and banked the jets abruptly, the pilots feeling like they were riding a

Coney Island roller coaster. The sensation of positive and negative g-forces would make most civilians toss their cookies.

Ace was *all in* for the low-level ingress. More importantly, the strike force was fully confident that the Prowlers would do their job of jamming any acquisition radar that might highlight the impending hell that they were about to unleash on the terrorist compound, now only a few minutes away.

It was a bit surreal, streaking through the early-morning darkness with patches of gray-and-white fluff cascading off his aircraft. *So beautiful*, he thought.

His mind briefly drifted back to early mornings at RAF Lakenheath Air Base in England, the main operating base for his F-15Es in the 48th Fighter Wing. As the 494th Fighter Squadron Commander, the deployment to Diyarbakir put him a long way from those he loved, and there was absolutely nobody more important to him than his wife, Cathy, and son, Matt.

They were undoubtedly still quietly sleeping while activity at the big air base slowly came alive, the servicing crews beginning the process of getting jets ready for their daily training sorties. Ace was a warrior, coming from a long line of warriors in his family tree. There was no doubt that Matt, even at only thirteen years of age, would grow up to be a warrior as well. His bedroom was already decorated with pictures of combat aircraft, plastic models of sleek fighter jets, and of course, the squadron and other organizational patches worn by his fighter pilot father.

He shook his head to get his mind refocused.

Enough with the reminiscing. Time to get every ounce of my attention on killing the target ahead and not getting our ass shot out of the sky.

Ace knew that with a bit of luck, the Prowlers would do their usual job, and if needed, his aircraft countermeasures would help avoid any surface-to-air missiles headed his way. He was very confident that he could lead his flight to the target, and then back to the safety of their Turkish base. He was also absolutely certain that the bombs hanging under each wing of his aircraft would pulverize their target, blowing it into oblivion. *This never gets old. It's always an adrenaline rush! I'm about to bomb the hell out of one terrorist bastard—and definitely disturb what little peace there is at this time of the morning.*

Fortunately, the forecast around the target was expected to be crystal clear. But that really didn't matter with all-weather GPS-guided bombs—the targets destruction was a downright certainty. Based on real-time intelligence information that was as solid as it could be, verified by one particular Special Forces team on the ground, the high-value target had been positively identified and his location pinpointed to one specific house. The GPS coordinates had been plugged in to the aircraft system's targeting computer and the data passed to the bomb's tail kit internal guidance system. Once released, the bombs would navigate their way to the designated target coordinates. Now, it was just a matter of minutes before the flight of four Strike Eagles inserted eight high-explosive bombs up the ass of Abdul al-Salaam. This notorious terrorist's time on the planet was growing very short.

In spite of being a seasoned combat fighter pilot, Ace had conflicting emotions about what they were about to do. He knew that there was a strong possibility of collateral damage as a result of the upcoming attack. That meant civilian casualties. It created a moral dilemma for him. Was the death of a heinous terrorist worth even one innocent life—maybe more than one? He thought about it often and sometimes woke from a dead sleep thinking about it. But he had a job to do.

"We'll turn to 030 degrees at the IP in thirty seconds," remarked Moe.

"Roger, let's get this done," replied Ace as he performed a final check of his instruments, verifying that the targeting information was correct and weapons were ready. He commanded his flight to arm their weapons. Ace's senses were now fully engaged, knowing that they were about to make their final turn that would lead his strike force into Syria.

Chapter 8

In the darkness of the Syrian countryside, the terrorist leader slept soundly in the village, snugly located outside of Shaykh al-Hadid. Basim, had chosen the perfect home there—most suitable for sheltering the leader of Back Dawn. Abdul had had no trouble confiscating the village chieftain's home for the night. As was almost always the case, even the highest-ranking Syrians in the village tribal pecking order knew what to expect if they even hinted at rejecting Abdul's request. Abdul insisted on being treated royally, like the prince he envisioned himself to be.

Earlier that night, Abdul and Basim had spent the evening planning for the following day's campaign in Shaykh al-Hadid. Things were going quite well for his radical Islamic group. Ever so slowly, Abdul's effort to swell his ranks with new healthy men was reaping the rewards he desired, resulting in a wider net of sympathizers that would ultimately support his cause.

"I have looked closely at the men in this town and believe they will make fine warriors in our holy jihad," remarked Abdul. "This area seems untouched by the Syrian Army forces that populate Aleppo, across the hills from here. Apparently, this is so close to Turkey that Assad doesn't want to prompt any conflict between them."

"My brother, we will harness the wealth this town provides and continue to build our army. Allah will indeed be proud."

As the evening wore on, Basim had other thoughts in mind besides building an army. He had questioned the village leader about Fatima. Had he seen her? Did he know if she was in one of the small buildings? Basim had gotten the information he needed.

Almost a month had passed since he had held her, the beautiful Fatima, in his arms. He yearned for her now more than ever. He waited for Abdul to fall asleep and then slipped away from his brother. He desperately sought the woman who would make all his tension from the past weeks disappear. Basim resisted the urge to run the one hundred yards to the village outskirts, where he knew she waited for him. He wanted no undue attention from either his men or any villager that might be up at this late hour.

Walking quickly through the darkness, he approached his destination. Looking around to ensure he was not being watched, he gingerly entered the house. He saw Fatima in the dull light of the room. Even in the darkness, he was astounded by her beauty. His heart began pounding, his mind racing with thoughts of what was to come. She had prepared the bed and herself for this occasion. As he walked toward her, he smelled her fragrant perfume wafting in the air, and smiled. He tried to resist the urge to tear off her abaya. As if Fatima could read his mind, she gracefully slid out of the clothing that hid her beautiful body. He reached out to her and pulled her gently to him, and they tumbled together across the small bed.

"I have waited forever for these weeks to pass," he said. "All I have thought about since we met is this night, this moment, this encounter."

"Basim, I too have longed for this night. You are the man I have dreamed about. Everything I have is yours."

They reacquainted themselves in carnal bliss, clinging tightly together in each other's arms. He quickly forgot about everything but the pleasure he was now experiencing and was quite pleased that this beautiful woman would do all that he asked—and more. The two lovers had no idea of the approaching violence from the sky.

———•———

The closest dwelling to where Abdul al-Salaam slept, about fifty yards away, housed Mohammad Ruffa, his wife, Nayifa, and their four children. They believed Allah had blessed them with a fine home, better than most. Many villagers lived in far less, in simple structures made from mud-and-rock walls, with flimsy roofs that sometimes left them exposed to the elements. The forty-five-year-old father understood his place in the hierarchy of this rigid society. He would never be one of those who enjoyed the best that was provided to the corrupt Syrian government's inner circle. He was content to live his life, raise a family, and follow the true tenets of the holy Quran.

He had scraped together a meager but adequate living by raising goats and selling the milk, and occasionally the goat meat when the goats were no longer able to produce milk. His disability had not hindered his success. Years had passed since his left arm had been permanently damaged from a rebel attack that had nearly taken his life. He thrived nonetheless, by Syrian standards. That helped him eventually take a young Assyrian bride and begin to raise four children as devout Muslims.

Mohammad was proud of the family he had raised, despite the constant struggle all common Syrians endured in the embattled country. He ensured that his sons received a rudimentary education in the local school and avoided getting on the wrong side of either the Syrian Army or rebel groups like Black Dawn. His two oldest sons, Ahmad and Jamil, through Allah's great blessing, had grown to be strong and faithful to their religion. As the boys neared their fifteenth birthday, Mohammad feared the Syrian Army might forcibly recruit them into their ranks. A far worse fate would be their coercive absorption into Black Dawn, a path of no return for any young man unlucky enough to be recruited.

His two youngest children, Ana and Khalil, were the light of his life. Seven years after the birth of his first children, Mohammad and his beautiful wife were blessed with twins born minutes of each other—first another son, and then a daughter. As the two children grew, he could see that Khalil was indeed special. The boy seemed intelligent beyond his years. At eight years of age, he questioned things that even his older brothers couldn't quite comprehend.

Mohammad believed that Khalil was destined for greatness and would become a leader of his faith—if he could avoid being cannon fodder for Assad or Black Dawn.

How fortunate could a man be, Mohammad thought, *to have Allah grace me with such a fine family?*

Dinner had been special on this clear night, as it was Nayifa's birthday. Following prayers to Allah, thanking him for his benevolence, a sumptuous meal of goat meat, potatoes and flat bread was voraciously enjoyed by the entire family. The two youngest children celebrated fancifully and presented their mother with a small bracelet they had made from woven pieces of vine, soaked in oil and then dried in the hot desert sun. Khalil said a special prayer, promised her his undying faith to his religion, and wished her a long, happy life. The stars sparkled in the sky as their celebration ended. The happy family retired for the night.

Chapter 9

In the dark cockpit of the Strike Eagle, Ace awaited the final signal transmission that the high-value target was still in the expected location. The large airborne warning and control system aircraft orbiting off the coast of Turkey received the message from the Special Forces team leader, confirming the spot Abdul al-Salaam had chosen for the night. The encrypted message was immediately passed to the strike force. The coordinates matched those the aircrew had previously entered into the aircraft.

"We're a go," Ace said seconds after the encrypted signal was received.

"Roger, Eagle One," came the secure communications reply from within the flight of four.

At the precise time, the strike force made their final turn, this one taking them directly toward the fertile valley that separated Turkey from Syria. Coming off the rocky ridgeline, the valley ahead was barely illuminated. He led his flight of fighters in a high-speed six-hundred-mile-per-hour low-level dash across the valley floor toward the town of Shaykh al-Hadid.

Optimal altitude for release of the guided bombs on this clear night was six thousand feet, a bit higher than the fighters wanted to be as they penetrated the Syrian airspace. The Prowlers were overhead, doing what they do best—sending out powerful waves of electromagnetic jamming signals along the foothills of the mountain chain east of Shaykh al-Hadid. Hopefully, the strike force would not be acquired and targeted by Syrian missiles. At least, that was the plan.

Streaking across the fertile valley, the pilots saw a few flickering lights, mostly from small fires intended to keep predatory animals away from goat herds and other livestock. Any secrecy at this point was eliminated by the piercing noise made by their jet engines, guaranteed to awaken anyone within a few miles of their flight path. The town of Shaykh al-Hadid was now just minutes away.

The strike force was now clearly visible to Syrian air defense acquisition radar. The SAM sites along the mountain chain east of their target had not yet reacted to the intrusion. Moe was all concentration, scanning the radar warning receiver for any threats.

Ace Black began his bombing run, with the other three jets following seconds behind. Moe verified the target coordinates one last time. Weapons release was now automatic. It would be only a matter of moments before the world would have one less terrorist bastard to deal with.

As they approached the target, Ace pulled his jet into a pop-up maneuver to get to the optimal altitude for weapons release. At the right moment, the deadly ordnance explosively ejected from the bomb racks.

"Bombs away," said Moe.

Ace felt the steel-encased weapons release with two noticeable thuds from the bomb racks under the sleek fighter, signaling that they had begun their guided descent to their target. He quickly pushed the throttles forward, pulling up and to the left rapidly, and began his egress from the target area. The bombs raced toward the earth, falling at a rate of over two hundred meters per second, and zeroed in on the terrorist's compound.

Abdul stirred in bed, not sure if a pesky insect was gnawing on his face, bedbugs munching on his leg, or if it was something else that was not as it should be. His battle-hardened senses, even in sleep, told him something was off. He awoke with a start, sitting up immediately in his bed. It was almost as if he expected the carnage about to befall him. Not seeing his brother across the room, he called out, "Basim, Bas—" It was the last fragment of sound coming from his throat.

The flash from the bombs impacting directly on the house lit up the village like the sun at noon. The violent explosions instantaneously decomposed Abdul's previous physical form into a million unrecognizable pieces of shredded flesh and bone.

Ace looked over his shoulder in the confines of his cockpit as he continued his climb away from the target. He grinned as the blast below spewed a glowing crimson fireball that towered high into the night sky.

Ace thought for a second. Was it true about all those virgins that jihadi martyrs claimed they got? *I wonder if Abdul is going to get lucky tonight.*

"We nailed it," shouted Moe. "Let's get the heck out of here."

They both caught a glimpse through the clear glass canopy of the subsequent Strike Eagle's weapons impacting their targets, taking out other homes where Abdul's army had scattered for the night. The explosions of each set of bombs, as if in some terrible yet beautiful synchronization, obliterated everything left standing and guaranteed that the target was completely destroyed.

Unfortunately, while Mohammad Ruffa's home provided protection from the elements, it was certainly never built to handle the blast of a single five-hundred-pound bomb, much less eight of the deadly munitions. Mohammad and his family never felt the initial or subsequent blasts that impacted a scant one hundred yards away. The first two exploding bombs produced a violent concussive blast wave, rapidly expanding out from the center impact point. The massive blast obliterated anything within four hundred yards, flattening a dozen small clay brick structures, including Mohammad's home. Whatever was left standing from the first strike was subsequently destroyed by the string of follow-on bombs that homed in on the terrorists.

In an instant, the lives of a devout Muslim family were changed forever. Mohammad, Nayifa, and the two oldest children were killed instantly, brutally crushed in the collapsing debris of their stone and concrete house. They never stood a chance with the blast-fragmentation bombs striking a target that close to them. By some miracle, the two youngest children, Khalil and Ana, were spared, having been sleeping in a hollowed-out concrete basement enclave of the home used to store their vegetables and fruit. The collapsing concrete walls had swept over them, and while the blast rendered them unconscious, beyond scratches, bruises, and ruptured eardrums, they were alive.

Also within the rubble, Basim and Fatima lay dead, crushed by the same blast waves, now and forever, together in each other's mangled arms.

As the remaining F-15Es climbed from the target area into the night to rejoin their lead, the radar warning receiver panels in the center of their aircraft multifunction displays lit up. The flashing monochrome light that a pilot hopes he will never see blinked crazily, and the missile warning aural message sounded loudly through the crew's helmet communication system. The strike force was now being painted by Syrian missile batteries.

What the heck? thought Ace, angrily believing that the Prowlers had not done their job to suppress the enemy missile acquisition radar. The annoying red flashes bounced eerie images off the Strike Eagle's canopy glass, now mixing crazily with the green from the multifunction displays. Up to this point, the Prowlers had, in fact, effectively enabled the strike force to hit their target and destroy it with seeming impunity. However, a clever Syrian air defense commander had kept his acquisition radar off until the Americans were egressing the target area, and then activated it.

The Prowlers locked on to the Syrian SAM radar and launched two anti-radiation missiles at it. The Navy pilots hoped it was in time to defeat the Syrian missiles before they launched and raced toward the Strike Eagles.

"Stand by for countermeasures," commanded Ace as he maneuvered his jet on a trajectory he believed would move them further away from the Syrian missile batteries. Instantly, the aircraft aural warning indicated "missile launch." Now the strike force was in the high-intensity self-defense mode, trying to avoid the explosive warhead atop the Syrian SA-6 surface-to-air missile that was streaking toward them. The flight of Strike Eagles began executing their aircraft countermeasures and tactical maneuvers. They hoped the chaff and flares ejecting from their aircraft into the early-morning darkness would deceive the SAM and direct it away from their jets.

"Moe, keep sight of that bastard," shouted Ace.

There was no need, since Moe knew his survival depended on outmaneuvering the missile. As Ace continued the tactical maneuvers he had been trained to do to avoid being hit, his weapon system operator craned his neck to keep the flaming telephone pole–sized SAM in sight while barking commands to his pilot to try to avoid it.

"Break right, break right!" shouted Moe as he sought to turn inside the SAM's path with a high-G turn that would make the missile overshoot and hopefully avoid a direct hit on their aircraft.

"We're going to make it," said Moe—his last words to Ace.

The high-explosive SAM warhead detonated within fifty feet of the jet, the bright fireball instantly encompassing the aircraft and its crew. In milliseconds, the blast tore off the left wing, sending hot flaming shrapnel into the conformal fuel tank on the left side of the jet, causing a second massive fireball that obliterated the canopy and rendered them both unconscious. Major Roger Dean, pilot of Eagle Two in the strike force, observed the explosion while maneuvering wildly to avoid another SAM blazing toward him.

"Eagle One, eject, eject," Dean shouted over the radio.

"Shit," he said to his WSO while watching the flaming pieces of the doomed jet tumble though the sky. "There's no way out of that."

The Prowler's anti-radiation missiles finally found their mark on the Syrian control center, making the other SAMs already in flight blind to their targets. But it was too late for Ace. All the remaining F-15Es had successfully initiated their defensive maneuvers and countermeasures and avoided the same fate of Eagle One. None had even a scratch as they began their egress from a now-very-pissed-off Syria. The stunned aircrews in the surviving Strike Eagles had all seen the missile explosion and knew that the ill-fated crew had had no chance to bail out. They watched in unbroken silence as what remained of their flight lead's aircraft spun crazily down through the clear early-morning sky, impacting the ground in a bright yellow explosion.

The disciplined team of warriors performed precisely as they had trained. Eagle Three immediately assumed command of the flight to get his strike force home. In the short minutes they had before departing the target area, they used their infrared displays to search desperately for any signs of chutes or life. There were no chutes, nor were there any responses from Ace or Moe. The Prowlers likewise searched for evidence of the F-15E crew and found nothing. Eagle Three knew that his loiter time in the area was running out, and the aircraft were rapidly approaching the point of having the minimum fuel required to return home safely. They transmitted the tragic loss of the aircraft and requested search-and-rescue support—but there was no one to be rescued.

Syrian air defense was now doing everything they could to acquire the American invaders. As the radar warning receivers in the flight of Strike Eagles lit up again, identifying the threat of additional SAMs, the pilots were forced to egress the Syrian airspace, minus one of their own.

Chapter 10

As daylight broke in the rubble-strewn outskirts of Shaykh al-Hadid, the scene was tragic. Only hours before, the small vibrant village of simple stone and frame homes, market stalls, and corrals that caged chickens and goats had effectively serviced the large town adjacent to it. Now, the area was scarred with deep, wide craters and almost unidentifiable debris from the disintegrated structures. There were also plenty of broken, distorted bodies and numerous human body parts. The village was effectively erased from the map.

The Sisters of Charity were committed to help the less fortunate and to spread the word of God. The Christian missionary volunteers were willing to risk their lives in the predominantly Islamic country—and there was plenty of need to be addressed by these caring, selfless Sisters. Fortunately, they had been only a few miles away when the bombs hit the village, and they had immediately headed for the disaster area.

A few survivors had dug the two unconscious children from the rubble. Initially, they'd thought the children were dead and had placed them on the ground next to their dead parents and older brothers. As the devoted Sisters checked for any signs of life, they saw some slight, almost imperceptible movement from the children. The missionaries called loudly for help, attracting the attention of the two medical personnel who were treating the injured. Although the children were still unconscious, by some miracle, they had escaped major injury. They were quickly moved into one of the few temporary small huts erected to separate the living from the dead.

When Syria's newest parentless children regained conscious-ness, Khalil and Ana had no real memory of what had happened the night of the blast. Khalil vaguely remembered having a nightmare. He remembered the screaming, the loud shrieks—and then nothing else. He had briefly awakened in the darkened rubble, large pieces of jagged concrete perched precariously over his head. The screams were not a nightmare, but the terrified sounds coming from his own throat. Underneath the pile of debris, when his screaming stopped, he passed out.

The devout missionaries knew these children would be aban-doned, just like so many other orphans they had seen across the embattled countryside. At eight years of age, they were of little use to anyone. But these two children would not face the same fate. The staff of religious volunteers hurried them out of the destroyed village, moving them to a nearby clinic for additional treatment. Nearly as quickly as the Sisters had arrived there, the waifs were whisked away to a safe area near the Turkish border. It was far from where they had previously called home, and away from the Syrian Army that was quickly descending upon the area.

The Sisters of Charity were well networked across the Middle East. They contacted their Christian counterparts in Turkey and arranged for Khalil and Ana to cross the border and reach an orphanage in Kirkhan. That was to become the children's home for months, or at least until good fortune might possibly descend upon them.

A Christian-run orphanage in Turkey was a rare sight, but there was plenty of demand from the flood of refugees coming out of Syria, from people whose lives had been torn apart by constant war and the brutality of a despotic regime. The facility was clearly a better option for the children than trying to survive in their homeland. They were fed nourishing meals and lived in conditions that were as good as or better than their home in Syria. While there was some hope that Khalil and Ana would be adopted by a good family, the odds were stacked against them. Most children grew to adulthood there, praying daily for a miracle. Sometimes, miracles happened.

Dr. Mahmoud Ruffa, Mohammad's older brother, had escaped Syria many years earlier after finishing his medical training at Cairo University in Giza, Egypt. He was one of the fortunate ones. He had married the daughter of a wealthy Syrian military officer who had financed his college studies and then, eventually, their travel to England for Dr. Ruffa to pursue advanced medical studies and start up a successful practice in Westminster.

He heard of the attack on the terrorist compound while watching the BBC news and seen the devastating film footage. He immediately recognized the name of the town and became extremely concerned over the safety of his beloved brother and family. Through his contacts with the Syrian military, he discovered the unthinkable—the family had perished. Torn by grief, he vowed to find the family's remains and ensure they had been given a proper burial. Through sheer determination, he obtained approval to travel into the war-torn country. The surviving senior member of the Ruffa family set out for Syria. Upon arriving at the international airport in Damascus, he used his travel documents, along with his old Syrian passport, and gained entry into the country. After going through a convoluted interrogation by the Syrian Army as to his intentions, he arranged for transport to Shaykh al-Hadid.

Two days of driving through Syria had its risks. Numerous army checkpoints made travel a crapshoot, given the widespread corruption in the military. People were stopped at random and often held for no reason other than how they looked. However, cash bribes, especially big ones, usually did the trick, and Dr. Ruffa had that part covered. More problematic was the possibility of a spontaneous attack by radical rebel factions intent on plundering wary travelers for anything of value, or protecting their established territory.

While Dr. Ruffa avoided any rebel encounters while en route, he was stunned by what he saw. He had seen televised evidence of the ongoing civil war's destructive nature, but seeing it firsthand shocked him. Homes had been reduced to rubble by barrel bombs Assad used against his own people. The devastation from apparent indiscriminate targeting of schools, churches and village homes was everywhere. It brought a tear to his eye. By the afternoon of the second day, he approached the town of Shaykh al-Hadid.

Bomb craters in the town were graphic evidence of the widespread damage caused by the explosive blast waves that had eliminated everything in their path. Dr. Ruffa's heart ached as he thought of his dear brother's last moments of life—of the terror from the blast—and then the crushing, horrific deaths the family must have endured. Walking through what was left of the village, he observed women and children, wandering through the rubble, searching for anything of value. He began asking them if they knew his brother and family. They did indeed. An old woman in a dust-covered abaya, hearing the questions he asked, approached Dr. Ruffa.

"Are you his family?" the old woman asked.

"Yes, I am Mohammad's brother. I have been told by the Syrian Army that my brother is likely dead. But I prayed to Allah that he has survived this terrible blast. Do you know if he is alive?"

The old woman shook her head and said that all had perished except the two young children.

Stunned by her admission, he said, "I was told they were all killed. Where are the children?"

"Missionaries took them to the clinic in Azaz."

"My brother, where is he buried?"

"He and his family were buried outside the village."

Dr. Ruffa headed over to the burial site and knelt next to his brother's grave. His tears flowed as he looked at the small mounds with nearly indecipherable grave markers, the only visible evidence of Mohammad Ruffa's family. After a short prayer, he rose, knowing he must waste no time.

He set out for Azaz, wanting desperately to find his nephew and niece. He luckily avoided any army checkpoints and arrived at the city's outskirts. After gaining directions to the clinic, he saw a large

Red Crescent emblem ahead. He rushed into the canvas-covered medical center and approached two women whom he presumed to be missionaries. They were more helpful than he had imagined. They explained that the children were in good health after being treated for minor injuries and had been taken to a home for orphans outside Syria, across the border into Turkey.

"Where is this facility located?" asked Dr. Ruffa.

"Not far from here. Follow the road that leads to the Turkish checkpoint, and then a few miles into Kirkhan."

Chapter 11

June 2008
Fort Stockton, Texas

I t was graduation day at his high school in Fort Stockton, Texas, and Matt Black was pretty excited to move on to the next phase of his life. Of course, he would have liked his father to have been there to celebrate this great day. But he had grown used to being the son of a single mom and a war-hero dad who had been tragically taken from him years before. While his dad had long since been physically gone from his life, he was *never* really gone in Matt's mind and heart.

As the young child of an Air Force fighter pilot, Matt was thrilled being around the world's top aircraft and weapons technology. He relished the many opportunities his dad provided him to see fighter jets up close, to climb into the cockpit and pretend to be soaring through the clouds, trying to get the bad guys in his gun sight and blast them out of the sky.

When his dad transitioned from the F-16 Fighting Falcon to the F-15E Strike Eagle, Matt was pretty excited. Beyond getting an up-close look at the fighter aircraft, his father had let him fly a combat mission in the flight simulator, with his dad at the controls. Matt was awestruck at how realistic it was, almost as if he was actually soaring through the sky, able to do things that few people ever got a chance to do. He relished it all—climbing, diving, doing barrel rolls, making a bomb run, and strafing targets. He knew that there was absolutely nothing better in the world than this.

As he grew, Matt became adaptable, as kids of military families had to be. They moved from base to base, often quickly packing up everything they owned on short notice, and leaving friends behind. This constant movement was tough for most kids, especially when they were young and had made special bonds with friends. Luckily, making new friends came easy to Matt, as he had the same rugged good looks and outgoing personality as his father. As he grew, Matt focused all his energy, his entire consciousness, on becoming a fighter pilot like his dad. There was no question in his mind that he would succeed in that objective, and in any other challenge that faced him. After all, he was the son of Ace Black. Failure was not an option.

Matt could still remember the day his father was shot out of the sky, and the knock on the door by the fighter wing commander and the chaplain. The torn look on his mother's face and her flow of tears was almost too much for him to bear at that time. He remembered his mother crying a lot, but also that he had not cried. He remembered being angry. At the tender age of thirteen, he couldn't believe that his dad, his hero, had been killed.

He recalled being told how Syrian missionaries had gathered what little remained of the two aviators from the crash site. The remains had been transferred across the border into Turkey and eventually found their way to England. He also remembered the memorial service at RAF Lakenheath. The chapel was packed with the men and women who served with his father. He remembered the wing commander giving the eulogy, explaining how his dad had been a fearless leader, a man respected by all, who by his own actions had set the example of what was expected of his comrades-in-arms. His father had believed in the critical and dangerous role of serving his country.

Following his father's memorial service at Lakenheath, Matt and Cathy Black accompanied the remains of Lieutenant Colonel

Alec "Ace" Black back to the United States. The burial had taken place in a small Texas town—his mother and father's hometown of Fort Stockton.

The funeral, Matt remembered, was the absolute low point in his life. He could still remember watching the honor guard remove the flag of the United States from his father's coffin. They carefully folded it in a tight triangle with only the white stars visible on a blue background, no red showing, and reverently presented it to his mom.

He remembered the solemn words spoken by the officer. "This flag is presented to you on behalf of a grateful nation, for your husband's faithful service to his country." In his mind, he could still see the officer standing at attention in front of him and his mother, offering a slow white-gloved salute to them both.

That was the worst day of Matt's life, a day that seemed to repeat itself in his mind for many months, and then years, as the excruciating pain of the loss of his best friend lingered like a crushing, stabbing weight on his chest. The only thing that got Matt through these thoughts was forcibly shifting the gears in his brain, remembering only the great times.

Cathy and Matt Black had officially moved from the air base in England back to the United States. After all, they were no longer tied to the military and could no longer live on an Air Force base. They had to face the awful fact that their lives were going to change significantly, forever.

Fort Stockton had been the obvious choice for them to live. His mom headed back to a town she was familiar with, where she had grown up as a child—where she had first met her husband, and where her sister still lived. The town now held a special meaning to her. It was where her cherished husband was buried.

It was quite a change for Matt, going from a vibrant air base, surrounded by kids who had similar interests and upbringings, to a place where he stood out from the rest as an outsider. Most Fort Stockton kids had never even seen a fighter jet up close, had no idea what the Air Force *really* did, and had nothing in common with a former military family. On top of that, moving to the middle of the western Texas desert, an absolutely desolate place, was just about the worst thing a thirteen-year-old boy could imagine.

The next four years were tough without a father. Sheer determination got Matt through it all. He focused on being the best at everything, as his dad had taught him to be. He excelled in all his studies, and upon entering high school, continued his strong trend in academics, achieving the top grades in his class each year. His teachers admired his intense focus and commitment, never accepting anything less than perfection on coursework or exams. Anything less, of course, was just unacceptable to him.

On the social scene, the prettiest girls in school migrated to him, not just due to his handsome looks but because he was very different from the other West Texas boys, who never ventured further than thirty miles from the town. He carried himself confidently, and it showed in how he looked and dressed. He did especially well on the athletic fields, as a solid infielder on the baseball team—but in football he had no equal. He was named All State for the Fort Stockton High Panthers for his last two years in school, and at six feet three inches and 240 pounds of solid muscle, Matt knew that he had a great future in athletics ahead of him.

While colleges had been actively courting him, Matt had counted on attending the Air Force Academy in Colorado Springs and presumed that as the son of an Academy graduate, and having lost his father in combat, he would be accepted for admission.

———————•———————

When the graduation ceremony ended, he and his mom headed out for a celebratory dinner at the local steak house. She could not control her emotions, knowing that her strapping young son would soon head off to college. Applications had been sent to many of the state colleges and universities, and to the Air Force Academy. Responses had come from a few, but they had not yet heard from the Academy.

Days later, Matt was putting in his normal rigorous exercise routine.

"Matt, you've got some mail," Cathy Black shouted into the garage. He was on the weight bench, finishing his bench press of the three-hundred-pound barbell. He grabbed a towel and wiped the sweat from his face. When his mother handed him the envelope with the Washington, D.C., address, Matt beamed.

"Is this what I think it is?" He stared at the envelope a minute before opening it. He thought about its contents. His future, hopefully, was inside the envelope—perhaps his destiny.

Good news or bad news? he thought.

He noted that the envelope had the return address of his Republican senator from Texas.

"Honey, I hope this is what you've been waiting for," his mom said sweetly.

Matt tore it open, hoping that it would be the best gift ever for graduation. A broad grin crossed his face as he read the official notification.

"I did it!" he shouted happily. "This is exactly what I wanted."

He wrapped his strong arms around his mother and gave her a loving hug. The letter was his Congressional appointment to the Air Force Academy. Cathy Black could not have been prouder of her son than at that moment.

Chapter 12

2008
Westminster, England

L
ife in Westminster the past five years has been so much better than in Syria, Khalil thought. Except for not having my parents and brothers with me—but my uncle and aunt have been a true blessing to me and my sister.

He remembered the day Dr. Mahmoud Ruffa had arrived at the orphanage in Turkey, after which their lives had changed forever. Khalil had seen others before him come to browse among the hundreds of young children with shattered lives, looking for the least damaged child, both physically and mentally. They didn't really understand the horror witnessed and endured by most of these orphans—nearly unimaginable for anyone who had not walked the combustible Syrian landscape.

Khalil had seen the *perfect* ones quickly taken—the lucky ones. He was smart enough, even at eight years of age, to realize that he and his sister had to be as perfect as possible to escape their temporary home.

I must not speak of my dreams, Khalil had thought.

His nights were often terrifying. He relived the horror of his parents and brothers so violently taken from him. The startling nightmares slowly crept into his sleeping brain, and then suddenly tearing at his subconscious, awakening him instantly. Sometimes he awoke still thinking he was buried under the rubble of what was once his home. Khalil knew that any talk of these dreams would make him less than *perfect* in the eyes of potential adopting parents.

When Dr. Ruffa appeared, Khalil had somehow noticed a difference about him. He carried himself in a way that expressed deep concern, even pity for the children that ran to him. The man talked with the headmaster, asking many questions, but not the usual ones. The headmaster had explained the story of how Khalil and Ana had been brought to Turkey. Their family, tragically, had been killed by American bombs that took innocent lives. He described what the missionaries said they had found—the torn bodies of Dr. Ruffa's brother and wife—nearly unrecognizable from the violent blast.

Dr. Ruffa had held his anger in check. *Another example of the willful use of excess power by the Americans, with no regard for innocents.* As his eyes welled up from the sudden thought of his brother's horrible death, Dr. Ruffa looked at the two children the headmaster pointed toward. He headed their way.

As this stranger walked across the crowded, dusty floor, Khalil had thought he looked familiar. There was something that reminded him of his father.

He remembered thinking, *Who is this strange man, and why is he walking toward us?*

The headmaster escorted Dr. Ruffa to where Khalil and Ana were sitting. He introduced the doctor to the children and left them to talk privately. Dr. Ruffa sat down and asked them if they were well, and if they felt they were getting adequate care from the orphanage staff. As they gradually opened up to him, he produced a picture of their family, with Khalil's father and mother, his two older brothers, standing, smiling with Dr. Ruffa. Ana burst into tears at the sight of her mother and father while Khalil stared intently at the picture. Dr. Ruffa explained that he was their father's brother, their uncle, and that he lived in England. He explained that he was now their only remaining family and that, if they would agree, he would take them from the orphanage and raise them in a new life.

The missionaries were elated that Dr. Ruffa wanted to take his niece and nephew into his charge and bring them to England. Things like that rarely happened. Khalil and Ana had been indeed lucky that their new life would begin in a country far away from the horrors of Syria.

Now, after five years in England, they had adapted quickly in their new home. At thirteen years of age, Khalil felt like their lives had a purpose, albeit without their true parents. Mahmoud Ruffa and his wife provided the best for the children that a successful doctor in England could provide. Khalil and Ana learned to speak English, and their formal education in the fine British schools ensured that they would fully assimilate into Western society. While both children had progressed well through school, Khalil stood out from the homegrown British students. He had a sharp mind and excelled in mathematics and computer technology. He had even begun to write his own software programs and designed interactive games using his creative coding skills. He had quickly become a favorite among the other boys.

Dr. Ruffa had never talked much about the children's past terrible experience. The tragic loss of their parents was enough to weigh on their minds. After the tragedy, Dr. Ruffa had sought to find out information about the bombing. The Royal Air Force had been reluctant to share much information for security reasons. But there had been enough publicity that he discovered the organization that had conducted the strike. The unit responsible for his brother's death was located at RAF Lakenheath Air Base in England. In the months that followed, he sought out more details.

As Khalil grew, he began to question his new father about the incident. It had angered him to think that while an evil like Black Dawn had been eliminated, the Americans had killed his family as well. It didn't matter whether the air strike had deliberately killed his family or the deaths had been collateral damage, as the Americans called it. He vowed that he would never forget, or forgive, that action.

The children's lives, however, were about to take another turn—a very good one. Dr. Ruffa found an opportunity to expand his medical practice in America and escape the burdensome British taxes and problems that socialized medicine brought with it. He decided to relocate just outside of Dallas, Texas, in the town of Mesquite, to set up a new medical practice with his family. While Khalil still internalized the anger he had carried about his parents' death, the move to the United States excited both him and Ana. They had read so much about a country that touted itself as the most powerful nation on earth, a country where there was never a shortage of anything, where people had the freedom to do anything they desired and become whatever they wanted.

The Ruffa family was determined to ultimately become United States citizens and would immediately begin the process upon arriving. The doctor's impeccable credentials as a British citizen and a professional in the medical field would help to streamline and speed up the process. He hoped his children would integrate seamlessly into their first year of high school in Mesquite and adapt quickly to their new environment. Within weeks, they were on their way to a new life in the United States.

Chapter 13

July 2008
Colorado Springs, Colorado

Colorado Springs was absolutely awesome in the summer. For most residents and vacationers, it was a paradise for hiking, mountain biking, camping, and fly fishing in some of the most beautiful streams and rivers you could imagine. For Matt Black, at the beginning of his college career at the Air Force Academy, the first year would turn out to be far from awesome. It was definitely not a vacation.

Matt was pretty well hyped when he arrived at the Greyhound bus station. He had caught a special shuttle bus from there that took him through the secure Air Force Academy entrance gates and on to the assembly area for all new cadets. As he came onto the expansive Academy grounds, he couldn't help but be stunned by the beauty of the surrounding environment. In the distance, on the southern front range of the Rocky Mountains, he could see Pike's Peak, with patches of snow still on top. He was struck by the gorgeous scenery around him, with the Academy sitting on gradually rising foothills that eventually rose to the peaks of the Rockies. This was prime real estate for a government institution, he thought, and land that the state of Colorado would have loved to get their hands on to develop commercially. Matt's brief stint of daydreaming was jolted back to reality as soon as he stepped off the shuttle.

"Put all belongings over here, next to the letter posted on the building column that matches the first letter of your last name.

That includes your suitcase, cell phone, your laptop computer if you brought one, and basically anything that you are not wearing. Ditch your hats as well. You'll see this stuff again next year." The sharp-looking cadet upperclassman directing all of the new cadets was not kidding. Anyone who groused about the direction given was roughly helped along with the task.

The upperclassman then directed the crowd of young men and women to line up in formation. If they didn't know what a formation was, they learned immediately. For the next few hours, the new Doolies, as the incoming class of cadets were called, were indoctrinated into the basics of marching in a formation, and how to respond to the drill commands. Most of the cadets had forgotten to eat before arriving. Their stomachs growled and sweat poured off their young faces in the hot Colorado summer sun, the heat intensified by the Academy's seventy-two-hundred-foot elevation.

The incoming cadets were marched to Vandenberg Hall, where they were ordered to line up. Most expected what was coming next. The buzzing sound of the barber clippers quickly relieved them of whatever hair they had on their head. Matt cringed as his long blond hair dropped to the floor. He thought briefly about what his old girlfriend might think if she saw him now. He looked in the mirror and thought he looked like a prison inmate. The cadets next to him looked no different. He reached up and rubbed the stubble on top of his head.

"I hope you guys don't expect a tip for this ten-second haircut," he laughed. "Guess I don't need a comb anymore."

The barber didn't laugh. He just motioned to Matt to move along.

"Hey, man, you look like you just escaped from Alcatraz," another cadet said to Matt.

"Well, you are *one* homely-looking dude. Good thing there aren't any datable women around for you to scare."

The good-natured ribbing continued until the hairless men were ordered to again line up. He now blended right in with all the other Doolies. The haircuts were a step in taking away their individualism and their identities as civilians, as they were no longer a member of *that* particular fraternity. Now, if they survived the rigorous four years of Academy life, they would become members of a very special fraternity—the fraternity of comrades-in-arms. They would become part of a fellowship that would stay with them for the rest of their lives.

The academic year began with vigor in August. Matt didn't fully understand it yet, but the coming year would bond him inextricably to his fellow first-year cadets, all of whom would do their best to help each other survive the ordeal in front of them. The challenges they would face were imposed deliberately, sometimes harshly, by the upperclassmen. There was no hate in their actions. Only those cadets who overcame the first year's initiation could continue to seek membership in the exclusive club.

Matt knew it would be tough, and he was ready for it. He had been contacted by an old friend of his father after word of his Congressional appointment got out. The friend, an Academy graduate and fellow squadron-mate in his dad's F-15E Strike Eagle unit, spent time with Matt to make sure he was prepared for the challenge of a lifetime. He was told what to expect, how he should behave, what he would have to overcome, and how to demonstrate that he had the right stuff to be an Academy graduate. Matt was a natural leader, and he was determined to be the absolute best. He had something to prove to himself, and to his father.

This was nothing like any college his buddies in Texas were attending. No girlfriends, no time off, no car—no freedom! Although he'd thought he was prepared, Matt was a bit stunned at the absolute rigor and discipline that accompanied virtually every aspect of his life this first year. While the academics were a snap for him, the rote memorization of endless streams of minutiae was mind-boggling and often seemed without a real purpose to him.

"You've gotta be shitting me," he remarked to his classmate as he thought about having to recite from memory the day's dining hall menu, the front page of the daily newspaper, and any detail from their Academy "Contrails" handbook when commanded to do so by an upperclassman.

"I don't know how anyone can keep all this crap in his head and then squirt it out when ordered," he said to Matt.

"Well, we better figure out a way to do it." Matt wasn't too worried, knowing his near-photographic memory would come in handy.

They both knew that failure to be able to recite anything on demand would result in a swift rebuke. Further failure to meet overall standards of discipline could be met with demerits and/or marching tours if the infraction warranted it. Worst among the penalties was the incessant hours-long marching that ate up the limited, if any, precious hours of free time they had.

What really bothered Matt was the simple things, though, like eating—something that he truly loved to do. Mealtime was ruined as far as he was concerned. Doolies were prohibited from eating until all upperclassmen had been served their meals. When the first-year cadets were allowed to eat, they sat at attention, stared straight ahead, and never said a word. It left little time to enjoy a meal, or even finish it.

This is a royal pain in the ass, he thought. *I can tolerate a lot of this bullshit, but I've gotta have time to eat my chow! I'm not sure I can function on all cylinders without a full stomach. But I'll get through this—nothing will stop me from becoming an Academy graduate.*

As the end of his first year drew near, Matt prepared himself for the ordeal of Hell Week. The Academy preferred the more socially correct phrase, Recognition Week. It involved intense engagement by the entire staff to break down anyone not yet fully committed to their future as a member of the select fraternity of warriors. During Hell Week, the cadets endured it all—constant room and uniform inspections, formation runs, intense exercise regimens, knowledge tests, incessant marching, and a great deal of in-your-face supervision from the upperclassmen.

While many of his fellow classmates got a bit overstressed with the constant harassment, Matt kept his cool. He could easily handle every aspect of the "torture" the upper-class cadets placed on him. *They'll never break me. I can do this standing on my head*, he thought arrogantly.

When Hell Week ended, the grand finale of the first year was recognition that they had met the stringent military training requirements, and were prepared for the next several years. Upper classmen formally welcomed them into their ranks, signified by the award of the Prop and Wings. This insignia identified them officially as brothers in blue. They would wear it proudly on their uniform for the remainder of their Academy time. Matt tried to contain his smile when the insignia was pinned to his uniform.

I made it, he thought to himself.

———•———

The next three years were tough on academics, essentially exposing each cadet to everything from thermodynamics and physics, to engineering, mathematics, and a sprinkling of liberal arts. Matt focused on aeronautical engineering as his chosen area of study and major and concentrated on the rigorous curriculum that would get him there. At the end of his third year, beyond being at the top of his class in studies, he relished finally being able to get a car. For the past three years, the cadets were restricted from having a car on the Academy grounds. If they wanted to head to "the Springs," they hitched a ride with a Firstie, as the senior class cadets were called.

While many of Matt's classmates put their orders in for new cars, with the Corvette and Camaro topping the list, Matt chose another path. The old hot rod in his mom's garage in Texas had originally belonged to his dad, who had special-ordered it from Ford and then had it modified by Kar Kraft in Michigan to its current configuration. His Boss Mustang had a 375-horsepower 429-cubic-inch V-8 engine that could produce 450 pounds of torque at 3400 rpm. The original Grabber Blue paint was faded, but the car had no rust. Matt had done his research and found a small company in Colorado Springs, Restoration Motors, that specialized in making old automobiles new again. He had shipped the car from Texas and had been making payments for the past two years to rebuild the 1970 Boss Mustang.

Matt had tracked the car's progress, and now it was ready. As he looked at the final restored Boss, he smiled. The black scoop on the newly painted Grabber Blue hood and the chrome Magnum 500 wheels definitely made this baby stand out! He couldn't wait to open it up on the long stretches of Interstate 25 when he was sure there were no troopers around.

Three years at the Air Force Academy had seemed like an eternity. The rigor and discipline instilled in all those that were willing to stick it out were the driving force that got them through the tough academics and physical fitness regimen. There had been times, especially that first year, when Matt was ready to punch out a few upperclassmen, not willing to put up with the constant harassment and belittling that was the yoke all Doolies had to endure. His only outlet was intramural sports, where he excelled, and eventually varsity sports on the Falcons' football team. As a tight end, he had the size and speed to stand out and was a key factor in the Falcons' winning seasons. Up to this point, Matt believed he had proven himself worthy of being an Air Force officer. He still had his final year ahead of him to get to graduation and to pilot training.

As a Firstie, Matt had it made. The senior class had the most freedom in their curriculum. In their extra time, they could do pretty much what they wanted. Matt took advantage of the time to fine-tune his hot rod, making added modifications to the Boss Mustang. The car, while not totally original to its manufacturer's specs, was perfection in Matt's mind. He wasted no time in testing the limits of the big engine's performance on the highway, and on the winding roads that surrounded Pike's Peak.

Chapter 14

August 2008
Mesquite, Texas

The dusty Texas countryside reminded Khalil of his home in Syria, at least a bit, from what he could see looking out the window of his father's BMW. As they drove outside Dallas on long stretches of deserted highway, Syria seemed to fade from his memory like the early-morning haze hanging in the air around Mesquite. His formative years in England had given him the tools to blend in quite effectively with an English-speaking population, even though he had to work a little to understand the nuances of the English language as the Brits used it. Texas was going to be yet another challenge, at least at first, since the Texas twang sometimes took a sharp ear to understand exactly what was being said.

The BMW pulled into the Arapaho High School parking lot. It was crowded with buses unloading students, as well as cars and plenty of pickup trucks maneuvering around them to try to get a choice parking spot in the dusty gravel lot.

"Come on, Ana. It's time to begin a new chapter in our lives. Who would have ever thought we'd be going to school in Texas?" Khalil smiled at his sister.

"I'm nervous, Khalil. I'm not sure that anyone will like me here."

"Are you kidding? You're beautiful, and I'm sure you'll have lots of friends. Just wait and see!"

"Have a wonderful day, my children—learn all you can," Dr. Ruffa said, looking lovingly at them.

Ana leaned forward, kissed her father on the cheek and jumped out, while Khalil nodded and joined Ana on the steps of the school's entryway. Dr. Ruffa watched his young children, now thirteen years old, as they walked toward the main entrance to the school. He believed that he had done his best to raise them, instilling in them the absolute imperatives of a strong education, pride in their heritage, and faith in their religion.

They should do well, he thought. *They have a good grasp of the English language from their education in Westminster, and they are better educated than most of the students here and more mature than their peer group.*

Dr. Ruffa believed his children would have a slight edge in this new society, but he knew that they would still have to overcome some bias on the part of die-hard Texans who would always see them as very different—as outsiders.

As an internal medicine physician, Mahmoud Ruffa knew the value of education, especially in a civilized society. He knew the respect it brought to those who succeeded, to those who rose to the top of their chosen profession, and the doors it opened to both opportunity and wealth. His children were well prepared, having attended the best schools in Westminster, supplemented by the good doctor's personal tutoring. They should easily assimilate into the Texas school system and quickly establish themselves at the top of their academic classes.

Likewise, embracing their Syrian heritage was extremely important. Mahmoud was proud of his ethnicity, proud that a boy raised in a poor village, through both good fortune and his own intellect, could rise from the desert like a phoenix and become a well-respected doctor. In many respects, Khalil and Ana, through tragedy, had been given the same opportunity. They had been whisked away from relative poverty and given a chance beyond the reach of most Syrian children.

Dr. and Mrs. Ruffa made sure to raise the children the way they had been raised. After all, the values instilled in Mahmoud by his own parents, both now long since deceased, were at the very core of his mental and physical being. He was proud to be Syrian, first and foremost. He knew that if he adhered to the Quran, to the key tenets of Islam, he would always have the strength to overcome any obstacle. Allah would never give a devout Muslim a task that was beyond his ability to handle. The children would have to tackle the obstacles they encountered and persevere.

The Texas school system was a rough environment. Any weakness, whether physical size, mental acuity, or lack of good looks—pretty much anything—might prevent a kid get from being accepted by classmates. In fact, there were enough predators to make a kid's life miserable. Khalil and Ana stood out. Their outward appearance and accent were undeniably not typical "Texas born and bred."

But both children had been blessed with astonishing good looks. Khalil was big for his age, with the muscle tone of an athlete, and his piercing brown eyes stopped people in their tracks. He made friends quickly. Ana was extremely attractive but had chosen to adopt the clothes of her Islamic culture, wearing the hijab typical of girls her age in Syria. This made her stand out from other girls—and not in a good way. A pretty girl would otherwise become the center of attention, resulting in quick integration into a new environment. However, her head covering caused a discomforting measure of disdain amongst most of the students and resulted in Ana's alienation from both boys and girls alike.

Most girls steered clear of her. Others simply stared or pointed at her. The boys were another story. Attractive girls were ordinarily surrounded by boys whose rampaging testosterone made them do and say almost anything to get a girl's attention. But it worked the other way if a girl appeared different from her peers.

Although the deadly September 11 attack on America was seven years in the past, the United States' global war on terror was in full swing. The Muslim community as a whole was often undeservedly targeted. And it took very little time before the hatred for all things Islamic came Ana's way. Insulting comments came from some of the more ignorant students seeking to draw attention to themselves.

One particular bone-headed Texas boy had been relentlessly taunting Ana for weeks. "Hey, get that rag off your head. We don't dress that way in Texas. If you want to wear that crap, why don't you go back where you came from?"

Several of his friends had laughed at the remarks.

"I am American," Ana responded proudly. "But I am also very proud of my heritage and my faith."

The remarks hurt her deeply. They also made her a bit fearful for her safety. While her father had prepared her for the possibility of anti-Muslim sentiment, it still shocked her, as she had not experienced this kind of treatment in England.

The insults cast Ana's way were almost always done when Khalil was not around her. On one occasion, a burly Hispanic youth openly cursed at Ana, taunting her to become his sex partner, to be subservient and submissive to him as he claimed all Muslim women were to Syrian men. Unfortunately for the arrogant, ignorant youth, Khalil heard the outburst. In the school parking lot, he meted out his version of justice on the kid that insulted his sister. Khalil beat the boy severely. Fortunately for the unlucky youth, other students intervened to stop his punishment. It served its purpose, and subsequently, Khalil's presence was ominous enough to silence anyone that would even think of publicly demeaning his beloved sister. Unfortunately, his action only further alienated her from her peers, and Ana struggled to make friends over the course of her first school year in the United States.

Both children, with the constant encouragement of their parents, focused on their studies above all else. The Ruffas strongly reinforced the children's need to excel and insisted that their education was their first priority. Their intolerance for anything less than top grades was enough to keep his young children on track for success in the future.

As Khalil approached the end of his first year in high school, he was noticed by one man in particular. The football coach at

Arapaho High was always looking for new talent. As he perused the possible new recruits, he spotted a tall, muscular boy in the hallway.

Hmm, this kid ought to be out on my field, he thought as he watched Khalil talking with some pretty young girls.

"Young man," said Coach Wiley. "Have you ever considered playing football? You've got the size and build of a potential running back. Why don't you give it a try?"

Khalil turned and looked at the coach, a bit surprised that he would be asking him that question. *I'm not sure what a running back is exactly, or pretty much any of the player positions on the team.*

Khalil had no real desire to play, as he had never touched a football in his life. But he had witnessed how most of the students at Arapaho High School behaved during football season. It seemed like it was the most important thing on earth to them. In England, he had heard that Americans, especially Texans, loved their American-style football. Through his freshman year studies, he had been caught up a bit in the football frenzy. He had attended a game and began to realize the importance Americans placed on the sport. He was amazed at how crazy the Arapaho students acted before, during and after the games. It reminded him of similar behavior he had seen in England during soccer madness. Khalil started to realize that if he was to succeed socially, he needed to learn a lot more about American football. For now, he politely dismissed the coach's request.

"Thanks, Coach, but I'm really not that interested. I appreciate you asking me about it. Right now, I'm still trying to get myself focused on the coursework here. It's a bit of a change from England."

Khalil was embarrassed that he didn't know that much about football or the rules, unlike every other Texas boy at the school.

I need to concentrate on my studies, he thought. He firmly believed *that* was the secret to success in the United States. *That is my true focus, my near-term goal. I don't have time for any nonsense, or football.*

Coach Wiley shook his head. He would eventually figure out a way to get this new student onto the team. *Maybe next year.*

Chapter 15

Khalil spent his summer taking online courses to improve his software skills. He also rigorously worked out at home and in the school gym, which opened early to accommodate preseason training for the football team. As he prepared for his second year of high school, he was on track to achieve the tough goals he had set for himself. He prided himself on both his exceptional mind and his powerful physique. He built up his endurance running on the Arapaho track—easily sprinting a mile or more with barely a heavy breath. On one particular day, while he was putting in his daily run, the football team was conducting a practice session. The kicker sent towering punts down the field, and as Khalil jogged by, one ball bounced crazily toward him. He stopped to pick it up while the punter shouted for him to throw it back on the field. Not exactly knowing how to throw a football, Khalil took a hard look at it.

This is a prolate spheroid. I've studied these engineering design shapes before. He immediately understood the ball's aerodynamic properties and how he could make it sail through the air. *This is just another engineering analysis. Apply the principles and it should work.*

He threw a perfect pass, a fifty-yard bullet to the punter.

Coach Wiley saw the pass and was astounded. He immediately ran toward Khalil, recognizing him as the same boy he'd talked with in the hallway the previous year—the big kid he believed had real prospects as a football player.

"Son, you've got quite an arm. I know you didn't have much interest last year when we talked, but I think you should give our team a shot. Come practice with us, and let's have a look at what you can do."

"Coach, thanks, but I don't really know much about the game. I've never played it before."

"No problem. What's your name?"

"Khalil Ruffa. But, Coach, I've got to tell you that this idea is not going to go over big with my father."

"Look, worst case, you get a good workout with us, and it looks like you're already into working out. Best case, you make the team and open up a new chapter in your life," replied Wiley. "Talk with your dad, and if you'd like me to talk with him, let me know. I'd like to see you out here for practice on Monday."

I don't know how I'm going to break this news to my father, thought Khalil.

As he looked around the field, he saw that he had not gone unnoticed by the cheerleaders practicing on the field. They were clearly enthralled with both his good looks and muscular build. A couple of them waved at Khalil, big smiles on their faces. He waved back.

At home, Khalil decided to ask his father, his mentor, what he should do. He was somewhat conflicted by anything that would interfere with his razor-sharp focus on his studies. He fully expected some major pushback about anything that would get in the way of his schoolwork.

"Father, I have a dilemma and need to get your opinion," Khalil explained over dinner. "The football coach thinks I can be a great player and asked me to come to practice. I'm not sure what to do."

"I think you would be an excellent football player," said Ana. "You're bigger and stronger than most of the boys I've seen playing."

"I know I could learn the game and the rules pretty quickly," he said to Ana. "It doesn't seem that difficult."

He looked into his father's face for some kind of reaction. All he got was a solid stare—possibly a look of astonishment—or maybe just a questioning expression about why Khalil would want to do such a thing.

Dr. Ruffa was a wise man and knew what it took to excel in a modern society, and especially in a technically advanced country. He believed that football was an unruly, violent American distraction from the primary purpose for which his charge was on this earth. But he knew that there were other benefits.

"Khalil, you are an exceptionally smart boy, and you will go far in this country as long as you continue to apply yourself to your studies to the maximum extent possible. You can do anything you set your mind to."

Dr. Ruffa also knew that a successful athlete was readily accepted and welcomed socially by most people, that being a top athlete could supplement a brilliant mind as a surefire ticket to success and open doors that might not otherwise be opened.

"You can never forsake your studies for football," he warned, "but success on the athletic field can help you more fully integrate into American life. It can open doors for you."

Khalil had the weekend to figure out what the game was all about. He headed to the Mesquite public library and read everything he could get his hands on related to football. He had the rules and all the nuances of the game down pat in his head by Sunday night. After classes Monday, he rushed a workout in the weight room and headed over to football practice.

After a few short weeks, Khalil had dumbfounded both the coach and the entire team with how quickly he picked up the game. For someone as intelligent as Khalil, it was no big deal. The practice sessions helped him quickly translate what he had researched to near-perfect physical execution of the sport. After only one game on the sidelines, the coach put Khalil in as a sub for the normal starting quarterback, Cody Stallings, after the junior-year student took a rough hit by a blitzing linebacker. It was as if Khalil had been playing the game all his life. After he took a few violent hits by aggressive defensive linesmen and linebackers, he understood the need for using the protection of his offensive line, staying in the pocket, and quickly releasing his passes before the threat was upon him. When the pocket collapsed, Khalil had the speed and agility to get out of even the toughest situations and sprint down the field. Coach Wiley was so impressed that he kept him on the field the rest of the game, even though Cody was ready to go back in.

"I can't believe this foreigner is taking my place, after all I've done for this team," Cody remarked in anger and disgust.

After their win, Coach Wiley had made a key decision about changing his usual starting quarterback for the Arapaho Stallions' next game. Khalil performed brilliantly, throwing three touchdown passes and running for two more. The team trounced their opponents and were now fully embracing their new superstar. Khalil tried to talk with Cody about Coach Wiley's decision to play him at the starting quarterback position. He knew that Cody was pretty angry about it, but it was a decision the coach had made, not him. Khalil felt bad about it, not really wanting to create any bad feelings between him and the rest of the team, many of whom had grown up with Cody. The benched quarterback would have none of Khalil's explanation.

A week later, another victory without Cody at the helm just made matters worse. "This just isn't fair, that some nobody *walk-on* can just show up out of nowhere and ruin my scholarship chances at the peak of my high school career," Cody complained to his buddies.

"Yeah, it sucks, Cody," his friend remarked. "But you've gotta admit, Khalil is damn good! And we're scoring more points than ever with him."

"Fuck off, asshole," Cody shouted. "Football is my ticket out of here and onto a good college team. I can't be sitting on the bench for my last two years!" Cody was about ready to explode.

His teammates all agreed that this was a shitty deal for him, but they certainly didn't mind the wins. But Texans were a loyal bunch, and no outsider was going to come between the tight bond of friendship developed over many years.

Ana couldn't believe that her talented brother, who hadn't even known what a football was a couple of years ago, was now the star of the team. She gained newfound attention from the cheerleaders now that her brother was a star, and suddenly the young girl in the hijab was getting almost as much attention as her brother. *I know they now pretend to like me only because of Khalil,* she thought. *They are not really my friends, and I don't think I should trust them.*

But Ana had to admit, it was kind of nice to finally have people to talk with. It was quite a change from feeling socially isolated, trapped in her own loneliness and need for friendship.

There wasn't much to do in Mesquite on most nights, but during football season, Friday nights were game nights. The sleepy town was hopping with late-night activity after another Arapaho win. The streets were choked off with mud-splattered pickup trucks cruising down the main street, horns blasting. Rowdy shouts of beefy football players were aided by cheap Jeremiah Weed whiskey mixed into their twelve-ounce plastic Coke bottles. Even though the kids couldn't legally buy booze, Patsy's liquor store looked the other way when it came to taking good care of the Mesquite football players. The team generally congregated at the Denny's restaurant, mainly due to its isolated location in the north part of town. Their large broken asphalt parking lot always turned into a noisy post-game tailgate party. The cheerleaders knew the drill and quickly paired up with their boyfriends. The girls enjoyed the celebration and the overload of testosterone flowing from the boisterous players.

There was no celebrating going on in Cody's mind. He had been relegated to the sidelines during the game yet again, picking up splinters on the bench while Khalil led the team to victory. Cody's girlfriend wasn't too happy either, believing *her* future ticket out of Mesquite was also being cancelled before it could ever get punched. Her hopes that her boyfriend would ride a football scholarship to A&M and, with luck, get drafted by a professional football team, were being dashed by this *foreigner* who, in her mind, had no right to be here.

"You need to man up and do something about this," she angrily told Cody.

"Darlene, what the hell am I supposed to do? The coach thinks this transplant from Syria can do a better job. He just won't listen to me." Cody tilted the half-empty Coke with its Jeremiah Weed mix to his lips and took a long draw from it.

"You need to man up!" she yelled loudly at him, as if the liquor had made him a bit hard of hearing. "Just don't screw up everything that we've been planning for, our future."

"Yeah, yeah. I hear you. I'll figure something out."

With a bit of help from the intoxicating effects of the cheap whiskey, Cody knew that he had to do something. He couldn't take the ribbing from Darlene or anyone else. He also knew he could never take on Khalil one-on-one. There had to be another way. Everyone knew that Cody was angry with the overall situation, and the finger would be pointed directly at him if anything were to happen to Khalil. Besides, he had seen Khalil's strength demonstrated in the weight room. Cody, while riding the ego of a consummate athlete, was actually a bit of a coward by himself and wouldn't think of taking on Khalil alone, or even with a couple of his friends. No, there had to be another way to get inside Khalil's head and shock him into the reality of Texas life…to rattle him so badly that he wouldn't be able to focus on football.

After a big win a week later against the Plano Reapers, the party was going strong at Denny's. Darlene, the head cheerleader, had finally persuaded Ana to attend, even though she knew Ana would never drink alcohol, nor show any overt affection to any boy in public. Ana was a good Muslim, and true to her Islamic faith. In spite of how American boys and girls behaved in public, she would never allow a boy to touch her the way she saw other girls do.

Cody and the rest of the team were already letting loose at Denny's and loudly proclaiming the power of the Arapaho Stallions. At this point in the season, it looked like they would easily take the division championship. This night was especially important for Cody, since he'd actually gotten to get onto the field late in the game after Khalil had taken a painful hit from an aggressive linebacker. The hit was facilitated by Cody's friend on the offensive line, who'd deliberately allowed the linebacker a direct lane for the brutal tackle, hitting Khalil just below the knees. Khalil had come limping off the field, and Cody had led the team for the remainder of the game. Cody's plan was coming together nicely. The injury kept Khalil away from Denny's that night, and prevented him from keeping a watchful eye over his sister.

Chapter 16

The strategy Cody had devised seemed perfect, at least in his twisted, evil mind. Darlene got Ana to leave Denny's with her to drive back to the school to pick up her purse, which she claimed to have left there accidentally. Once at the school, Ana waited in the car while Darlene walked in to retrieve it. In the dark, unlit parking lot, three of the biggest football linemen hid in the darkness with nylon stockings pulled over their heads.

They snuck up to Darlene's car, pulled the door open, and grabbed Ana, dragging her from the front seat. It happened so quickly, Ana had no time to scream. A large hand quickly clamped over her mouth. The three boys had no problem carrying her around the side of the building, out of sight of any passing cars. In the remote school zone, there would be little likelihood of anyone hearing any screams from the terrified girl. The boys ripped the hijab from her head. Ana's long, silky black hair tumbled down her shoulders, highlighting her beauty in the moonlight, even though stark terror flashed in her dark eyes.

"C'mon, Dirk, let's teach this bitch a lesson! Her stinking brother brought this on. Nobody messes with us and gets away with it," shouted one of the boys.

"Hey, asshole, shut the hell up and don't use my name!"

"Oh yeah—right."

The boys wasted no time trying to tear Ana's clothes off. The biggest of the group shouted, "You Arab whore, you're gonna get what you deserve."

They had rape on their mind. But they underestimated the strength of their intended victim. Even with two boys holding her down, Ana struggled with all her might and was able to break their grip and land a few blows on her attackers. They were startled at the intensity of her counterattack. She was almost out of control as she swung her clenched fists, hoping to land enough strikes to fend off her attackers. Her screams couldn't be muffled by their attempts to keep her mouth covered. Any hand that got close to her mouth was rewarded with a painful bite.

"Ouch! The bitch bit me!" one of them shouted, jerking his hand from her mouth.

His large fist swung down hard against Ana's cheek. The punch to her face was followed by successive hard strikes to her head, chest, and stomach. The boys were now in a rage. Their interest in rape had shifted to beating Ana nearly to death. Ana passed out quickly as the assault progressed, the horrifying ordeal continuing for fifteen minutes.

Ana lay unconscious, her face so badly beaten that she was nearly unrecognizable. Her cheekbones had been fractured, her jaw broken. The beating to her body had broken several of her ribs, one of which punctured her lung. Her kidney was lacerated, and she had internal bleeding around her stomach cavity. The brutal attack was finished.

The three football players ran from around the building, hopped into their car, and headed back to Denny's. They slipped unnoticed back into the ongoing rousing party. They saw Cody standing by his car and waved at him, giving him a thumbs-up. The deed had been done, and Cody smiled.

He thought to himself, *This will take care of Khalil. Screw with me and you get screwed—and your sister too!* Laughing out loud, he raised what remained of his cheap alcohol mixture to his lips and took a long swallow.

Darlene waited for twenty minutes in the school for the boys to finish and then came back to the car. Not seeing Ana, she headed around the building and found her unconsciousness. When she saw her, she was stunned. She hadn't realized how brutal the assault was going to be. Darlene began to sob.

"Oh my gosh, what happened, Ana?" she screamed. "I was only in the school for a few minutes!"

Ana couldn't hear a word. Darlene began to dial 911 on her phone. She hesitated briefly, knowing that she would be questioned by the police. But after looking over her shoulder at the shattered girl on the ground, she dialed the number. There had been an assault, and it was her duty to report it. At least that was the plan.

The local Mesquite police department and medical unit wasted no time getting to the school. Darlene's explanation of events to the police officers was completely believable. She stated that there was nobody else in the parking lot when she'd left Ana and that she was only in the school building for about fifteen minutes. She said that she had trouble opening her locker, the combination not working properly. That delayed her getting back to Ana. She said she had done her best to help her friend.

The paramedics hadn't seen anyone beaten this badly before. Ana was breathing, but just barely. They did their best to stabilize her and gently lifted her onto a portable gurney and into the ambulance. Within ten minutes, they were pulling into the emergency entrance of the Mesquite Hospital.

At this point, there appeared to be no witnesses to the attack, as far as the police could determine. Darlene was in the vicinity of the attack but had seen nothing. The officers took a lengthy statement from her and then told her she was free to go, but they might want to talk with her again. As the officers talked among themselves, one mentioned that he knew Darlene's father. She came from a respected Texas family, was an honor student, and had been friendly to Ana prior to the assault. They felt that Darlene's story was plausible, and likely an accurate explanation of what had happened. They chalked the assault up as a potential hate crime and would do their best to determine who had committed the horrendous assault.

Upon receiving the phone call from the police, Khalil and his father raced to the hospital. They were stunned by what the emergency room staff told them about Ana's condition. They had to wait a couple of hours before they could see her, while the hospital trauma staff did all that they could to determine the extent of damage done to the young girl.

As Dr. Ruffa and Khalil sat in the waiting room, the police talked with them both. From what they knew, there were no witnesses to the attack. They would begin their investigation and gather whatever DNA and other evidence was available. Maybe there would be a DNA match with any number of known criminal elements that frequented the Mesquite area. The police questioned the Ruffas about any known threats that might have been made to Ana. Did they have any idea who might have done this? The family couldn't provide any relevant information to assist the police.

Chapter 17

The investigation into Ana's assault proceeded for weeks without a breakthrough. Once Ana had regained consciousness, she couldn't provide any detail, other than knowing there were three men who had attacked her. She had no recollection of any names being mentioned during the assault, in spite of the mistake made by one of them, who had shouted out the name "Dirk." Ana's mind had shut down early—she remembered nothing but the violence prior to passing out, and then waking from the ordeal.

Additional statements taken by the police from Darlene were a bit sketchy but, absent any other evidence to the contrary, they were believable. She had seen nothing. And she was adamant about knowing nothing about any threat to Ana. After all, Ana was one of her newest friends. The perpetrators, at least for the time being, had evaded capture. No suspects—no evidence—no charges.

Dr. Ruffa was crushed by what had happened. The child that he should have protected had been brutally beaten. He had failed his brother. He spent the next two days at the hospital with Ana. The attack had left Ana experiencing episodes of catatonic-like behavior, unable to speak. She was occasionally alert, and when she was lucid, she moaned about being ashamed of herself for the terrible violation of her body, and especially the disfigurement of her face. She believed that her life was over. While her father did his best to comfort her, it was clear to him that the tragic event might have a lasting impact on his daughter's life.

Dr. Ruffa thought about how he had raised her since rescuing the two children from the orphanage in Turkey. How could Allah have allowed this to happen? *I have done everything I could to raise her according to the Quran's principles. I have kept my faith and prayed to Allah daily. Yet this is the result of my faith*, he pondered.

Mentally, Khalil was trying hard to come to grips with the brutal act—likely Americans, in his mind, who had no honor, no respect for anything in their lives, and who only lived for the moment. It was also unfathomable to him that the scum who had assaulted his sister hadn't been quickly caught and punished. Punished in the way of Islam. Punished in a way that would send a message to all who committed such atrocities.

Here in Texas, he thought irrationally, *the law is on the side of the attackers, not the victim. And, of course, we are different from the rest. We are foreigners in a land that makes it formidable for anyone who is different to be treated fairly.*

His rage continued to grow. The intensity of his anger took over his mind, his usually rational thinking being displaced by irrational thoughts. But what would be his ultimate release of this rage? He suspected that boys from his school might have been involved in the attack on his sister, but there were no witnesses. Nobody on the football team was talking, other than a few expressing feigned sympathy.

For weeks, Khalil stood by her hospital bed. Each visit brought tears to his eyes ears as he stared down at Ana's horribly disfigured face. What he saw tore through the fabric of his heart, his psyche. His head was spinning with random thoughts. He was thankful that Ana was alive, but his heart pounded as he struggled internally about what to do. *I must do something to avenge my sister. I can't stand idly by and do nothing.*

The only real outlet for Khalil was the Abdallah Mosque, south of Mesquite. His father had taken him there on multiple occasions to help bring Khalil closer to his faith, and to the true tenets of Islam. Sheikh Rahainee, the imam there, offered not just the answers to some of the Quran's most difficult concepts but also the guiding principles for any devout Muslim who wished to live his life in the way that Allah prescribed. In the past, the sheikh had offered the opportunity to discuss what Khalil was struggling with, his conflicts between his new life in America and his true identity as a Syrian devoted to Islam. Now, Khalil sought the kind of guidance that he could not get from his father. The imam understood the struggle Khalil had in his mind and heart, the conflicts every Muslim might encounter while living in the United States.

"My imam, a terrible thing has happened to my sister. Once again, my family has experienced horror no one should ever endure."

He explained the assault on Ana and the fact that it was very likely that nobody would be held to account for her brutal attack.

"I'm doing everything I can to integrate into American society, into their culture. But if this is the result, I question my true direction in life."

Sheikh Rahainee patiently listened to all Khalil said and tried to read his face, his heart, his soul. The imam spent time explaining how devout Muslims could shape their lives and even their odds in favor of Islam.

"The Quran is your guide to life," he explained. "It must become the basis for all that you do in spite of your assimilation into this American culture. You must return to your roots, to the teachings of Mohammad and your *true* culture—the way of life taught to you by your birth father, who was so ruthlessly taken from you and your sister at such a young age by these same people that you have now called friends."

These crucial messages would make a lasting imprint on Khalil.

———————•———————

The imam had seen great potential in his young scribe. This young Syrian had all the necessary elements needed in the struggle to establish radical Islamic ideals within the United States. The religious cleric was a master at manipulation. After all, he himself had been recruited and trained at a young age to be a warrior for Islam—a warrior whose duty it was to eliminate all that was evil and corrupt in the world—a world stained and tainted by the impurities of thought and deed, fostered by countries that would not ever embrace Islam as the true religion. Rahainee had fought on the battlefields of his country at the young age of fifteen, recruited to fight for his faith. He had survived, and in fact flourished, for ten years as a brutal combatant in the struggle to eliminate the curse of Western influence. He had been personally tutored by one of the most notorious radical Islamic factions, who had seen in him a future imam to lead the cause against all infidels. Over time, the imam would use these skills, learned on the battlefield and in his intense training, to shape Khalil in a way the boy never imagined.

———————•———————

In the weeks that followed the attack on Ana, Khalil had difficulty concentrating on anything, and as such, his high-energy football performance suffered, much to Cody's delight. When he wasn't at school, every trip to the mosque had Ana foremost in his mind. Khalil found ways to visit the mosque on his own, keeping his trips secret from his football teammates, being careful not to draw any further alienation to his family than he already felt existed. He had his own way of getting around now, having picked up an old but reliable Chevy truck with help from his generous father's wallet.

When Ana had recovered enough to undergo reconstructive surgery, the specialists went to work to repair the extensive damage to her face. Unfortunately, the violence of the beating ensured her beautiful smile would never be recreated. Since the assault, she had retreated psychologically into herself, creating a cocoon-like barrier in her mind—there was no room for any more pain. She refused to leave the house for school, to go anywhere. She carried the shame of the assault deep inside her, mainly due to the damage done to her previously beautiful face—and the fact that no justice had yet come to her attackers. She believed her life was over, that no man would ever want to take her for his bride.

Khalil's rage grew with each visit to the mosque. His sister's brutal assault had fundamentally changed him, triggering a seething cauldron of hate for Americans. It built upon the bedrock of hatred and anger already present from his parents' and brothers' deaths. He sought some comfort, some understanding, from the imam to help him deal with the anger. The cleric did not offer the kind of support he needed. Instead, Sheikh Rahainee found a fertile mind that was ripe for the kind of manipulation that formed the basis for transitioning otherwise rational people into something that most of the intelligent world could not understand. He found a mind traumatized by tragic life events, a mind that could be shaped for the greater good of radical Islam. With these continued discussions came Khalil's indoctrination into the more violent aspects of a religion he had once believed was a means to live a peaceful life. It was a religion by which his father and mother had lived their lives, raising their children in holy Islam's fundamental concepts. But now, Sheikh Rahainee would deeply implant the mutated seeds of Islamic extremism in Khalil and shape his future—his destiny.

Chapter 18

June 2012

He looked across the crowd of starched uniforms—the graduating class of Air Force Academy cadets—his family. They had a common bond that just didn't exist in a normal university environment.

"We've waited a long time for this," Matt remarked to his buddy sitting next to him. "Man, there were times when I wondered if this day would ever get here. Time to get on with why we came here in the first place."

Tim Beamon nodded at the comment and smiled broadly. "I know just what you mean. Let's just get through this long-ass ceremony and then leave this place as a traumatic memory in our rearview mirrors."

He and the rest of his classmates had now earned the right to become officers in the United States Air Force. *All to prove you're the best*, Matt thought, as he patiently waited for his diploma.

He was proud as hell that his mother was in attendance at the graduation. She absolutely beamed with happiness as she watched her son walk up on the stage and get his diploma. The soon-to-be second lieutenant in the United States Air Force was the spitting image of her late husband. Tears flowed down her face as she envisioned Alec watching with pride from the heavens.

He would be smiling, I just know it, she thought.

Plenty of requisite pictures were taken to capture this important moment in Matt's life. It seemed that Cathy Black wanted to memorialize the day her son officially picked up the baton left for him by his father. She knew her son would be incredibly successful in the Air Force. He had the same drive and determination her husband had demonstrated for the cherished years they were all together. When the official graduation ceremony ended, Cathy and Matt headed into Colorado Springs for a special dinner.

The Chop House was packed. Matt had made the reservation months earlier to ensure he would have a table on this crowded graduation night. The steak and grilled shrimp were renowned at this high-end downtown restaurant. Matt chose the bison steak, seasoned and blackened to perfection, with plenty of sautéed mushrooms. Cathy Black decided on the petite filet, with spicy marinated shrimp on the side.

"Mom, I'm so glad you could make it here for my graduation. I know it was a long trip from Fort Stockton, but this is truly a special day."

"Are you kidding? I wouldn't have missed this day for the world," she exclaimed, her smile as big as Matt had ever seen it. "You looked so handsome in your uniform. And the gold bars on your shoulders are terrific. Your father would have been so proud of you."

"I know he would, Mom."

He reached across the table and took her hand gently in his. "I know it's been pretty hard on you for the past nine years without Dad. But your father taught us both how to be independent—to survive—no matter what."

"He did. I remember him constantly reminding me about how I could do anything I set my mind to." He paused. "He was right."

A tear trickled down Cathy Black's cheek. Matt knew that in spite of what she said, his mother still missed Alec Black terribly.

As dinner came to a close, Matt glanced around the dining area. Many of his classmates enjoyed the same celebratory wrap-up to their four-year stint at the Academy. It would be a while before he would be able to do this again, given the rigorous military schedule that this new second lieutenant was about to undertake.

THOMAS BELISLE

Matt headed back to the Academy after dinner for a few good-byes with his classmates. Many of them were cleaning out their dorm rooms and packing up what little they had, and Matt did the same. When he was finally done, he cranked up the throaty Boss Mustang and pulled out of the dormitory parking lot. He would miss this place.

Okay, maybe not so much.

Some long-lasting friendships had been made, but a few of the instructors he would rather not see again. Nor would he miss the hazing he'd endured early in his time at the zoo.

Yeah, he thought, *there's a reason the cadets call this place the zoo.*

Matt couldn't wait to head on out of Colorado Springs and on to pilot training. Hopefully, with a little luck and a lot of determination, he would become a fighter pilot just like his dad. The drive to Vance Air Force Base in Oklahoma, where Matt would undergo his training, would not be particularly long. He would make every minute count before the next big step in his career.

He drove the scenic route out of Colorado Springs, adding some much-needed time to chill out a bit before going into the high-pressure program that awaited him at Vance. He traveled southwest along the Fort Carson perimeter, reaching Route 50. This was a gorgeous drive, west through the mountains, across the Continental Divide and Monarch Pass, and over to Montrose. There he picked up Route 550 southbound until branching off to eventually arrive outside Telluride. Matt loved this area, remembering the times his father had taken him camping there. The awesomeness of the location, from Matt's perspective, was almost indescribable, as he was surrounded by mountain peaks ranging from ten thousand to over fourteen thousand feet. A week by himself in the abundant wilderness area was just what he needed. *Summer in the mountains is as good as it gets on earth.*

He left his car in a National Forest parking area, the steering wheel of his precious automobile secured with a lock so that it wouldn't be easily stolen, or so he hoped. He talked briefly with the park staff, who assured him that his car would be safe and that cameras spanned the lot from the visitor's center. Grabbing his pack loaded with outdoor provisions, including enough water to sustain him for days, he headed up the trail that he thought would attract the fewest hikers. Matt needed some *alone* time. It wasn't the easiest hike, obviously not the best for day-hikers. But that was exactly what he was looking for. In fact, in some areas, the trail was pretty rugged, grown over with tangled brush, and clearly hadn't been used anytime recently. After a vertical climb of at least fifteen hundred feet, he came to a clearing near a large rock formation.

Great place to stay for the night.

The view was spectacular, with no evidence of any other hikers for miles. Camping in the wilderness was blissful peace, beneath the endless array of glittering stars, with just his own thoughts to entertain himself. The ultimate in chilling out your mind and body, he believed. Matt enjoyed the solitude, the quiet of the night, interrupted only by the sounds of the natural environment, the wildlife that called this area their home.

His first night was about as perfect as it could be. Lying on his back, looking up through a large break in the tall green aspens that surrounded him, he watched the universe above come to life. From his high-altitude vantage point, the stars seemed to reach down to him. The planet Saturn was extremely bright, bigger than he had ever witnessed before. He didn't want to close his eyes and miss any of the natural wonder of the brilliant night sky. He could just make out what appeared to be the constellation Orion, seeming to beckon him to leave the earth and approach the sparkling string of stars. Before he dozed off, a single meteor streaked across the dark sky, entering the earth's atmosphere in a blaze of burning light.

An omen, he thought. *This is definitely a sign from my Dad. I'm right where I'm supposed to be.*

Matt spent the next few days hiking up and down the steep crags and walking along crystal clear, fast-running mountain streams. The water was still extremely cold in midsummer, the snow melt keeping the temperature of the streams brisk. Brown and rainbow trout were occasionally visible near some of the warmer, shallower spots, constantly looking for insects to light upon a clear calm pool near a fallen tree.

The detailed trail guide he used was not the usual type acquired by everyday hikers. Matt had gotten it from the Bureau of Land Management. The maps provided plenty of options that would allow him to get deep into the wilderness area—and make him less likely to run into any other human. One early afternoon, Matt sat on a large boulder that appeared to have cascaded down from the craggy peaks above. His position overlooked a winding, fast-moving stream. About one hundred and fifty yards away, just outside the tree line adjacent to the stream, a large black bear was visible. It slowly walked from the protection of the spruce-fir tree line and approached the water's edge, standing motionless for about five minutes. The bear seemed to be staring at the water—waiting, perhaps, for an unlucky trout to get too close to the gravel-strewn edge of the stream. Matt watched it for nearly thirty minutes. Occasionally, the big carnivore turned its head, looking in Matt's direction, but if it saw him, it seemed unfazed.

"Not today," Matt said softly. The water was moving a bit too fast, and the fish were perhaps a little wise to the bear's intentions. He wished his time there would go on forever.

After five days of hiking and enjoying the beauty of the rugged, magnificent Rockies, he reluctantly began his hike back down the trail toward the National Forest parking lot. He was happy to see that his car appeared to be untouched. His trusty Boss Mustang started up with a roar, and Matt pulled out onto the twisting two-lane road that would take him out of this dreamland and back into reality. The Mustang handled the altitude pretty well, never bogging down on the steep grades and cruising effortlessly down from the Colorado heights until he was in the flatlands of Oklahoma. Enid, the town closest to where Matt would attend pilot training, was in the middle of nowhere, or at least that was what he thought as he drove through the town. He headed to Vance AFB, made his way through the main gate, and followed the directions he had been given to the bachelor officers' quarters. This outpost in the Oklahoma prairie was to be his new home for the next year.

Chapter 19

June 2012
Dallas, Texas

K halil walked from the mosque where he had just spent the last several hours. The stifling late-afternoon sunshine felt like an oven compared to the welcoming dark coolness of the mosque. His mentor, Sheikh Rahainee, watched him as he headed for his truck. The imam saw greatness in this young man. Like a piece of soft clay that needed to be carefully shaped, the imam would build this man into a warrior for Islam. He smiled to himself, thinking that the challenge to realign Khalil's focus, his desires, his true identity, had been made a bit easier after the attack on his sister. The sheikh used the brutal attack to continue building the anger in Khalil, like stoking glowing hot coals in a fire pit to get *just* the right results. He preached that the attack was but another example of Western corruption and of the disregard for the sanctity of one's body and of life in general. The sheikh also constantly refreshed Khalil's memory about the attack, years before, that had killed his family. He produced example after example—members of the Muslim faithful—slaughtered by Americans. The young Syrian's mental state made it relatively easy for the imam.

Khalil's hatred for his adopted country had been growing for the last three years, ever since his sister had been reduced to a hollow shell of the person she once was. Before the vicious attack, she had been a vibrant, intelligent young woman with great potential—now she was unable to integrate into any activity outside her home. Ana was so withdrawn that Dr. Ruffa sought extensive professional help through the large Dallas area physician network. One of the best psychiatrists in the area was treating her. They had seen this condition before, and the prognosis was most often, not very good. Ana had undergone constant intensive therapy using the latest medical approaches to unlock minds that had shut down—minds that had been so traumatized that a patient could remain locked in a state of complete retreat, often impenetrable to even the most advanced forms of stimulation. The specialists tried everything they could, but to no avail. They hoped that over time, Ana's mind would be able to get past the horrific shock she'd endured and somehow emerge from the lonely, isolated darkness where it currently resided.

The cleric stroked his gray beard and smiled ever so slightly as he thought about the future, the plans that would be formulated and ultimately executed by Khalil. The career path for this bright young Muslim would need to be managed carefully. He would need to guide Khalil to ultimately become a useful tool in the struggle for promulgating Iran's Islamic Caliphate within the Middle East. Iran had been busy laying the groundwork for years. Their Supreme Leader had declared the religious edict—the fatwa—as fundamental to Iran's future destiny. And the Caliphate was thus born. There was a constant need for intellectual warriors whose lives had been shaped at a young age—they would become the catalyst for radical Islamic change. The seeds for Khalil's college education, and his future, had been firmly planted by the sheikh.

As Khalil drove away from the mosque, he thought about his conversation with the imam. It seemed to him that every recent meeting with Sheikh Rahainee ultimately had one purpose. While Khalil was looking for explanations about why his life was in turmoil, the advice he was being given didn't seem like it was helping him reduce the seething anger he felt. Instead, the sheikh's messages stoked Khalil's rage and shaped the way he thought about his future—in a manner he had never intended. The end result would ultimately produce something much more satisfying for both him and for radical Islam.

———————•———————

Khalil hadn't needed much prompting about his upcoming college plans. His brilliance in high school and mastery of nearly every technical subject he tackled guided him to the best place to leverage his abilities. Prompted heavily by Sheikh Rahainee, he had done his research and investigated the best colleges, universities and technical institutes that would afford him the greatest opportunity for success. The school that his imam believed would be the catalyst for his greatest technical growth was nearby.

The program of studies offered by the prestigious Institute of Applied Science in Dallas seemed to be tailor-made for Khalil. The coursework was unlike any other technical college in the state. Poring through the detailed explanation of the curriculum, it was crystal clear to him that at the Institute, he could significantly expand his knowledge in cutting-edge software development and coding. While in high school, he had been intent on learning everything he could about this important area of expertise. He was especially interested in the latest advances in machine learning and artificial intelligence.

The Institute was acknowledged as one of the most demanding engineering, science and technology programs in the country. Only those students that had demonstrated near-Mensa-like academic skills were admitted—and Khalil easily met that criteria. Sheikh Rahainee knew the Institute's technical training would be invaluable to Islam, and ultimately to restructuring the world order, led by Iran.

Khalil was elated when he was accepted into its exclusive program. He already knew that software was at the heart of nearly every advanced piece of machinery—from cell phones, to cars, to airplanes, to satellites. He wanted to be on the cutting edge of technology—to do things with software programming that nobody else had even dreamed about. *How cool would it be,* he had thought, *to be able to develop a program that could perform, when properly stimulated, in ways that were never expected? The absolute power that can come from this technology could be astounding.*

His mentor, Sheikh Rahainee, encouraged Khalil's ambitions. He knew the power of software. He knew that future wars would be dominated by those who controlled that environment—and he recognized in Khalil the potential to be the catalyst for that control.

Khalil's anger with America now had a channel—perhaps he would use his expertise to get even with the country that had already taken so much from him. Up to now, it hadn't given him anything of value—only pain. He thought about the possibilities. *At the Institute, I can hone my skills in software development and leverage the vast intellectual property of this arrogant capitalist country to achieve my goals and do great things for Islam.*

When he began his studies, it was evident that Khalil was among elite groups of students. All of them were extremely intelligent. As a result, competition between them was stiff, and often a bit combative. But that type of environment appealed to Khalil. In fact, he almost relished the conflict, the battle to demonstrate who among the highly educated class was truly the best.

The Institute would help him continue to expand his knowledge in a wide array of electrical, mechanical and—more importantly—computer-based engineering, machine learning and AI. Applied mathematics, and especially all aspects of computer sciences and software coding, had come easy to him, the advanced concepts easily grasped by his sharp intellect. His analytical mind astonished the Institute's professors, who were amazed at Khalil's ability to develop solutions to problems almost before the problem was fully understood. The labs at the Institute excited Khalil the most.

The advanced capabilities of the software development and integration laboratory facilities were one of a kind. Generous donations by Dallas philanthropists, and some funding from the wealth generated by Texas oil, ensured the national ranking of the Institute. Other large donations came from Middle Eastern contributors, eager to gain access for their prospective students.

Institute attendees had nearly fifty percent of their education centered on every possible software-related area, including the latest research into artificial intelligence, cryptological programming, morphing code, spoofing—and the methods to defeat it. It seemed tailor-made for Khalil.

The faculty quickly recognized Khalil's incredible intellect and accelerated him through their most advanced classes and programs. He excelled and would be a prime candidate for a bright future in this highly advanced field of study. Khalil was fortunate to be living in the Dallas area, a hotbed of technology, science and research. Most technical schools in the sprawling desert city tailored their programs to help feed qualified graduates to the booming technology industry—the Institute of Applied Sciences happened to be one of them.

The dean of the Advanced Studies Program, himself a close friend of Sheikh Rahainee, arranged for Khalil to intern during his summers at the Omega Company, one of the leading software developers in the nation. Their expansive lab facilities occupied a central location in the heart of the Dallas technical district, and this internship was to be Khalil's first opportunity to really test his ability. He quickly proved his value, becoming their star intern and demonstrating skill sets beyond those possessed by many of their experienced engineers. Like most companies looking for prospective employees that would help drive company profit, Omega saw a limitless future for the young Syrian.

Khalil felt like his time at the Institute of Applied Science had flown by—in fact, he had advanced through the difficult curriculum much quicker than any other student. As a result, he was on track to complete his degree requirements in three years. Khalil's future employment was now predetermined, since he had successfully mastered the Institute's difficult course load and proven his value to the Omega Company.

The young Syrian engineer already knew where he wanted to work after graduation. His internship at Omega immersed him in the world's latest software development technology. It excited him to imagine the possibilities ahead. The company had gotten an in-depth look at a man with incredible intellect and seen a potential future superstar. They intended to plant their hooks deeply into him and bring him into the company following graduation.

Sheikh Rahainee also continued to mentor his young protégé. When Khalil told him of his desires to continue with Omega after graduation, the imam smiled broadly. The mosque's Islamic leader knew his strategy for Khalil was executing perfectly to the plan.

Chapter 20

2013
Vance AFB, Enid, Oklahoma

The instructor pilot in the sleek aircraft tightened his stomach muscles and grunted during the aggressive vertical pull-up as the jet completed the aerobatic maneuver recovery. "You've got to watch your airspeed and g-forces coming out of the Split S," shouted the instructor pilot. "You know damn well these old T-38 Talon airframes are not built to handle the constant overloading—not to mention pissing off the maintenance guys who'll have to do the added inspections."

He shook his head, continuing, "These jets have had a lot of abuse by you and your buddies over the last couple of decades. At some point, they just aren't going to fly anymore."

"Roger that, sir," Matt Black replied. "But I sure love this old beauty's speed," he said, raising the nose and putting the stubby-winged jet into a gradual turn to bleed off speed.

The student, one of the best the seasoned instructor had ever trained, was sure to keep his number one position in his pilot training graduating class at Vance AFB in the coming weeks. In spite of Matt's occasional lapses in following the flight manual, the operating bible for the jet, the instructor knew that this future fighter pilot had that special something—a sense of oneness with his aircraft, to take it to the limits, the outer edge of its performance capability. A great fighter pilot needed to fully understand his aircraft, to know every boundary of the aircraft's performance and not be afraid to push the limits if the situation demanded. The instructor, an experienced fighter pilot himself with over one thousand hours of combat time in the F-16 Fighting Falcon, knew that to survive in a life-or-death aerial duel with the enemy, you had to not only be a better pilot but be able to handle your aircraft in ways that the enemy would never risk doing themselves.

Taxiing in to the large concrete parking ramp, Matt couldn't suppress his grin. He knew he'd passed his final check-ride with flying colors. After many months of intensive training, he and his instructor pilot were close. The feedback Matt was getting from him on his rank among other students meant a first choice in his next assignment. There was only one choice in his mind—the F-22 Raptor, the first fifth-generation fighter in the world and still the only fighter aircraft in existence possessing awesome stealth capabilities and advanced sensors. Matt also knew that his dad, his hero, was looking down on him at this very moment with an equally wide grin, acknowledging his son's current success at Vance and his bright future as an Air Force fighter pilot.

The graduation ceremony in July 2013, nearly a year after his arrival at Vance AFB, was a rousing event, with Matt's mom proudly pinning the silver wings on his chest. She couldn't hold back the tears as she looked lovingly into her son's blue eyes. As she gazed at him, Cathy Black could see her husband, Alec, in the eyes of her strapping son.

"Don't hold them back, Mom," he said, putting a comforting arm around her. "I'm having a tough time not choking up on my own," he added, giving her a warm hug. "I couldn't be more excited, heading to Tyndall AFB to get qualified as a Raptor fighter pilot. I'm *absolutely* ready to follow in Dad's footsteps."

"You are your father's son for sure," replied his mom. "I'm so proud of you."

———————— • ————————

Two weeks later, Matt was on his way. While he had established a tight bond with his fellow student pilots in *Nowhereland*, Oklahoma, he was more than excited to be getting out of there. From tumbleweeds to seaweed, this was definitely going to be a welcome change for him. Panama City, Florida, was considered a top vacation spot for most tourists and students hoping to escape the northern winter cold and was also a summertime mecca. The pure white sand beaches, the warm aqua-blue Gulf of Mexico water, the wide assortment of high-rise hotels and condos, and top-notch seafood ensured that things were always hopping in this coastal resort area.

Panama City was to be Matt Black's home for the next year. He had driven through the night from Enid, hoping to avoid any traffic, especially the steady stream of tractor-trailers that clogged the interstate highways. Arriving at Tyndall's main gate late on a Saturday morning, he received the obligatory salute from the security forces staff sergeant guarding entry. After Matt's credentials were verified, he drove into the base and over to the Bachelor Officers Quarters, or "Q" as it was known. He checked in, dumped his bags in the room, and quickly changed into his preferred Florida attire—his Academy T-shirt, baggy bathing suit, and weathered leather sandals. He was a bit tired from the overnight drive, but sleep would come later. He hopped back into his Boss 'Stang and drove to the beach. *I'll bet the sand is inundated with good-looking honeys today.*

First, he needed a meal. As he drove along the road adjacent to Panama City Beach, he had a choice of any number of great seafood restaurants. He saw what he was looking for—Get Shucked, a perfect seafood joint on the water. It was definitely not one of the usual chain-type tourist places. He pulled in and found himself a small table with a wooden bench overlooking the Gulf. He wasted no time feasting on several dozen famous Apalachicola oysters on the half shell and then washed them down with some of the tastiest draft beer he had had in a long time. His appetite temporarily satisfied, he gazed out across the white sand and watched the surf pounding gently on the shoreline. A slight breeze blowing in off the Gulf made the air smell sweet to him—the distinctive odor of ocean surf. He smiled. It was quite a change from the fragrant, pungent odor of fresh cow chips that dotted the prairie surrounding his previous base.

Waves are only about a foot today, he mused. Matt surveyed the crowded sand and saw his guess about the possibility of babes on the beach had been correct. There were dozens of attractive women sunbathing. *God bless the guy that invented the string bikini.*

He kicked off his worn leather sandals, walked down the weathered wooden steps, and planted his feet on the warm white sand. Matt hadn't had much contact with eligible young females in the cowboy town of Enid. Most of his time was spent making sure he finished *first* in his pilot training class, and when he was free to roam off base, he just hadn't seemed to click with the local Oklahoma girls. But here was a new opportunity to test his skills—to prove to himself that he hadn't lost the touch.

He walked up to the three attractive girls lying on their large beach blanket, the large University of Michigan logo prominently displayed. All of them were slathered in suntan lotion, intent on getting the brown hue of their life in the short time they had from their home up north. Matt put his best "killer" smile on his face and tried to strike up a conversation.

Before he could get a word out of his mouth, the cutest of the bunch turned her head toward him and smiled.

"Hey—you're missing some great waves today," he said to them. "But, then again, your tans are coming along beautifully. Given the blanket you're on, you probably haven't seen much of this kind of weather in Michigan."

The cute blonde raised her sunglasses to get a better look at Matt. "Thanks. We've only got a few more days before we have to head back north, and so we're trying to soak up as much sun as we can."

"Well, I don't know what's more beautiful today—the aqua surf, the blue sky, or the three of you."

"I haven't heard that one before, and I think I've probably heard them all!" Her friends laughed as she smiled and motioned him over to the spare corner of the blanket not otherwise occupied. "Have a seat if you want. You look like you could use a little sun. Where have you been hiding out—in a cave?"

Matt blushed a bit and stared at his pale arms and legs. "Oh, yeah, I've been pretty busy for the last year. Never got much time to enjoy the sun." He sat down on the blanket and pulled off his Air Force Academy T-shirt. The three bikini-clad girls looked quickly at each other, clearly impressed with what they saw. While Matt was pretty pale from lack of sunshine, he was solidly built, his physique cut by the years of weight lifting and athletics.

"You better put some of this lotion on or you're going to burn up in fifteen minutes," the cute blonde commented. "If you need some help with your back, I think I can make the sacrifice," she said, a coquettish smile on her face.

"Thanks. I *really* appreciate it," he said.

She seemed to spend just a bit longer than needed to get his back well oiled, and Matt knew that he was likely to make a stronger connection to her as the day progressed. The conversation on the sandy beach reminded Matt of what he had been missing during his *internment* in Oklahoma.

The rest of the day and the evening activities with the three Michigan girls made him realize why Panama City's beaches were so famous.

Chapter 21

The exciting new chapter in Matt's life unfolded as he reported to the training squadron at Tyndall Air Force Base to learn to fly the F-22 Raptor stealth fighter—America's premier weapon system. The expansive base housed two F-22 squadrons of eighteen aircraft each, the only training base in the world for the radar-evading stealthy jet. Three large state-of-the-art flight simulators were constantly in use to certify that future fighter pilots could safely handle the aircraft before they strapped into the cockpit.

Matt knew how critical the simulators were and was intent on maximizing his time in them. He knew that he alone would have to master the aircraft. *It will be all me,* he thought. *There won't be an instructor pilot sitting with me in this aircraft like the T-38. There's only room for one pilot in the Raptor!* Matt actually relished the challenge, knowing that new Raptor pilots would go straight from the simulator directly to the flight line! All pilots knew that there was no second chance in the F-22. They had to get it right on the first flight.

Flight simulator instructors had an extremely important job, teaching a Raptor pilot how to fly the most advanced fighter jet on the planet. Fortunately, all of the instructors were experienced combat pilots with thousands of hours in fighter aircraft. They ran every possible flight scenario with their students before having the confidence to release them to the flight line, and only then after they had demonstrated the required proficiency. A pilot's reaction to emergencies and execution of emergency procedures, or EPs, had to be so automatic that it became second nature, like scratching your nose when it itched.

Matt quickly got into the operational tempo of the training regimen. He immersed himself in the rigorous academics until he absorbed every detail. Sticking to his plan, he took advantage of every opportunity he could to log "sim time." Fortunately for him, he didn't need much sleep, a characteristic he had inherited from his father. Consequently, he was able to get extra simulator practice in the wee hours of the morning, when his buddies were still sleeping. Instructors were pretty flexible scheduling extra hours, especially when they recognized a student who clearly had the right stuff to be one of their best.

Matt proved he had mastered all required aspects of handling the jet more quickly than any other student. He constantly pressed the instructors to stretch the boundaries of the jet's performance, to give him emergency situations beyond the usual ones that he might encounter. They made it their personal challenge to fluster him with extremely difficult problems. While he broke a sweat a few times, he never hesitated in taking the right actions quickly and decisively.

After a late-night training session, the instructor approached Matt.

"Lieutenant, I think you're more than ready to handle your first F-22 flight. You've already proven your ability to fly the jet in the sim, and handle it like an experienced pilot. I've been impressed at how well you dealt with every emergency situation we've thrown at you. You've got great reactions and phenomenal situational awareness. You've worked hard enough tonight—go get some sleep!"

"Thanks for the good words," Matt responded. "I feel good about handling the jet. Hopefully that will translate pretty closely to my actual first flight." He shook the instructor's hand. "I think I'll take your advice and hit the rack for a few hours of shut-eye."

As he walked out from the cold air in the F-22 simulator building, the warm, humid air hit him, immediately warming him, taking the chill off.

"What a beautiful night," he said aloud to no one but himself at this early hour.

The moon had already moved down toward the horizon.

It'll just be a few more weeks of training before I'm strapped in the cockpit, he thought to himself.

He pulled his Boss 'Stang out of the parking lot and headed down the dark, deserted air base road. He passed the flight line on his left and caught a glimpse of the F-22s parked in rows on the ramp. They were already being prepared for the first launches of the day—he saw some activity under one of the aircraft.

The grease-stained aircraft maintenance guys have a tough life, he thought. *They're out here at all hours making sure these jets are ready to go. Thank God we've got airmen willing to bust their ass at this early hour.*

He smiled to himself, an acknowledgement of their dedication and commitment to prepare their aircraft for future Raptor combat pilots.

———•———

The day of Matt's first flight came quickly. The hours of studying, the constant sim time, and of course his daily regimen of exercise to keep his fitness level at its peak rapidly ate up the days and weeks preparing for this thrill of his life.

As Matt walked across the aircraft parking ramp to his jet, Staff Sergeant Jeff Bosworth saw him coming and walked toward him. Bosworth offered Matt a sharp salute.

"Sir, your aircraft is ready for acceptance," he said.

Matt greeted the crew chief with a big grin, returned the salute and then offered a hearty handshake.

Sergeant Bosworth had been quite busy for the last couple of hours. In spite of his past eleven years in the Air Force, every day he spent preparing a jet for flight was an exciting challenge to him. In his mind, there was no better job, even on the days that things didn't go so well. Now he was one of the top aircraft maintenance Raptor crew chiefs at Tyndall. He considered it a privilege to get this powerful aircraft ready for the young pilot who would take his first flight.

I'll make sure that his jet is as perfect as it can be. This lieutenant's first sortie is special, and it's my job to give this newbie the best ride of his life. All he has to do is not fuck it up, he thought to himself.

The crew chief looked over his shoulder at the dark gray Raptor. The morning humidity had left glistening droplets of moisture on most of the jet's surface, but not on the canopy, which Bosworth had wiped clean.

"No maintenance issues to affect your flight," he said to Matt. "The jet is fully serviced and ready."

Bosworth had checked the aircraft forms contained in a ruggedized laptop computer known as the portable maintenance aid, or PMA in Raptor parlance. He'd ensured proper documentation of all the servicing actions, including fuel, nitrogen, gaseous oxygen, hydraulics, oil, and tire pressure. He handed the PMA to Matt.

"Thanks, chief," Matt replied. "This is one beautiful bird."

As he paged through the various electronic forms, he quickly got a thorough understanding of every aspect of his jet—all critical systems, fuel status, components changed, major and even minor repairs completed. The deferred maintenance problems were minor and would be fixed at a later date.

Matt spent plenty of time reviewing the aircraft status. He wasn't going to take the word of his crew chief, although he had the utmost faith in him. After all, once he was airborne, if there was a problem that he should have caught while reviewing the forms, it was on him for not bringing up the deficiency to his crew chief before the flight.

Once he was confident the aircraft forms indicated his jet was good to go, it was time for a closer look. He began his walk-around inspection of the aircraft, knowing full well that the final visual inspection was critical. He moved slowly around the jet, inspecting the aircraft completely, thoroughly, almost obsessively. He examined everything that might affect the condition, the readiness of his aircraft, and its flight-worthiness. Jeff Bosworth walked around with Matt. As the lieutenant moved by the gaping wheel wells, Bosworth pulled the landing gear pins and showed them to Matt. Visual confirmation was extremely important. Matt didn't need an in-flight emergency due to a pin left in on his first flight—or any flight for that matter. His jet was ready!

Climbing the boarding ladder of the jet for his first flight, Matt was almost overcome with excitement. After he stepped carefully over the canopy rail and settling into the seat, his crew chief helped him strap in and handed Matt his helmet. When he was ready, Matt reached down and pulled the ejection seat safety pins and handed them to his crew chief. After Bosworth climbed down from the aircraft, he gave Matt a thumbs-up.

Bosworth lifted the ladder away from the jet and set it on the parking ramp away from the aircraft. Once he had his communication headset on, he plugged the comm cord into it. The sharp crew chief turned the aircraft battery on, and instantly, the intercom system between him and his pilot was activated. Matt spent the requisite time looking over all cockpit switches and settings. When he was confident that everything was in order, he signaled Bosworth.

"Sir, are you ready to fire off the auxiliary power unit?" Bosworth asked.

"Ready to go," answered Matt.

Bosworth checked the engine intakes a final time before giving Matt the clearance to start engines. No mistakes here, he thought. He had seen the result of objects getting ingested into an engine. The damage was often extreme. Engines were outrageously expensive, and repairs sometimes ran into the millions of dollars.

Matt began the verbal sequence to prepare for engine start.

"Chief, clear fore and aft, fire guards posted, chocks in place, ready to start," he said over the intercom.

"Sir, you are clear to start engines."

Matt lowered his canopy and started the auxiliary power unit, bringing it to life. A burst of white smoke exited the left exhaust port. The low howl from the building air pressure indicated the big jet was awakening.

Matt Black could feel the excitement almost exploding within him as he started the number two engine, followed by the number one engine.

Just like in the simulator, he thought.

The powerful stealth fighter quickly spooled up its Pratt & Whitney F119-PW-100 jet engines, the rumble through his ejection seat causing a wry smile on Matt's face as he readied for his first flight. He glanced over his electronic consoles. Every critical aspect of his engine's performance and all key systems, including electronic, hydraulic, and life support, were giving him optimal indications that his jet was flight-ready. Next, he proceeded to verify the integrity of his flight control systems. As Matt operated the fly-by-wire flight controls, his crew chief confirmed that his pilot's physical stick inputs were correctly matching the deflection of the Raptor's large aerodynamic surfaces.

Time to go, thought Matt as he watched his crew chief disconnect the comm cord from the aircraft.

Bosworth moved in front of the jet to marshal his pilot out of the parking spot. Once Matt Black had clearance to taxi, he gave his crew chief the signal to move the large yellow chocks from each wheel. Bosworth verified that the taxiway was clear and motioned with his arms for Matt to pull away from his parking spot for a couple of feet and stop. The assistant crew chief manning the fire bottle checked the tires one last time for any cuts and, finding none, quickly moved away from the jet. Matt had practiced this a hundred times in the simulator and was gratified that the real thing was pretty close to how he had trained.

Hope the takeoff is just like the simulator, he thought, knowing that there was no margin for error in your first flight in a hundred-million-dollar jet.

Matt's instructor pilot was in the jet parked next to him and would accompany him on this and many subsequent flights. This was a key part of the transition between simulator and aircraft. There was no way to simulate *every* possible condition a pilot might encounter, and an experienced IP could help bridge any potential gap in training by flying as a wingman during these sorties.

Staff Sergeant Jeff Bosworth gave Matt a sharp salute and a thumbs-up as the big stealth fighter headed down the taxiway to the end-of-runway area, called the EOR, where a final check of his jet would be performed by the arming crew. Once the jet's readiness for launch was affirmed by the crew, he received his clearance from the tower. Matt pulled onto the active runway and stopped the big jet. He waited for his instructor pilot, Captain Rufus "Mad Dog" Mays, to taxi in behind and left of him.

"Ready to roll?" asked Mays.

"You bet," blurted out Matt, his excitement over his first flight breaking up his usually calm composure and making his voice rise a few octaves.

"Tower, Ajax flight of two, ready for takeoff," May's said.

"Roger, Ajax flight, cleared for takeoff, Runway Two Six, winds, southwest, fifteen knots. Change to departure frequency."

Matt pushed the throttles forward while holding the jet steady. It shuddered as the engines reached the desired rpm, and all instruments indicated his Raptor was ready to launch.

What a difference in engine power this jet has over the T-38 in pilot training, he thought briefly.

He shook his head and brought his mind back to the inside of his cockpit and the importance of getting this first ride right. Releasing the brakes, the big bird surged forward, picking up speed quickly as Matt kept the nose of his jet on the runway centerline. The Raptor's powerful engines moved the gray jet quickly, the runway markers rapidly becoming a blur. His speed hit about 160 knots and he pulled the stick back, gradually lifting the Raptor's nose off the ground. The jet rose gracefully into the air. He was still accelerating as he raised the landing gear. He put the aircraft's angle of attack at precisely the right attitude and climbed into the mottled cloud-spotted sky of Panama City, Florida. Matt set his heading toward the large training area over the Gulf of Mexico.

No time to be looking over my shoulder at the beautiful shoreline of the Gulf Coast, he thought as he soared across the white sandy beaches. *I want this first ride to be perfect.*

The training areas supported both Tyndall and Eglin AFBs and as such remained off-limits to commercial aircraft traffic. Mad Dog was confident that this young, talented flyer was going to do just fine on his first flight. He had received the glowing reports from the sim instructors on Matt's proficiency. Nonetheless, he would keep a sharp eye on his protégé to ensure that the flight went safely and according to plan.

"Ajax Two, great takeoff and climb-out—how does it feel so far?" Mad Dog asked through the comm system.

Matt grinned beneath his mask as he responded, "Outstanding, Ajax One—absolutely outstanding!"

"Okay, take us to the prescribed altitude and heading, and let's get some training done in our flight area."

"Roger that, sir," Matt replied.

———————•———————

Lieutenant Matt Black continued to excel through the rigorous training program, and by the time graduation rolled around, he was champing at the bit to get to an operational squadron and test his mettle in the *real world*. He had proven he could handle the Raptor in the training environment. His next step was to prove he could handle the deadly jet in combat.

Before he departed Tyndall, the instructor pilots assigned Matt the call sign "Ace," an acknowledgement of his phenomenal skill in handling the advanced aircraft. The young lieutenant's performance was unprecedented, quite unlike any other previous graduate of the Raptor training unit. It reminded one of the instructors of a man he had served with at Lakenheath—Matt's father, Alec

Black. The fighter community had great respect for the Strike Eagle pilot lost in battle. "Ace" was the perfect fit for this new Raptor pilot, and for Matt "Ace" Black, earning his father's call sign was an honor like none other.

Chapter 22

August 2014
Langley Air Force Base, Virginia

Tyndall AFB was a pretty good gig for any pilot learning his trade. After all, living near Panama City's prime vacation real estate and absolutely gorgeous beaches wasn't a bad way to spend your time when you weren't flying the Raptor.

While the training was often pretty intensive, Matt "Ace" Black was ready when he was reassigned to his first operational base. The 1st Fighter Wing at Joint Base Langley-Eustis in Hampton Roads, Virginia, was a plum move. Langley was located just off the tributary of the Back River, on the opposite side of the historic James River from Norfolk, itself a sprawling center for several Navy installations. Langley had a long history dating back to 1916, beginning with lighter-than-air dirigibles and biplanes, and had been home to many fighter, bomber, reconnaissance and seaplane aircraft through its history. The F-22 Raptor was its newest resident.

He checked in to the 94th Fighter Squadron, sometimes referred to as the 94th FS, late in the afternoon, and noticed the Hat in the Ring emblem that was prominent in the entryway. It was a reminder of the famous aviator Eddie Rickenbacker, who had served in the original 94th Aero Squadron. During WWI, Rickenbacker had flown with his fellow aces, called the "Hat in the Ring Gang," in the Lafayette Escadrille, and thus the emblem was born. Matt was proud to be joining the squadron, known as the "SPADs," and knew from its heritage that it was the second-oldest fighter squadron in US military history. Walking into the squadron building, he was greeted by the Operations Officer, Lieutenant Colonel Jerry "Jammer" Welsh.

"Hey, you must be our new guy," Jammer called out. "Great to have you as part of our family," he said, extending his hand and shaking Matt's hand vigorously with a firm grip.

"Glad to be here as well, Colonel," replied Matt. "I go by Ace."

"Your timing is perfect, Ace. Our commander just came in off the flight line from a training sortie."

Jammer hustled Ace toward the commander's office, the necessary first stop for every new pilot coming into the squadron. Ace came to attention as he walked into the office and saluted, and before he could get any words out of his mouth, Lieutenant Colonel Brewster extended his hand. With a big smile, he welcomed Ace to the fold.

"Lieutenant, it's great to have you here. You're indeed fortunate to be in the best fighter unit in the Air Force, and also the *top* squadron at Langley."

"Thanks, Colonel Brewster. Langley, and in fact this squadron, was my absolute first choice for a combat unit. I feel pretty lucky getting it," Ace replied. "The 94th has a terrific history, and I'm really proud to be a part of its future."

"From what I've heard about your performance at Tyndall, I'm sure you'll fit in nicely. You'll be matched up with Flamer Lightner, in 'A' Flight, who will be your shadow for your spin up. Flamer will make sure you get all your required training, your simulator time and flying schedule—and he'll be flying with you."

Captain Fred "Flamer" Lightner had gotten the heads-up that the new guy was in the commander's office and, having been pre-briefed on his assignment with Ace, walked over to the doorway and signaled the commander that he was there.

"Come on in, Flamer, and meet your new shadow, Ace Black," Brewster called out.

"Been expecting you, Ace. Great to meet you. You'll have a fantastic opportunity to fly with the best fighter squadron in the Air Force, and luckily with the *best* fighter pilot in the Air Force," Flamer said with a bit of a swagger and smile.

After a brief discussion with the commander, Flamer led Ace out of the office. He gave Ace a quick tour of his home for the next three years, showing him where everything was located. They finished the tour and Flamer spent some time talking about the squadron's history. He didn't want to overwhelm Ace in the first hour, so he finally focused on the essentials of life in an operational unit. Due to the late hour, all flying for the day had been completed. Most of the pilots were milling around the squadron bar, waiting for the light to flash on, signaling the bar was open for business. Flamer and Matt headed toward the gathering crowd of thirsty pilots.

"Hey, guys," Flamer called out across the room. "Come on over and meet our newest squadron-mate—Ace Black."

A few of the flight suit–clad pilots came over to welcome Matt and quickly ushered him to the bar for a drink. Matt saw the bell hanging over the bar and made sure not to put his flight cap on the varnished mahogany bar surface. He remembered his dad talking about Air Force bar etiquette—the cap would trigger someone ringing the bell, and Matt emptying his wallet to buy everyone a round. He immediately noted the vast array of beer mugs across the back wall of the bar. Each belonged to one of the 94th FS pilots, their call signs prominently displayed on the side of the mug—he noted "Snake," "Buzz," "Rupert," and "Flamer," among the collection. He didn't notice an "Ace" and was thankful for that—after all, there had to be room for him, and there could only be one Ace. Matt also noticed the vast array of plaques that commemorated squadron achievements. A few of the aviators offered plenty of friendly ribbing about his time at Tyndall, which most of the operational base pilots considered to be a vacation—even though they had all endured the tough training regimen to prove their own ability to handle the Raptor.

Hours into his orientation into the squadron, Matt's head was spinning, not only from the beer he had consumed but from the dozens of men he'd met, their stories about combat training flights, and of course his eagerness to get engaged in everything as quickly as possible. After a bit, Flamer guided Ace out of the building and pointed him in the direction of the Bachelor Officers Quarters.

"Get yourself checked in, and then I'll pick you up and drag you to the house for dinner. My bride is expecting us and wants to show off her cooking prowess. And I can attest to that," he said, patting his lean stomach.

Ace headed out to his 'Stang, cranked it up and then drove over to the Q. After stowing his gear and cleaning up, he walked down to the lobby and saw Flamer waiting.

"Ready for some first-rate chow from the prettiest little cook in the state?" Flamer greeted him.

"You bet, Flamer. I haven't had a home-cooked meal in a long time."

With that, they headed to Flamer's home in Yorktown.

Matt appreciated the invitation, since all his meals for the past year as a Tyndall bachelor had involved going out to get something—either chowing down on fast food, the occasional steak dinner at Outback Steakhouse, or some choice seafood. The evening with Flamer, his wife, Colene, and their toddler, Sean, was a refreshing break for him. Fred "Flamer" Lightner had been at Langley for a year and was a flight commander. He had spent a couple years at Nellis Air Force Base prior to Langley as part of the operational test and evaluation team. He spent part of the evening filling in details of Langley's operational life and the overall high-speed tempo of the squadron. Ace had plenty of questions, and as the evening wore on, he knew that he was in *exactly* the right place at *exactly* the right time in his life to hone his skills as a fighter pilot.

"Stick with me, Ace, and I'll teach you everything I know. If you're lucky, you might actually become as good a fighter pilot as I am," Flamer said with a laugh.

Matt "Ace" Black quickly plunged himself into squadron life. In his first few weeks, he was deluged with briefings, training, getting fitted with his life support gear, and most significantly, he was put on the flight simulator schedule. The time in the simulator was critical, as it was geared for flying the Raptor in the Langley area in both training *and* operational flight scenarios.

His first flight on a two-ship mission occurred during his third week. He and Flamer had briefed the mission—a pretty basic local area orientation flight to get familiar with the airfield layout, the key landmarks, and the crowded sky around Langley that was kept busy by air traffic from both Norfolk International Airport and Newport News Airport. Additionally, Ace and Flamer would head out over Chesapeake Bay to the tactical training range before finally turning back toward the Langley airspace.

Matt walked with Flamer across the aircraft parking ramp toward their war birds, smiling as he caught the scent of jet fuel and engine exhaust. While doing the preflight on his big jet, Ace was thorough with every aspect of his aircraft's readiness. He made a point to spend some time talking with his crew chief. He had learned at Tyndall how important it was to bond with crew chiefs, and he wanted to build a strong rapport at Langley with the folks who were critical to his survival in the powerful fighter. After introducing himself, Ace asked him if the jet was ready. The crew chief's quick thumbs-up made Ace feel good. He reviewed the aircraft status on the portable maintenance aid, scrolling across multiple status screens. This jet was pretty clean, from a maintenance standpoint. Even the deferred maintenance items were minor in nature and wouldn't affect the jet's performance.

"Chief," Ace said, "I see that this jet has a pretty good performance record—that's an excellent string of consecutive Code One flights."

His crew chief had a broad grin on his face. "Yes, sir, I take pretty good care of my baby here, and she performs well as a result.

The jet's record of mostly *no defect* Code One flights attests to my top-quality maintenance," he bragged. "Just don't go and break it on your first flight," he laughed.

"Okay, then, let's get this show on the road," Ace remarked, smiling as he climbed the ladder to get into the tight cockpit.

When all checks had been performed, Ace started the big engines. After all systems appeared flight-ready, he gave the crew chief the signal to pull chocks and taxied out of his parking spot.

Ace and Flamer made it to the arming area, had their final checks completed, and then pulled out on the runway. The wide grin on Ace's face was completely concealed by his oxygen mask as he accelerated down the long stretch of concrete on his first operational F-22 stealth fighter sortie. Flamer followed close behind and the two joined up in the clear morning sky for their mission. He and Flamer headed out to the Mid-Atlantic over-water training area, about twenty miles due east. Ace was proud of himself for not honking anything up in the first real demonstration of his flying ability with his new squadron-mate.

The time went by so fast that when Flamer indicated they needed to head back to the airfield, Ace was disappointed. As the two aircraft approached the runway, Ace was in the lead. He performed a perfect flare to settle the large black rubber main gear tires on the concrete, a short squeal coming from them as they roughly left a skid mark before spinning up to finish the roll out of the jet.

As the two pilots unstrapped and began to extract themselves from their aircraft in the Hat in the Ring parking area, Flamer gave Ace a big thumbs-up and a wave, acknowledging a successful first flight. Ace thanked his crew chief, handing him his helmet before he climbed down the boarding ladder. Flamer wandered over and shook Ace's hand, and the two fighter pilots headed to the squadron.

"Ace, you did well," said Flamer. "I'm just glad you didn't screw things up so badly that we would have had to declare an in-flight emergency. That would have been pretty embarrassing for *me*," Flamer said, trying to keep a straight face, but not being able to hold it in, he busted out laughing.

"Very funny, Flamer. You're lucky I didn't have to guide you back to the base," Matt laughed. "You older fellas sometimes have some memory lapses." They both had a good laugh.

In debrief, Ace reported that his aircraft performed just as his crew chief had said it would—another Code One sortie. He made it a point to shake his crew chief's hand and thank him for the top-quality jet.

Over the course of the next twelve months, Ace proved he was the airman that his father was. His integration into the 1st Fighter Wing and its proud combat heritage was intensive. Like all new fighter pilots entering their first operational squadron, he followed the prescribed training syllabus for spinning up to the requisite proficiency level.

His training began with visual and instrument approaches to the runway, then moved on to the demanding challenge of flying tactical formations, performing intercepts, and finally, into defensive and offensive flight maneuvers. He effectively demonstrated his aircraft handling skills while flying air combat tactics, where two aircraft faced off against two other aircraft. He proved that his ability to make the Raptor perform in ways that other pilots struggled with, set him apart from the crowd. The Raptor was the first aircraft to be specifically designed to synthesize, analyze and understand feedback from all of the critical aircraft systems that in previous generations of aircraft, had to be analyzed in the pilot's brain—and decisions made based on that analysis. It enabled the pilot to make more critical offensive and defensive decisions almost in the blink of an eye and focus on the pilot's primary job—to defeat the enemy.

As Matt got more comfortable with Langley's combat training program, he relished every opportunity to climb into the seat of his Raptor. He realized that he was truly happy—he was right where he needed to be at this point in his life.

Chapter 23

2015
Dallas, Texas

As graduation day approached at the Institute of Applied Science, the CEO of Omega made his move and produced an offer that Khalil couldn't refuse—a generous salary and a signing bonus as an engineer in their Advanced Software Development Lab. Khalil had proven himself over his internship as a *must-have* new acquisition for the company.

Upon hearing the news, Dr. Ruffa could not have been prouder of his adopted son's achievements. "Khalil, you have honored me, as well as your blessed father and mother, with your accomplishments. Allah has clearly had a hand in your success and will continue to guide your future with Omega—and beyond."

Khalil grinned. "I am truly blessed to have you as my mentor, my father on this earth. You have placed your faith in me, and I will never let you down. I will honor you and my departed parents by doing great things in the name of holy Islam."

At the Abdallah Mosque, Sheikh Rahainee beamed with pride. His plan was coming together rather nicely. Very important, well-connected people linked inextricably, albeit secretly, to Iran hoped to benefit from Khalil's accomplishments at the Institute and the promising future for this talented Syrian engineer.

While Khalil's studies were the imam's primary focus, he encouraged regular visits to the mosque. Sheikh Rahainee knew the ingredients for Khalil's future destiny—the advanced technical education, the indoctrination and training he personally provided, the careful shaping of the youth's, mind, and most importantly, his will to accomplish any task for his faith—would turn Khalil into a powerful force for advancing Iran's radical goals.

Sheikh Rahainee wasn't terribly worried about being discovered as a simmering hotbed for radical activity. The mosque had never raised any undue attention. Nothing would have given any indication that terrorist activities were being carefully fomented and would eventually be developed into full-scale plans. In fact, the opposite was true. The imam had made a point to ensure that the mosque's overt actions and activities were consistent with the growing Islamic culture in the United States. Many of the mosque's attendees were distinctly American, distinctly Texan. As far as anyone knew, the Abdallah Mosque was no different from dozens of other places in the greater Dallas area where the Muslim faithful gathered, prayed, and fit into the local communities. There had been no indication of anything unusual going on at the mosque.

The tentacles of Iran's reach in the United States had no bounds and extended into the building blocks of America's technical skill base. Khalil's ultimate placement at Omega following his graduation from the Institute of Applied Science wasn't *solely* a function of his demonstrated talent and intellect—and definitely *not* just a lucky break for him. It actually had been part of a longer-term Iranian plan to embed key engineers into companies that were closely tied to the United States' defense industries, especially those companies that were at the cutting edge of software development.

Many publicly traded companies were influenced to hire specific people in a variety of ways. In Omega's case with Khalil, Senator Edward Wright, the Texas Democrat and Armed Services Committee member living in the Dallas area, had received significant political contributions over the years from one particular donor. Beyond the senator's subtle help in steering contracts in Omega's direction, the contributions were a major leveraging tool that helped get brilliant people like Khalil Ruffa placed in key companies. The donor had expected, and received, a quid pro quo favor—Khalil was that favor, and Omega was the recipient.

As one of the nation's leaders in software design and development, Omega had accomplished a major breakthrough in combat aircraft identification—that is, the ability to identify friendly aircraft from enemy aircraft. Aircraft IFF systems—Identification Friend or Foe, or interrogator systems—had evolved over the years, becoming more powerful in their ability to prevent fratricide among friendly aircraft during the heat of battle. But like most software-based equipment, aircraft transponders were only as good as the latest breakthrough in technology that either protected their ability to transmit and receive or made them more vulnerable to enemy spoofing.

Omega's proprietary technology enabled military aircraft IFF systems to perform at enhanced distances, protect the friendly aircraft from a spoofing counterattack, remain cryptologically secure in combat, and most importantly, align its capabilities to enhance the survivability of America's fighter and bomber aircraft. Virtually everything that happened in modern military aircraft was tied to the ability of its software to function effectively. Omega was at the top of its game in upgrading weapon systems using the most advanced software concepts, and became the beneficiary of the fast-tracked interrogator system improvement program for their premier fighter aircraft—the F-22.

If capturing that program wasn't enough, Omega's success was destined to continue. Twelve months prior, the company had bid on another major software upgrade program planned for the jet—the Raptor central computing system. It was an integration hub that controlled most of the advanced fighter aircraft's key functions and was the primary means for the stealthy jet to perform the way it did—in ways that other aircraft couldn't. The down-select between Omega and other contenders had been completed, and Omega had recently been awarded the program based on its solid proposal and past performance. The new contracts, valued at almost $1.1B, had made investors happy when the decisions were announced—the stockholders had gone wild and the share price had nearly doubled.

———•———

Khalil had faced a major hurdle in his initial placement within Omega. When he was an intern, he had been given access to only those programs that were at lower levels of classification, since he possessed a temporary security clearance. In order to be of significant use to the company as a full-time employee, he would definitely need a permanent US government security clearance—one that would grant him access to some of America's most sensitive military programs and secrets. The process to obtain his clearance had run into some initial roadblocks—mainly concerning the details of his formative years, and some scrutiny of the recent activity he had been engaged in with his imam. With the help of Dr. Mahmoud Ruffa, and the doctor's own personal contacts in the government, Khalil was able to build enough of a detailed personal history to get past the initial pushback from the Defense Investigative Service, or DIS.

It certainly helped that Khalil had graduated at the top of both his high school and college classes, had glowing recommendations from his teachers, and had a strong sponsor in the Omega CEO—and one particular Texas senator. The fact that Khalil frequented the Abdallah Mosque was not a showstopper but required a more detailed look by DIS investigators. Fortunately, Sheikh Rahainee had never been flagged by the government as being anything other than a devout religious leader in the Dallas area. After a short delay, Khalil was granted an official US government security clearance at the top secret level. He was subsequently cleared for certain special access programs as well.

During the first year of his employment with Omega, Khalil worked hard to demonstrate the reputation he purportedly had as a star new hire. His brilliance often overshadowed the manager of the Advanced Development Lab, especially on hard-to-solve technical issues.

A problem encountered in a major avionics update to the B-2 Stealth Bomber was proving difficult to solve by the team. They had struggled for two months trying to isolate and correct numerous integrated software faults.

They just waste time, Khalil thought. *I can fix this problem, if they just get out of my way and let me work the solution.*

On his own time, he worked tirelessly in the lab until he was sure of a solution that would work. It was a bit unconventional, not clearly following established approaches to isolate and solve complex integrated problems. But after working on it intensely for only thirteen hours, he had it solved.

His manager, a senior software engineer with over twenty years of development experience, wouldn't even consider discussing Khalil's approach, writing it off as a risky nontraditional application that was ultimately doomed to fail.

"We should test this approach," Khalil insisted to his boss. "I know it will solve this issue, and we can then move on to finishing the update and get it done before the deadline."

The manager reacted angrily, his disdain for this young engineer and his recommendation evident. He brushed it off as just another means for Khalil to tout his value to the CEO who had hired him. Khalil was a clear threat to his manager, and no way was he going to help him. He knew that this new guy had obvious talent and would get plenty of recognition over time—and, at some point, prompt the company to give Khalil *his* job. Foolishly, he ignored Khalil's recommendation and continued to work with the rest of his team to try to reach a solution that was unlikely to happen.

The Omega CEO was getting tremendous pressure from the Air Force to get the B-2 problem solved and was growing tired of the delays. The negative feedback had to stop. Aircrews were angry, constantly having to deal with the B-2 bombers' performance issues. The complaints resonated all the way to Air Combat Command Headquarters at Langley AFB and then on to the senior acquisition official for the bomber program. The old adage *shit flows downhill* applied to this situation—and it was about to flow directly onto the CEO. An especially nasty discussion took place between the USAF colonel running the B-2 program and the Omega CEO. The senior company executive was raked over the coals for lagging performance and inability to solve the problem. The company's cash performance incentives were now at risk—and reducing anticipated cash flow was not in the CEO's equation.

The Omega senior executive subsequently gathered his lab manager and a few members of the team to assess the constant delays. The manager quickly made excuses about how hard the team was working and how they were doing their best to solve the problem. The red-faced CEO was hot and looked like he was about to boil over.

"Why the hell can't you fix this damn problem—you have the best engineers in the country working for you," he chastised the manager. "You claim that you've been working hard on this problem for over two months, and you aren't any closer to solving it *now*! Hard work that produces nothing is *failure*!"

The silence in the room was deafening. "Do *any* of you have any clue about moving this forward?"

After a minute of silence, Khalil piped up. "I believe I have an approach that will isolate the problem and solve it quickly. I've tested it and it appears to work."

"Then why the hell haven't you done it?" demanded the CEO, his anger just short of a full-tilt boil.

Another minute of silence passed as Khalil stared directly at his manager. "I've explained the approach to my manager but was told not to proceed," he said. Khalil watched the CEO's face turn from red to an awful shade of purple, his jaws tightening, veins on the side of his head now plainly visible.

"Clear the room!" shouted the CEO. "Everybody out but you!" he said, pointing to the manager.

The shouting from inside the closed conference room echoed through the door and into the hallway. After ten minutes, the manager exited the room looking like a whipped puppy and sheepishly told his team to head back to the lab. They would try Khalil's approach.

Within four hours of running his tests and making a couple of adjustments to the code, Khalil proved he had quickly solved that particular problem.

Following the ass-chewing he got from the CEO, the manager was never the same. After a few more delays on other programs the manager directed, the CEO had lost confidence in him to effectively lead the software group. The entire development team was becoming more and more dysfunctional. Friction continued to escalate between Khalil and his frustrated manager, who believed the young engineer had thrown him under the bus. But he knew that Khalil was clearly more qualified for the job than himself.

Believing that he would soon be replaced, and embarrassed one too many times, the software manager turned in his resignation and decided to seek other employment. The opening in this key managerial position didn't last long. They quickly offered Khalil the software development manager position and leadership of the Advanced Development Lab. After only two years from the time Khalil had come on board, leadership within the company saw great potential in this mature, brilliant youngster.

Omega's large staff of outstanding software engineers, experienced system development specialists, and a team of integrated testers had been brought to the company to assure the future success of the Advanced Development Lab. Now the lab had a new boss. Leading the ranks of the development specialists on the F-22 central computer contract, Khalil fully understood the critical tasks, and even more so the immense pressure on him and his team to execute this project flawlessly. With well over two million lines of software code in the powerful jet, the task of making every aircraft system work seamlessly now fell to Khalil and his army of crack software engineers. The two-year central computer upgrade program, from start to finish, had the eyes of his company CEO and senior USAF leadership directly on him.

Chapter 24

2017
Tehran

The Supreme Islamic Council had flexed their military muscle when sanctions were lifted. The free flow of critical imports necessary for the regime to resurrect their weapons programs, and the influx of $150 billion in cash, previously tied up by the United States, had given Tehran the funds to rebuild their military forces, erasing years of atrophy.

The United States believed the six-nation nuclear deal—the Joint Comprehensive Plan of Action—had the rudimentary teeth to slow Iran's nuclear development efforts. In actuality, it gave the Persian nation the needed breathing room to continue moving their program forward, mainly due to the lack of effective oversight by signatories to the agreement. Almost any evidence of an agreement breach could be hidden. Months-long advance notice was required for inspectors to visit Iran's key facilities, during which Iran could effectively hide the basic elements required to build nuclear weapons. Additionally, all military installations were off-limits. Thus, while the world breathed a tentative sigh of relief that the Gulf region would remain nuclear-free, Iran systematically developed weapons of mass destruction right under the very eyes of those that were trying to prevent it from happening.

Two superpowers had their fingers deep into Iran. China and Russia were actively helping facilitate the Ayatollah's efforts, both hoping to establish stronger economic and military ties to the region and increase their sphere of influence. Both superpowers had been only too willing to sell Iran many of their older high-performance fighter aircraft, some with minimal stealth capability, in an effort to generate the cash needed to move forward with their own advanced stealth fighter development programs. The injection of this advanced weaponry now represented the majority of Iran's combat fleet and gave the Ayatollah a huge edge over any other Persian Gulf country—and some Western nations. Their robust military force was a key building block in Iran's military plans. The foundation of Iran's defense posture ultimately relied on more than advanced fighter aircraft and defensive systems—nuclear weapons were the desired ultimate foundation.

But the combat edge, the gap between their newly acquired fighters and those of any likely major adversary, was not yet in Iran's favor—and might never be. The country's Supreme Leader sought the technology needed to effectively identify and target its enemy's advanced weapons systems—especially those likely to attack their homeland and deny their efforts to become the next nuclear power.

Their emerging nuclear capability had to be protected at all costs. That protection relied on their ability to counter stealth aircraft—especially the F-22 Raptors that always led an air assault. The Raptor could break through an enemy's defenses, opening the way for other, less stealthy aircraft to enter the combat fray with less risk. If they could stop the Raptor, their defensive forces had a chance to even the playing field. Iran also knew that strikes were very likely to come at the point when the Americans had hard evidence that the Iranian nuclear program was a real threat. Time was of the essence. They were fortunate that the technology they sought was, in fact, accessible.

Months before, Ayatollah Batani, Iran's Supreme Leader, had approached their Chinese military benefactor with a request for a significant increase in support. In secret meetings between Batani and China's president, Xi Jinping, the Ayatollah explained his plans for rapidly advancing Iran's nuclear program. When completed, its ballistic missile fleet would move Iran into the nuclear community, alongside its neighbors, India and Pakistan.

Xi was stunned at first. Adding a rogue nation to the small community of nuclear powers was not high on his priority list. But Batani sweetened his request for assistance, offering in-country air force basing rights and naval port access to China's military, giving Xi a major foothold in the Persian Gulf region. Xi reluctantly decided to hear him out.

Batani explained that nuclear weapons would provide their already-formidable military with a deterrent capability to counter any aggression against their country. Iran knew that no country possessing nuclear weapons had ever faced a major threat to their sovereignty by an aggressor for fear of a retaliatory nuclear response.

Both leaders knew where America stood and knew Israel's position as well—neither country would permit Iran to become a nuclear power. Xi began to understand what Iran was really asking him. Batani knew of China's efforts to develop stealth aircraft and suspected they were on the leading edge of technology to defeat the stealth advantage of their own enemies. He needed China's help to deter, and in fact defeat, any near-term attacks and complete the final stages of their nuclear program.

Xi agreed to do what he could for the Ayatollah.

———————•———————

Stealth technology was, in fact, a top strategy in the world's most populous country. China poured billions of dollars into the development of their own stealth fighters, but their efforts still were not yet proven to equal what the Americans had in the F-22 Raptor. Stealth was the one major advancement the Western world had that was difficult to match, and even more so to counter. But China had reprioritized its military spending since the US had introduced the F-117 Nighthawk stealth attack aircraft in 1988. Stealth was clearly the technology that gave any nation that possessed it a military edge over those that didn't.

China's aircraft development program had been proceeding quite well, thanks to plenty of technology stolen from the United States. Using every source they could acquire to experiment with the fundamentals of stealth technology, they were able to steadily move forward and build their first stealth aircraft, the J-20. Reverse engineering was an art that the Chinese engineers had advanced to the point that they understood almost as much as the United States about the technology. No wonder their J-20 fighter jet looked surprisingly like an F-22! Since the birth of their first stealth jet, China had moved forward with two newer development efforts, constantly improving on their previous design.

Beyond building stealth aircraft, China focused much of their fiscal and intellectual capital on counterstealth technology. No country in the world had as yet determined a way to build an effective system to target and kill stealthy aircraft. Some limited success had been gained using low-frequency radar. That was, hopefully, about to change.

In a most secret location deep in the heart of China, Dr. Lee Yu led a remarkable group of scientists and engineers whose goal was to develop a counterstealth radar capable of detecting, identifying, tracking, and targeting aircraft from their primary adversary—the United States.

The team had developed a working model. The essence of the radar's capability centered on a transmitter/receiver that could sweep across the frequency spectrum, from low to mid to high, and, using complex algorithms, detect stealth aircraft. Dr. Yu was ready to test his newest radar development, called Shengdau. Its first test would be against China's newest stealth aircraft. If it was proven effective, then the next step would be to test it against their adversary, the United States.

Advanced radar systems were only one piece of China's efforts to gain tactical advantage over their adversaries. At the core of advanced weapon systems, software made them perform in incredibly powerful ways. As aircraft became more advanced, the lines of software code needed to achieve enhanced performance levels increased exponentially. Dr. Yu knew very well that whoever was at the leading edge of software design and development would likely produce the most powerful weapon systems—and control the skies.

China had some of the best software design and development capability in the world. Yu had a sizable part of his scientific team focused on how to corrupt otherwise-secure software code, the essence of which kept airliners in the air and military fighters and bombers leading attacks on adversaries. His team did not disappoint him in their creative, almost unbelievable products. Of most significance were the advances his team of development engineers had made in software code reformation. Yu envisioned opportunities in the future where software code could be made to change within itself, to reform, morph, or repurpose itself based on triggering signals. The team believed they could build a morphing code, but they needed a way to insert it into an American stealth aircraft.

———————•———————

President Xi Jinping was excited to hear the news of the Shengdau radar's successful test. Of course, it was difficult to tell if the tall, distinguished Chinese gentleman was excited from the look on his face. Not one to show much emotion, his expression never seemed to change. Many of his own staff struggled to determine their president's feelings about anything. Was that a smile? A frown? Contempt? Anger? But in this case, when the head of his defense services explained the details of the test, he smiled ever so slightly. He thought about how this major step would put China on an equal footing with its primary competitor, the United States, when it came to military prowess and the ability to defend China's rightful territories.

"How will we prove Shengdau works against the Americans?" he asked his chief of staff.

"There is an opportunity to test it in a way that will keep the United

States from knowing we possess this technology," replied the general.

President Xi listened to a detailed briefing on how his newest technology would be proven. The military strategy was brilliant, albeit with some risk. China planned to use Iran. Xi knew that the Americans already suspected Iran of importing technology. The US would not be surprised if Iran produced yet another new threat that they would have to deal with. Xi believed the radical Middle Eastern country would make a great proxy for China and provide a place to test the Shengdau radar against American stealth aircraft that routinely patrolled the Persian Gulf.

———————•———————

China's leader nodded his head in concurrence. President Xi liked what he had heard. Xi waved most of the attendees from the briefing room but asked his chief of staff and Dr. Yu to remain.

"Very interesting," he said. "You insist that two of our most important developmental capabilities in stealth technology can possibly be tested against American aircraft." He paused a moment as he stared down at the dark mahogany conference table. "*If* it is possible, it must be done in a way that keeps China's involvement on the sidelines, away from any criticism by the US.

"I must hear more. If successful, it would likely eliminate a major concern I have over how to blunt an American response to our expansion in the South China Sea."

Xi Jinping continued, "With a proven counterstealth radar, and additional advances in disrupting the critical software systems in American aircraft, we could move more rapidly in our military expansion across Indo-Asia."

The Chinese president sat back in his beige calf-leather armchair and thought quietly to himself about how this strategy could be executed. His staff remained silent. They were used to their leader's habit of thinking through major issues and knew never to interrupt his thoughts.

He contemplated how this could be a major win for China's

near-term planning. If done correctly, it could conduct an actual test of counterstealth capability against America's primary stealth aircraft. But there was little time to execute the plan. As soon as the Americans had enough intel on Iran's nuclear development, they would try to eliminate it before it can become operational. Secrets like nuclear weapons development aren't kept secret for long. If the United States didn't strike Iran soon, Israel would. It would be too late to test any of its counterstealth plans.

"How soon can we have the Shengdau ready for operational use?"

The chief of staff stared at Dr. Yu. The scientist responded, "We will be ready soon with three radar systems. Of course, we will need to get them to Iran, set them up, and operate them for the Iranians. Soon after that we would be ready to test them against American stealth systems."

Xi nodded. The timing should be sufficient to begin running tests of the radar in Iran. But he needed to understand more about corrupting the Raptor's software. He knew that no country had done more research and development than China in software innovation.

"Tell me about our progress in counterstealth software." Xi wasn't smiling anymore, if that had even been a smile. "From what I understand, we are far from ready to implement that kind of a solution to defeat stealth."

For years, Chinese engineers had developed the means to hack into airborne platforms and even figure out ways to overcome the protections that were intended to prevent hacking from happening. But it had yet to be actually proven—tried in a way that would clearly show it could succeed in defeating a stealth platform.

"It is a very bold step to believe that American stealth can be defeated by tampering with their software," Xi stated. "I understand that you have figured out a way to make this happen?"

For the next two hours, Xi heard his staff explain how a plan to defeat stealth with corrupt software could be successful. Unlike the Shengdau radar, which could be tested in its current configuration against an airborne stealth aircraft, corrupting American stealth aircraft software would require a more insidious approach. It would require somehow inserting a morphing code into the Raptor's encrypted, highly classified software and then devising a means to trigger the code to change. The change could conceivably cause a stealthy jet to emit unintended signals that would give away its location. With the location known, it could be targeted and the aircraft shot down.

Xi's own head was spinning from the level of detail he had been given. While he didn't need to fully understand the basic elements of developing a morphing code, he was more interested in knowing exactly how it could be inserted into the Raptor, and how it could ever get by the number of checks all software code was exposed to before being sold off and certified for installation into an aircraft. He was advised that Iran had an insider in the company currently modifying the Raptor's code. There was high risk in the plan, but it could work. The risk would have to be carefully managed.

The president's general staff believed that China had been afforded a great opportunity to significantly advance their counterstealth capability. Iran provided that opportunity.

Xi was only somewhat concerned about helping move Iran into the relatively small but growing nuclear weapons community of nations. He believed Iran would acquire the capability regardless of whether China helped them or not. North Korea was more than willing to help, as was Russia. Why not take advantage of the situation? Why not gain the basing opportunities offered to China by the Ayatollah?

It was very evident to China's leadership that Iran was in a new era of military growth and expansion. Adding to that were clear indications of a coming Caliphate within the Persian Gulf, led by Iran. None of the Chinese leadership believed the United States would allow Iran's aggression, and they all were in agreement about the likelihood of another war in the region.

They would propose to Ayatollah Batani that the software

development efforts be completed in Iran. They would leverage the insider managing the F-22's software to use corrupt code to target the Raptor's ability to remain invisible to radar. At the same time, the Shengdau radar would be tested in Iran, providing a redundant means of defeating the American stealth capability. The plans needed to move forward without delay, as Xi believed it was likely that combat actions against the country of Iran would occur in the near future.

An amazing opportunity presented itself.

"Execute the plan," President Xi Jinping ordered his staff, "and do not delay our effort for any reason."

The Chinese president then made a secure telephone call to his counterpart in Iran. The deal was on!

Chapter 25

The Supreme Leader of Iran, Ayatollah Batani, was delighted when he received President Xi's telephone call. An unprecedented opportunity now presented itself into countering stealth technology. With China's commitment to help, the odds for success had improved substantially.

Beyond the subsequent influx of Chinese technical expertise into Iran, the transfer of critical information to support their own counterstealth research and development efforts had been migrating surreptitiously from key contacts in the United States. It was done through extremely careful, secure means to prevent discovery by snooping US intelligence agencies, always on the lookout for theft of critical intellectual property.

Sheikh Rahainee, from his mosque in Texas, was one of the prime sources of budding intelligence gathered from around the United States that would prove useful, and in fact crucial, to the plans being developed in Tehran. After all, the sheikh was centrally located near the Dallas-Fort Worth area, the location of the factory where the Raptor was supported, and where the newest stealth aircraft, the F-35, was being built. The area was also a hotbed of advanced technical information, and often the target of clandestine eavesdropping and theft of classified information.

Rahainee appeared to have a potential key to defeating the Raptor's stealth. He had Khalil Ruffa, whom he had effectively recruited and groomed so that the young engineer was now in a singularly pivotal position to help further Iran's plans. But the path forward was complicated and depended on more technological help than Iran possessed.

Omega provided the perfect breeding ground—the interrogator improvement program had enormous potential for getting insight on how the United States was going to operate in combat—and the F-22 upgrade was a potential gold mine of information on the inner workings of the Raptor's performance software. The value was clear to both Iran and China. Khalil Ruffa was a primary player as the Omega central computer program manager—and his links to the IFF program were critical. Khalil had an inside track to a full understanding of the complex code that was at the heart of the advanced fighter aircraft's capability. The young Syrian would be embedded in every aspect of the Raptor's performance software. While Khalil Ruffa didn't know it yet, he was now an Iranian agent and an integral part of Iran's strategy.

The scheme would nonetheless take careful planning and execution. An obvious level of secrecy had to be maintained—but the result could indeed be rewarding in ways that would shake the Western world.

———————•———————

Iran had kept their activity hidden, even from the prying eyes and ears found in the best intelligence sources available to the United States. They prosecuted an immense program, with China's technological help, focused on countering the critical stealth technology that made the US military so effective—and so feared.

The bulk of their critical research and development was conducted in a large underground facility just north of the Kavir Desert, near the foothills of the Elburz Mountains. Iran had covertly constructed a three-hundred-thousand-square-foot facility under two hundred feet of the valley soil, all while US and allied satellites peered down on the area. The Supreme Islamic Council had planned and executed an elaborate ruse involving the construction of the largest textile production facility in the country at this location. With few international sanctions applying, and others simply ignored by Iran's benefactors, their activity didn't seem to create any undue concern by all who were closely watching Iran.

Suspicions constantly raised by the Western world about potential Iranian efforts to hide the development of weapons of mass destruction were never confirmed. Even the name of the research facility given by the Supreme Islamic Council was designed to downplay any possible chance that it would divulge the facility's true function. The People's International Commerce Center, as it was called publicly, was widely advertised. The ruse included the positioning of large amounts of raw materials essential to the textile industry in open storage areas around the fenced facility. Likewise, the constant movement of delivery vehicles into and out of the area actually moved empty containers of "textile products" to major towns and cities in Iran.

This had not gone *completely* unnoticed by the National Security Agency. Within the ultra-secure briefing room, the director received his daily update on the Commerce Center's activity. The collection of intel sources produced photographic evidence of apparent wholesale commerce taking place—trucks moving in and out of the large set of warehouses arranged around the complex. Analysts did their best to surmise what exactly was happening there. Even the electronic sensors designed to intercept voice communications appeared to reveal nothing other than routine chatter about textile product deliveries to locations around the country. When his briefing concluded, the NSA director nodded his head in concurrence and moved on to the next subject. For now, Iran's covert activity near the Elburz Mountains was still a secret.

Meanwhile, deep below the dusty surface, Iranian and Chinese scientists worked side by side to develop the technology that would break the stealth barrier.

Chapter 26

Khalil had his hands full managing the crew of egg-headed software engineers at Omega. They were brilliant, talented, and focused on the incredibly detailed code development within their current contract. But they would often diverge on a tangent from their objective—meeting the stringent Air Force requirements for the central computer upgrade. Instead, they constantly added what they believed was additional, enhanced functionality for the jet. Every addition beyond the requirements added cost, undesired complexity, and unnecessary time to complete the project on schedule—all big negatives in the eyes of their customer.

The Air Force central computer program manager was a young attractive female—First Lieutenant Rebecca Casey—and from her youthful looks, she appeared barely out of college. While she wasn't a software engineer, she had a computer technology degree and had earned her acquisition management credentials through the rigorous academic program at the Air Force Institute of Technology. She performed so well that she had been a natural choice for the top secret Raptor modification effort. Working primarily from her office in the town of Fairborn, Ohio, at Wright-Patterson Air Force Base, she had frequent contact with the Omega development team, and with Khalil Ruffa. She knew that in spite of her academic credentials, Khalil, her counterpart, was the key to the program's overall success.

Lieutenant Casey worked hard to establish a close working relationship with Khalil, having recognized his brilliance over time in numerous program status reviews. Beyond admiring his obvious intellectual capacity, she was also a bit attracted to his striking good looks. Rebecca would never admit that to anyone, of course, but the more she was around him, the more she felt a growing emotional connection to this talented man.

Khalil was confident he could succeed with or without his Air Force lieutenant's oversight. But he also realized that this pretty lieutenant might play a role in his success, if he *managed* her correctly. He noticed the way Casey looked at him when she didn't think he was aware, and he planned to leverage the way she felt about him to the maximum extent. He made sure that he used his best smile when addressing her. When he shook her hand, he held on warmly, just long enough to help build on the growing emotional connection. He really wasn't naive enough to believe *that* was all it would take to manipulate her. But he understood that he could use these feelings of attraction to his advantage.

While Casey was an intelligent young officer, her growing emotional attraction to Khalil would lead to some critical management mistakes in the most important aircraft upgrade program in decades.

———•———

Over the course of the first year, the team's progress was nothing short of outstanding. Not only was every critical measure of performance met—in most cases, each was exceeded, making their Air Force customer very happy. Lieutenant Casey couldn't contain her enthusiasm upon completion of the first annual contract review.

"Khalil, we make a great team, and I owe you a lot of credit for our success," remarked Casey.

Always gracious, Khalil made it a point to publicly praise her exceptional guidance and leadership to her boss, Colonel Hampton.

"Sir, Lieutenant Casey is a slave driver. She's tough but fair, and she's the main reason for our team beating all these critical milestone requirements, including budget!"

Colonel Hampton turned to Casey and gave her a wink and a nod of approval. "I'm delighted to hear that. We can't afford any mistakes as we move forward. This program is of immense importance to the Air Force, as you are well aware. I expect you two to keep us on schedule and be mindful of any cost growth. There's no room for an increase in funds—so manage your technical risks carefully."

"Yes, sir," remarked Casey. "Khalil and I are conducting daily how-goes-it reviews—making sure the team has a clear understanding of the day's objectives, and how we're addressing problems carried over from the previous day."

Khalil nodded and added, "Omega is fully committed to deliver on schedule and under budget. We know what's at stake."

Not only did the program execution team know the pressure they were under, the Omega CEO knew full well that the large Air Force contracts would positively leverage plenty of future business if done successfully. Khalil's CEO and CFO were ecstatic and couldn't contain their praise of this talented young manager, now turning out to be the star of Omega. With the right man running the Raptor development program, their world-class labs would help accomplish the rest.

Omega's software development labs *were* world-class—in fact the best in the country. The company had positioned itself as first in its industrial niche, with a lay-in of capital infrastructure over the past fifteen years that had given this facility enormous capability. The Raptor central computer upgrade program occupied one-quarter of Omega's lab footprint. Built of special construction materials to withstand the most invasive external electronic eavesdropping, the lab also had multiple levels of security at key entry points. Only those technicians with the highest-level security classification and need to know were granted access. In the most secure area of the development activity, retinal scans were the only way to gain access.

Khalil spent most of his days at Omega monitoring the incredibly complex software build. It came easily to him. His brain was wired to think, analyze, and conclude how entire systems were codependent and integrated by each line of code. That level of intellect drove him to micromanage his team, getting into every engineer's work, much to their frustration.

The chief technology officer at Omega had watched Khalil operate, and he was impressed at what the young manager had accomplished in a short time. The interrogator program was not nearly as complex, but there was much riding on its success as well. The executive knew it had to be carefully integrated with the central computer software—an extremely difficult effort due to the interdependency in lines of code. While he was a little hesitant to overload Khalil, he insisted that the Khalil be heavily involved in the interrogator software integration.

"Khalil, you're a natural at understanding virtually every nuance associated with code development and integration. I'm giving you full authority in monitoring the IFF software development. I've already cleared the way with Dave Ballard, the program manager." He paused for a moment and continued. "While Ballard's not too happy with someone outside his program sticking his fingers in, he's okay with you if it increases the likelihood of success of both key programs."

"Thanks, boss," Khalil responded. "I know I can handle it. It's a lot of responsibility, but I was likely to be heavily involved anyway since the interrogator is managed through the central computer."

Khalil loved a challenge and seemed to relish the added work being piled on top of him. He had already established a strong reputation within the company as a workaholic. He was at the lab day and night, but then again, he loved it—the environment, the technology, the opportunity to do things that he believed most engineers couldn't fully comprehend.

During the few spare moments when he wasn't at Omega, he got plenty of encouragement from his mentor, Sheikh Rahainee, his imam in the Abdallah Mosque. He advised Khalil to spend every waking hour in the lab—build a pattern of behavior that would never draw attention by anyone. Khalil began to wonder about Rahainee's intense interest in his performance. His work habits and long hours in the lab, though not encouraged by his boss, were acknowledged as the way this successful young engineer operated.

The imam tried to keep him solely focused on his job, although he knew Khalil wanted to visit his parents and sister more often—but Rahainee knew Iran's plans had to come first. The sheikh mentioned an upcoming meeting that Khalil would be attending. The young software genius had not yet been informed by Omega or the Air Force about his future overseas travel to an important conference. Rahainee explained that he would meet a contact there who would discuss the incredible challenge that lay ahead for him.

Chapter 27

Friday nights at the Langley Officers Club drew the usual crowd of tired airmen from across all squadrons on the base. The bars in the club were stocked with every brand of liquor imaginable, along with plenty of beer options, and provided an opportunity for pilots to chill out a bit after a grueling week. Matt and Flamer made it a point to join the fun. Flamer's wife, Colene, met them there.

The beer flowed freely, with most of Langley's squadrons represented to commiserate about the week's events, talk some bullshit, and drown out their tension before the weekend began. It was an old tradition to meet at the club on Fridays. It gave many of the younger officers a chance to socialize a bit with their more senior bosses in a casual environment. Of course, socializing was done carefully, respectfully, since Monday would come around soon enough and not everything that was said at the bar was forgotten.

The west side of the club had a small bar and a number of crud tables that were always the scene for plenty of friendly squadron competition. Crud was a game adapted from a pool table, with only two balls, no cues, and at least two competitors at a time, although teams usually had at least four players each. To the uninitiated, the game looked a lot like a free-for-all among fighter pilots. The rules were simple. A "shooter" rolled a cue ball from one end of the pool table and tried to strike the striped ball at the other end. The "receiver" on the other team must grab the cue ball after it hit the striped ball and, from either end of the table, strike the striped ball with the cue ball before it stopped moving. A "judge," normally holding a drink, stood by the side of the table and could rule the play dead if the striped ball wasn't hit before it stopped rolling. Players were eliminated as they accumulated three lives lost due to failure to execute their play in time and for other violations of the crud rules—like bumping into the "judge" and spilling his drink! And so it would go until there was only one team member left standing.

As was almost always the case, squadrons put together teams to compete against each other and claim bragging rights, at least for the next week. A few of the larger aircraft maintenance and support squadrons, and many of the flying squadrons, had teams of women who could play the game just as well as any man.

A group of single ladies had gotten together and challenged Ace, Flamer and his mates to a crud match. They had instigated the competition using an offhanded "lack of manhood" remark—sure to get cocky fighter pilots sucked into a game.

Flamer turned to Ace. "You better watch out for these gals, Ace. I've seen them in action before. They play plenty dirty, and they can whip our asses if we're not careful."

"I've got this, Flamer!"

I'm sure I can handle these babes, Ace thought to himself.

He smiled broadly at the ladies, bowed awkwardly at the waist, and agreed graciously to the match, insisting that he and his buddies would try not to make them lose *too* badly.

"Okay, what shall we play for?" Ace grinned broadly, then turned his head and winked at his teammates.

"What have *you* got that *we* would want, other than bragging rights for beating a bunch of drunk flyboys?" replied the cute blonde. "I'd be surprised if you guys can even keep up with us," she laughed.

Ace was smitten with her smile but kept his composure, in spite of the three beers he had already downed.

"Okay, guys, let's take it easy on these gals," he said, huddling with his three buddies. "But let me be crystal clear about one thing. Stay away from the blonde in the tight jeans. I believe that she and I may have future plans together, and *she* doesn't even *know* it yet."

The crud match involved a lot of running around the table, trying to get in the best position for a shot at an opponent's ball. Blocking your opponent without being obvious was legal, and at times there was plenty of contact between the young pilots and their pretty challengers. Ace had a hard time trying to concentrate on the game—he just couldn't keep his eyes off those tight jeans! As players were eliminated on both teams, it finally got down to Ace and his attractive blonde opponent.

"Hey, since we're the last ones standing, at least let me know your name. I'm Matt, but everyone calls me Ace."

"I'm Julie, happy to *beat* you," she said with a smile. She paused for a moment and put on her best coy facial expression. "It's getting pretty warm in here," she said as she unbuttoned the top two buttons of her blouse, deliberately revealing plenty of herself to Ace. She pretended to fan herself to cool off.

Ace couldn't help but be immediately distracted by the ample bosom spilling out of the black lace bra now in plain view. At least, that was Julie's sly plan. Wide-eyed, Ace grinned and tried hard not to stare. He missed the fact that Julie had already played her shot. He ran around the table, trying desperately to get to the ball to make a kill shot. But Julie had gotten in a blocking position. Ace quickly reached in front of her, accidentally brushing his hand across her breasts as he tried to get to the ball.

"Hey, buster, watch those hands!" she said with a squeal. Ace dropped his ball on the floor, a stunned look on his face—and the match was over.

"I can't believe you fell for that," she said, laughing loudly.

Ace just shook his head, his face still a bit red from blushing at her last comment about his hand.

"Well, I guess you win," he said. "Can I buy you a drink?"

"I think you've had enough beer, and besides, I don't drink. But I'll sit down with you to catch my breath," she said.

They headed over to a quieter spot, found a small table, and sat down.

"You don't want to desert your friends, do you?" said Julie with a flirtatious smile.

Matt didn't seem to hear the words as he stared into her deep blue eyes. He suddenly realized she had asked him a question.

"Oh, sorry, I didn't mean to stare, but I just can't get over how beautiful you are. I know that may sound a bit corny, and you probably hear it all the time, but it doesn't make it any less true."

It was Julie's turn to blush a bit, surprising herself with her reaction to his comments. She had seen her fair share of fighter pilots out to put another checkmark in their record book of conquests. But for some reason, she felt Ace was different. He seemed sincere from the look on his face. She hadn't been expecting this kind of reaction from Ace, a guy she had just met and had whipped in a friendly crud match. Julie did find him ruggedly handsome but was surprised that he wasn't just another obnoxious fighter pilot looking to score for the night.

As he reached across the table to hold her hand, she said, "Hey there, buster, let's slow down a bit. After all, we really just met, even though you're a little familiar with my territory," she said, pointing to her breasts. "You did manage to cop a free feel at the crud table," she laughed.

Ace uncharacteristically blushed again, embarrassed that she would think he brushed across her on purpose. She continued. "Tell me a little about yourself. What's a boy like you doing in a gin joint like this any way?" she asked with a flirtatious smile. "I want to know who this big lug named Ace *really* is."

The rest of the evening was magical as the two seemed to mesh together. A perfect fit, it seemed, and the beginning of a budding romance between Matt and Julie. The more they talked, the more they discovered about what they had in common. Not just the obvious physical attraction, which was pretty strong on both sides, but they seemed to be connecting on a deeper mental level and appeared just perfect for each other, although they had yet to fully realize that.

Julie was a Florida Gator, having attended the University of Florida in Gainesville, and they both came from families whose parents had served their country in the military. Julie's father had retired after thirty years in the Army. He had two combat tours, in Afghanistan and Iraq. After graduating from UF with a degree in business administration, Julie snagged a job as an assistant manager at the Base Exchange at Langley, a department store found on almost all military bases. She had a few flings with fighter pilots in the past, but never anything serious, and nothing recent.

Matt explained how he'd spent his formative years growing up without a father and how his mother had done her best to raise him as a good Christian kid. She helped guide him to achieve his full potential—to become a fighter pilot like his father, and to continue the legacy of service to his country. He took the time to explain his life at the Air Force Academy, and all the "fun" he had while there. He talked about his love for the outdoors, especially the Rocky Mountains. Julie could see how Matt's face seemed to light up when talking about his last hike at Telluride. Then he explained how his time in Oklahoma and Panama City had eventually gotten him into a Raptor cockpit at Langley.

"I'll bet you were pretty distracted during your spare time at Tyndall," Julie said. "I've been down on the strip, and I'm sure you probably got pretty well acquainted with the college girls escaping winter for some Florida sun."

Ace blushed again, mostly from knowing that he did have a pretty good time there. But hey, he was a single guy—no rules! Now that he'd met Julie, that might change.

"Julie, I definitely behaved myself down there," he said with the most innocent and sincere expression he could muster. She looked straight into his eyes, and then they both started laughing.

For Matt and Julie, it seemed that their union was predestined. Their subsequent courtship moved at lightning speed. At first, Matt thought that maybe things were moving a bit too fast.

After all, he thought, *I'm a fighter pilot, at the absolute peak of my testosterone growth period. It just doesn't get any better than this. Am I ready to settle down?*

But every time he looked into those deep blue eyes, Julie made him feel like nothing he had ever experienced before, and it was a feeling that he wanted more of, constantly, every minute of every day!

Unfortunately for Matt, Julie was off to see her folks the next week. Her father's birthday just happened to be the following Saturday, and she wasn't going to miss the short drive to Fredericksburg. When her dad had retired from the Army, he'd settled near the National Military Park, where in 1862, during the Civil War, the Confederate Army had defeated the Union Army in the Battle of Fredericksburg. Julie's father was a rabid American history buff, and the hallowed ground of Fredericksburg was rich in history. It made him feel truly alive, in spite of the blood that had been spilled in the Virginia soil. Julie said her father could almost feel the presence of Union and Confederate soldiers who'd lost their lives near the stone walls on Sunken Road.

Matt counted the minutes until she got back. Meanwhile, it was back to the operational training regimen at Langley. Climbing into his jet for another training sortie, Ace shifted gears in his head. He could compartmentalize the special Friday night's excitement with Julie from the job now at hand. Minutes later, he headed down the taxiway to the end of the runway. When he got his clearance to go, he pushed his Raptor's throttles forward and streaked down the long gray concrete runway, lifting gracefully into the early-morning sky. He smiled inside his oxygen mask as the orange glow of the slowly rising sun peeked over the horizon.

Chapter 28

The annual International Aviation Development Conference was planned for Riyadh, Saudi Arabia, this year. Every major aircraft manufacturer and most of the key technology experts from around the world attended. Lockheed Martin and Boeing were the largest US companies represented. Also present were the key European aircraft companies and their major suppliers. Neither Omega nor the Raptor Program Office had participated in the past, but their major F-22 contract captures had prompted both Lieutenant Casey and Khalil Ruffa to attend.

The conference agenda included a full day devoted to the latest advances in open architecture systems and the challenges of software code integration. While the F-22 central computer and interrogator requirements were already fixed in concrete, gaining a more complete understanding of what was going on across the industry was vital to staying one step ahead of the competition. Sometimes, the competition *was* the enemy.

Khalil and Lieutenant Casey flew coach class out of Dallas-Fort Worth International Airport on American Airlines, nonstop to Riyadh. Throughout the long late-night flight, there was only small talk between them as they both struggled to get some sleep. It was nearly impossible, with flight attendants on a regular schedule passing out free drinks, snacks, and meals and constantly asking if they needed anything. Casey had resisted having some wine, not wanting to offend Khalil, but Khalil insisted it wasn't a problem.

"Go ahead and have some wine. It will help you sleep, Rebecca."

"Oh, all right, but just one or two glasses," she replied.

"I'll make sure you don't overdo it and get a little bit crazy." As soon as he said it, he thought he might have overstepped his bounds. He was about to apologize when Casey just burst out laughing.

"I can absolutely control myself after a couple of drinks," she announced, squeezing his hand.

Before long, she was slumped against Khalil, her head resting on his broad shoulder. He gazed down at this young officer, the flowery scent of her hair pleasantly appealing to him. The engine's drone eventually caused Khalil to fall asleep as well.

Both Casey and Khalil were awakened by the aircraft cabin lights abruptly coming on, along with the pilot's announcement that they were beginning their descent into Riyadh. Casey blushed a bit as she pulled her head away from Khalil's shoulder, apologizing with a smile for leaning on him throughout the long night flight.

"Sorry for using you as my pillow—but I sure slept great."

"I was honored to offer you anything that would make your flight more comfortable," replied Khalil with a smile and a gentle bump against her shoulder.

After disembarking, they both proceeded through Saudi customs and caught a cab to their hotel. They checked in, freshened up and met in the lobby. They couldn't wait to eat something other than airline food after the fourteen-hour flight. The Royal Hilton dining room helped satisfy their hunger.

There was plenty of time to get acclimated after the flight since the conference wasn't supposed to start until the following day. So they decided to explore the area to get a taste of the Saudi culture.

Rebecca Casey's idea of the best attractions didn't involve looking at the local historical sites or going to a museum. She had read that the gold souk markets were famous in Riyadh, and a *must* for jewelry shopping. She wanted a bargain on some ornately carved twenty-four-karat gold jewelry, and perhaps even to have some made for her and her mom.

"Khalil, the gold souks are my top shopping priority on this trip. Today may be the only opportunity we might have while we're here, before we get immersed in the conference activities."

Khalil knew a bit about the Middle Eastern jewelry markets, and while there was plenty of opportunity to buy gold from high-end souks near the hotel, he knew they needed to venture out a bit from the city center to find the best value.

Khalil checked with the concierge, got directions, and met Casey at the hotel door. "Let's grab a cab and head to the outskirts of Riyadh. The concierge told me right where to go.

"Oh, and don't forget your hijab. There will be plenty of the Saudi religious police just looking for an opportunity to harass a foreigner," remarked Khalil. *No need for any unwanted attention,* he thought.

"I've got it in my purse—I came prepared after my country briefing back at Wright-Patterson."

They ventured out of the city to the southwestern perimeter and encountered a stark contrast in conditions. While the kingdom clearly put its bountiful oil revenue into making central Riyadh a striking example of a modern economic growth engine, the outlying areas reflected an obvious class distinction. Saudi nationals living in the inner city enjoyed all the benefits of a relatively high standard of living—free medical care, free education, and the opportunity to live in well-equipped modern homes. In contrast, outside the central Riyadh area was a huge population of third country nationals who represented the country's labor force. The opportunity for them to work in Saudi Arabia often was far better than in their own homelands. Many were also superb craftsmen—in fact, some of the finest goldsmiths to be found in the Middle East.

They directed the cab down a few side streets into what appeared to be a shanty town. Casey nervously looked around, not really comfortable with what she saw.

"We're out in the middle of nowhere," she exclaimed.

She momentarily worried that she might be kidnapped, tortured for her secrets, or worse, sold to some wealthy Arab to be his sex slave. *Stop thinking ridiculous thoughts,* she told herself. *Besides,* she mused, *Khalil looks like he can handle himself, and I'm sure he won't let anything happen to me.*

"It's okay. Let's walk from here," Khalil said to her. "The cab will wait for us to finish shopping."

They both exited the cab and headed down the street, past fruit, vegetable, and meat stalls. The pungent odor of raw chicken permeated the already sizzling dusty air. They passed the small food market and continued walking. A beggar on the side of the street squatted, his head lowered, a small tin in his hand. His tattered, filthy clothes and dirty bare feet provided clear evidence of his hopeless condition. Rebecca felt sorry for him and dropped a few rials into the tin. He murmured something and nodded in thanks.

As the two continued down the street, in between what appeared to be two ramshackle buildings, an alleyway seemed to explode with a bright yellow light, in sharp contrast to the surroundings. They turned into it, their path illuminated by stall after stall of every form of gold jewelry hanging from ceiling to floor. Casey was stunned at what she saw.

"How can this possibly exist in such a run-down area?" she asked Khalil.

"Markets like this are everywhere, even in the smallest villages. Saudi women wear their family wealth on their arms, wrists, fingers and around their necks." He looked at Rebecca. "You just can't see the jewelry under their abayas."

Casey found some great bargains and had fun trying to communicate while asking cryptic questions about quality, weight and price. The merchants definitely understood the universal language of selling gold. She found some nice pieces and asked Khalil his opinion on how they would look on her.

Khalil, always working it, said, "With your beauty, anything you buy makes the jewelry look good."

Casey smiled, a slight blush on her face, and proceeded with her purchase, managing to get the best price, at least in her mind, while not trying to come across as arrogant or greedy. When she had charged enough to her credit card, it was time to go.

They walked down the street to their cab and headed back to the center of the city as the glowing orange sun began to set on the cloudless brown horizon. Casey was beaming in the back seat of the small cab. The glow on her face brightened up the seemingly mazelike path through the run-down neighborhoods on Riyadh's outskirts and on to the main thoroughfare that took them back to the Hilton.

She's quite lovely when she's happy, thought Khalil, trying to decide in his mind how their first evening in-country would end up.

Chapter 29

They met for dinner at the Royal Hilton dining room after cleaning up from their day exploring Riyadh. Rebecca had changed into a beautiful red dress with a plunging neckline and bare back—a bit bold for the ultra-conservative Saudi culture. When Khalil saw her across the room, he quickly looked around to see the reactions from any hotel staff that might have been offended by Casey's attire. Seeing no obvious attention being given to her, he walked briskly toward her.

"Rebecca, you look absolutely beautiful."

"Well, I just wanted you to see the real me!" She smiled and turned slowly around like a fashion model on a catwalk. "Doesn't this look better than me walking around with my head covered?"

"For sure, but you need to be careful in this country. There is very little tolerance in this culture for women who expose themselves—even for a beautiful Westerner. But I must say, I *really* like what I see."

"Thanks, Khalil. You're quite the handsome gentleman yourself," she said, reaching out and stroking his arm.

They headed into the dining room as Khalil continued to wonder where the night was headed. They ate a delicious dinner that was capped with an equally sumptuous dessert. As they rose to leave, it became apparent that the time zone change and full day of activity had worn them out. They headed back to their respective rooms and got some much-needed sleep.

The next morning, following a short breakfast, Khalil and Casey headed over to the large exposition center that was hosting the International Aviation Development Conference. Their entry badges were waiting for them, along with their introductory packets with the agenda, key speakers, conference breakout sessions, and a listing of companies and executives attending. Khalil took special note of the sessions involving major advances in software development and, in particular, military applications involving offensive and defensive systems in aircraft and space-based systems.

Lieutenant Casey split away from Khalil and meandered through the packed conference display floor to make some introductions with other Air Force officers and senior civilian representatives in attendance. As there was no one else from Wright-Patterson AFB planning to attend, Casey had been told by her boss to get acquainted with as many of the key folks associated with the Raptor as she could while on her "boondoggle" trip. Her boss had insisted she make it worthwhile to justify the cost of her excursion to the world's largest sandbox. Casey knew her program in detail and had been briefed on the IFF program progress as well, in the event any questions came her way.

The Lockheed, Boeing, and Northrop Grumman booths, known for their colorful graphic displays and scale models of the latest in military aircraft technology, drew large crowds and a preponderance of US representatives. Casey had to physically push her way through just to say hello to the F-22 Raptor and F-35 Lightning II representatives at the Lockheed display area and make sure they knew she was representing the Raptor's latest major upgrade. The Lockheed business development team kept a sharp eye out for the military attendees. The company was eager to promote their technologically "superior" products that they insisted were just the right application for any prospective customer's needs.

"Hey, Lieutenant, great to see you here," said the tall, rather distinguished-looking gentleman wearing his Lockheed star emblem brightly affixed to his suit jacket.

Rich Masters, a former F-22 Raptor pilot with four thousand hours of overall fighter time, including three hundred and fifty combat hours, looked like he was fit enough to jump right back into the cockpit. He likely would have been happier *there* rather than standing in front of the Lockheed display area. But on the bright side, his paycheck was a lot better! Rich extended his hand to meet Casey, a warm smile on his face.

"Hi, Rich Masters here, welcome to our display area."

"Hello, Mr. Masters, I'm Rebecca Casey, from the Wright-Patterson F-22 Raptor Program Office. Great to meet you as well."

"Awesome," shouted Masters over the noise of the crowd. "It's really great that you could make it to the conference."

Rich's face beamed on hearing that a Raptor representative was here. He knew that while the F-22 was putting on some age after nearly fifteen years of flying, there was still nothing in the world that could touch this stealthy, lethal platform in terms of capability. Given the Air Force's wise decision to perform the critical upgrades, this old bird would continue to dominate the sky for years to come.

"Yes, sir, I got lucky, along with my Omega program manager. The Air Force usually won't fund trips like this overseas. But the conference agenda seemed tailor-made for us given our Raptor central computer and interrogator upgrade programs."

"First, some protocol. Don't call me 'sir.' I gave that up when I retired from the Air Force. You're the officer here, ma'am—not me. But to your point, both programs are essential to improve the Raptor's performance and enhance its capability." He paused a moment. "From what I hear, they seem to be progressing quite well. I'd like to meet your Omega rep if you can free him up from the other conference activities. I want to thank him in advance for what his company is doing."

"He's wandering around the display area. I'll try to find him later and link you up."

Casey and Masters talked for about ten minutes until the crowd around the Lockheed area got so large that Masters had to disengage to work his potential future customer base. You never knew when the next opportunity for another big sales opportunity would present itself. And while the F-22 wasn't on the market to foreign entities, the F-35, the newest stealthy Lockheed fighter, was currently being sold to allies of the United States. The Lightning II avionics capabilities, high performance, and stealth made a compelling potential acquisition program for any country looking to exponentially increase their air force power.

The European consortiums were also in place, showcasing their aircraft, support systems, and latest capability upgrades to either protect their homeland or take the fight to their enemies. Casey wandered through a number of display areas, impressed with the French Rafael and Russian United Aircraft Corporation booths. For a young Air Force acquisition officer, Casey felt like a kid in a candy store as she scanned the multitude of technological innovations on display.

An hour into her exploration, Casey heard the chimes ring out throughout the facility, signaling the start of the conference sessions and encouraging the attendees to head to the large briefing area. She made her way to the southwest door to meet up with Khalil, as they had prearranged.

In spite of the massive crowd, Khalil quickly found his lieutenant and helped usher her to the rapidly filling seats in front of the podium. They both wanted to be close enough to ask questions during the "Critical Software Advances" discussion, presented by Harris, one of the leaders in the world of software coding. While these presentations really had nothing to do with the F-22 programs, Casey was advised by her boss to be alert to any key words in the briefs that might signal the development of potential emerging threats to her weapon system. Of course, nothing classified would be presented at these conferences, especially in Riyadh, Saudi Arabia, and no contractor worth their salt would publicly and freely give up their "crown jewels" of innovation or intellectual capital. These presentations were meant to whet the appetite of potential customers and draw them into more detailed future contract discussions that would hopefully follow on from conferences like this.

Khalil listened intently to every word of the briefing. He smiled inwardly. The technical details being presented were likely well over the heads of most of the conference attendees. Most people in the audience who were not in the software business already had their eyes glazed over. Many looked for any distraction from the excruciating details of the briefing, some information coming across like unintelligible gibberish to them. After two hours, the first set of briefings ended.

The coffee bar was a concession the Saudis made for their foreign guests. During the break, Khalil and Casey met there first, and then she headed in a different direction. He looked for the strongest brew he could find, hoping to get a little caffeine jolt—a bad habit he'd developed after joining Omega. As he reached for a cup, a well-dressed gentleman with a neatly trimmed gray beard approached.

"You would think that in this modern city, we could at least get some decent coffee," the stranger said.

Khalil glanced over his shoulder at the gentleman. *Clearly not a Saudi*, he thought, *maybe Iranian*. "Well, this is not Starbucks. That would be much preferable to this weak, tasteless liquid," he responded.

Smiling at Khalil, the gentleman extended his hand. "Dr. Abu Katari," he offered.

Khalil shook his hand. "Khalil Ruffa," he responded, then thought about the name of the gentleman he had just met.

The name *Katari* rang a bell in Khalil's head. It was a name mentioned to him some time ago in his detailed indoctrination with his Texas imam. This was no chance meeting. Khalil had been told that his future would be tied to important people, trusted operatives who had the skill sets, the knowledge, the connections, that would enable him to change the world order. The imam had said that true change would require him to develop and embrace these new relationships and use them to reach Islam's true common goal across the planet.

The two walked away from the coffee bar, sipping their tasteless brown liquid, and headed to a quiet corner of the exhibition hall. Dr. Katari looked into Khalil's eyes, searching for a sign of recognition, of understanding from Khalil about why this "chance" encounter had taken place.

"I see that you have a Raptor pin on your lapel," replied Katari. "That is a powerful aircraft with unbelievable technology, and of course, the stealth!"

"Yes, I am the program manager with the Omega Company for one of Lockheed's major upgrades. It's quite exciting to work on such an exceptional weapon system."

"The F-22 is a truly awesome aircraft. The best in the world," replied Katari. He paused, looking around at the crowd.

"We have plenty of time before the next briefing begins. If you would, walk with me a bit," said Katari.

Khalil wasn't quite sure about what was going to happen next. He was smart enough to know that they were likely being watched, surveilled by one of the dozens of cameras and microphones positioned around the large facility. The two men headed down the long hallway, away from the crowded passageway toward the exit doors, and found a relatively deserted corner to have a discussion that would not be overheard or filmed. No cameras or microphones appeared to cover the area.

"I saw a note of recognition on your face when I introduced myself," said Katari.

"Yes, I have heard your name before." Khalil remembered his lengthy conversations with Sheikh Rahainee. "My imam told me about you. He said you were very important to the future of Islam—and that I should trust you implicitly." Khalil waited for a response.

"You have been briefed correctly," said Katari. Looking over his shoulder to verify they were alone, he continued. "I want to discuss an incredible opportunity for you, a cause in the name of Islam that I am sure you will embrace with your entire spirit."

Khalil looked into Dr. Katari's eyes—dark eyes that seemed to pierce his soul—eyes that drew Khalil closer to him. The conversation was astonishing as well. Khalil listened intently as Katari explained that his position in Omega had been carefully orchestrated. In that position, he was going to be a great enabler for Iran, to move the rapidly emerging military power to the forefront of the Muslim world. Khalil would be asked to use his brilliance, his intellect and his access in Omega to help defeat the capability of America's greatest weapon system, the F-22 Raptor. His task would involve the critical software of the Raptor's central computer program. And it would involve Iran's best scientists and engineers using technology that Khalil would help provide to Iran.

Khalil was shocked—and then a little bit frightened. He kept glancing over his shoulder, afraid that they were being overheard. The last thing he wanted was to be caught in any discussion that would likely land him in prison. But he kept his composure. After all, the imam at Khalil's mosque had advised him of the great role he was to play, and the likely involvement of the F-22 program. As he listened to Katari, he didn't fully realize what was actually in store for him—or how dangerous his task would be.

He thought about what this stranger was telling him. He had expected to be playing *some* important role for Islam, but not *this*. His brain was struggling with how he would ever be able to do what Katari was asking. Khalil, of all people, fully·understood the levels of security surrounding his program. The redundant checks and counterchecks on virtually every aspect of the software build would make any task he was being asked to do extremely difficult. Maybe impossible.

They chatted for some time before the chime signaled the beginning of the next briefing session in the conference hall.

"Perhaps we will talk again," said Katari.

"I would like that." Khalil shook the doctor's hand and headed back to his seat to join Lieutenant Casey. As he headed toward the conference area, he kept thinking about what Katari had said, about what he was being asked to do. What actually was the task? Was it something that could even be done? Why should he do it? He wondered about what Katari had said about getting his position in Omega. Had Iran been behind that? Would there be consequences if he turned the task down? If he accepted it, he would be, in essence, a traitor to the United States. His first gut reaction was to push back on the task—to refuse to do it. He had come too far in his life to risk everything.

His mind was spinning as he walked back toward the briefing room. Khalil began to realize the significance of his meeting with Katari. It was as his imam had predicted. He had been chosen to use his skills, in concert with those who could best apply the advantages of his position in Omega.

The two men met again on the following day, during a similar break in the briefing activity. In a quiet part of the conference facility, Katari gave Khalil *all* the details of his tasking.

Chapter 30

Six months after the crud match that brought them together, Matt and Julie were married in the old historic Langley Air Force Base Chapel. While the church had been rebuilt from its earliest construction in 1935, it still retained the beauty of a true colonial-style building. Many of Langley's structures, like the chapel, were on the historic registry of facilities that were strictly controlled by state and federal laws, with explicit rules that prevented any changes to the exterior facade. As such, the chapel retained its original luster, the steep slope of the roof making it appear as if it were reaching to the heavens. The weathered red brick construction showed some signs of age, and green vines clung to parts of the side—but it still gave off the treasured appearance of Langley's history.

Matt and Julie had not wanted a big wedding, but planned for only a small gathering of close friends, and of course, Matt's mom, and both of Julie's parents. The plan for a small ceremony quickly went to hell in a handbasket as Matt's family of aviators boisterously indicated they would be turning out in force—first to celebrate the marriage of one of their own, and second because they knew the reception at the Officers Club would be a great one. After all, what respectable fighter pilot would turn down a free delicious buffet dinner, serving up the best seafood that Chesapeake Bay had to offer? Even more compelling, there would be a massive open bar! Did someone say, "Free drinks"? Nothing was going to stop the thundering herd of fighter pilots from attending.

Cathy Black insisted that Matt wear his formal ceremonial Air Force uniform, as opposed to a locally rented tuxedo. It served the same purpose but looked a hell of a lot nicer than the civilian counterpart. She vividly remembered the day that she had married Matt's father, Alec Black, many years back. Alec and Cathy had said their vows on a military base, her husband proudly wearing his ceremonial dress uniform. In her mind, it was the way it ought to be—Alec would have wanted it that way. Julie's parents thought it was a great idea too, especially the thought of having a military wedding in the Langley Chapel. Julie's father reluctantly agreed to wear his Army dress uniform as well. It still fit him perfectly. He looked like he hadn't gained a pound since retiring.

The wedding ceremony was beautiful. As her father walked Julie down the aisle, Matt couldn't believe how lucky he was to marry this stunning lady. The priest presiding over the marriage smiled broadly as the couple turned toward him to begin the biggest chapter of their lives. Matt was nervous. For a guy who considered himself to be a fearless fighter pilot, he could feel his heart pounding as the priest asked each of them to repeat their wedding vows.

His voice broke a little while repeating his lines, almost forgetting what the priest asked him to repeat: "I, Matthew, take you, Julie, to be my lawful wedded wife—to have and to hold from this day forward, for better, for worse, for richer, for poorer, in sickness and in health, to love and to cherish, until death do us part."

As he looked into Julie's loving eyes, he immediately calmed down, his heartbeat slowing.

After Julie stated her vows, the priest concluded, "I now pronounce you man and wife." He turned to Matt. "You may kiss your bride."

Matt gave Julie a gentle kiss, and the newly married couple headed down the aisle amidst raucous cheering from Matt's buddies that drowned out the organ music.

The wedding reception was nothing short of phenomenal. The 94th Fighter Squadron was there in force, with every one of Matt's buddies showing up to rib him a bit on getting tied down at the tender age of twenty-five. More important, they were all comrades-in-arms, members of an elite fellowship of warriors that would always be there to support a teammate. And of course, they showed up to drink some free-flowing premium whiskey, eat dozens of large salty Chesapeake Bay oysters on the half shell, and raise some aviator hell!

———————•———————

Two months after the wedding, Julie found out that they were going to have a child. "I'm pregnant," Julie said softly, looking for the *right* reaction from Matt.

His response was a stunned one at first, and then a big smile spread across his face. He grabbed his beautiful wife around the waist, drew her toward him and spun her around like a doll.

"Whoa!" she yelled. "Be careful, you big lummox. After all, I'm in a motherly way now."

"Baby, I love you," he exclaimed, planting a big kiss on her lips. "I couldn't be happier that we're starting a family. I had really hoped for that, and now I can hardly control myself."

He looked deeply into Julie's blue eyes and saw tears of happiness begin to flow.

"Don't cry, baby, this is the happiest day of our lives! I can't wait to tell my buds at the squadron. But I've gotta pick up some premium stogies before I show up, or I'll catch all sorts of grief. I think Flamer brought back some *primo* Cuban leaf on his last vacation cruise. I'll bet I can tempt him to sell them to me for this special occasion."

"You're supposed to hand out cigars *after* the baby comes, not before."

"It's a squadron tradition, before *and* after the baby comes. You know these guys won't *ever* pass up any opportunity to celebrate."

"So, I suppose you'll be doing some celebrating tonight at the squadron bar," she replied, more as a statement than a question.

"Well, you know I can't just tell them my news, hand out the cigars and then leave," he said. "I'll pick up some decent Scottish whiskey, Macallan 15, and have it ready. Nothing but the best for my squadron-mates."

"Don't get yourself stopped by the cops," she said.

The Langley gendarme were famous for staking out the routes from the Officers Club and the fighter squadrons. A few unlucky fighter pilots had made the mistake of thinking that their perceived invulnerability in the air existed equally on the streets of Langley. Aside from the obvious embarrassment, being pulled over by a cop for drunk driving was a career-ender. The military dealt out harsh punishments for driving while intoxicated, and for officers especially, it seemed that an example had to be made to discourage anyone else from making the same big mistake.

"You'll ruin your career if you're not careful."

"No problem. I know my limits—and where they hide," he grinned.

———•———

Their first child came quickly, nine months to the day after Matt and Julie had gotten "really acquainted" shortly *before* their wedding. A beautiful daughter named Claire was now the pride of this family. Nothing made Matt happier than coming back from flying and picking up his curly-haired blonde baby, making her laugh ecstatically as he lifted her high over his head.

It was sometimes tough for Matt to head to the squadron, as he constantly had his daughter on his mind. As the months sped by, he was amazed at how quickly she changed from a tiny, seemingly helpless baby to a constantly smiling energetic toddler trying to crawl, and then walk. She squealed happily every time he came into the house after a hectic day of flying. Her voice melted his heart. Anything that bothered him from his day was melted away by this precious child.

Before Matt could fully assess that his life was now all about his bride and daughter, Julie announced that she was pregnant again. It wasn't necessarily part of their plan, since they had hoped to put a little space between the first and second child.

"Baby, how exactly did this happen?" he exclaimed when he found out the news.

"Very funny, Matt," she said, crinkling up her face with a half-smile, half-frown. "It happened the usual way, or don't you remember how cold it was three months ago? Remember, the freak snowstorm, roads closed, nothing to do but hunker down for two days?"

"Oh yeah—forgot about that," he said sheepishly, a wry grin on his face.

"There's more news. The doctor believes there are two heartbeats."

Matt's face blanched almost white, the instant realization of having twins sinking deep into his chest. The shock on his face brought an instant response from Julie.

"Aren't you happy that we're going to have twins?" she exclaimed.

His face began to return to its normal pink color, and he immediately reached down to hug his wife.

"Honey, I'm the happiest guy alive, even if you can't tell!"

Chapter 31

South of Tehran, Iran

The Supreme Leader of Iran was quite satisfied with the recent meeting of Persian Gulf coalition nations. The consensus they reached was unprecedented.

The strategy—some might have called it a wild scheme—to unite them in a common cause involved the clever leveraging of the rogue country's emerging nuclear capability. Iran's virtually unchecked development efforts to build nuclear weapons was a huge enabler for the strategy.

The multination nuclear deal, officially titled the Joint Comprehensive Plan of Action—JCPOA—had so many loopholes in it that Iran had proceeded with their nuclear program development at a rapid pace. It gave confidence to the coalition states that finally, a strong Islamic Gulf nation would possess the strength to influence world order and unite all Muslims under a common non-Western military defense umbrella. Time would ultimately be the measure of what could be accomplished by the union of religiously and politically diverse competing countries.

In spite of the growing coalition, the Iranian defense minister continued to have deep concerns about the rapid growth of their nuclear program and constantly expressed his thoughts to the Ayatollah.

"At some point, the Americans will realize their efforts failed to stop our nuclear weapons ambitions. They will surely have the evidence that we are about to become a true nuclear power—and will never stand for that. The US will try to impose restrictive sanctions to pressure us to stop. When that fails, they will likely conduct a military strike on us," he said. "That is, unless the Israelis attack us first."

The Ayatollah was not fazed by the defense minister's negativism and lack of confidence.

"That is precisely why our continuing efforts to eliminate the American military advantage are so important. Our defenses are now stronger than ever, thanks to several years of military buildup with advanced weapon systems provided by our Chinese and Russian friends. We can protect ourselves, and strike the infidels from the sky if they choose to attack." His intense focus on his minions had not changed.

"Our nuclear program is progressing quickly. Before long, we will have the ability to arm our ballistic missiles with nuclear warheads. Once we achieve that, we will be invulnerable to any attack. No sane country would dare strike a nuclear-capable nation for fear of a retaliatory response by those very weapons."

He continued, "For now, we are not encumbered with anything other than the useless visits by weapons inspectors who will find nothing."

He looked intently at the defense minister. "But we must eliminate the American stealth advantage. *That* is the wild card that could threaten our efforts if the United States were to attack. *That* is where we are most vulnerable. The Americans have used their stealth capability in the past to gain an advantage in the opening days of an attack. They will surely lead any strike on our territory with their best stealth fighter, the F-22 Raptor. We must be able to neutralize that capability *when* and *if* the Americans choose to attack us. As far as the Israelis, our defenses are now formidable enough to deter their attack—if they were foolish enough to do so."

There were more than a few concerned looks among the Supreme Leader's staff. They all knew Israel was unpredictable and might act in ways that defied logic, especially since Iran had threatened them in the past with complete annihilation.

The looks on the faces of the defense minister and the general staff did not scream confidence that they could actually thwart an attack by the Americans or the Israelis.

"Once our nuclear missiles are ready," he continued, "the Gulf nations, under our coalition, will no longer need the Americans for protection. We will instill fear and uncertainty in the United States, and in any non-Muslim nation that tries to place its filthy footprints and corrupt behavior in our holy lands."

"We are still months away from producing our first nuclear warheads," the defense minister stated. "We need more time. Even though our ballistic missiles are already tested and ready, the warheads are not yet complete. We must do everything we can to accelerate production. As you must know, the American spies likely already know we are close to completing them. Their president will not tolerate this."

"His talk is hollow," replied the Ayatollah. "The United States said the same of North Korea and did nothing while Chairman Kim proceeded rapidly with his nuclear program while laughing in the Americans' face." He smiled and continued. "Even their diplomatic actions and recent military threats to eliminate Kim's weapons are unlikely to actually result in nuclear disarmament of that country."

There were now nods coming from around the executive chamber. The Ayatollah thought to himself about how his country could actually stave off an American preemptive attack on the most important program in his country's history. He knew that to be successful, he had to take away the offensive advantage the US had over Iran's military.

"Nothing must slow us down from executing the Epsilon plan," Batani threatened, citing the name given to the code that he expected would cripple the Raptor's stealth capability.

Chapter 32

onths before, a meeting on counterstealth efforts had taken place between the Iranian and Chinese scientific and engineering leadership. They knew that any future American conflict required the playing field to be at least leveled—to take away any stealth aircraft advantage—allowing Iran's potent military to engage in a reasonably fair fight.

Dr. Katari was deeply involved in discussions with the other key scientists at the underground Khamenei Development Lab near the northern Iranian city of Rostamabad. The subject was the particular design of software programming code labeled Epsilon.

Dr. Lee Yu spent some time explaining the concept.

"China has experimented with ways to make the basic elements of software—that is, lines of code—actually repurpose themselves, or morph based on external stimulus. Essentially, a software program embedded in an aircraft system that was intended to perform a specific function could be externally triggered to perform a very different function than it was originally designed to do."

"I don't see how that is possible," Katari remarked. "There are protections built into most critical aircraft systems that are designed to prevent an external electronic intrusion from tampering with or disrupting its function."

"In order to make Epsilon work, the special software code would need to be placed into an aircraft's system. We believe that our agents, embedded in key American aircraft companies, have determined a way to accomplish this. They are able to access the fundamental software programs of some of the top fighter aircraft possessed by the United States.

"But to succeed," he continued, "Epsilon still requires an insider currently working in critical American defense contracts—the F-22 in particular."

Katari knew full well that Dr. Yu was referring to Khalil Ruffa. He thought about the discussion.

How do the Chinese even know we have Khalil in a position to do what we are talking about? Do they know he is in Omega? Do they have agents embedded there as well?

Dr. Katari and his Chinese counterpart continued debating the likely success of inserting the disruptive Epsilon morphing code into the F-22 Raptor software without being detected by any of the US government software design engineers who would have critical oversight of the central computer program.

"If this is done correctly, we can disguise the code as a redundant piece of the primary software program—perhaps as a repair function, which to all outward appearances would operate when a particular type of fault in the original code occurs. Only when activated by a signal, a satellite pulse stimulating the code, would it morph into its primary function, which is to trigger the Raptor's interrogator system, the IFF transponder. It would emit an interrogation signal from the aircraft, creating noise. That noise eliminates the advantage the Raptor has over non-stealthy fighter aircraft," stated Dr. Yu.

As he listened intently, Dr. Katari thought about what the Chinese scientist had said. Dr. Yu was brilliant, an expert in the field of stealth. China had been closely following the United States in their development of stealth technology for years and had surreptitiously gotten their hands on elements of the critical top secret data to advance their own program. Dr. Yu's specialty was the F-22 Raptor, having worked in ancillary US government-related software labs during the formative years of the aircraft's development.

As Yu continued, Katari wondered if this scheme would really work. Did the plan have any chance at all to be successfully executed without the Americans having any idea that their most important weapon system software had been penetrated?

———————•———————

It had been almost too easy for a country that *knew* and *lived* the virtue of patience. For decades, China had embedded their brightest young citizens in key cities and towns in the United States. Students spent years in the US building their credentials as law-abiding residents and eventually legal citizens through the generous American immigration laws. They were carefully groomed in some of America's best schools from an early age and attained advanced degrees. These young overachievers were subsequently placed in centers of academia, at key universities like Cal Tech. They were given but one objective—to absorb from the United States every available ounce of technological knowledge and every piece of American intellectual property related to cutting-edge aerospace programs. While their spoken allegiance was to the United States, their real allegiance was to Mother China.

They subsequently gained employment with major defense corporations that worked on some of the nation's most advanced military programs. Obtaining work visas following graduation, the best of their best migrated to America's top aerospace, scientific and technology companies. Their goal was to further position themselves to gain the right access to the latest developments that the strongest military in the world had available. In fact, Dr. Lee Yu was a top graduate from Cal Tech and later worked at two of the biggest defense companies in the US for years before eventually heading back to China.

Advances in American stealth technology had been carefully watched since the very first introduction of stealth aircraft. In spite of the best attempts American industry made to protect its most precious secrets, data migrated to China, enabling their own advancements in developing and building stealth into their own fleet of military aircraft. China had been playing the long game— one that counted on decades of preparation. Astoundingly, this migration was made somewhat easier by the large-scale theft of the Raptor's basic architecture containing the original software design code. Extremely tight checks and balances existed in the ultra-secure industry laboratories to guard against the likelihood of espionage, but it was not enough.

The highly intelligent Chinese software engineers had been bred for just this kind of opportunity. They were not just inculcated in all aspects of American life but became trusted friends to the citizens who made up the middle class of the United States. Familiarity bred complacency, and in fact, over time, a culture of complacency thrived in the ultra-secure industry software labs that produced the US military's most sensitive programs. Their efforts were facilitated by the careful insertion of China's top software engineers into the key labs of America's industrial base. Some of these brilliant engineers looked and acted like any other next-door neighbor. Most importantly, they earned the trust of their colleagues and supervisors. Many obtained top secret security clearances. Some gained employment on contracts associated with building the Raptor.

China's long-game strategy consequently resulted in the surreptitious theft, over time, of America's stealth technology.

———————•———————

Katari wasn't alone in questioning the true viability of the plan. Dr. Yu also had a few doubts, especially about the ability of the Iranians to pull it off, even *with* his help. After all, understanding the Raptor's software architecture was one thing. But that was still a long way from being able to develop and insert a disruptive code that would actually work in the *current* F-22's software program—a program they didn't have. They would need access to the *current* code. They would need a means to insert Epsilon without suspicion and would likely have to adapt the code in Iran to meet any system software architectural design changes the US had made in the program.

It was a long shot. The Chinese government saw an advantage for themselves remaining intricately involved yet carefully hidden from the prying eyes of the Western world—a world already suspicious of Chinese military intentions, a world that already had their eyes and ears focused on what was going on in China's labs. Iran was the perfect environment for this important test. No one believed the Iranians had the technology to do anything at this level of advanced software development. Dr. Yu was the right man to help Iran move this counterstealth effort forward. Why not let the Iranians prove or disprove this project?

This will keep Chinese fingerprints off it until it works, thought Dr. Yu. After all, F-22s were not flying anywhere near China. But here in the Gulf, a counterstealth test could easily be accomplished due to the ongoing Raptor jet flights in the area. American combat air patrols were a regular occurrence due to aggressive Iranian naval activity.

As he talked with Katari, Dr. Yu couldn't help but think about how dangerous, how risky it would be to get the key technology embedded in the Raptor software. Success or failure of the first important step rested on one man—Khalil Ruffa.

"It would be a notable achievement, if you can execute it. But I believe there is high risk for discovery by the US government before we ever get to use it," remarked Dr. Yu. "I also don't fully understand the true capabilities of this *genius* of yours, the software engineer you have at Omega, or his ability to pull off this monumental effort. If he fails, how will you ensure the disaster doesn't trace back to you, or more importantly, to China?"

"Khalil Ruffa is one of the most brilliant engineers we have ever seen. He is dedicated to the cause of unifying the Muslim world under a single holy Caliphate." Dr. Katari continued, "His commitment to this task is beyond question. He fully understands the consequences of failure and also understands the extreme secrecy involved. He knows the value of China's support in our holy cause and would give up his own life before revealing anything about this effort, or allowing it to be discovered."

Yu thought about what Katari had said. The Chinese scientist couldn't care less about a unified Muslim world. There already existed a significant level of disdain for Muslims in general within the world's most populous country. He was more interested in the capability of the man who was going to pull off this task.

Dr. Katari shook his head, holding back his contempt for this arrogant Chinese scientist. He had never liked Yu to begin with. The self-righteous, superior attitude the Chinese brought with them into Iran was barely tolerable. But he needed China's help. They were far ahead of Iran in understanding stealth technology and how to potentially defeat it. They had developed Epsilon and were already a key part of Iran's rearmament efforts.

Dr. Yu had brought the latest Chinese information on counter-stealth technology. His team of engineers had worked with the Iranians to disguise the true purpose of the engineering efforts from the outside world. It was important that it appeared to those whose business was all manner of spycraft that the Iranians were doing nothing more than advancing their communications capability. They were making improvements to a woefully inadequate infrastructure within their country. With much assistance from China, Iran spent a fortune developing a set of satellites that appeared to be for telecommunications use. The actual use of a strategically placed satellite would be quite different. The true purpose of one *special* satellite was to trigger Epsilon and eliminate the Raptor's stealth advantage.

The extremely complicated and dangerous plan was going to be heavily dependent on triggering, at a precise time, the behavior of the aircraft's radar return—making it a ready target for an Iranian missile kill. This part of the plan had to succeed, because if for any reason it didn't make it visible to radar, the Iranian aircraft and their key defensive systems would be sitting ducks to the attacking F-22s. The enlarged radar return, or bloom, was essential to stop the Raptors.

Dr. Yu guaranteed that the Iranians would have the necessary support to pull off the risky effort. The risk-reward equation looked very good to Chinese leadership. If Iran failed to corrupt the Raptor software and was discovered by the Americans, the US would go after Iran with a vengeance—no big change there in the current geopolitical balance of power. If Iran succeeded, they would likely still get pounded by the Americans in the end, but the Chinese would obtain verification of key counterstealth advances they didn't currently have.

Lee Yu smiled to himself as he continued to think this through. Success would be quickly leveraged by China's military, clearing the way for their unopposed expansion throughout the South China Sea, and Indo-Pacific! *These Iranians are dupes and they don't even know it. It's so easy to manipulate them,* he thought. *But Katari is a smart man—he has to have some idea about our true intentions. He must wonder about why we chose Iran to try to prove our strategy to defeat the American combat advantage.*

Chapter 33

Since his return from Riyadh, Khalil was more determined than ever to drive his program toward the targeted completion date. Dr. Katari had given him his specific task: provide the most up-to-date version of the Raptor central computer software to Katari as soon as possible. Complicating the task, he had to figure out how to get it out of the Omega lab without setting off any alarms, without being discovered.

He still didn't know how he was supposed to pull that off. He couldn't very well put it on a hard drive and walk out of the building with it. The program was extremely large, classified at the top secret level, and encrypted at that. Any attempt to download it onto another device, another computer, would immediately raise a red flag and set off the internal antitampering alarms. Khalil's mind seemed to spin around in a fog whenever he tried to dissect the problem into its individual elements. But like any good engineer, he needed to analyze every key piece of the problem and figure out how best to solve it.

A few weeks after Khalil returned to Omega, a successful program review was completed with the Air Force, and in spite of a few very minor software integration issues, his military customer was extremely happy. Lieutenant Casey was especially pleased. She had been nervous that the preparation would not happen in their absence. But Khalil's team had been all over it while he and Casey were in Riyadh, and the results indicated that the program was on track and under budget. The Air Force program manager, Colonel Hampton, complimented Khalil on his deep grasp of every aspect of the complicated software build.

"Great job, Khalil," said the colonel. "Your team performed superbly, and I couldn't be happier." Hampton continued, "Hopefully the rest of the development efforts will proceed just as successfully."

They ought to be happy, thought Khalil. *I spend enough time reviewing virtually every action by my team, including fixing their occasional screwups.*

"Thank you, Colonel. I've got the best team in the world, and they know how to produce when given a challenge," he remarked. "But Lieutenant Casey has been instrumental in providing me with the right guidance and oversight. She deserves plenty of credit." Khalil motioned toward the lieutenant.

Rebecca Casey wasn't prepared for the compliment, but she smiled at Khalil and nodded her thanks. The meeting adjourned, and the Air Force and company representatives headed for the door. Rebecca pulled Khalil to the side and thanked him for the impromptu public accolade in front of her boss.

"Khalil, you really didn't have to say that. I'm still trying to keep up with the rapid pace. You and your team deserve all the credit."

"Rebecca, don't undersell your role in the success. You're extremely talented, and it's evident you know how to drive this effort to the finish line." He hoped he wasn't laying on the praise a bit too heavily.

Khalil knew full well that there were times when Casey didn't have a clue about what his team was doing. That didn't matter to him. She was *perfect* for the job. At this point, Khalil knew precisely how to manipulate her to avoid any concern that she might have about anything he was doing, or was going to do. He was building the relationship—carefully, slowly, but with very deliberate objectives. Her unequivocal acceptance of his actions would be extremely important in the near future.

———•———

The afternoon prayers were over, and most of the Islamic faithful had departed from the Abdallah Mosque in southeast Dallas.

Among those who fervently believed in the power of prayer was Khalil, lingering back in the corner of the large, ornate hall. With the pressures of his job at Omega, he normally didn't have the time to visit the mosque for anything other than weekend prayers.

Sheikh Rahainee walked toward Khalil. As he approached, he turned his head and stared intently around the dimly lit hall for any others that might be lingering.

"*As-salamu alaikum*, my most holy imam," said Khalil as the sheikh stepped toward him.

"*Wa alaikum assalaam*," replied the sheikh, motioning Khalil to follow him down the darkened hallway toward a small room. "I received communication from Dr. Katari. He indicated you are now aware of the great opportunity that awaits us all once you have completed your critical tasks at Omega."

"It was a good meeting in Riyadh, but dangerous to discuss such things in a place like the conference center," replied Khalil. "I am concerned that we may have been observed, in spite of our precautions. There is no way to know if the Saudis had cameras, microphones and perhaps even spies who were watching and listening to our conversation."

"You don't have to concern yourself with that possibility," replied the imam. "Dr. Katari is a brilliant scientist and would not have even broached the conversation with you if there had been any threat of discovery."

"Still, I must be extremely careful with whom I converse, especially in a forum that was attended by my Air Force program manager, and plenty of other military representatives. There were a few odd reactions by military officers when my program manager introduced me. Nothing openly hostile, but more like a questioning look. They were likely wondering why a Muslim was managing the most critical Air Force contract in existence."

The reality, of course, was that throughout the Air Force, and across most of the military and government agencies, Muslim men and women held positions of authority and responsibility. Khalil knew this, but his suspicions about what was *really* in most American hearts occasionally made him think irrationally.

"You must stay focused on successfully completing this project and sticking to the schedule," replied the imam. "That is critical, as your timing is woven into Iran's planning for achievement of their nuclear program. You, Khalil, are integral to that achievement."

What? This is about Iran's nuclear program? Khalil questioned himself.

Rahainee saw the puzzled look in Khalil's eyes.

"Iran is on the verge of achieving greatness on the world stage. The completion of their nuclear weapons development is most sensitive, and their most closely guarded secret."

He explained what was at stake—the ability of Iran to lead a holy Caliphate to unite all Muslims, backed by a weapons capability that would ensure the Caliphate would never be challenged. He further explained the threat posed by America's stealthy military aircraft. For Iran to succeed, stealth must be defeated. Khalil was integral to that effort.

"America's greatest weapon system will be brought to its knees."

Khalil stared intently at his sheikh.

"You have something to provide Katari, soon," directed the imam. "The current version of your central computer software program is essential for our scientists to move forward with the testing of our great weapon. You must find a way to provide it to Katari in three weeks. Again, the timing is crucial for our plan to succeed."

Khalil still couldn't believe what he was being asked to do.

"How can I do this without being discovered? The program is extremely large, over one million lines of code. There is no portable device that can be used to load the software and still allow me to get it out of the lab without detection," replied Khalil, trying to control his elevated voice.

Sheikh Rahainee nodded knowingly at Khalil.

"You will be meeting again with Katari, soon. He will provide more detail on your task, as well as the device you will use to pass the program to our scientists. This device is your means to success. It contains the latest achievement in miniaturization, de-encryption, and compression of software code. Our Chinese friends developed this device to support their own efforts to obtain data from the Americans. It has the ability to compress and store the massive amount of software you are developing," he finished.

"It absolutely *must* have the ability to de-encrypt," responded Khalil, "or the data will be meaningless. Also, the central computer program has protections that keep it from being copied or transferred. The barriers are built in to prevent tampering with the code. How will this device get past this problem?"

"You are a clever man. You have the necessary skill to build bridges across the antitampering protections—and the device will work as I have described. I have been assured by our Chinese experts that it will enable you to bypass all protections built into the system."

And if this plan turns to shit, my life in the United States as a free citizen will be over, thought Khalil. *I'm sure the Americans would relish capturing a traitor to their country. Especially a Muslim traitor.*

Khalil, deep in thought about what lay ahead for him, was gaining a growing understanding of the key role he would play in what was likely to be a major blow to the United States. A part of him was actually excited to be an integral player in gaining some measure of retribution for what America had done to him and his family.

"The Supreme Council in Iran is aware of your sacrifice, dedication and commitment to our holy cause. It has not gone unnoticed," replied the imam.

Chapter 34

The next three weeks at the lab were intense. Khalil was doing his best to keep his team from slacking off the rigid schedule in front of them. He knew they couldn't rest on the last program review's success but had to retain a sharp focus on the rapidly developing code. The thought of what lay ahead weighed heavily on his mind.

On a rare Saturday that Khalil was not working, mainly due to a Muslim holy day, he was contacted by Dr. Katari—a call that he fully expected, given the timetable Sheikh Rahainee had described.

"I was expecting to hear from you," Khalil said.

"Time is of the essence," Katari responded. "We must meet as soon as possible for a very important discussion."

"I am at your disposal," said Khalil.

"You remember our conversation in Riyadh," replied Katari. "I know you are committed to the cause of returning Iran to its dominance in the world, to be powerful as it was in the days when Persia ruled most of the civilized world. Meet me at the Abdallah Mosque today at three o'clock."

Khalil quickly agreed, knowing that he was now going to move forward on what was likely the most important mission of his life. He headed for the mosque a bit early, not wanting his arrival to be delayed by any traffic or highway construction.

Coming in from the bright Texas sun into the darkened hallway of the Abdallah Mosque, Khalil removed his shoes, stepped into the prayer room, and gave his thanks to Allah, who after all, he believed, must be guiding his every move. Dr. Katari appeared out of the shadows and walked over to him, putting his hand on his shoulder.

"Come with me. We have much to discuss."

One hour later, Khalil sat staring into dark eyes, looking almost dumbfounded at Dr. Katari.

"This sounds like an impossible task," Khalil said. "I thought my task was to provide only a current version of the central computer code. A plan like this to actually corrupt the final code in order to defeat the Raptor's stealth is likely not achievable, considering the levels of secrecy and the cryptological protections. The stealth properties and the technology that enables them are like nothing ever seen before. Countries outside the United States have been trying for years just to come up with ways to *see* this aircraft in combat. Thus far, they have failed to come close to achieving that goal."

"One step at a time. You must have faith, Khalil. Put your trust in the guiding hands of the Supreme Leader, our Ayatollah—and of course, in the hands of Allah."

Katari went over the detailed plan with Khalil. He explained how the latest Raptor software build could be surreptitiously loaded on a device and spirited from the Omega lab.

"You will use this," Katari said, handing a small package to Khalil, "to load the software and provide it to me."

Khalil stared down at the innocuous-looking package.

"It is essential that you provide the complete software build. This is necessary for our scientists to ensure the disruptive code they are developing will effectively interface with it."

Khalil opened the small package and was astounded at what he saw.

"I've heard of the Chinese advancements in miniaturization, but I was not aware that such a device existed."

As he looked at the credit-card-sized device, he wondered how something so tiny could hold a massive software program that could run the Raptor's central computer. Embedded in the card was a chip slightly larger than those found in ordinary credit cards.

The chip was also slightly raised from the face of the card, not enough to make it stand out too drastically from common credit cards, but clearly larger. He picked it up and found it heavier than a credit card. It also had a tiny flat slot on the short edge. A short wire was in the box as well.

Katari explained that the card was the latest in micro-miniaturization. It had the capacity to store a petabyte of information. It also had decryption capability. "The card has the capacity to hold the entire Raptor central computer software program. It was proven in China on an earlier version of the F-22 software."

Khalil noticed that there was something else in the small box. He stared down at a slim gray silk pouch in the container. He picked it up, loosened the drawstring that held the pouch closed, and slid out a black pen. It was, in fact, a Mont Blanc pen. Khalil noticed an inscription on it—his name.

The Mont Blanc was not actually a typical pen. It had a small ink reservoir so that anyone picking it up could, in fact, write with it, but two-thirds of the pen's body was designed for another purpose. The pen had a small circular hole on one end.

"The pen has the ability to wirelessly interface with a mainframe computer. Positioned correctly, with this thin cable attached between it and the card, it will be able to transfer the central computer program data to the card." Katari paused, looking intently at Khalil.

"While the software program that you will transfer to the card is not developmentally complete, it is far enough along to support the feasibility test of Epsilon." He paused. "That is the name given to the special repurposing code that will be embedded in the Raptor."

Katari continued with the discussion. "Getting the downloaded central computer software program out of the Omega lab will be simple and give you no problems getting past security. Khalil, as you can see, once the program is loaded on this card, simply insert it into your wallet. It will not draw any attention and will appear as just another credit card." He went on, "Place the Mont Blanc pen in your shirt pocket. The personalized engraving and ability to function as an actual pen will mean it draws no attention. You will then provide the card to me for immediate transport to Iran."

Khalil now knew the brazen plan. First, he had to discreetly download the current central computer software build onto the card, in the next few days at the latest. Katari would arrange its passage out of the United States without drawing attention to this major transfer of technology from the world's primary superpower to one of its main belligerents. When the card arrived in Iran, the program would be transferred onto a mainframe computer, where software engineers intended to integrate the Epsilon code. That would be quickly followed by testing that was already ongoing with their satellite burst efforts.

Once the satellite's success was demonstrated, the Epsilon code would be provided to Khalil. Then, the trickiest part of the plan had to proceed without a problem. Khalil would need to insert the disruptive Epsilon code into the *final* software build without being detected.

Once he had completed that critical step, American engineers would certify the code. When the upgrade was finally accepted by the Air Force, installed in the Raptor aircraft, and operating as it was designed, the Iranian plan to cripple the F-22's stealth capability could be executed. At the right time, likely during an American attack on Iran, a burst signal from the Iranian satellite would trigger the latent code in the Raptor software and conceivably activate Epsilon. The lines of code would morph from its previous configuration, execute a disruptive program in the central computer, and trigger the aircraft interrogator system to pulse signals that would be visible to Iranian missile acquisition radar. Then, death to the Raptors.

Khalil was busy thinking about the plan. *This is a tall order. How can I embed this disruptive code into the Raptor's central computer software, make sure it is undetectable to both the Omega and government software testers, and ensure it is unnoticeable in the operation of the myriad systems controlled by it? This is extremely high risk! Any mistake I make, or any chance discovery by the government, ends this whole scheme. And it ends my freedom! Maybe my life!*

The success or failure of this plan would hinge on his expertise on the code's functionality and its application across all the Raptor systems. Given that his knowledge was unmatched by anyone in Omega, and likely anyone on the planet, it could *possibly* be accomplished. Still, there was some reason for concern.

"I'm not sure it isn't too late for the code to be inserted without being detected," he said to Katari. "As you know, we are already at the second iteration of code build. Dr. Katari, my program is moving forward rapidly due to the Air Force's urgency in getting this software onto their aircraft. My software has already passed its first major milestone in development, and the configuration of the code is pretty well set. The next stage of development we are entering may be the last opportunity to make any major changes without visibility to the testers."

"Don't worry about the Epsilon code. You will have it within two weeks from the time you provide me the current software program on the card," replied Katari. "The early testing of our satellite pulse effectiveness on one of our fighter aircraft is ongoing as we speak."

Khalil shook his head in confusion, the motivational speech by Katari still not quite convincing him. "How can you be testing the Epsilon code on software that I haven't even given to you yet?" responded Khalil.

Dr. Katari explained in detail how his Chinese counterpart had provided the Raptor's rudimentary early test software build to the Iranians. It had been stolen by deep-cover Chinese software engineers involved in the original build of the Raptor's software program.

"But the code they are using is not the final software program that will be installed in our F-22 aircraft," explained Khalil.

Staring intently into Khalil's eyes, Katari responded, "It will be close enough to the correct program to perform our current testing with the Epsilon code and the satellite. We believe that you can make any minor changes to it once we provide it to you, in order for it to correctly interface with your current software configuration. As long as we know what you change, we can make the adjustments and do the final tests in Iran. Do not waiver on this task, Khalil. You have been singularly chosen. This is your jihad. You must not fail."

Khalil nodded his head, affirming his acceptance of the task, and the jihad.

"Remember what I have said. Epsilon will be the key to destroying the American stealth. Iran is on the verge of greatness."

"I understand," replied Khalil.

Then Katari left and went to talk with the imam. Khalil sat in silence as he tried to fully comprehend this seemingly impossible task. The obvious risk actually excited him. The opportunity was unprecedented. At the same time, he wondered if he was going to be up to the task. He believed he could do it. Yet nothing of this magnitude had ever been done before, as far as he knew. One thing was certain—he didn't yet fully understand the ultimate consequences of his actions.

Chapter 35

Julie stirred in half sleep and abruptly woke, feeling uncomfortable. The bedsheets she lay on were soaked. "Honey, I think my water just broke," she said loudly, tapping Matt's shoulder. It was two o'clock in the morning.

Matt jerked awake from his otherwise sound sleep, threw off the sheets and leapt from the bed. "We've got to get you to the hospital right now," he shouted. Bolting across the room to the closet, he started pulling his clothes from the hangers and then ran quickly back to Julie's side.

"Calm down, we have some time," she said firmly, "but you do need to get my small suitcase out of the closet while I get dressed. I put some clothes and things I'll need in it a few days ago, so I think we're ready. Just grab my makeup bag from the bathroom. I don't want to look horrible when visitors show up after our sons are born," she said.

"Honey, you couldn't look any more beautiful, with or without makeup, but I'll grab it anyway."

Matt was a nervous wreck. He was not the cool, calm fighter jock anymore but a concerned husband worried that he might not make it to the hospital before Julie gave birth. His heart was actually pounding, and he was sweating profusely.

Holy crap! What about Claire? Gotta call Flamer right now.

He grabbed his phone, and fortunately, Flamer answered on the second ring.

"No problem, Ace, I'm headed over right now to get her. Colene and I will take care of everything. Be there in two minutes."

"Thanks, Flamer, I really appreciate it. Thought we had a few more weeks before this big event."

"No worries, buddy. Everything is going to be just fine. Just try to relax a bit—no use getting your bride any more nervous than she already is."

Matt wasn't afraid of many things, actually. In his line of work, fear was healthy but controllable, and it took a back seat to decisive action. But right now, he was doing his best to keep his emotions in check, with the growing fear of Julie giving birth in the car. She was yelling loudly as her contractions began, and he knew they would soon be coming more frequently.

Flamer and Colene showed up moments later. Colene gave Julie a few words of encouragement. "Hang on, Julie. You're going to do great. You'll see. You've got enough time to get to the hospital—it's not far from here."

"Get going, Ace. Good thing the hospital is close by. Good luck," said Flamer. "We've got Claire and she's in good hands." They bundled up Claire in her blanket and took her across the dark street to their home.

"Let me help you to the car," Matt said, guiding Julie gently down the hallway and into the new minivan they had recently purchased—just the right car for a growing family.

The trip to the hospital emergency room likely broke the land-speed record as Matt raced the minivan down the dimly lit, deserted streets.

I've got enough to worry about without being stopped by some cop that just woke up from his night shift snooze, Matt thought.

Fortunately, the race to the hospital was uneventful, with nobody on the road to complicate things. Matt had called ahead to alert the medical staff that they were on their way. As he pulled up to the emergency room drop-off point, he slowed the van, careful not to cause a jolt that might just start a chain birthing reaction. He came to a gentle stop. Julie winced as her contractions indicated she was getting closer to the time when she would give birth. They were greeted by two smiling attendants dressed in their starched blue hospital scrubs.

Matt delicately helped his wife out of the car and turned her over to the emergency room attendants.

"I'll be back in a flash," he yelled, jumping back in the car and heading to the mostly vacant inpatient parking lot.

As the staff led Julie to an available examination room, she gasped in pain from the cramping contractions she had been experiencing since her water had broken. They were coming pretty quickly now, and the staff immediately called the attending obstetrician on duty.

Matt wasted no time sprinting across the parking lot, leaping the curbs like a hurdler on a track. He slowed only slightly as he got to the hospital doors. He quickly asked where his wife had been taken and was guided to the delivery room. He actually could have found her without the nurse to guide him there, as he could hear her loud screams of pain from each contraction. Entering the room, he walked over to her side, held her hand, and tried his best to provide support, keep her calm, and hopefully keep her breathing steady. Julie would have none of it, screaming loudly with the rapidly increasing painful contractions. The obstetrician was now standing by for the impending births.

As another severe contraction hit her, Julie dug her fingernails deep into Matt's hand and squeezed it hard, making him wince slightly.

Jeez, this woman just about crushed my hand with that grip, he thought.

"Baby, everything is going to be just great," he remarked with the most encouraging facial expression he could muster.

"No, it's not!" she screamed at him as the next severe contraction hit her.

Whoa—that is one angry woman, he thought. *Okay, gotta help as much as I can.*

"It won't be more than a few minutes," the doctor said, "and everything looks like a normal delivery so far."

Matt could see the obvious pain in his wife's eyes, and there was nothing he could do about it but hold her hand and tolerate her vise like squeeze every time a contraction hit.

Within an hour of their arrival at the hospital, Matt was a father again, this time to two sons. As the boys lay cradled in Julie's arms, she beamed with happiness. In spite of her pain, she was thankful that the labor had proceeded as quickly as it had. Matt was thankful too that the boys had waited for him to get to the hospital.

As she gazed lovingly at the two pink boys, she smiled and said, "They are absolutely perfect—thank God."

"They *are* perfect," remarked Matt. "I think they look just like me!"

The two proud parents sat in silence for the next few minutes. They gazed at the newest members of their family, both in joyful wonderment about the blessings they had in front of them. Matt thought about how lucky he was to have such a beautiful family. At this moment, they were the most important thing on earth to him.

"Julie," he said softly. "I love you more than anything. I just don't know what I'd do if you and our children were not in my life."

"You big lug. I love you too. Now you really have something to celebrate with your buddies," Julie said as she smiled at Matt.

"Baby, the only thing I care about right this minute is that you are okay, and my sons are healthy! And by the way, you look beautiful!"

"Nice try, Matt, but I know I look dreadful. Get my brush out of my overnight bag so I can fix my hair a bit. And I need a wet face-cloth and my makeup. I don't want anyone else to see me like this."

The attending nurses gently took both boys from Julie, giving her some time to make herself a little more presentable for visitors. She knew that her neighbor would be coming by with Claire at the break of dawn.

Flamer and Colene showed up at the hospital with Claire a couple of hours later. "Congratulations, buddy," Flamer shouted to Matt as he gave him the standard man-hug, consisting of a handshake and chest bump.

"You too, Julie," he shouted, "you still look ravishing after your little ordeal!"

"Shhhh, very funny," she said quietly, trying not to disturb the two boys that were now back in her arms. The boys had just finished their breakfast, with Julie successfully nursing them both. Their eyes were blinking now after the noise brought them out of their light sleep.

Claire ran over to her mother's bed and peered at the two tiny pink babies swaddled in soft white blankets. Matt lifted his daughter up to the bed so that she could get a good look.

"Say hi to your new brothers," Matt said to his young daughter.

At almost two years old, Claire did her best to welcome them into the world. Matt balanced Claire on the edge of the bed so that she could touch them.

"Be careful, honey. You must be real gentle. Touch your brothers softly," Julie encouraged Claire.

As Claire reached out to touch the small hands of her new brothers, their little fingers tightly grasped hers. A big smile came over her, and she began to laugh uncontrollably.

Chapter 36

After Dr. Katari left the mosque, Khalil wandered around the darkened halls, his mind trying to come to grips with everything he had heard. The faint smell of incense wafted into his nose, the sweetness of it interfering with his thinking.

He thought about a number of things. The man who had raised him to adulthood would not approve of what he was being asked to do—in spite of what had happened to his brother in Syria. He had never heard one hateful thought come from him. Would he disown him if he believed his son was involved in potential terrorist activities? Khalil wondered how all of this could possibly work out. How could he keep from getting caught, and if he was arrested, how would the Americans treat him? He would surely be a traitor in their eyes. Would they confine him at Guantanamo? He shook his head to clear his thinking.

He decided to heed Katari's advice and headed back to the Omega lab. There was little time to waste. If it was at all possible to do what he was being asked, he must get the software program downloaded quickly onto the special card he was carrying and get it back to Katari. Any delay added undue risk in being able to incorporate the final Epsilon code into the Raptor's software.

Khalil was familiar enough with the guards at the primary access points not to raise any suspicion when coming in on a weekend. The card was tucked away in his worn leather wallet, and he was never asked about what he brought into or out of the lab. Tonight, thankfully, turned out to be no different.

Khalil still worried that alarms would be triggered if any part of the software program being electronically monitored was transferred, copied or otherwise tampered with. But he had the authority to override the built-in barriers within the computer system's architecture and enable the transfer of this critical classified code to the card. His late-night work, mostly alone in the lab, gave him the opportunity to build coded bridges across the barriers. He looked carefully for electronic markers that could trace all actions back to the individual making any change. He would have to overcome those as well.

The design of the card was brilliant. It would actually mimic part of the existing F-22 firmware and, due to its architecture, should readily accept the current, though not completed, central computer program software build. The only markers that would appear would make it look as if the program had just been run as a test. Khalil experimented with the Mont Blanc pen on an unclassified program to verify that it worked to wirelessly transfer the data. He smiled in relief as it appeared to work as intended.

Khalil checked that the latest version of the IFF interrogator system upgrade had been fully integrated into the existing software build before the program ran. As he started the transfer, the program appeared to run smoothly, appearing like another verification of the software's integrity. Thankfully there were no alarms. The bridges he had built across the alarm barriers had worked well. After a few hours, the transfer was complete.

This seems too easy. Am I missing something? Khalil expected that armed guards would appear at any time, put him in handcuffs and drag him away to some dark hole to be interrogated. He nervously looked around, then caught himself, thinking he was giving the appearance of doing something illegal. He tried to calm himself. He knew he was alone in the lab. And even if he wasn't, anyone observing him wouldn't conclude anything different from what they observed on all the other weekend days and nights he had spent there.

Khalil's only concern now was that the card had hopefully retained the configuration of the program and the code hadn't been scrambled by the encrypted software architecture as it had migrated from the Omega mainframe system. Satisfied that he had successfully completed his task, he slipped the card into his wallet and placed the pen in his shirt pocket.

While he tried to look normal leaving the Omega facility, he couldn't help but begin to overthink what he was doing. He was committing a treasonous act at the moment he left the facility with the F-22 software. Actually, it was treason at the moment he'd transferred the software program to the unauthorized device. He began to perspire heavily as he walked past the guard, nodding to him as he always did on his way out. The guard didn't seem to notice the beads of sweat on Khalil's forehead, and simply said, "Good night, Mr. Ruffa," with a courteous nod.

Once Khalil was back in his car, now well past midnight, the card safely secured, he headed back to his apartment.

I don't want to get stopped by the police, he thought, believing for a moment that he was weaving as he drove the winding two-lane road toward the expressway.

He was momentarily not in control of his thinking, not behaving as he always did; normally he was *always* in full control of his mind, his actions. He shook his head vigorously to try to jolt himself back to reality.

"Get a grip, Khalil," he said out loud to himself, looking in the rearview mirror and noticing nothing but the dark, deserted road behind him. As he cleared his mind, he dialed Katari's secure line and was rewarded with an answer on the first ring.

"Yes, Khalil?"

"Dr. Katari, I have the card ready for you."

"Excellent. Did you have any trouble? Did it appear to anyone at Omega that you were doing something that was out of the ordinary?"

"No, in fact it went extremely well, almost too well. I believe I have left no trace of this transfer."

"Perfect," Katari replied. "Meet me at seven a.m.—the same place we met before."

Jeez. It's coming up on two o'clock now. Maybe I can catch a couple hours of sleep.

"Okay, Dr. Katari. I will see you at that time."

The first part of the plan devised by the Supreme Leader of Iran was now successfully completed.

Chapter 37

For Captain Matt "Ace" Black, nearly three years at Langley seemed to have flashed by. It was almost a blur in his mind how time had gotten away from him—the constant intense focus on honing his Raptor skills had consumed him. Days and months of training sorties, short cross-country flights, deployments, and endless operational exercises melted away the time. His ultimate goal was always the same—become one with the jet and feel the aircraft almost as if it was an extension of his body, like his hand or foot. Only then could Matt hope to get the maximum output from this warbird. It was the same way he pushed himself physically, always to his limits, constantly working out in the base fitness center, making sure his body was always in peak condition.

The Raptor could humble a person if he wasn't in top physical shape, especially when the aircraft itself was pushed to the limits of its own aerodynamic design. The gravity forces sustained during thrust vectoring turns brutally compressed vital organs and worked to drain the blood flow from the brain. The more fit a pilot was, the better prepared he was to counter the beating his body took and stay focused on his enemy.

After a short morning refresher in the simulator, and now fresh off the flight line from his afternoon training mission, he finished up a few things in the squadron and headed home in his Boss 'Stang. Matt burst into the house and grabbed his wife, pulled her toward him, and planted a firm kiss on her lips.

"Well, what's gotten into you today?" she exclaimed happily.

"Baby, you won't believe what happened," he shouted, his voice rising a bit uncharacteristically from his outward image as a head-strong fighter pilot. "You know the squadron is selecting the jets and pilots to head out to Nellis Air Force Base outside of Vegas for Red Flag. Even though I'm not very senior in the squadron, my commander picked me to go. He said that I'm more than ready to sharpen my combat skills over the tactical training range there and mix it up in a major wartime scenario. Also, I'm going to be a flight lead for our first Red Flag mission there."

Julie had never seen Matt this excited before, almost losing his composure, especially when it came to talking about the Raptor.

"That's terrific, honey. I know you've been putting your heart and soul into your flying. In fact, sometimes I think that's the most important thing in your life," she said, pretending to be hurt.

"You're not kidding, baby. No! Wait! I *meant* that I'm putting everything I've got into my flying *when* I'm flying. But *you and the kids* are the most important thing in my life. That will never change."

Trying to recover, he continued, "The squadron has been training for weeks on the various scenarios we're likely to see there. I'm more than ready to go."

"Are you?" Julie replied with a smile and a wink.

"Are you kidding me? I've been training as hard as I can, hoping to get the chance to show them my stuff!" He continued, "Now I can take more of a leadership role and maybe teach some of these young fellas, *and* some of the older ones, how to really fly this jet."

"Don't get too cocky, big boy," she said. "I'm sure there's a lot more you can learn about flying as well, and I want you to be careful."

"Always." Matt just grinned back at her. She saw the familiar look in his eyes. "Where are the kids?" he said with a broad smile on his face.

"*Oh no*, you don't," she said, knowing full well what was on his mind. "Claire is playing next door with the Lightner kids, and the boys are taking a nap. Colene is taking good care of her. But she'll be coming back any minute, since I just baked these cookies."

"Cookies?" Matt quickly became distracted, making a beeline for the rack of warm chocolate chip cookies. Before Julie could say a word, his mouth was stuffed with two of the delicious treats.

"Well, I guess I know what's really important to you," she responded, pretending to pout.

He glanced over his shoulder looking at Julie, his mouth still full of half-eaten cookies.

"Wait, baby, I need this extra energy since I skipped lunch today—I only had an apple and a granola bar. Do you think Colene can watch Claire for a little longer? I'll call over and ask her to hang on to her for a bit."

He wasted no time dialing up his buddy's wife.

As Matt turned around, he caught a glimpse of Julie heading toward the back of the house, unbuttoning the back of her sundress.

Matt tossed the remaining cookies back on the rack and quickly followed his bride toward the bedroom.

"We don't get this kind of opportunity very often," Julie whispered into Matt's ear as they pulled each other close together under the large canopy-covered bed's satin sheets.

"I know, baby. It's my fault, since I'm always at the base—and when I'm not, the kids seem to want my constant attention."

She smiled and whispered back, "Well, then, let's make the most of this!"

When they were together, it was as if the rest of the world didn't exist, and it really didn't, at least for these few minutes of bliss. Their time together when the kids were temporarily out of the picture was precious and didn't happen often enough in Matt's mind. The closeness they shared at times like this was the most important thing in their lives. Except for the kids, of course.

Their thirty minutes of privacy ended abruptly. As if on cue, the doorbell rang, and Colene Lightner called out to them that she was dropping Claire back from her playtime. Noticing that nobody was in the living room area, she called out loudly as she headed for the door, "Hope you're finished with *whatever* you were doing!"

As the screen door slammed closed, Claire came running into the bedroom. As if on cue, the babies' cries on the monitor alerted them that nap time was over.

"Daddy's home," she shouted, leaping onto the bed and throwing herself on top of Matt.

"Ouch," yelped Matt as one of her knees found its mark in his groin.

Nothing like a crushed set of nuts, he thought, but then he smiled quickly since he had clearly finished his primary task at hand before being interrupted.

Matt gave his daughter a big hug and kiss.

"Run out to the nursery and check on your brothers. Let's see if we can find some ice cream and cookies that need eating," he said to her. Claire scrambled from the bed and ran out of the bedroom.

"Well, I guess that was our afternoon matinee," Matt said to his beautiful wife. "I'm going to throw on some sweats and bring the kids to the playroom for some more fun. And some ice cream! Why don't you just rest up a bit? I feel the need for a rerun later tonight," he said with a smile.

"Are you sure those jewels of yours survived the knee?" she asked.

"We fighter pilots have balls of steel," he replied, giving Julie a grin and a wink as he limped toward the kids.

Chapter 38

The next few weeks raced by as the fighter squadron focused intently on their upcoming challenge. They were mobilizing equipment and people, as well as prepping the Raptors for their deployment to Nevada.

The Raptors had been to the Red Flag combat exercise before, but this would be a first for Matt. He relished the opportunity to fly in a regime that was as close to real combat as you could get without actually being in a war. It also had the advantage of being a great environment to hone his skills, develop new tactics, and maybe even learn a few things.

As the date for the deployment came, Matt had gotten to the flight line early, wanting to spend some time talking to the maintenance team. He knew that the secret to his success in the Raptor was getting the absolute best from the guys and gals that worked on his jet. He had established a solid rapport with them all, gaining their respect and to some degree establishing a modicum of friendship with many of them.

His crew chief, especially, was singularly important to him. Matt made it a point to know as much about him and his family as possible and always thanked him for the countless hours spent making his jet "war-ready." Today, another team of maintainers was responsible for the launch. Matt's crew chief, along with the others supporting the Raptors that were deploying, had already headed to Nellis Air Force Base. They were busy setting up the parking ramp designated for Red Flag exercise aircraft. A large C-17 Globemaster cargo aircraft had taken them there, loaded with the equipment, tools, and other support the aircraft maintenance crews needed to conduct simulated combat operations at the desert base.

The sprawling base occupied some prime real estate with a distant view of the Las Vegas casino skyline. The high desert landscape, dry air, massive amounts of unrestricted airspace in the Nevada Test and Training Range (NTTR), and spacious facilities at Nellis were ideal for deployments like this and the subsequent war games executed there.

Six Raptors launched midmorning, heading west. Matt was the lead for the second flight of three aircraft for the deployment. He had rolled down the Langley runway hundreds of times over the past three years, but this time, the launch was pretty special. He knew that he was taking his teammates to Red Flag and that the eyes and reputation of his squadron were at stake. He wasn't at all worried in spite of the pressure to do well. After all, Captain Matt "Ace" Black was now an accomplished aviator in the F-22 and well respected by his comrades in the 94th Fighter Squadron for his unparalleled flying skills.

The flight across the country toward the dry, desert air of Las Vegas went off without a hitch. All the jets landed at the large fighter training base in the afternoon and found their home away from home at their designated parking area. As they taxied in, an array of allied force aircraft were parked across the wide expanse of concrete reserved for Red Flag participants—Royal Netherlands Air Force F-16s, a few Typhoon EF-2000s from Spain, and some French Rafale fighters. Nearby, he spotted some F-15C Eagles out of Kadena Air Base, Japan, and F-15E Strike Eagles from Seymour Johnson Air Force Base in North Carolina.

His crew chief marshaled him into the parking spot, and Matt pulled to a stop at his command. All of the arriving pilots were similarly met by their maintenance teams. As Matt raised his canopy, his crew chief, Sergeant Kyle Jacobson, brought the boarding ladder to the jet, climbed up, and handed Matt a cold bottle of water.

"Thanks, Kyle. I really need this right now," he said, tilting the bottle up and downing nearly two-thirds of its contents in a couple of swallows. "Man, it's pretty toasty here," he said, glancing around the parking ramp. He noticed the heat waves shimmering off the dark tarmac. "Bet you could fry an egg on that."

"Yes, sir, but it would taste like shit," replied Sergeant Jacobson.

Matt laughed and climbed out of his jet. He enjoyed every discussion with Kyle, never knowing what might pop out of the young crew chief's mouth.

"How'd our baby do on the flight over?" asked Jacobson.

"This little lady is Code One, as usual, thanks to your great work on her. The Raptors have all been flying pretty well. I didn't hear any chatter from the rest of my flight about any maintenance issues, so hopefully you guys won't have to spend much more time today out here on this hot ramp."

"Great, sir. I'll give her a thorough once-over and make sure she's ready for your first Red Flag sortie."

"I appreciate it, Kyle."

Matt headed toward the debrief building to officially finish his day. While he was in debrief, Flamer came over and sat down next to him at the computer terminal. They input all their critical flight information into the electronic database. After debriefing, they caught a ride to the base dormitories earmarked for the deployed aircrew members. They would both get some rest before beginning the next day's initiation into the closest thing to combat a pilot could experience in the States.

Matt began to think about the days ahead of him at Red Flag, and hopefully the opportunity of his life to get really "down and dirty" with air combat tactics—and of course, to show everyone what he was *really* made of. Red Flag had been around for years and was well known in the Air Force fighter pilot community as the true essence of training, outside of actual combat, which was in itself a means of training—but one you might not survive. As a member of the Blue Force "good guys," a Raptor pilot could make some mistakes and commit a tactical error that would get him "shot down or killed" in the simulated world of combat. The pilot would survive the "kill," but it was tough to survive the ridicule he would likely get from his buddies for committing a foolish error.

I'm not here to make any errors, Matt thought, lying in bed on his back, staring up at the ceiling. *And there's no way I could live down getting "killed" by guys I know I can beat.*

As he thought about the tactics he would likely employ, he knew that Red Flag was a deadly serious enterprise for combat pilots. It was one of the few realistic training venues in which all previous training was put to the test. Tried and true tactics could be employed against the Red Force, or adversary forces in the simulated aerial battlefield. The 64th Aggressor Squadron adversaries were formidable and included advanced fighter aircraft—F-15s and F-16s, along with French Mirage variants. Other battlefield threats included simulated ground-to-air missiles called Smokey SAMs, and other antiaircraft threats whose sole job was to disrupt the attacking Blue Force from accomplishing their mission. New tactics could also be developed and employed by the Blue Force pilots, providing the exercise participants with a golden opportunity to fine-tune their combat skills.

As he tried to sleep, an almost impossible task due to the time zone change, his mind kept him awake with thoughts about what was to come.

We'll see how this goes. Gotta keep my concentration, keep my cool when mixing it up with these guys. I know that the Red Force is just looking for an opportunity to brag about taking out an F-22.

Matt thought about the previous encounters that Red Forces had had with Raptors in combat exercises. In the past, it had never been a fair contest—that was exactly what the United States expected if the country was engaged in a war with an enemy. Kill ratios of ten to zero in favor of the Raptor were common—and expected.

I'm not going to be the one that changes that ratio. No friggin' way! Another thought popped into his mind that had nothing to do with flying. *Gotta call the family!*

Matt always made sure to call home so that Julie knew he had arrived safely. Quickly dialing his cell phone, he heard three rings before an answer.

"Hi, honey," Julie said. "Did you make it?"

"Hey, baby! Yeah, I made it safe and sound. How are you and the kids?"

"Well, I guess you haven't figured out the time zone difference. They're already in bed. And I'm getting ready myself."

"Oh yeah. Sorry about that."

They talked for a few minutes, Matt catching up on what the kids had done during the day, and then about Julie's activities, which pretty much revolved around tending to the kids.

"I'll let you go and call tomorrow when the kids are up. I love you."

"Be safe, Matt. I love you, too."

In spite of the thoughts about Red Flag spinning through his head, he quickly dozed off.

———— • ————

The exercise week began with a blur of high-intensity activity. It started with an initiation into Red Flag operations, the rules of engagement, and flying in the Nellis Test and Training Range located north of the sprawling base. Also, time was spent reviewing the types of threats they might face and the most critical aspects of Red Flag during the intensive mass debrief process. After every day's mission, the aircrews were assembled in the large debriefing facility. Here, every aspect of the day's missions would be reviewed, including initial planning, launch, ingress to the target areas, threats encountered, tactics employed, and the results of the combat exercise. Of utmost interest to fighter pilots was the accuracy of their simulated missile launches at "enemy" targets. A fighter pilot's success or failure was literally dissected for all to see, and to learn crucial lessons from. Once the indoctrination was complete, it was time to fly!

Matt's first Raptor mission turned out to be a real eye-opener for him. At home, he was usually training with pilots he knew, with aircraft he was familiar with. He knew what to expect, and how to react. Here at Red Flag, Matt was part of an overall mission plan that included a complete package of air superiority aircraft—his F-22s, and the Netherland F-16s. The Strike Eagles would be performing in a strike role to hit specific targets with high-explosive ordnance. The Typhoons were tasked with taking out any enemy ground air defense threats that would surely be in the target ingress area. Of course, enemy fighters, the Red Force adversary aircraft, consisting of F-16s with special paint schemes, would be waiting to pounce on the Blue Force aircraft and do their best to disrupt their mission and "kill" as many of them as possible.

Matt had heard the stories from other units of the capabilities possessed by these experienced combat adversary pilots. A handful of unlucky "good guys" had been on the receiving end of a Red Force "missile." But getting shot down was not even a stray thought to Matt.

I'll kick ass and show them what this Raptor can do when in the hands of an expert, he arrogantly thought to himself.

His first mission did, in fact, open his eyes wide to what an experienced adversary could do. While his Raptor performed admirably under his skilled control, the Red Forces surprised him twice with their unexpected tactics, placing Matt in a compromising position that might have made his jet vulnerable to attack in actual combat. The post-mission debrief dissected every move he'd made for the consumption of all Red Flag pilots. After all, this was combat training. You had to learn from your mistakes, and Nellis was the preferred environment for learning.

Matt was a bit embarrassed—he vowed *never* to let anything like that happen again. He knew he was too good to let any adversary get the best of him.

The remaining missions proved out Matt's belief in himself. His Raptor dominated the sky over the NTTR, "killing" the adversary aircraft, one after another, before they ever had the Raptor on their radar.

As the Red Flag exercise wound down, Captain Matt "Ace" Black was ecstatic. He had expected to perform well in the sky over the northern Nevada desert, and he had. In fact, he had performed so well that in spite of his first mission mistakes, he picked up the honors as "Top Gun." He almost couldn't contain himself as he celebrated with Flamer.

"I feel pretty fortunate to have gotten this honor," he told his buddy. "I know I'm the best, but now I have proof!"

"Yeah, yeah. Just don't let your head explode from the recognition," remarked Flamer sarcastically. "The margin between *the best* and *the rest* was pretty close. In fact, I had a shot at it," he said.

"Hey, Flamer, I get it, believe me. You're a damn good fighter pilot. I'm just a bit better," he laughed.

Chapter 39

K halil passed the special card with the Raptor's central computer software to the Iranian scientist during his morning meeting at the darkened Texas mosque. From there, Dr. Katari and his precious cargo headed south in a rental car that reeked from cigarette smoke. The drive out across the dusty, barren landscape would have been boring if not for the importance of the package being carried. While travel by car was not the quickest, it provided the least noticeable means of moving the stolen software across the border into Mexico—then on to Mexico City International Airport, formerly Benito Juarez International Airport. There, the Ayatollah's trusted scientist would board a flight that started his trek across the Atlantic, through Munich, and then on to the final destination in Tehran.

Dr. Katari booked a first-class seat on Aeromexico and made sure never to let the special card out of his possession. He had it in his black leather computer bag with his Quran and other essentials for his flight. It passed seamlessly through the X-ray screeners and stayed in his hands the entire flight to Munich. He had thought about the importance of this mission—how critical it was to the Ayatollah, and to his country's future.

The flight from Munich to Tehran landed on schedule. Katari wasted no time finding the car and driver sent to meet him. An hour later, he was at his destination, where a collection of scientists and engineers eagerly awaited his arrival.

Near the town of Shamam, just east of Rostamabad, he was met by the town's ruling mullah and a number of security personnel dressed as common laborers. They escorted him to a discreet entryway to one of the most secret locations in Iran. A large door stood amidst a dense grove of olive trees, under the canopy of tree branches that had been carefully pruned. As the group approached, the mullah made a call from his secure phone, and the door began to lift. Once it was fully open, the group proceeded toward it across a short path strewn with dropped overripe olives.

They descended underground on a steel staircase to a chamber. Two large elevator doors greeted them—a ten-digit code opened them. Katari was met by four heavily armed members of Iran's Islamic Revolutionary Guard Corps, the IRGC. One of them checked his credentials carefully and inserted a special key into the panel on the elevator's side. After turning the key, the IRGC soldiers punched in another code on the adjacent keypad. The doors closed and the elevator began its descent. Dr. Katari winced as his ears popped from the rapid two-hundred-foot drop to their destination. With a jolt, the elevator stopped, the doors opened and the mullah directed him toward the group of scientists gathered in the expansive hallway leading into the facility.

"*As-salamu alaikum,*" Katari said to his colleagues.

"*Wa alaikum assalaam,*" replied a diminutive bespectacled scientist as he embraced Katari. "We have been expecting you and are excited to begin this major step in our quest to elevate Islam to its rightful place in this world," he pronounced.

The scientists were ready to take the "special package" and begin running the next crucial tests. Here, deep underground, away from any peering eyes, Iran had established a test facility that was distinct from anything that existed in the world. It was carefully planned by brilliant minds, with much collaboration from China's best engineers.

Similar to the secretive research facility in the Kavir Desert, the Rostamabad underground test site was designed to fool anyone that kept watch over Iran's activities. It had been carefully built right under the nose of American and British satellites that constantly focused on the Iranian countryside. The construction was performed under the guise of a major agricultural collective operation. Around Rostamabad, some of the richest agricultural lands provided a convenient cover for large trucks moving *product* to the three-hundred-thousand-square-foot covered *distribution* facility just east of the tunnel entrance. The eavesdropping cameras of the orbiting satellites tracked the large trucks that constantly moved in and out of the apparent agricultural distribution building, not knowing that the real product they were carrying was construction debris from the massive underground facility being built.

Dr. Lee Yu had played a pivotal role to quickly modify the facility for Epsilon testing. The design was nothing short of genius. Its purpose was to test a satellite's ability to activate a software program installed in an in-flight aircraft. Astoundingly, here, deep beneath the desert surface, a three-mile long tunnel had been built, laser-aligned to keep it perfectly straight, with two laboratories, one at each end. At one end, an Iranian communication satellite was suspended from a test stand, able to be fully powered up to replicate its operation in orbit. At the other end, a Russian-made Sukhoi Su-35 Flanker aircraft was suspended as if in flight, a phenomenal engineering feat. The Iranians had disassembled the aircraft at Esfahan air base, transported it to the rear tunnel entrance and service elevators, lowered it beneath the ground to the test facility, and reassembled it. The aircraft could power up all systems, absent the engines operating, to replicate an aircraft in flight. The engineers had great faith that within such a facility, they would be able to run tests of the satellite's ability to send a signal to the aircraft and, in doing so, activate the software code within the jet. The use of the shielded tunnel would safeguard against American sensors attempting to discover the true purpose of Iran's activity.

The card containing the Raptor's central computer program was quickly delivered to the massive software lab adjacent to the tunnel. Talented coders worked intently for a week. They carefully dissected the program, inserted Epsilon, and verified that the code retained its ability to repurpose itself. Finally, they installed the program into the specially modified suspended Flanker fighter aircraft containing equipment that closely replicated the F-22's brains.

There was a leap-of-faith here by both the Iranian and Chinese engineers. They knew that many modifications, both software and hardware, had been made to the Raptor over the years. A successful test here didn't guarantee Epsilon would work in the lethal jets at Langley. Khalil would ultimately have to make it work in the current aircraft configuration.

The pivotal test was about to begin. The pulse from the stationary satellite at the far end of the tunnel lasted but a few seconds. Receiving the signal at the opposite end, the Su-35 instrumentation registered the incoming pulse. The aircraft's interrogator system was set in the in the expected F-22 combat configuration. The pulse triggered the aircraft to immediately begin transmitting an interrogator system signal. Had the Flanker actually been a Raptor flying against an enemy, the transmission would have been a telltale *bloom*, an unwanted signal coming from the Raptor that would violate its ability to remain stealthy.

Dr. Katari smiled broadly as the engineers and scientists in the control room slapped each other on the back. Dr. Yu, in particular, cracked the slightest of smiles, knowing full well that the ultimate Chinese strategy was beginning to bear fruit.

Within days, Iran was ready to run the test as it would be done in wartime—from twenty-three thousand miles above the earth's surface—the *true* measure of success. They wasted no time getting the actual satellite ready to blast into orbit. The routine launch was previously announced to the international community as just another in a series of communication satellites. It took place days later, putting into geostationary orbit the weaponized satellite and making ready the first critical test—could it trigger Epsilon in the purloined Raptor code now loaded on an airborne Flanker fighter aircraft?

———————— • ————————

Much was riding on this test. In fact, a pretty large portion of the Iranian defense budget had been consumed in this risky venture. To fail would likely mean the execution of some key engineers and scientists, including Katari. After all, there was little tolerance for failure, and even the Ayatollah was at risk if he plundered the nation's wealth in a failed venture.

The Flanker pilot stared intently at the multifunction instrument display within his cramped cockpit. A transmission from the ground station initialized the start sequence within the satellite, and seconds later, in its cold, dark orbit, a short satellite pulse beamed a signal to the aircraft. The display lit up, indicating activation of the aircraft's interrogator system transponder.

"We have a successful engagement of IFF," the excited pilot communicated to the tower and to the underground command bunker where Iran's ruling party leadership waited eagerly for the news.

"We now wait for the next step in our great plan," the Ayatollah stated. The gray-bearded cleric looked directly at Katari. His gaze seemed to pierce him to his core.

Dr. Katari knew what he had to do next. His mission was to get the modified central computer program with the embedded Epsilon code back to Khalil. The Syrian must extract Epsilon and carefully integrate it into the final Raptor software.

———•———

About the same time the satellite test was ongoing over the Persian Gulf, the odd-looking American military aircraft with the strange elongated nose cruised along, operating parallel to Iran's border. The RC-135 signals intelligence aircraft routinely flew in this area, constantly looking for indications of military activity by the world's leading sponsor of terrorism.

"I just detected a strange signal coming from Iran. The odd thing is that it came from space, not from the ground," reported the mission crew member sitting intently at his sensors' display console in the large reconnaissance aircraft. "It lasted for only a couple of seconds. I've never seen anything quite like that before."

"What do you think it was?" asked the commander.

"Could have been some sort of signal from a satellite to a ground station in Iran. I know they recently put up another communications satellite into that constellation they've been working on."

"Log it in for the record," replied the commander. "Any other activity being picked up?"

"No, sir, not anything unique. Just the usual chatter."

Chapter 40

The day began as it always did. He awoke minutes before his alarm clock rang, his brain internally programmed with its own precision timer that never failed him. Khalil went through his early-morning routine—one hundred pushups, one hundred sit-ups, and then out the door for a two-mile run. His path was usually in silent darkness, lit by only a few remaining stars and the widely dispersed bug-covered streetlights. He grabbed a quick shower and then wolfed down a breakfast of granola and blueberries. He would get coffee on his way to Omega. On the twenty-minute drive to the software lab, Khalil thought about how far he had come in his life. And he thought about his family. What began as a normal day was about to take a major detour, although he didn't know it yet.

Since he'd left college and started working for Omega, his focus had been primarily on achieving his professional goals and succeeding in his chosen career path. His free time had been limited. While he tried his best to visit his parents and sister, the demands of the job kept him from those he loved the most. Visits were infrequent, and even the phone calls he placed were sporadic. He had been determined to do better. Maybe after he got through the challenge he had been given by Sheikh Rahainee and Dr. Katari, he'd have more time to visit, to help his sister. He knew that she needed his encouragement to come out of her shell. Ana, his lovely sister, still struggled in her recovery from the brutal assault years before. But his father had told him that she appeared to be doing better.

Ana had been doing remarkably well with the rigorous therapy to reset her brain's electrical connectivity. The erratic firing of her brain's neurons had triggered the reclusive behavior her doctors so desperately wanted to change. They hoped she would regain a normal life over time—to socially interact with people, as most of the world did. Ana had made enough progress that her doctors recommended she take on the challenge of getting back into the public arena. It was a small step, but important to get her life restarted. Ana was actually excited to get out of the house, even though she still had a few doubts about being able to handle herself in the downtown Dallas department store crowds.

On that special day, she dressed the way she believed she should, very conservatively, as a Muslim woman, including her hijab. Mrs. Ruffa had gently objected, concerned that her clothes might bring stares and maybe even vocal criticism from ignorant people who wouldn't accept the goodness that came with cultural and religious differences. She recommended Ana wear clothes worn by most Texas women her age—jeans, a nice colorful blouse. Ana would have none of it. She was proud of her Syrian heritage. She was ready to engage with the outside world again.

Her father had done as she asked. He dropped her off at the entrance to the large department store set back on one of Dallas's busy streets. She insisted she wanted to do this on her own. She told him to leave her, do some of his errands, and come back in about an hour. She was adamant that she was all right—she was ready to engage with people in the relatively benign department store environment.

This particular store had been carefully chosen by Dr. Ruffa. It had just opened for the day, and there would not be large crowds. The staff was known for being friendly to their customers. He believed it was the perfect setting for his daughter to hopefully take the first big step in recovering from her darkness.

Ana browsed through the wide array of colorful summer clothes. She saw much that caught her eye. She didn't notice the stare she was getting from the young lady at the checkout counter. She never expected the event that would send her reeling back into the deep, dark recesses of her mind.

It was, perhaps, just an innocent comment—perhaps not. "You might want to try on some of these." The sales lady pointed to the rack of colorful clothes. "These blouses would look a lot better on you than what you're wearing."

Ana saw the look in the young sales clerk's eyes. *A look of contempt*, she thought. *She doesn't think I belong here. She thinks I look like a freak.*

Ana's mind was now racing, crazily, irrationally. She felt nauseous. Then more horrific thoughts ripped through her mind. As she stared at the clothes the sales lady pointed out, her memory flashed with thoughts of wearing similarly styled clothes during a horrible time in her life. Her mind screamed at her...the clothes were again being torn viciously from her body, the foul-smelling man forcing himself onto her.

Ana was in escape mode. *Get out of the store—now!* She ran toward the door, nothing stopping her. She knocked over a display of jewelry as she bolted through the aisles. Exiting the store, she ran across the sidewalk and into the busy downtown street.

It was now midmorning, only one hour after she had made her first foray back into the public arena. The traffic was steady, with morning commuters, taxis and city metro buses moving the mass of Dallas's population to and from their destinations.

Ana never saw the metro bus coming. Her mind had pushed her to flee as fast as possible. All she wanted was to get away, far from the foul-smelling man and the brutal attack. The bus driver had a fraction of a second to react, even if he had been looking toward the curb where a young woman bolted from in between two parked cars. His reaction wasn't quick enough to keep him from impacting her before he could hit the brake. It wasn't quick enough to keep the six-ton bus with its front steel grill from hitting Ana forcefully enough to throw her broken body over twenty feet forward onto the oil-stained concrete street.

The white light was the most peace that Ana had known since her assault, even better than the prescribed cocktail of drugs taken over the past years to control her emotions. Now there was no more pain. Her thoughts were a blur of images reflecting the happy times in her life. She saw her brother, Khalil, and her long-since-departed family in Syria. Of course, her brain was firing off images of what had been the joy in her life as it was shutting down. Her crumpled body lay distorted on the street. Traffic stopped, crowds formed, and a few people on their cell phones made calls to emergency responders. Some warped bystanders took pictures.

Dr. Ruffa was running just a few minutes late. Traffic was more backed up than he had anticipated for this time of the morning.

Must be another fender bender, he thought. It happened frequently in the busy Dallas downtown area as people jockeyed for the curb to park or drop off passengers. Looking ahead, he saw the flashing red lights of an ambulance. *Somebody is injured. Hope not too badly.*

As he approached the prearranged pickup spot he and Ana had agreed upon, he didn't see her waiting. A bit worried, he looked intently on both sides of the street, searching for his beloved daughter. Then he saw her.

The paramedics were bending over her, performing CPR, doing what they could to keep her alive. Dr. Ruffa pulled abruptly to the curb, ignoring the police officer who was waving him along, to keep moving with the traffic around the accident site. He jumped from the car and ran to her. The officer tried to stop him, but Dr. Ruffa screamed that his daughter was on the ground. She was the victim of the accident. He had to get to her. As he approached the paramedics, they were already beginning to put their equipment away. It was clear to him that he would never have another conversation with Ana. She was gone. The pain he felt was indescribable, immense, and crippling. He dropped to his knees and sobbed uncontrollably.

———————————•———————————

By late morning, Khalil had already reviewed the progress his team had made on some small software patches to fix minor anomalies. He had also completed his morning phone call to Lieutenant Rebecca Casey. He assured her that everything was proceeding on schedule and under budget. He sat back in his ergonomic office chair and tried to catch up on the endless email messages from his boss.

He never expected the call from his father about his sister. The shock to his system was nearly instantaneous, the news hitting him like a ton of bricks. He was speechless for several moments as the horrific news sank in.

This can't be happening, he thought. He felt gut-punched. He gasped for air. His heart pounded in his chest. He almost couldn't hear the rest of his father's words. After he ended the call, he screamed as loud as he could in a mix of utter anguish and intense rage. Beyond the loss of the only one he had left from his original family, he felt tremendous guilt. He had wasted the precious time he might have otherwise spent with Ana. He would never be able to talk with her again. To hold her delicate hand. To reassure her that everything would be all right. To let her know that he would always be at her side, whenever she needed him.

He met his parents at the hospital emergency room, where Ana had been taken by the paramedics. They would have one last look at Ana—and complete the paperwork on her tragic death. Dr. Ruffa would subsequently make the arrangements for her funeral. Her final burial place would be in Syria, next to her birth parents and older brothers.

As the excruciating grief from the loss of his sister continued to torture him, the growing hatred for his adopted country seemed to take over his mind. America had destroyed everything meaningful to him—his birth-father, his mother, his brothers, and now his sister.

Khalil was now more committed than ever to exacting retribution from the country that had ripped away the fabric of his life. He headed for the one place that he knew he could find refuge from the pain—the one place where he would receive the advice he so needed to help him get through his immense grief. It was the place where his mentor resided, where his imam stood ready to help him chart his way—to achieve the satisfaction, the revenge he needed.

Sheikh Rahainee welcomed Khalil with open arms into the dark incense-scented halls of the Abdallah Mosque.

Chapter 41

Eight weeks after the aircraft returned from Red Flag, the 94th Fighter Squadron Commander called an urgent meeting in the squadron Ready Room. The pilots assembled quickly, not sure what all the fuss was about.

"Flamer, what's going on?" asked Matt as he pushed his way through the crowd of pilots, grabbing a seat next to his buddy.

"Ace, I heard there's a real nasty dustup across the pond, and our Raptors are on a short list of fighters to head over and lead a potential strike force."

Matt's eyes brightened as he quickly thought about the opportunity to take his aircraft into combat. "Let's hear what our leader has to say," replied Matt.

"Make the room secure," decreed the commander. The crowd of pilots quickly jumped from their seats, double-checked that they had deposited their cell phones outside the room, and reassembled. When the door was finally closed, the briefing began.

"The Russians have overstepped their bounds again in Syria, and our president is not going to take it lightly. He has ordered a squadron of F-22s to prep for deployment to support potential combat operations in a yet-to-be-disclosed classified location. This is in anticipation of beginning limited strikes against Assad's brutal regime.

"Vladimir Putin is clearly supporting Assad's forces, albeit under the cloak of targeting rebels who are slowly picking apart the Syrian Army through their guerrilla hit-and-run tactics. Most recently, Syrian fighter aircraft were flying protective escort for modified cargo planes and helicopters that are dropping barrel bombs on anti-Assad rebels. The collateral damage caused by the bombs is indiscriminately killing hundreds of innocent men, women and children. Assad has been warned a number of times by the international community, and more importantly by the United States, about the consequences of his actions against civilians.

"Yesterday, for the second time in a week, they hit US forces working with coalition partners and the Free Syrian Army. While we don't think we were targeted specifically, the movement of a contingent of Russian Su-34 Fullback bomber aircraft into the region poses a growing threat to our guys. That's the primary reason for sending the Raptors."

The briefing went on for a couple of hours, including time for questions from the group of combat pilots. If the air tasking order, or ATO, was issued, the squadron would initially deploy to Incirlik Air Base in Turkey. The base had been a United States forward deployment location over the years and had plenty of parking ramp and aircraft shelters to handle the expected arrival of F-22s and other strike aircraft. It also had extensive munitions bunkers to support their assault on Syrian targets if they were called on to do so. The deployment and potential offensive actions would send a strong message to Assad and his Russian supporters to cease and desist all offensive actions.

Matt was excited about finally getting an opportunity to demonstrate his skill in combat. He craved it, almost more than anything else. He had something to prove to himself.

The squadron anticipated the order would be coming at any hour, and they were not disappointed when it arrived at three o'clock the next morning. The Base Command Post immediately set in motion the recall to duty of all military personnel. Matt literally launched himself out of bed when the phone rang. He pulled on his flight suit and quickly headed out the door. He would say his family goodbyes later.

Luckily the trusty old Boss Mustang cranked up on the first key turn. Shifting into reverse, he backed out quickly, turned down the street and then floored the accelerator. His tires screeched as they gained traction on the dry roadway, and Matt roared away. He was sure the neighbors heard him, the unruly vibration from the howling Mustang's throaty Flowmaster mufflers putting out enough decibels to wake anyone from a dead sleep.

He quickly arrived at the base and parked near his squadron. Walking through the Ready Room, he saw Flamer and waved at him, smiling widely in spite of his shortened night of sleep.

"This is it," Matt shouted excitedly to Flamer, his loud voice clearly an irritant to quite a few of the sleepy-eyed pilots assembling around the room.

"Shut the hell up, Ace," a voice out of the crowd yelled. "Don't you know it ain't quite daybreak yet?"

"We can sleep later," Matt remarked. "It's time to get serious about our business."

When the room was secure, the commander began the brief, first reading the tasking order, and then proceeding through the detailed deployment plan. While this was going on, the rest of the support personnel on base were extremely busy. The aircraft maintenance folks were inspecting all of the aircraft for any problems that would prevent the Raptors from deploying. Most of the jets were in great shape, having had two months to recover from Red Flag. The focus right now was to get them ready for a long flight.

Munitions technicians, known affectionately as "Ammo" troops, were busy in the Bomb Dump, the name given to their munitions storage area. They were opening the earth-covered concrete-hardened igloos and pulling out the prescribed combat load of ordnance. Escorted by the base security forces, they began convoying the deadly munitions to the airfield parking area and the awaiting F-22s.

The flight line was a well-choreographed blur of activity. The air tasking order indicated the Raptors needed to deploy in a "hot" configuration and be prepared for a potential combat tasking in Syria before they arrived at their destination. The Raptor's deployment configuration was one Sidewinder heat-seeking missile loaded in each internal side weapons bay, and two advanced medium-range air-to-air missiles, AMRAAMs, in the internal center bay. Two one-thousand-pound high-explosive joint direct attack munitions, JDAMs, were also loaded in the center bay in the event that ground targets needed to be eliminated during the flight into the combat theater of operations. Yellow-tipped 20 mm high-explosive incendiary ammunition was loaded in the internal gun.

Concurrently, the supporting cargo necessary to keep the stealthy jets operating at Incirlik was being mobilized. Wooden supply crates and aircraft equipment were loaded onto large, flat, square steel pallets and secured with red nylon mobility nets. The loaded pallets were then transported to waiting C-17 Globemaster airlift aircraft that were steadily arriving to pick up the cargo.

After the briefing, Matt headed back to the house to grab his prepacked mobility bag that contained pretty much everything he would need. Julie was waiting for him as he burst through the doorway. He stopped cold for a moment, now remembering how early in the morning it still was, but happily surprised that his daughter and the boys were all up.

"I've got to head back to the squadron pretty quickly," he said to his bride, "since we have to get the mission planned."

"Have some breakfast with the kids first," she said. "It may be a while before you get to see the children again, and the food is already made. We were expecting you."

"Perfect," he said. "Come on, kids, let's chow down on this great food your mom made for us."

The kids did their best to show some eagerness for breakfast, but it was only six o'clock in the morning, and it was a Saturday. The two boys pushed the scrambled eggs away and squealed for some Honey Nut Cheerios. Matt had to compete with cartoons on the TV that ran seemingly nonstop at their home.

Having completed a noisy breakfast with his young children, he sought a private moment with Julie.

"Baby, I'll call you from the squadron before we launch. Won't be a lot of time before we go. Hey, it's not like we're going to some desolate hellhole in the world. Just a staging area, and it's not too bad a place to stage. They even have a Baskin-Robbins," he said with a wide grin.

"I know. I just worry when you deploy. You never know what might happen," she said.

"Don't worry," he whispered gently into her ear. "I'm the best at what we do. I won't let anything keep me from coming back to my family, especially you," he said, drawing her closer to him and giving her a long, tender kiss. He grabbed each of his children and gave them a bear hug and a kiss.

Julie could never hold the tears back when Matt left for any deployment, and this time was no exception.

He waved back to her as he headed to his Mustang, mobility bag slung over his shoulder. The last image he had was of Julie sobbing softly, his daughter clutching her leg and the two boys in her arms.

Chapter 42

I t was as perfect a launch as anyone could script. In pairs, the Raptors lined up at the end of Langley's long main runway and thundered down the concrete. As the runway lights flashed by their cockpits, the jets slowly lifted off from the base. The evening departure was spectacular for those watching from the ground. The yellow-orange glow from the twin tailpipes and the muted wing position lights faded as the Raptors gained altitude. They rose slowly into the darkening eastern sky with their full load of ordnance and fuel.

Matt and his wingman, Flamer, headed to the predetermined assembly point over the Chesapeake Bay to begin their long air bridge over the big pond called the Atlantic Ocean. The air bridge was a series of tanker aircraft extending across the ocean to refuel the fighters multiple times all the way to their intended destination at Incirlik.

When not preparing to take fuel from the big KC-10 aircraft, Matt kept busy monitoring his aircraft systems. The other fighter pilots did the same. To help kill the time, frequent discussions occurred between pilots over their secure comm systems. Any subject was fair game to keep them occupied and their minds off the monotony of the long flight. Football, politics and, of course, *women* were the standard topics. Matt and Flamer spent time seeing who could tell the funniest joke.

Fortunately, they had an uneventful flight, refueling like clockwork and thankfully experiencing no major aircraft issues. Some had only a few minor problems that did not affect safety of flight.

Had a major problem arisen, there were only a few options for diverting the aircraft over the large expanse of dark blue ocean. The flight path took them off the coast of Newfoundland, past Greenland, Iceland, and then across Europe into southern Turkey, home to Incirlik Air Base.

As the jets arrived in Turkish airspace, Matt's adrenaline was up, like most of the pilots in his flight, all of them eager to get on the ground. The trip across the Atlantic had been a long haul, and even though fighter pilots were quite fit, fatigue always managed to set in when one was confined to a cramped ejection seat for twelve hours. But the rigor and concentration required for landing at an airfield in another country, one that most of these pilots had not been to, helped boost cognition and kept their minds and senses razor-sharp as each jet touched down. The bright Turkish sunshine and light brown dusty landscape made Matt squint. Even with his dark polarized helmet visor down, he could see the shimmering waves of heat coming off the taxiway, the bright midsummer sun's rays at their peak.

Pulling into the parking area, Matt saw his crew chief marshaling him toward the taxi line that separated the jets from each other, and aligned them for their next launch. As he shut down his engines and raised his canopy, he waved at Sergeant Kyle Jacobson.

As Kyle placed the ladder on the side of the jet, the nimble crew chief scrambled up. "Long flight, huh, sir?" he said as he handed Matt a cold bottle of water.

"You bet, Kyle. I can't wait to get off my ass. Feels like lead about now."

"How'd the jet do on the flight over the pond?"

"No real problems. Just glad to get out of this jet," he said, handing his helmet to Kyle.

Once all the jets had landed, the maintenance crews who had arrived earlier on the C-17s did their best to prepare the aircraft for their first combat mission, which might happen soon. A few needed repair, but for the most part, the fleet of Raptors was in great shape. The stealthy coatings on these war birds got a close look by the maintenance team. It was one thing to fly training sorties at Langley or Red Flag and trust stealth to keep a Raptor invisible. It was clearly another when there was a real threat, an actual enemy who wanted nothing better than to bring down an F-22 with an advanced surface-to-air missile. The Raptor's stealth, among other capabilities, was essential to the effectiveness of this weapon system.

———————•———————

The early-afternoon sun blazed at the Turkish base as the pilots assembled in the deployed forces briefing room. Matt had taken a seat near the front, Flamer at his side. After the room came to attention with the arrival of the deployed detachment commander, everyone took their seats and the briefing began.

"Here is the tasking order for today. Yeah, you heard it right, today! Sorry for the quick turn for you guys, but the target can't wait another day. We are to lead a force of Strike Eagles and F-18G Growlers to take out a factory that we suspect is manufacturing barrel bombs. We'll stay in Turkish airspace as long as we can to help mask our intent. We'll begin our turn toward Syria just south of the town of Batman, ingress the Syrian border just west of Al Qamishli, and continue heading south. Our target is south of Ar Raqqah, across the Euphrates River, outside the area currently occupied by Kurdish forces. We expect that there will be Syrian fighters in the area, and possibly some Russian aircraft.

"The Russians will be notified of our intent as we cross the Syrian border, shortly before we strike the factory. They will be strongly advised not to interfere, or risk getting hit by our fighters. Up to now, they've been compliant with our advice. We don't believe they really want to risk a combat engagement."

Ace turned and looked at Flamer, who quickly returned the glance. Both fighter pilots were likely thinking the same thing.

Matt didn't say anything but was thinking, *It looks like we may be hanging it out a bit in that area. Plenty of threats are likely to be waiting for us. And who really knows how some crazed Russian fighter pilot will react?*

From the murmuring around Matt, clearly he and Flamer weren't the only ones thinking about this possibility. As if on cue, the intelligence brief began. It highlighted the location of Syrian airfields where known fighter aircraft were based, including Russian jets that hopefully wouldn't choose to engage the Americans. Additionally, along the route to the target area, the intel officer highlighted the known location of Syrian surface-to-air missiles and commented that the strike force could expect other SAMs in covert mobile launch sites that had not been identified. Finally, the weather brief indicated that there should be no issues that would adversely affect the mission.

"Launch is planned for twenty-two hundred hours," added the colonel.

The late-evening takeoff would provide a modicum of cover and concealment during the mission.

"Good luck, and good hunting."

After the briefing concluded, the group of stirred-up but tired fighter pilots headed for the exit.

Matt knew that this mission had to be perfect. He would get only one chance to lead a *great* first combat mission. As the thoughts spun around his brain, he headed for his home away from home, affectionately known as his hooch.

A quick snack, a nap, and then the alarm woke Matt from his brief rest. He caught the aircrew shuttle that took him to the squadron life support building to pick up his gear. Once he checked everything, he headed to his jet. Like clockwork, he completed his preflight checks, climbed into his Raptor, and at the prescribed time began the long taxi to the arming area. Everything was ready for launch, and the takeoff proceeded as planned.

Airborne with his strike force, Matt was all confidence as he headed south toward the Syrian border. His flight joined the Strike Eagles, and he began leading the way toward the target. The four-ship of Raptors in this mission looked for threats and weaknesses in the defense and then directed the attack to achieve optimal results. The Raptors would ensure that the ingress to the target by the strike force would avoid as many threats as possible, to the greatest extent possible. If a SAM site radiated an acquisition radar signal, the Navy Growlers would take it out. If the Raptors' radar detected enemy aircraft as a threat, the stealthy aircraft would eliminate them before they even knew they had been targeted.

The Strike Eagles enjoyed their dark realm—their terrain-following radar and precision targeting would ensure they delivered their ordnance on the barrel bomb factory with pinpoint accuracy. As long as they weren't threatened by enemy fighters, Syrian or Russian, the mission seemed pretty straightforward.

Approaching the Syrian border, Matt wanted no signal emanating from his attacking force that could give the enemy a chance to target them. He also knew the interrogator system had had problems in past training sorties. Matt and the other pilots had seen some spurious flickering, and the fix was on the list of improvements that Air Force had underway.

"We have some activity near the target area," Matt indicated over his secure link.

The Strike Eagles and Growlers copied the transmission, having recently been modified to integrate this secure communication system into their aircraft. The Raptors advised their strike package that a flight of what appeared to be Syrian aircraft was just north of the target area.

"We can't avoid drawing their attention as the Strike Eagles head to the target. Their aircraft will pick up our fighter bombers pretty quickly. If they turn toward our guys, we're going to light them up," Matt calmly transmitted.

The other Raptors copied the transmission. The Strike Eagles had begun to drop in altitude as they proceeded to their primary turn point that would take them straight to their intended target. Meanwhile, the advanced acquisition radar in the F-22s easily picked up the four Syrian fighters.

Matt's focus was now fully committed to the task—to successfully execute the mission. He had trained for this, practiced this again and again. He had proven he could do it at Red Flag, and certainly hundreds of times while training at Langley. Now, all his training was coming to this critical test. *Real* combat. *Real* missile launch. *Real* death to an enemy that *surely* wanted to kill him.

The F-22s picked up the Syrians miles before they even knew the Raptors were there. Bad news for the Syrians—when they turned toward the Strike Eagles on an intercept heading, their fate was sealed. At the right moment, the center bay doors underneath Matt's stealthy jet snapped open, but only for a moment. It was long enough to launch two AMRAAMs at two Syrian fighters—then the bay doors quickly snapped shut. Flamer performed a similar action seconds later, targeting the other two Syrian jets.

"We have incoming missiles!" shouted the lead Syrian pilot over his radio to his comrades.

"Where did they come from?" screamed his wingman. "My radar shows no indication of aircraft in that area."

Two of the targeted Syrian aircraft began immediate evasive maneuvers, using the limited tactics taught by the Russians to help them stay alive. The other two Syrian aircraft rapidly turned away upon hearing the calls from their comrades.

The Syrians grunted as they pulled the maximum g-forces, trying desperately to evade the incoming missiles. Two bright explosions eliminated that hope. The other two who had turned away saw the explosions, and by now their radar had picked up Flamer's incoming missiles, which were soon to find their marks. As the Syrian jets diverged from each other, one pilot believed it better to fight another day and promptly ejected from his aircraft. Within seconds after the ejection, his jet exploded in a bright orange fireball from Flamer's missile. His partner in the other jet failed to eject and became another casualty of war. The Russian-made fighters flown by the hapless Syrian pilots were no contest for the Raptors.

Meanwhile, the Strike Eagles raced low-level at six hundred

knots towards Ar Raqqah. The automatic release of their ordnance sent their JDAMs plummeting down toward the darkened barrel bomb factory. Instantly, the night sky was brightly lit by the expanding fireballs as the bombs found their mark.

The attacking force wasn't out of the woods yet. With the destruction of four Syrian aircraft, and explosions violently rocking the Syrian landscape, the country's air defense network was now on full alert, canvassing the sky for the attacking aircraft. The Raptors weren't under any major threat, as they had skillfully evaded the known concentration of SAMs. As the Syrians tried to acquire and target the incoming aircraft, the Growlers worked their magic on the SAM sites that tried to target the egressing Strike Eagles. The Growler's high-speed anti-radiation missiles destroyed the acquisition radar control centers that posed a threat, leaving the SAMs blind for all practical purposes. Without direction from their control centers, the missiles veered wildly across the sky, hitting nothing of value before exploding.

Matt smiled. The job was done, target destroyed, mission accomplished. No friendly aircraft were lost or struck by enemy fire. The strike force headed for home.

As the group of US fighter aircraft crossed over the Syrian border into Turkey, Matt activated his interrogator system. Minutes later, it flickered on and off—a reminder to him that the intermittent problem still existed. He thought about the new central computer, soon to be installed in the F-22, that would provide the Raptor even more combat capability, and the IFF mod that would hopefully fix the vexing inconsistent interrogator system performance.

Matt transmitted to his team. "Great job, guys. Let's get these birds back to Incirlik."

Captain Matt "Ace" Black had led his first successful combat mission. Overall, it was a major success.

Over the next few weeks, it was evident that the Syrian Air Force would not be a threat again, at least not for the near term. The assault by the Raptors and other strike aircraft had sent a strong message to President Assad. Not willing to risk losing any more of his aircraft fleet, and with the primary barrel bomb factory decimated by the Strike Eagle attacks, he ceased all air operations. Although no formal declaration of war existed, it was apparent that the United States was unwilling to stand by and watch civilians be slaughtered—or its own forces be threatened. Of course, the US was also not willing to accept any verbal assurance by Assad that he would discontinue his air operations against the enemies of his regime. Continued missions over Syria were established to eliminate, if necessary, any continued indiscriminate strikes on their population.

Almost as soon as the deployment of the Raptors had begun, it ended. The order to head home came after forty-five days of air operations, and Matt was heading back to Langley.

———————•———————

The ongoing problems with the Raptor's interrogator system, including those from Syrian strike reports, were significant enough that Headquarters, Air Combat Command at Langley AFB, made it Omega's top priority.

They were very concerned. If there was a bug in the software that was causing the flickering problem, there was no telling what other problems might manifest themselves at precisely the wrong time. Could the bug inadvertently activate the IFF? If a Raptor was all of a sudden sending unintended electronic signals while engaging with the enemy, its stealthy signature would be compromised.

Omega was directed to accelerate their programs and get the modifications into the Raptor fleet as soon as possible.

Chapter 43

D r. Katari flew a circuitous route from Tehran that took him to Frankfurt, Germany, then across the Atlantic Ocean to Montreal, Canada, and finally into Dallas–Fort Worth International Airport. He carried a credit-card-sized device of immense value, priceless in the eyes of the Ayatollah and crucial to Iran's holy Caliphate.

He had contacted Khalil from Montreal while changing planes and arranged a time and place to transfer the card. With final testing completed in Iran, it was time to move this project forward. The two met late in the afternoon at the Abdallah Mosque.

"I trust you understand the importance of your task," remarked Katari, his tone ominous as he looked straight into Khalil's eyes. "This effort cannot fail—too much has been invested. You must now quickly embed Epsilon into the Raptor's software." Katari paused. "It cannot be discovered."

Katari knew there was high risk in these next steps. First, there was the chance that Khalil's treasonous activity would be discovered—and Epsilon compromised. And second, without Epsilon, Iran had little chance of stopping a preemptive American military attack on Iran. The results of such an attack would be devastating to the Caliphate. Years of military buildup would be wasted. The final element necessary to establish Iran as a world power—nuclear weapons—would be lost.

"You *must* keep the code protected at all costs." Katari spoke his last words softly, but with deadly intonation.

Khalil stared back at Katari, knowing full well the pressure that was being placed on him. He would be a hero to Islam if successful. But he would be a traitor to his adopted country.

Khalil nodded and reached out to accept the precious card. He had been told that Epsilon was cleverly designed to mimic a key part of the Raptor's interrogator system code, to appear innocuous—like it was supposed to be there.

He was already thinking about how to discreetly work Epsilon's deadly string of code into the Air Force's top fighter aircraft software. It had to be undetectable to the engineering oversight groups, both in the government and in Omega. Most significantly, he had to get it to actually integrate and work in the *latest* version of the central computer software, a very different version than that tested in the sky over Iran. While he understood that the risks were formidable, he knew he had the skills to pull it off.

———————•———————

As he continued to exhibit his usual late-night work habits in the Omega lab, Khalil was certain that nobody took any undue notice. Nothing was overtly unusual or out of the ordinary. He was extremely careful anytime he opened the central computer software lines of code. It was normal to verify the code accuracy, to work on an anomaly, or to certify a previous fix to the code. As he worked diligently in the lab, he continued to think about what Katari had told him—how China had been able to develop the capability that Epsilon represented.

Chinese engineers had been trying to spoof IFF for years. Once they discovered, almost by accident in testing, a means to make an interrogator system perform in the way they intended as opposed to how it was designed, they knew this technology could be a game changer in a future potential US conflict.

In fact, within the most secret of China's core intellectual property development centers, the Epsilon code had been deemed the most significant technological breakthrough of the decade. Incredibly, the code could actually morph within itself, to repurpose itself. Once activated by the right external input, the software would change from its intended design into a sinister, altogether different set of coded messages. It would command the IFF to emit signals that the pilot never intended. If it happened in the heat of battle, as planned, the Raptor's interrogator signal would be plainly visible to enemy radar in spite of the aircraft's stealthy shape. The resulting Raptor bloom would likely result in the jet's destruction.

The real ingenuity of Epsilon was that, after repurposing itself for the critical few seconds needed to highlight the Raptor's position to the enemy, it would transform itself back to its previous configuration, thereby making it virtually undetectable within the aircraft's software program—and extremely difficult to trace and fix.

Khalil was one of the few engineers in Omega that fully understood the complex software architecture that made any changes to this warbird extremely difficult. Besides the hundreds of obvious integrated systems that could be affected by even the simplest code change, firewalls protecting critical and noncritical, classified and nonclassified systems were designed to prevent unapproved tampering with the massively integrated software.

He had studied the interrogator code extensively along with everything that either touched it or was touched by it. The levels of complexity could be mind-boggling to even the most skilled engineer. But Khalil was better than even the most skilled individual in this field.

Weeks had passed since the Epsilon tests in Iran. Significant changes in the program had taken place at Omega as the team accelerated their effort to deliver the final product. Khalil had to understand how Epsilon worked in the old version of software in order to have a chance of successfully integrating it into the current program.

This can't be done here, thought Khalil. *The risk of being discovered is too great, even if I do it in a different Omega lab. They'll know I was working in a lab we don't use for this upgrade—and that will draw plenty of unwanted questions.*

He had to plan this effort carefully. He would need to take the old program loaded on the special card and somehow run it on a separate set of computers, disassociated from the current Omega labs. But where?

Dr. Katari had anticipated this problem after his lengthy discussion with both the Chinese and Iranian engineers. The solution would be found on the west side of Dallas, at Texas Tech University. Katari had arranged to buy some lab time in their extensive secure facilities, one of which was fully capable of running the Raptor software. Texas Tech labs had been used by companies in the defense industry before, having been certified to handle military programs with the top levels of security classification. The labs also possessed the infrastructure and capability to run large, complex programs. An extremely generous financial donation made to the institution by a nameless foreign donor, on top of the usual fee for lab time, guaranteed that Khalil would have sole use of the facility for as long as he needed it.

Saturday morning, Khalil arrived at the Texas Tech laboratory. It was pretty well deserted. Some students who might have thought about using it were still sleeping off their hangovers from a hard night partying, an often-necessary break from their demanding course of study. Khalil was surprised to find no one milling around the building.

Khalil knew what a stretch it was to presume that the successful testing of the Epsilon code in the old software version meant that it could actually work in the new software program he'd developed at Omega. After all, he had no idea what the scientists had actually done to it in Iran. He needed to find Epsilon first.

Then there was the issue of unintended consequences. Khalil was quite sure that Iran's scientists didn't fully understand the central computer code's complexity—and the impact of any change like Epsilon on the hundreds of integrated systems the software touched. Any function might be negatively affected by even a simple change. That analysis would take some time. And, at some point, he knew that the only place he could truly test it was in the Omega lab, and then on the actual aircraft.

Upon verifying that the lab's mainframe system was fully operational, Khalil loaded the software and began the program run. He had been told precisely where the Epsilon code would be. After an hour, he plainly saw where it was embedded. It appeared as an innocent, unremarkable interrogator system code patch in the central computer program. In fact, it was embedded in one of the many redundant repair functions.

Software programmers routinely built redundancy into their programs, especially where critical functions of the aircraft had to perform perfectly. When a system failed, the redundant code was intended to provide the messaging to keep the system operating. The location of Epsilon avoided the critical lines of code that directed the primary interrogator functions, hoping to prevent any discovery that it had been altered. Instead, it was placed in a benign area of the software.

This is pretty clever, he mused. *What a perfect spot to place a corrupting piece of code, in an area that is unlikely to draw much attention in any review process. It looks as benign as any other structure within the code.*

Khalil continued examining the program. He didn't yet understand how the software was able to morph within itself after receiving the satellite's signal. Additionally, he wondered how it could trigger its intended function from a noncritical part of the code.

It appears so simple in its architecture, and it looks so benign. Yet it supposedly has the ability to repurpose itself, to activate one of the primary interrogator functions.

As he dug deeper into the system architecture, he lurched upright in his chair. Even as one of the nation's experts in software development, he had some initial trouble understanding what he was looking at.

There's a unique combination of code that I don't recognize. This must be the heart of Epsilon.

As Khalil continued for the next few hours to dissect Epsilon, he began to understand what had been done, how it was structured, and why it performed the way it did. He knew he must understand it so thoroughly that he could integrate Epsilon into the actual Raptor program back at Omega.

Time seemed to slip by, and Khalil didn't realize he had been there for over five hours. His concentration was broken by a voice coming from one of the lab's overhead speakers. The facility was closing in thirty minutes.

Fortunately, he had studied it enough to understand what had been done. *This is brilliant*, he thought. *It's AI! The Chinese and Iranians have somehow integrated elements of artificial intelligence into this code.*

Khalil had studied AI extensively in the past and had even written a couple of technical papers on the subject for various think tanks.

The trigger for Epsilon is within the AI code structure. He smiled to himself. Khalil could only surmise how the code actually morphed itself, messaging the IFF transponder to begin broadcasting its interrogation signal.

He had learned enough. As he left the lab, Khalil's mind was accelerating at breakneck speed. He was confident—no, absolutely certain that he understood enough about Epsilon that he could pull off the task at hand. He understood precisely where the differences were between this old version of the program running in the Texas Tech lab, and the current, actual Raptor software program his team was working on. After all, he had essentially designed them both and could see in his mind the changes that had been made. The time in the Texas Tech lab had produced exactly what he had hoped. He was now confident he could make it work back at Omega. But he also knew there was plenty of danger.

I've got to be careful and not make a stupid mistake in moving forward integrating Epsilon, he thought. *I've also got to bridge the classified tracking system—trick the demon security guard in the software architecture that watches for any change being done to the code. That's going to be my top priority to avoid detection.*

Khalil was confident he could do it and not draw any undue attention when he breached the Raptor's classified software. He had developed a way to bridge the firewalls and prevent being discovered. Khalil planned to use his firewall bridge to insert unclassified code into the classified program without detection.

Once back at Omega the following Monday, Khalil managed to bring Epsilon into the lab without raising any suspicions. He got the usual wave from the security guard on entry and returned it with a nod and a polite thank-you for the courtesy. With the special card containing Epsilon secured in his locker, he began to run the current program. He questioned his engineering team about the changes they had made in the past weeks and, after getting a detailed review of their changes, dismissed his staff.

He spent the next few hours analyzing the program architecture, keen to understand any differences from the old version that he'd seen with Epsilon incorporated. He found what he was looking for. Khalil wanted to ensure there would be no mistakes when he tried to modify the actual Raptor code. This insertion had to be done right the first time. He decided to come in later in the evening, when the facility was less occupied, and begin his work. He grabbed the card from his locker and left.

———————•———————

"This is Khalil. I want to update you on my progress with Epsilon," he said over his cell phone to Dr. Katari.

"Yes, Khalil. I was hoping to hear some good news from you. As you know, our schedule for completing this effort is extremely tight. Have you begun integrating Epsilon into the Raptor software?"

"Not yet. I finished my analysis at Texas Tech as planned. The facility worked out quite well for what I needed." He paused for a moment. "I'm ready to begin the initial integration at Omega this evening!"

"You are now at your highest risk of being discovered," Katari warned. "There can be no mistakes at this point. The consequences of your failure are extreme."

Khalil paused before responding. He was getting a little irritated with the constant reminders about the *consequences of failure*.

"I *understand* what's at stake. There will be no problem with the integration," he blurted out a bit irritably.

"I know you realize how important Epsilon is to the holy cause. We must have Epsilon to defeat any American effort to destroy all that we have done. Our nuclear weapons development is very close to completion, but it won't be long before those who despise us try to eliminate our labs, our centrifuges, and our uranium enrichment facilities. Once we have Epsilon embedded in the American aircraft, they will not be able to penetrate our defenses without being shot out of the sky. You must accelerate your efforts and complete the task."

Khalil thought for a moment before responding, "*Inshallah*—as Allah wills it, I will accomplish the task."

After he had finished the call with Dr. Katari, Khalil sat silently in his small apartment. He gazed out the window at the orange glow from the setting Texas sun and wondered briefly if he could really do what had been asked of him.

Chapter 44

The Omega parking lot was nearly empty shortly after midnight. Aside from guards and the cleaning crews, the facilities were unoccupied. The company didn't normally conduct twenty-four hour operations. That was usually reserved for the infrequent times when a program was behind schedule or a crisis presented itself—like a war—to put a demand on their workforce that would drive extended hours. The Raptor upgrade was ahead of schedule, and its dedicated team of engineers had gone home for the night.

He had explained to his team that he was not completely satisfied with the software integration activity within the latest code update and would be working late that evening to verify all the changes they made. Of course, that wasn't what he actually planned for this night. Tonight he would begin the dangerous task of inserting Epsilon into the Raptor's code. He told them he didn't need their help. His singular night activity would draw no attention.

The software laboratory was quiet except for the dull hum of the air-handling system providing the constant blast of frigid air that kept the equipment cool. The lab support equipment had been specifically built to simulate the aircraft. It included actual radar and avionics parts from the Raptor, along with banks of simulators designed to make the operational flight program running in the central computer think the lab was an aircraft in flight.

Khalil never could get used to the constant chill in the labs. It distracted him sometimes from thinking clearly and focusing on his primary task. With a shiver, he sat down at the lab station.

Confident that there was no one else in the large facility, he got down to business.

The current Raptor software normally ran on the mainframe computer system. Khalil moved it to an offline system where it would avoid any tracking fingerprints caused by his code manipulation. He pulled the card containing the Epsilon code from his wallet and connected it to the Mont Blanc pen with the slender wire. He placed them in position near the offline computer and began to transfer Epsilon into the Raptor code.

He understood the system program architecture thoroughly enough that he could insert Epsilon as a trial run of debugging software. He would carefully embed the code and look for any anomalies, any perturbations in the program that would indicate an unintended consequence that might be immediately noticed. He would immediately see if there were major issues caused by Epsilon and could correct the problem—and eliminate any lasting evidence of this corrupting code.

In the remote hours of the night, Khalil continued to integrate the Epsilon code in the separate, offline operating station. *This will take a bit of restructuring*, he thought. *I'll address the primary failure mode that is causing the interrogator system perturbations in the aircraft and then patch the Epsilon code into a benign area of the architecture. Then I'll integrate it fully into the central computer software. But I'll provide a path for Epsilon to enter the signal generating code within the interrogator. Whatever I do, it's got to look and act like part of the fix—so much so that neither the current IFF program manager nor his engineers will know what I have actually done.*

He thought through every possible iteration of code integration, running and rerunning the program with various patches. Hours passed by. He was so intently focused, he had even forgotten about the chill in the sterile lab air.

I've got to have a fail-safe means to safeguard Epsilon from compromise, he thought, remembering the "threat" he had understood in Dr. Katari's message on the phone.

How can I keep the actual Epsilon code from being compromised, even if that is unlikely? Maybe I can build a close replica of Epsilon as part of the fix. The interrogator problem is not difficult to correct, at least not for me. I can add some additional "performance" enhancements that will help bury the Epsilon replica in the overall fix. It should be able to pass the oversight review, and if it doesn't, I won't have given up the actual Epsilon design. If it is discovered, I'll know why. I can probably explain it away as one of my rare errors. I'll bury the real code deeper. Make it truly undetectable.

Khalil knew this was risky, but then again, the entire scheme was risky. He just might be able to explain away his Epsilon patch if it was questioned in any way. The plan was coming together. Epsilon would be designed into the integrated fix of the IFF problem.

As the hours rolled by, Khalil worked tirelessly to understand all aspects of the replicated code he built, and the impact of its integration into the central computer software. On two attempts to embed the code, he failed to make it appear as a seamless fix to a redundant repair function. It appeared too obvious, easily detectable to skilled software engineers trained to dissect and understand the purpose of the code. On his third attempt, the code looked good. Almost perfect!

Not almost, thought Khalil, *but absolutely perfect*. He sat back in the chair, staring at the computer screen. He smiled.

He felt the slight pressure change in his ears first. Then the sound of the lab door closing caused Khalil to stop what he was doing. He jerked his head around, searching for who or what had caused the intrusion. At four o'clock in the morning, who was coming into the lab? He saw someone heading toward him through the dim light. One of Khalil's brightest young software engineers had come in early to pick up some technical papers for his trip to Fairborn, Ohio. Steve Brooks walked over to the station where Khalil was working.

"What's going on, boss?" asked the engineer with a sleepy smile. "I forgot my data for the Program Office visit this afternoon at

Wright-Patt. My flight is at seven this morning, so I'm just here for a minute."

"Steve! You surprised me for a second," responded Khalil. "I didn't expect to see anyone this early. I've been working all night on cleaning up errors in the code. As you know, my most creative time is early morning, by myself, with no distractions. I'm also just reviewing some of last week's work by the team, in case anything comes up at the review," he said, trying to look like all was normal.

Peering past Khalil's shoulder, Steve noticed his boss was working at one of the offline system integration test stations, which seemed a bit unusual. Seeing the questioning look on the young engineer's face, Khalil kept his back to the terminal as he quickly made up an excuse that he hoped sounded plausible.

"We're so close to locking down the final version of the central computer program upgrade, I decided to run it offline rather than risk undoing any of the great work you guys have done," he said.

The young engineer was pretty sharp and noticed part of the program running on the terminal.

"Is that the IFF program?" he asked. "I didn't know we could run that offline."

Khalil's anger started to boil up, but he caught himself as he answered, "I'm not actually running it—I'm just doing a test on a number of code fixes."

Brooks kept the puzzled look on his face.

Khalil blurted out, "You better get going, or you'll miss your flight. I've still got a lot of work to do. In any event, I'll be linked in to the meeting via teleconference and will give you all an update on what I've come up with."

Steve turned and walked across the lab to his desk. As he picked up his notes for the meeting, he looked back across the lab and saw Khalil still watching him as he left.

After a few minutes, Khalil stepped out of the lab, unlocked the box outside the secure area where his personal cell phone was stored, and tapped in a text message to Dr. Katari. He felt it essential to advise him about the awkward encounter with the engineer. Despite the early-morning hour, Katari immediately responded with a phone call. After listening to what had transpired, Katari believed Khalil might have tipped his hand as to what he was doing. Learning that the engineer was on his way to Ohio for a routine technical discussion, Katari knew there was only one thing to do to protect the continued secrecy of the Caliphate's plan.

"You were careless, Khalil. You were warned to take every precaution. This cannot happen again!" he shouted angrily. "As for this potential problem, it will be resolved." With that final message, the line went dead.

Khalil wasn't sure what to think about his conversation with Katari. *The problem will be resolved? I wonder what that means.*

Chapter 45

K halil finished the interrogator system patch with the embedded replicated Epsilon code. He was quite satisfied with his work. *Perfect, and undetectable,* he thought. He had managed to race back to his apartment a few hours after his conversation with Katari, just as the early bird employees were arriving in the Omega parking lot. He took a quick shower, ate some fruit and yogurt for breakfast, and was ready to head back in to Omega and get ready for the teleconference. *No sleep today.*

He worried a bit about what Katari had said to him in the early morning after discussing the lab intrusion by one of Khalil's sharpest engineers. By now, Steve Brooks was on a two hour American Airlines flight to Dayton, just a short drive from Fairborn. At the Dayton airport, he would pick up a rental car and head down the interstate highway to the large base that served as one of the most important research and development centers in the Air Force.

Dr. Katari had been extremely upset about what had happened in the lab. Khalil knew he had to be more careful in the future. All the work that had been done, both by him and by the engineers and scientists in Iran, had to bear fruit. It could not be squandered by any lapse in his ability to pull off this most important effort.

He tried to push the admonishment he had gotten to the back of his mind. *How much did Steve pick up on what I was doing? He knows how important the central computer program is. He's a smart guy, and he may be concerned about me running the IFF code offline, since we don't ever do that. Surely he won't comment on any of that while at the F-22 review.*

Khalil thought about what Katari had said to him about Brooks—the problem would be resolved. How was it going to get resolved?

———•———

The Technical Design Review at the F-22 System Program Office was set to start at three o'clock in the afternoon. Khalil planned to teleconference in from Omega, a routinely acceptable practice to reduce the travel budget. Today's review didn't require his physical presence, only that he be able to talk through the current status. His technical design manager had traveled to Ohio a day earlier and would be the Omega senior representative there. The manager expected to have another young engineer, Steve Brooks, flying in early on the morning of the review to give the briefing.

Steve Brooks stepped off his American Airlines flight and headed for Baggage Claim at the Dayton International Airport. Once he had his bag, he walked over to the Budget Car Rental counter, got his keys, and headed to the parking garage to pick up his car.

He was followed by two people—a man in a blue two-piece suit and a stunningly attractive woman. As Steve drove away from the rental car center, two Chevy Malibu sedans followed him out.

The travel time to Wright-Patterson Air Force Base was about forty minutes. Driving east down the highway on Interstate 70, Steve began to think about his presentation. He also was thinking heavily about the security breach he had witnessed that morning in the Omega lab. His boss had clearly violated all security protocols running the IFF program offline.

I should report this. Khalil knows better. The security procedures are quite clear. Was there something fishy going on here that I should report? Maybe bring it up to Lieutenant Casey at the review? I'll tell her about it in private.

He didn't pay much attention to the two cars behind him, as the road was always choked with traffic at this time of day. He signaled his turn and pulled into the right lane toward the exit that would put him on Osborn Road. On the two-lane exit, he was passed by a Chevy driven by an attractive lady who looked at Steve as she slowly pulled past him. He made eye contact during the brief glimpse of her. She smiled at him as she rapidly accelerated away. Several minutes and a few miles up the road, she stopped her car.

This part of Ohio had long stretches of undeveloped land containing beautiful oak and maple trees. Steve wasn't paying much attention to the landscape. He was deep in thought, thinking about the briefing he would give in a few hours. He saw a lady waving at him from the side of the road. Her extremely short red skirt and shapely legs were enough for him to slow down and pull in behind her apparently disabled car. Steve quickly looked at his watch. He knew he had to get to the base, but he still had plenty of time to make it before the review began.

He stepped out of his car and approached her with a smile.

Wow, what a knockout, he thought.

"Hi, do you need any help?" He believed it was the same lady in the car that had accelerated past him.

She had a beautiful smile, one that captivated him.

"Thanks so much for stopping. My rental car just died, and I was headed to Wright-Patterson for a meeting. I don't know what to do." She continued, "My cell phone just quit, and I can't even call for help."

Steve volunteered, "Well, you can use my cell phone. Or, if you prefer, I'm headed to the base for a meeting with the F-22 folks. I can take you to where your meeting is, and from there you can call the rental car company to get your car fixed and bring it to the base—or bring you another one."

"That is so kind of you," she replied, reaching out to touch his arm and giving it a light caress. "You don't know how much I appreciate you for stopping. Most people wouldn't do that. You're pretty special."

"Really, it's no big deal. I'm happy to help."

Steve detected a slight accent in the pretty lady's voice. Was it a bit Middle Eastern? Definitely not the usual Ohio inflection he was accustomed to hearing from most of the local Dayton crowd in his past visits.

"Well, you've saved me a lot of time, and kept me from being late for my meeting. I just don't know *how* I'm going to thank you."

She gave him the best smile she could muster. She had practiced it hundreds of times.

"I'm Kelly," she said.

"Steve Brooks. It's a pleasure to meet you, Kelly, although the circumstances might have been better."

He thought for a moment that Kelly seemed like an unusual name for a woman with that particular foreign accent.

"I really hate to be a bother to you, and I don't want you to be late for your meeting," Kelly replied.

"Hey, it's no bother. I have plenty of time before I've got to be there. It's really no problem getting you to the base. I'm just glad I came along when I did. Who knows if anyone else would have stopped at this time of the morning? Most people are in a big hurry to get to work, and this route is one of the less traveled ways to the base," he said.

"Well, let's get going if you're ready." As he walked with her to his car's passenger door, he couldn't help but again notice how shapely she was.

Steve thought that this was a stroke of good fortune. As a software engineer, and a single man at that, he didn't usually have time to mix it up with the social crowd back in Dallas. Even when he did get the chance, he never envisioned meeting someone like this!

Steve had no real idea of how much danger he was in. The seemingly innocent stop to help a fellow citizen in need was going to take a deadly turn. He didn't understand that Kelly wasn't at all who she seemed to be. Her background as one of the only females who had served in Iran's Islamic Revolutionary Guard Special Operations Unit would likely have floored him. She had been trained as part of their elite covert tactics unit. Her shapely build hid the fact that she was an expert in hand-to-hand combat and specialized in being able to quickly disable and kill another human being in mere seconds.

Steve opened the passenger door, being the consummate gentleman as his mother had drilled into him over his formative years. Kelly slid into the front seat, her skirt riding up a bit and briefly exposing the most beautiful pair of legs he had seen in some time. He closed the door and walked around the car to the driver's side. Right now, his mind drifted away from the F-22 meeting and to thoughts about this lovely woman. He thought that he might just be able to hook up with her later at the base. Maybe for drinks. Maybe more! After all, she seemed pretty grateful that he had stopped. As Steve got into the driver's seat and closed the door, he smelled the flowery scent of her hair.

Hmm, she smells divine, he thought.

"How long are you going to be at the base?" he asked. "I'm here a couple of days for a program review."

"Really? I'm staying at the Doubletree for two nights," she said.

"I don't mean to sound too forward, but if you're not tied up with your other business acquaintances tonight, perhaps we can get together for dinner. I'm flying solo myself." He'd make excuses to the Omega manager at the review—he might have other nighttime plans.

"That's a terrific idea," she said. "It's the least I can do for you after you stopped to help me."

Steve smiled at the thought of his upcoming nighttime rendezvous with this beautiful woman.

"Great. So, who are you meeting at the base?"

"My meetings are with one of the research labs," she replied.

"Which one?" he asked. "I'm pretty familiar with most of them, since our company does plenty of business with them."

She paused before answering.

Too many questions, Kelly thought as Steve started the car.

While waiting for her to answer, he looked left to make sure the lane was clear for him to pull back on to the roadway. He didn't notice the slender tube containing the hypodermic needle that Kelly had slipped out of her Gucci purse. As he waited for a car to pass, he felt a sharp pain in his right thigh.

"Ouch! What the heck," he yelled. Before he could utter another word, Kelly had shoved the car's shift lever into park and roughly pulled Steve toward her. She locked him in a choke hold while the fast-acting poison took its toll. In just about fifteen seconds, she released her grip on his throat as she felt his body going limp from the lack of air and the deadly injection.

Her partner in the other car pulled in behind her and began to scan the north-south roadway for any police that might come to investigate the parked cars along the road. Had Steve not stopped when he did, the second car would have continued to track him. Osborn Road wasn't that heavily traveled, and the two were fortunate that traffic was sparse. When no cars were visible, they pulled Steve Brooks's apparently lifeless body across the seat and out of the passenger door and quickly placed him in the trunk of the other car.

Kelly, known in Iran as Banu Sayeed, and her partner, Omar Khan, drove off, leaving Steve's car locked and abandoned by the side of the road. The two Iranian operatives drove east toward the Monongahela National Forest, specifically the Cranberry Wilderness area—the trails there encompassed over forty-seven thousand acres with elevations up to forty-six hundred feet. They headed to a heavily wooded isolated area and, once they arrived, carried Steve deep into the forested thicket, leaving the body under a pile of leaves. They presumed over time the local carnivorous wildlife—black bears and, recently, mutated coyote-wolves—would find the body and enjoy a meal, destroying the evidence of Steve Brooks. The Iranians quickly departed the area and caught a flight out of Ohio.

———•———

The heartbeat was ever so slight. Almost imperceptible. Steve Brooks was *alive*. An avid free-diver off the coast of Texas in his spare time, Steve had developed phenomenal lung capacity. His physiology was significantly stronger than the average man. The poison had left him paralyzed, but nonetheless alive! As he regained consciousness, his mind raced. He had some recollection about what had happened. He tried to move. He couldn't. He tried to shout, to call for help. Nothing. He hoped he would be found by someone. Or perhaps, once the injection effects wore off, he could get some help.

Chapter 46

"Colonel, it's good to see you today," Khalil said to the F-22 system program director, surprised to see him at this lower-level technical review. Khalil and a few of his other team members were sitting in the Omega Teleconference Center ready to proceed with the briefings. On the other end of the line, the Wright-Patterson Air Force Base F-22 Conference Room was full—mostly Air Force and government civilians attached to the program. The colonel's presence was a bit disturbing to Khalil.

Is there a problem that I didn't know about? As he thought about it, the colonel began the meeting with a quick introduction of the attendees.

"I don't normally sit in on these," he replied, "but my schedule opened up for an hour, so I thought I would listen in. As usual, my trusty program manager, Lieutenant Rebecca Casey, is running the show."

"Hi, Khalil." Rebecca waved to the camera in the conference room as she looked at him on the large-screen monitor. "Sorry you couldn't make it today, but I'll see you in a couple days when I'm down your way to review the program upgrade testing, including the IFF run."

"Sounds great, Lieutenant," he said, being careful not to get too familiar in front of the colonel and his staff. He was actually on a more-than-professional basis with Casey, but these formal meetings required some discretion.

"I thought you were sending one of your software engineers to the meeting," remarked Casey, looking first at Khalil and then across the table at the Omega manager present.

"Khalil, Steve never showed up," replied the manager. "I assume he got tied up in traffic or missed his flight. Not really sure. I gave him a call on his cell phone, but it went straight to voicemail. But no worries, we can press ahead without him, in my opinion."

"Agreed," responded Khalil, "as long as it's okay with Lieutenant Casey."

"Good by me," she said. "You know much more than anyone about the subject for today." She smiled, looking back at the monitor at Khalil.

"I can go through everything that Steve was planning on presenting and then some," responded Khalil. "Also, our IFF program manager is tied into the call as well. So, if you all are ready, we can proceed."

Khalil wondered if the engineer's absence had anything to do with Katari's comment about "resolving the problem." But somehow, this was better. No engineer meant no discussion about running a highly secure program offline. There would be no questions about whatever might have been running through the young engineer's mind as he'd viewed Khalil's early-morning lab activity.

The design review proceeded, with the colonel remaining quiet for the short time he was present. He remarked occasionally about how great Omega was doing on the upgrade programs. Khalil knew everything that the missing engineer was going to present, having approved all his slides. He easily conducted the review, with detailed explanations of the design progress, technical issues, and the solutions that had been incorporated. He also broached the IFF issue, indicating that he believed that he and the interrogator program manager had a solution to that as well and would be happy to run the program once Lieutenant Casey arrived in a few days. The colonel was elated to hear this and advised Khalil and Casey to let him know about the success of the fix as soon as possible.

When the meeting concluded, the video and audio connection to Wright-Patterson AFB was shut down, and Khalil headed back to the lab. The pressure was on to get this job done quickly, with representatives from the Program Office coming to Texas soon to review the software's performance. Khalil was confident that the replicated embedded Epsilon code would look like and, more importantly, *work* the way the Air Force intended.

It fixes the interrogator software problem, and at the same time it has the raw elements of the corrupt code silently and invisibly integrated into the build, he thought with a devilish smile. *Even if my work is somehow questioned by the government review committee, I know I can convince them of the need for the other enhancements I added to the code, at no more cost to the program.*

He wondered about the missing engineer. *What happened to Steve?*

When he'd made the call to Katari after being interrupted earlier in the lab that morning, Khalil hadn't considered what might actually happen. He knew the secrecy involved in his software effort was paramount. Katari had warned him of the dire consequences of discovery.

I wonder if the reason Steve is missing is that he has disappeared. Or is dead. He was about to call Katari but then thought better of it. *Leave it alone.*

Khalil couldn't get Steve off his mind. What could possibly have happened to him? The police had been notified by Omega of the engineer's disappearance.

Two days later, in spite of an intensive search, Steve had not been found. There seemed to be no trace of him after he had rented his car at the Dayton Airport. The car was found empty, locked, on the side of Osborn Road. The Ohio State Police kept the company informed of their progress trying to find Brooks. The entire Omega staff was reminded to contact the police if the engineer somehow tried to make contact with anyone back at the company.

There would be no calls, of course. Dr. Katari believed that the Iranian agents in Ohio had buried all evidence of Steve Brooks.

———————•———————

The darkness of the forest frightened him. Steve guessed that it had been almost two days since he had been left there. He felt weak from lack of water. Nobody had come anywhere near him, as far as he knew. While he couldn't move and couldn't speak, he could hear. The noise of something moving through the woods—definitely not human, likely an animal—startled him. He could hear footsteps, something walking slowly through the heavy brush around him. Twigs breaking. Leaves rustling. The sound was coming from two different directions around him. His eyes were flashing with stark terror now. He was helpless. The dark shapes approached him. He could hear their grunts, almost smell their breath. In seconds, they were on him. He couldn't even scream in pain.

Chapter 47

Days later, Rebecca called Khalil when she landed in Dallas. She would be staying at the Marriott and wondered if Khalil wanted to meet her there for dinner. She indicated they could discuss the next day's software review and anything else that he might want to address. Wanting to continue his professional and even more so his personal relationship with his lieutenant, he met her in the lobby at seven p.m.

"I missed you at the review," she said to Khalil with a shy smile.

"I know I should have been there, but I was really trying to concentrate on accelerating the program and getting the interrogator fix completed. I know how important it is to the Air Force." He paused as he looked into her eyes. "But, I'll make it up to you," he said sincerely. "*Whatever* you want, you can have it."

"*Anything* I want?" she said with a knowing look in her eyes.

Khalil had seen this look on her face before. This lieutenant clearly wanted far more than a technical discussion, and he was more than willing to go down that path if it meant helping ensure the success of his treasonous efforts.

"Dinner first, or…?" He left his sentence deliberately unfinished.

She grabbed his hand and led him to the elevator. They rode in awkward silence to the fifth floor and headed to her room.

"You know, we need to be careful," replied Khalil, smiling at Rebecca.

He didn't want there to be any possible complication that would get in the way of his primary goal, his critical work to ensure the success of Iran's Caliphate.

"Just come with me and be quiet for a minute," she whispered as they approached her room.

She looked down the deserted hallway, slid the key into the lock, opened the door, and pulled him into the room.

Khalil knew this woman was in need of him, but he didn't realize how wild she could get. She wasted no time pulling his clothes off and then pushed him onto the bed. Standing at the foot of the bed, she smiled at him. She teased him as she slowly undressed, making almost a ritual of stripping the clothes from her body. Khalil just lay there, admiring her beauty, enjoying the show. Rebecca leapt onto the bed, landing in his arms, and they enjoyed a pre-dinner dessert of sensual lovemaking.

They showered together, and that led to a few more moments of lustful bliss. After they were dressed, they headed out for dinner and then agreed to meet at Omega the following morning for a preliminary review of the day's agenda. They would have most of the morning before the actual meeting.

———•———

The design review began the next day in the software lab. Khalil ran the central computer upgrade program with the interrogator fix, and everything performed superbly. The civilian software engineering rep from Fairborn had arrived just prior to the review and was the real expert, if you could call him that. While the Air Force had a few extremely smart civilians to help Lieutenant Casey manage the program, this one was stretched thin due to his coverage of multiple programs. As a result, he occasionally overlooked things he might otherwise have caught.

Khalil spent plenty of time with him, briefing him constantly, overwhelming him with technical performance design details. He explained the progress—debugging the critical code functions, eliminating false signals, determining failures in the messaging, and finally how he had overcome the obstinate IFF problem the Raptor pilots were experiencing.

Khalil's replicated Epsilon code was embedded in the program well. It appeared as an innocuous system enhancement intended to provide redundant capability for powering critical systems in the event of a system fault. The civilian software engineer never raised an eyebrow at the enhancement.

In the end, the government rep had heard and seen the right things. Confident in the integrity of the program and the interrogator fix, he advised Lieutenant Casey that all was good. This successful Air Force review cleared the way for Khalil to proceed with the next important step in the plan.

At two o'clock on a Saturday morning, the Integration Lab was dimly lit, the temperature a brisk fifty-five degrees Fahrenheit. The constant droning hum of the forced dry air handling system and the massive lab test, simulation, and avionics equipment made it nearly impossible to hear a conversation, or someone approaching from behind.

He removed the replicated code and integrated the actual Epsilon code into the program. Extensive tests were run throughout his late-night foray to verify that the *true* Epsilon code could not be detected. He inserted fault after fault into the program to determine if it had any effect on the Epsilon code architecture. There could be no mistakes here. Khalil noted that for a few highly unlikely faults that might occur in the jet, all was good with Epsilon's performance. But he couldn't take a chance that in the event of even *unlikely* faults, Epsilon might not perform as intended. Khalil carefully developed the intricate work-around coding that would handle these types of problems. Once completed, he reran the entire program to verify its overall integrity.

Khalil finished up his work with the Epsilon code. He was now confident that the code could not be detected by anyone, having tested it in every way imaginable—certainly in more ways than the Omega team members or the government oversight team would do. He had designed Epsilon's integration into the program in such a way that it was all but invisible to even an expert who might delve into the individual packets of code. Epsilon was ready for its final review, when the entire central computer upgrade program would be sold off to the Air Force and approved for installation into the F-22 stealth fighter fleet.

Khalil expected Epsilon to perform as originally intended in actual testing on a fighter aircraft. Whether it would work as expected when triggered by a satellite signal was still another question in his mind. Nonetheless, his work, for now, was done. He loaded the program with the Epsilon code onto the card Katari had provided. The modified program was now ready to make its way back to Tehran for final testing. It would be reviewed one last time in the Iranian underground lab and then loaded on the specially modified Su-35 aircraft. The key test would come after another satellite launch. The subsequent activation of the satellite trigger signal would hopefully initiate the Iranian jet's IFF system.

No time was wasted in expeditiously getting the Epsilon code out of the country via Iran's most reliable courier—Dr. Katari.

Chapter 48

Tehran, Iran

The widely announced launch of two commercial satellites was billed as a massive improvement in communications capability, intended to provide broadband coverage to some of the most remote areas of the country. It was touted as a major breakthrough in the ability of ordinary Iranian citizens to openly communicate with each other over the airwaves. This joint venture with China would also provide them with greater electronic access to the world—albeit a heavily censored system to ensure the population wouldn't foment dissent for Sharia law nor be exposed to Western filth. The public announcement was further intended to desensitize the Americans to Iran's missile launches, especially those intended for peaceful purposes. One of the two satellites was far from peaceful.

The stage was set from the previous successful satellite test conducted deep underground. Epsilon had been activated while buried in the early version of the Raptor's central computer software code. It had worked well in the static setup within a long tunnel, and in the first flight test with a modified Su-35 fighter. Now Iran was ready to test Epsilon in a software version that had passed its final design review—a version that would ultimately be installed in the F-22 fleet. It would provide proof that Khalil succeeded in his task—and Epsilon was ready to violate the Raptor's stealth.

The software was analyzed quickly by both the Iranian and Chinese engineers. They viewed the subtle changes Khalil made and verified that they could trigger the code from the satellite signal. They jointly gave the go-ahead for the launch at the Bandier Complex.

At the spaceport, a large two-stage rocket had been prepared within the commercial launch vehicle assembly building. Once the satellites were ready, they were mated on top of the second stage, and the entire rocket moved to the launch facility. This routine had been repeated a few times, and observed each time by the spying eyes of US surveillance satellites overhead. For all appearances, this was going to look like just another in a series of communication satellite launches.

The countdown for liftoff of this high-value rocket proceeded normally, and at precisely one o'clock in the afternoon, amidst a gray-white plume of smoke and orange flame, the powerful rocket rose from the pad. Streaking through the azure-blue sky, the first stage separated at the intended time, and the second stage continued to push the satellites towards their target orbit. The final separation of the second stage was flawless. The satellites headed for their position approximately twenty-three thousand miles above the surface of the earth, entering a precise geostationary orbit that would keep their position constant over Iran. Meanwhile, the second stage fell back into the earth's atmosphere, burning brightly during reentry and eventually falling back toward an unpopulated area. The satellites joined with a smaller constellation put into position on previous launches.

———————•———————

It had been a relatively quiet day in the Peterson Air Force Base Space Control Facility. Sharing property with Colorado Springs Municipal Airport, the base was home to North American Aerospace Defense Command, or NORAD, the center for monitoring literally anything put into orbit. The facility kept a careful eye across the world using a variety of spaceborne, airborne and ground sensors that were monitored around the clock.

The officer of the day had just been called by one of his technicians. Colonel Andy Bell had been in the Air Force for twenty-four years. Getting the job at Peterson AFB was a plum assignment in his mind, especially after the overall responsibility for space operations had moved from the deep underground bunker at Cheyenne Mountain to the fresh air of Colorado Springs. Other officers of his rank were constantly being tapped for crappy assignments outside of their career field, some in remote locations like the Middle East or Africa. His job gave him a bit of immunity from that, at least for the three years he would spend in the job. He had a staff of lower-ranking officers, enlisted and civilian technical experts, manning the massive array of computer systems.

"Sir, we just picked up the launch of a ballistic missile from Iran. It appears to have pushed a couple satellites into geostationary orbit and joined up with a small constellation that was already up there."

Colonel Bell responded, "Let me see the tracking data on it. I know that there was an announcement made by Iran of their impending communication satellite launch, and this looks like it."

Protocol required that the National Security Agency be notified of all foreign rocket launches. Whether they reached orbit or not, the United States took no chances on any potential threat from anywhere on earth. Everything was identified, tracked, and characterized as to its probable intent. In this case, the call to NSA was made and the launch identified as a likely commercial enterprise supporting Iran's communication system upgrades. Colonel Bell was okay with the report to NSA, but in the case of belligerents like Iran, there was always a nagging question—was the real purpose of the launch something other than advertised?

———————•———————

One day after the launch, the F-22 Raptor software program made its way to the airfield where Iranian and Chinese engineers oversaw its loading into special equipment installed in the Su-35s. Several ground tests were run to verify the code operated properly within the fighter's interrogator systems. The actual success of the test was contingent on the satellite burst triggering the software to change.

Senior Tehran leadership gathered in the secret, underground facility, accompanied by key scientists, engineers, and their Chinese partners. The test on this day would determine the future of the Caliphate. If successful, it would set in motion a series of events and actions that would change the face of geopolitical power in the Middle East. If it worked, it would likely stop any future US military attack Iran's nuclear facilities. Success meant Iran could kill the attacking Raptor stealth aircraft. It would pave the way for the final stages of Iran's nuclear plans and elevate Iran as the leader of the Islamic world.

"Katari, how confident are you with your test?" the Ayatollah asked.

Dr. Katari looked at the Ayatollah, then at the other senior representatives in the control center.

He wondered about the Ayatollah's choice of words—*your* test. Was this his responsibility alone? Was he solely responsible for the myriad problems that could arise in the satellite's operation, in the Su-35 fighter's equipment, and in the Epsilon code? He could accept some ownership of the code operation, but what about the dozens of Iranian and Chinese engineers that had approved it? What about Khalil Ruffa's role? If it failed, wouldn't they all share culpability? And share the ultimate punishment that would be handed out by the Ayatollah?

"I have great confidence that we will succeed," he said, although the words seemed to choke him at the tail end of his statement.

"We shall see," Batani remarked, then directed the test to proceed.

The Su-35 Flankers accelerated down the runway at Esfahan airfield and gracefully lifted off into the clear, dry air surrounding the launch complex. The pilots, among Iran's best, pulled the nose of their jets up and pushed the throttles forward into afterburner. The Flankers headed to their designated flight training region near the Elburz Mountains. There they would likely not raise any suspicion by spying American overhead sensors that the flights were anything other than routine.

In the low earth orbit, the small constellation of satellites were built to survive the frigid temperatures of their hostile operating environment. Their power sources were driven by both solar and nuclear means, and their design, developed by Chinese technology, had been proven reliable over time. Currently, the satellite carrying the trigger signal was operating at full capacity, with no malfunctions. All indications of its condition were positive and were closely monitored in the control facility. The satellite was ready for its crucial test.

In the sterile darkness of space, the rogue Iranian satellite, equipped with advance imagers and X-ray sensors, seemed to be idle, silent, and nonthreatening. It was about to be tested in a way that would hopefully prove the effectiveness of Iran's newest weapon. Deep within the control room in Bandier, the lead engineer in charge of the test initiated the satellite's activation signal. Unnoticed and undetected by anyone on earth other than the Iranians, an internal solar-powered motor deep within the orbiting weapon opened a small door. As the motor whirred, an odd-looking black spiral probe extended outward and pointed down toward the earth's surface.

The Su-35 fighters orbited at thirty-five thousand feet in a ten-mile-long racetrack pattern within the large training area. Both pilots were well trained and knew there was plenty riding on the success of the test. They confirmed with each other and the control center that their central computer and interrogator systems were operating properly. The pilots placed their IFF transponders in the planned test position. They then waited for the indication that their aircraft had received the satellite's transmission.

At the precise moment, a burst signal was transmitted from the satellite down toward the earth over the central Iran training area. The signal was intended to run for only ten seconds, long enough to penetrate the software system of the Sukhoi fighters, but not long enough that any US eavesdropping would be able to identify the location, nature or intent of the signal.

The Chinese and Iranian scientists had bet much on the success of this risky venture. Over one-third of Iran's available funds were tied up in this activity. Failure was not an option, or at least not a survivable option if you were one of the unlucky scientists. Or if you were Katari.

The multifunction display panel in both Su-35 fighters flashed as their IFF transponders began transmitting an interrogation signal. The pilots, per their instructions, attempted to shut down their systems, but the transmissions continued.

"I have indication of code activation," remarked the chief test pilot over his encrypted radio communication to the eagerly awaiting control room.

"I also have code activation," replied the wingman flying opposite the test pilot in the racetrack pattern.

The control room was silent for a few minutes as the staff waited for the Ayatollah to react. Batani looked around the room, stroking his scraggly gray beard, and finally said, *"Allahu Akbar."* His proclamation was then followed by unanimous shouts of the same chant from all those present. The Epsilon code had been successfully triggered.

———————•———————

Back at Peterson AFB, Colonel Bell was called by the technician on duty.

"Sir, I just got a report from one of our assets. An RC-135 patrolling the Persian Gulf picked up a weird signal out of Iran. It wasn't like anything they'd seen before, and it only lasted about ten seconds."

"Where was it generated from?" asked Bell.

"Well, sir, that's the strange thing. The RC believed it came from space, not from another aircraft."

"Hmm, very interesting. Did they get any indication of who or what received the signal?"

"No, sir, it didn't last long enough for them to track it to its destination."

"Okay, make sure you get it into the daily log. I think it might have been a test of the last communication satellites they launched. Probably a verification test that they could transmit data back into Iran."

———•———

The next step in the Iranian Caliphate was about to begin.

Chapter 49

"This is a great day for the holy Caliphate. You have done well, Khalil. The Supreme Leader is pleased with your work," Katari announced.

The phone call announced Epsilon's successful test and sent Khalil into a temporary state of euphoria. He was relieved, to say the least, that the software worked as Iran intended.

"Thank you, Dr. Katari. I am ready to move forward at your direction." *Fantastic news*, thought Khalil, although he had been pretty confident that his brilliant efforts would produce success. Finally, there was proof of Epsilon's capability.

It was now up to him to keep his team focused. He had to keep a sharp eye on the final government review coming up and needed to prevent any overzealous engineer from tinkering with the code. There was always *one* engineer who overprepared for a review, looking for anomalies in the code architecture, trying to determine if there were any unintended consequences from all the work that had been done to make the code perfect. Khalil knew he couldn't afford to have anyone focus too intently on the interrogator system patch or perform too much analysis of the changes he made.

At this point, there was no turning back from his treason. Khalil accepted the fact that he would face the consequences if things turned really bad and he was discovered to have deliberately sabotaged the most important Air Force upgrade of the decade. He could get over being labeled a traitor by the people he had grown close to. After all, they weren't like him, and none of them would ever understand the cause he believed in with all his heart.

He still carried a deep-seated hatred for the Americans, given what they had done to his parents and siblings. He believed they were clearly responsible for their deaths. Even his sister's death he attributed to the sustained American hatred of his culture and his faith. Even though the perpetrators of the heinous attack on Ana had eventually been caught—a result of loose talk from too much whiskey—it didn't change anything in Khalil's mind. They were ultimately responsible for her death. No, he would have his revenge. His retribution would be a thousand times greater than the destruction of his family. And he swore to himself that he would not be caught.

His window of time was closing fast, with only mere weeks remaining before the software program's sell-off. The late-night hours on the Independence Day weekend found the lab empty. The company's facilities were mostly dark and quiet, shut down to give its employees time to celebrate with their families. There was one guard maintaining security at the single main entry door. He chided Khalil jokingly for not taking the time off to go enjoy the fireworks and other festivities around the greater Dallas area. Khalil gave him a couple good-natured excuses. He said he was looking forward to the fireworks, and hopefully he would be done checking his team's work on the most important project Omega ever had.

"I've got to ensure that the software we're selling to the government is perfect. After all, your pension is riding on its success," Khalil joked.

"Then by all means, Mr. Ruffa, press ahead. We really appreciate the sacrifice you're making," he said.

Khalil worked nonstop in the empty lab, moving at a pace that even surprised himself. But again, he knew this software better than anyone else. Within a twelve-hour period, he tested it multiple times. It was ready. But he continued to obsess over one thing. *The final review will be excruciatingly detailed, with intense scrutiny. Epsilon must stay invisible.*

He still believed that if it hadn't been discovered by now, it was unlikely to be detected. Khalil left the lab after spending the entire night there. As he exited the building, he saw that the guard had changed, the previous one replaced at the end of his shift. The new guard had been briefed that Khalil was in the lab and waved at him as he headed for his pickup truck.

The final weeks signaled the end of the upgrade program and the approval of the expensive Air Force project. Khalil's team was hard at work going through the final steps to gain approval by the government for the completed software program. The military had strict standards, checks and balances, required in each phase of the final integration, test, verification and delivery of the software upgrade program. Each phase had rigorous oversight by both government and Omega engineers. As such, Khalil spent an inordinate amount of his time in the lab—he would be ready if any issues arose.

The final review proceeded on schedule. Fortunately, nothing major was noted, and only very minor tweaks were subsequently needed. The Air Force approved the final version of the Raptor's central computer software in the Omega lab, with both the government and company representatives celebrating this major step. At this point, everything was set to load and certify the new software in a Raptor test aircraft.

Khalil made the trip out to Edwards Air Force Base, along with Lieutenant Casey, to support final testing. In the crisp dry air of this high desert location, he supervised every integration activity as well as its test in a static Raptor test aircraft. As they stood in the Edwards hangar watching the testing proceed, Khalil couldn't help but sweat a bit. He trusted that his criminal efforts would not be discovered as the test pilot verified the fidelity of the program through the lengthy criteria. The government oversight team, along with the lead pilot and test engineer from Edwards AFB, verified the operational integrity of the program over the course of a long day. Virtually every aspect of the code's function was tested in the jet, and the results could not have been better.

As the Raptor powered down, the pilot offered a thumbs-up. Casey was so excited that she inadvertently hugged Khalil, catching him off guard.

"We did it," she squealed excitedly and then, capturing her composure, reluctantly pushed herself away from Khalil.

She looked quickly around to see if anyone had witnessed her emotional outburst. Khalil smiled back at her and extended his hand to professionally congratulate his Air Force program partner.

"Congratulations, Rebecca. You've done an outstanding job guiding this program to fruition. It appears to work phenomenally, and you did it on time and under budget!"

"Our next steps are to proceed with operational test and evaluation at Nellis, followed by the aircraft upgrade—the retrofit of all the F-22s," she said. "You'll be a key part of that activity as well, Khalil."

The program plan called for aircraft retrofit installs—modifications—of the new central computer hardware and software to begin quickly. The production hardware kits were ready, their design having been frozen months before. Omega engineers would perform the aircraft modifications at each base to quickly bring the Raptors to their new combat configuration.

Casey smiled back at him and said, "Khalil, I know how hard you and your team worked to make all this possible. You have no idea how important this project is to the Air Force and to our country—and to me! I can't thank you enough."

She paused a moment, thinking to herself that they both were staying in Palmdale for the night. Rebecca did her best to hide the smile that was growing on her face but couldn't hide the slight blush on her cheeks as she thought of the potential evening activity. Khalil caught it all and just winked back at her. He quickly looked around, careful to not draw any undue attention to the obvious closeness that had developed between them.

After shaking hands with the test team in the hangar, the long day at Edwards was over, but the evening was just beginning. They drove down the desolate road out of Edwards, the dry desert lake bed zipping by on their left. They headed back toward Rosamond and then turned north toward Antelope Valley and Palmdale. They were both staying at the Marriott and arrived at the hotel forty-five minutes later. After standing in the warm hangar all day watching the testing, they headed down the hallway to their respective rooms to shower.

As Khalil passed Rebecca's door, he said, "I'll see you in an hour for dinner. Sound good?"

Before he could take another step, Rebecca looked quickly down the deserted hallway and then grabbed Khalil's hand, pulling him into her room.

"Let's conserve a little water," she said. "After all, we're in a drought here in California, and I'm *all* for doing my part. Are you?"

Khalil knew when to say yes to an offer, and this was one of those times. He slowly shut the door behind them, but not before hanging the "Do Not Disturb" sign on their door handle.

Chapter 50

Captain Matt "Ace" Black was excited about the important changes coming to his jet after a few years of flying the Raptor. The normal array of problems every maturing aircraft endures were finally getting addressed.

He glanced over at Flamer, who had just lifted a glass of his favorite amber-colored fifteen-year-old single malt Scotch whiskey to his lips. Ace grabbed his own glass, reached across, and clinked his against Flamer's.

"Here's to the success of our aircraft upgrade program. The central computer modifications are getting ready to ramp up, and I, for one, can't wait to put my jet through its paces with the all the new problem fixes, *and* the added capability."

"Roger that, Ace. We're *really* gonna be able to kick ass when it's done."

A few of their fellow aviators walked over, intent on joining Matt and Flamer for some Friday night camaraderie, fellowship, and bullshit. Every Raptor pilot eagerly anticipated the important modifications. They heard that the operational flight program, or OFP, consisting of the new Omega software and hardware had gotten through its initial certification at Edwards AFB. From there, it had been sent directly to the Test Group at Nellis AFB. After a thorough operational test and evaluation was completed on a Raptor test bird, the new modification was approved for installation into the entire F-22 fleet.

———•———

"Khalil, I think everything looks ready to start the installs," stated Lieutenant Rebecca Casey over the phone.

"Thanks to you, Rebecca, we are ready to move out," he replied.

"I'm glad *you* are going to be leading the first group of mods at Langley," she said, knowing that for these initial aircraft, it would be done right. She was certain that Khalil would guarantee success.

"Will you be joining me at Langley?" he asked. Khalil hoped that Casey would be there to further cement the positive bond he had been building with her, both professionally *and* personally.

"I'm not sure yet that I can make the initial kickoff, but I should be able to come down a few weeks into the effort."

With that conversation completed, Khalil pulled his team together and reviewed the central computer upgrade plans. The software program was solid, and included the interrogator improvements. There were enough hardware kits available to support all of the first squadron's requirements—undoubtedly the 94th Fighter Squadron, based on the information he had been given. He was absolutely convinced that his team could get the jets modified quickly, barring any unforeseen problems in the aircraft that he couldn't control.

———————— • ————————

When the team arrived at Norfolk International Airport, their rental cars were waiting. They luckily beat the rush-hour traffic that normally clogs the heavily populated area around the airport, home to a number of United States military installations. They headed through the tunnel under the James River towards Hampton and Langley Air Force Base. They had their access already prearranged by the Raptor Program Office and made their way to the maintenance complex adjacent to the flight line. Looking across the expansive aircraft parking ramp, they could see the Raptors under their sunshade shelters, some with Air Force mechanics performing maintenance, others with trucks pumping jet fuel for upcoming training missions.

Khalil headed over to the 1st Maintenance Group building to meet the officer who would facilitate the team's unrestricted access to the aircraft. As they entered the building, they were met by Colonel Brett Carswell, the group commander, and with him the top enlisted man in the group, Chief Master Sergeant Tommy Hartman.

"Welcome to Langley," the colonel said to Khalil and his team.

After a few brief introductions, he said, "The chief will take you to the maintenance hangar, where we've set up your temporary office area with Wi-Fi connectivity, phones, tables and chairs, and the other things you requested. Once you get settled, let's meet at sixteen hundred hours today to discuss the plan to modify my jets."

"Yes, sir, that should be no problem," replied Khalil. "We really appreciate the accommodations you are providing, and we'll be ready to brief you later today."

Chief Hartman led the Omega group to their work area and advised them that he would provide a familiarization tour after the briefing. He also told Khalil that all the modification kits for the upgrade had arrived, and were securely stored nearby. Air Force technicians would make sure the team had the parts they needed when they requested them and would also provide any additional technical and logistics support required.

Khalil wasted no time directing the team to set up their work area to help facilitate the modification planning and control. The installation on all twenty-four jets in the first squadron would likely take about forty-five days. Khalil planned to oversee every one, even with the teams working two eight-hour shifts.

Colonel Carswell and his maintenance staff assembled in the conference room late in the afternoon. Each squadron from the Maintenance Group was represented, along with senior officers from the three fighter squadrons. There were also a few of their sharpest, most knowledgeable Raptor pilots present. Captain Matt "Ace" Black fit into the latter category. He had plenty of experience putting the Raptor through its paces, both in peacetime and in combat, and knew firsthand what problems needed to be fixed. As such, his commander had made him the project lead for the 94th Fighter Squadron. Once the squadron had their aircraft modified, the Omega team would continue on with the 27th and 71st Fighter Squadrons.

Captain Black watched the Omega team enter the room and immediately picked out their leader. He could tell from the way the well-dressed and clearly fit man walking ahead of the group handled himself through the introductions around the table. Khalil took his seat next to Colonel Carswell.

Matt Black looked straight into the eyes of the Omega team leader, not quite sure why he was intrigued by him. He could feel a kind of strength emanating from him. And for some odd reason, he felt a common bond. *Weird*, he thought.

Khalil's lead engineer gave a thorough briefing on virtually every aspect of the retrofit plan. When he had concluded his presentation, he took questions from the attendees.

"Is this mod going to finally fix our IFF problem?" asked Matt Black, directing his question not to the lead engineer but to Khalil. "We've been told that the interrogator fix is integrated into the central computer upgrade. It's a really big deal to us." Matt didn't go any further in talking about the issue and waited for Khalil to respond.

"Sir, without a doubt, we've fixed the flickering system issue. I have personally worked the problem, and the patch in the code has been thoroughly tested. You won't have the issues you saw in combat anymore," Khalil said, telling the group exactly what they wanted to hear.

Inwardly, he smiled to himself, knowing how the embedded Epsilon code would actually work when activated. *What you will have is the destruction of your fleet when we trigger Epsilon in combat*, he thought to himself, keeping his emotions in check.

Chapter 51

T he first stealth fighter was in place before the team arrived at 0600 hours. They were met by their hosts, Air Force maintenance technicians, who had positioned the first retrofit kit on a table near the aircraft. The hangar was equipped with all the necessary equipment, including electrical power, hydraulic and other servicing capability, as well as other essentials to support the mod. This first aircraft already had the old central computer hardware removed and the bay prepped to accept the new equipment, per Omega's request.

Khalil conducted his pre-task brief with his day shift engineers, and once it was completed, they wasted no time getting started. His team was well trained in working with the new hardware and software modifications. They had gotten some time at Nellis AFB on one of the operational test Raptors and had already figured out how to cut off some schedule time. By the end of the second shift, the new equipment was in the first jet. Khalil was pleased with the first day's accomplishments.

The next day, the team was hard at work trying to wring out a couple of minor issues they encountered when loading the software program. They had expected as much, since Langley's operational jet configuration could sometimes be slightly ahead of the Nellis test aircraft configuration, but they quickly resolved the problems. Khalil was happy this first upgrade had gone pretty much as he had expected. He moved to the small portable cubicle in the hangar to prepare his daily brief to the colonel.

Just then, the door on the flight line side of the hangar opened, and Matt Black stepped in. He had just finished his debrief after returning from a training mission and thought he would check on the progress.

"How's my jet coming along?" Matt shouted across the hangar to Khalil.

"Hi, Captain Black. We're doing just fine. We just finished this aircraft ahead of schedule and are ready for the next one. Let me show you our modification flow plan on our display boards over here," Khalil said as he walked Matt over to the side of the hangar.

Khalil went through every step of the process to complete the mod, pointing to the various steps the team had completed, and the flow plan for the remaining jets. He clearly impressed Matt with his detailed explanation and his absolute knowledge of how the Raptor's complex software program operated.

"Impressive. If you keep the same pace with the rest of my jets, we may get these Raptors done well ahead of schedule," Matt said with a wide grin on his face.

"As long as the jets are serviceable when they roll in here and are prepped for us per the plan, we should be able to finish early," Khalil replied. "I'm headed over for an office visit with Colonel Carswell. He asked for a short update when we finished the first aircraft."

They both headed over to the Maintenance Group Commander's office, quickly briefed the colonel, and then stepped back outside. As they walked away from the building, the sun was low on the horizon and a warm breeze was blowing a salty spray from the east, right off the water near the end of the runway.

"Hey, if you have some time, come on over to meet some of the guys. They sure would like to know who is taking good care of our aircraft and *who* the guy is that's fixing that interrogator issue."

"I think I've got some time now. Lead the way, Captain."

Big cumulus clouds had been building up over the water, and the air was now beginning to smell a bit like a rain shower might be coming soon. As they approached the entrance, Khalil saw the red, white and blue Hat in the Ring emblem over the door. Upon entering, Matt introduced Khalil to several of the pilots, as well as his buddy, Flamer Lightner. Since it was well after 1700 hours, the light over the bar was already lit and the beer had begun to flow.

"What's your pleasure, Khalil, beer or beer?" the officer behind the bar shouted.

"Just some ice water for me," replied Khalil, getting some immediate hostile looks from some of the pilots around him. "My Muslim faith discourages drinking alcohol. But don't let me stop you guys from enjoying yourselves," he added with a smile.

Khalil got some curious looks from around the bar.

"Sorry about that," said Matt, not wanting to insult Khalil or his faith.

He was a bit surprised, though, for some reason, that a Muslim was leading one of the most classified efforts ongoing within the Department of the Air Force. His thoughts flashed briefly to one of the darkest days in America—September 11, 2001, and the attacks on his country. He shook his head to clear his thinking. He came to the quick conclusion that most Muslims were good, solid citizens of the United States. And *this* particular one was an expert on his jet. The nutballs, the terrorists with radical Islamic ideas, would never get the kind of access to the F-22 that Khalil had.

"Please, Captain, no offense taken," replied Khalil.

And with that, the beer flowed. Khalil and Matt sat on the barstools and began to shoot the breeze on subjects ranging from sports, to politics, and eventually to the subject every red-blooded guy likes to talk about—women!

———— • ————

As the weeks went by, the retrofit of Langley's F-22s proceeded superbly. Rebecca Casey came down from Fairborn to compliment her Omega engineering team on their performance—and of course, she wanted to spend some time with Khalil. She hadn't seen him in over a month and couldn't stop thinking of him. She still remembered their last sensual encounter and longed for another chance to light her fire!

Lieutenant Casey checked into the Courtyard by Marriott, just off Mercury Boulevard, the main thoroughfare running from Interstate 64 to the base. She dumped her bags on the bed, grabbed the keys to the rental car and headed back out the door. The drive to the base was a short one. She drove down Mercury, then turned on the short stretch to the old King Street gate and then across the rickety bridge over the small tributary of the James River that took her around the Officers' Club and toward the flight line.

When she reached the parking lot near the maintenance hangar where the retrofit team was working, she found the space reserved for her. She quickly crossed the narrow two-lane street over to the hangar, gained access to the restricted flight line area, and headed in. Khalil didn't see her enter, deeply engrossed in a technical problem he was intent on quickly solving. Rebecca came up behind him and tapped his shoulder with her hand.

"I'm busy right now. Don't bother me!" Khalil shouted over the hum of the equipment running in the hangar.

Rebecca slapped his shoulder harder this time, expecting now to get a reaction. She got a reaction all right, although not the one she was expecting. Khalil whipped around, his face a bit contorted in anger, thinking he was being interrupted by one of his team with an annoying question. He caught himself before he could utter anything he might regret.

"Rebecca—I mean Lieutenant Casey," he said, glancing around to see who might have heard him get too familiar with his government program boss.

"You better watch yourself," she said with a stern look on her face, which then melted away quickly into a smile.

"I didn't think you would be here this soon. Sorry for snapping at you."

"Don't worry about it, Khalil. You have been hard at it for several weeks and making great progress. I know you're under some pretty intense pressure by us and the 1st Fighter Wing leadership to get these jets done quickly."

"That's no excuse for my behavior. Sorry again. Let me show you on our display boards how we are progressing."

As Khalil covered the team's progress, he was pleased to show his lieutenant that more than two-thirds of the 94th Fighter Squadron jets were already done, and at the rate they were going, they would finish early. Rebecca had been closely following the daily situation reports coming from the team and knew how well things were going. Her boss and, more importantly, *his* boss, the system program director for the F-22, were both absolutely elated at Omega's performance. They were more than happy to up-channel that information to the Pentagon and Department of the Air Force, both eager to see the changes made in their most important fighter aircraft. The added combat capability that came with the retrofit was important to future battle planning, if combat became necessary. In the world they lived in, it was necessary all too often.

She spent a couple of hours in the hangar watching the Omega team install the upgrade on a Raptor. Rebecca was impressed with their knowledge and the speed with which they worked. She relished getting close to the action, to the work that put the capability she managed as an acquisition officer onto a jet.

Lieutenant Casey headed over to the 94th Fighter Squadron to make a courtesy call with her ultimate customers, the pilots who flew this warbird. She also stopped in to say hello to the commanders of both the Maintenance and Operations Groups, then made a visit to the wing commander, Brigadier General Butch McCoy. As expected, she was warmly welcomed and congratulated for the professionalism and competence of the Omega team.

When the day began to fade, she met Khalil, per their agreement, at the small lounge in the Courtyard Marriott. The concierge had just uncorked a nice merlot, and Rebecca grabbed a glass and found a secluded spot on a large red leather couch. Khalil arrived a few minutes later and, seeing her wave at him, wandered over to where she was sitting.

"Well, I understand your visits to the base big shots went well," he said, sitting down across from her.

"Let me tell you, Khalil, it couldn't have gone better. I hope you keep the team focused and get the other two squadrons done as quickly as the 94th. It would be great to have this same kind of response from the leadership once we're done. After all, if they're happy, my boss is happy." She looked devilishly at him with a twinkle in her eye and added, "And I'm pretty happy too."

Khalil knew exactly what she meant, having spent enough time with her to fully understand her ravenous desires to be with him.

He thought about how useful she was to his critical work on the F-22—work that would change America and elevate Iran to its rightful leadership role in the Islamic world. The sex with her wasn't too bad either.

He smiled at Rebecca as he thought about the encounter that was about to happen.

———————•———————

Two hours later, Khalil rolled out of the bed and told Rebecca that he needed to head back to the hangar to check on his team. Nothing serious, he told her, just routine stuff that needed his oversight. She was not at all pleased with Khalil leaving so quickly and tried her best to make him stay.

"It can't be *that* important, Khalil. It can wait till morning," she pleaded, displaying a pitiful pout and the saddest eyes she could muster. "I have to leave tomorrow to return to Fairborn."

Khalil insisted he had to leave and, after pulling on his clothes, told her he would try to call her in the morning before she left.

The sacrifices I must make in the name of my faith, he thought as he headed for the hotel door, smiling. *Especially with an infidel woman, one who clearly doesn't even respect her own body if she is willing to engage in these actions with me.*

He felt that his behavior was *truly* acceptable if it helped propagate the radical brand of Islam that his imam and the Ayatollah espoused.

THOMAS BELISLE

Chapter 52

t is sometimes said that, in very rare circumstances, the planets do in fact align. After nearly twenty years since their individual lives had been so tragically altered by a single event, what was the likelihood that the lives of two very different men, worlds apart in so many ways, would once again intersect?

One man was the son of an Air Force fighter pilot. He had been given pretty much everything in life by parents who wanted to ensure he had all the opportunities to succeed. Even after his father's death, he had continued to reap the benefits that the United States provided its citizens—a great education, access to world-class medical care, and of course, the opportunity to chase his dreams.

The other man was the son of a Syrian goat farmer, a peasant. He had been raised for his first few years in poverty, in a country torn apart by war. But in spite of their country's situation, his parents had made sure that there was always enough to eat. The tragic loss of his father, mother, and brothers, although horrific, had eventually resulted in opportunity he might never have realized in Syria. Some small bit of fortune had come his way through his adoption by his uncle. That had opened the door to him for opportunities to make something out of his life. Especially when his uncle had taken him and his sister out of Syria to Great Britain, and finally on to the United States. In America, they had been offered the same benefits that every citizen enjoyed.

Of course, neither of these two men had any real idea of the very personal connection that existed between them—their common bond. They were about to find out—the convergence of their lives seemed to be almost predestined.

———•———

Langley's Raptor fleet was already enjoying the benefits of the new upgrade. Captain Matt "Ace" Black couldn't have been more pleased. Nearly all of his squadron's twenty-four Raptors had been modified and were now being flown in the new configuration. Without exception, every pilot who strapped in to an upgraded F-22 was thoroughly impressed with its added performance capability. Additionally, it was clear that the nagging IFF interrogator problem finally appeared to be fixed.

Matt had been getting to know Khalil pretty well. Every few days, they got together for a meal and to discuss the progress, sometimes meeting at the Officers Club, other times at places that Matt believed were less of an offense to card-carrying Muslims who abhorred the consumption of alcohol. It didn't seem to matter to Khalil, or if it did, he didn't show it. Matt never seemed to get any indication that Khalil was in any way upset over him having an occasional beer. But regardless of what Khalil might have thought, Matt was sensitive to their respective cultural and religious differences.

During one quiet dinner they were both enjoying in a local Thai restaurant, the subject of their early childhood came up in conversation. From their previous discussions, they were both familiar enough with each other's professional background. Their childhood was new territory for exploration. They both headed down the path somewhat innocently.

"You are pretty fortunate to have such a senior position, one with so much responsibility," Khalil remarked. "I was impressed that you were given ownership for this key aircraft upgrade. That must be a true indicator of your importance and skill as a fighter pilot."

"Hey, I'm not a senior guy *or* that important in the overall pecking order! I'm just a captain. My boss just felt that I was the right guy to oversee this modification. But I *am* fortunate, Khalil. I've always wanted to be a fighter pilot since I was a small boy. My dad was a fighter pilot as well, and I wanted to be just like him. Jets always intrigued me—their speed, their lethality. When I was young, I had quite a few models of my favorite aircraft, and pictures of most of them were plastered all over my bedroom walls." He smiled as he thought about those joyous days.

"My dad would take me to his squadron to get a close-up look at the jets. It was awesome. We also went to air shows, and boy, the stuff Air Force fighter jets could do, even back then, was just extraordinary."

"Your father was a pilot just like you? He must be very proud of you and what you have accomplished."

"I'll never really know if he's proud of me, Khalil. He was killed when I was only thirteen. But I guess he must be watching me from the hereafter—and I hope he *would* be pretty proud of what I've been doing with my life."

"I'm sorry to hear that you had such a tragedy as a boy. We share a similar loss in our lives. My father was also killed when I was a boy," replied Khalil. "In fact, when I was only eight years old, my whole family, except for my sister, was killed."

Matt sat still for a few moments, a stunned look on his face. Khalil pushed his dinner plate away from him, his spicy Thai chicken and rice only half-eaten. The thoughts racing through his mind had ruined any remaining appetite he might have had. As they both sat in silence, Matt noticed a change in Khalil. The look on his face made Matt sit back in his chair. It wasn't so much the pain that he noticed but instead what appeared to be a slow, growing anger—something in his facial expression that looked almost like rage.

"That's awful. I'm so sorry to hear that, Khalil," exclaimed Matt. "It must have been pretty hard for you. I know it was hard for me, but at least I had my mother to raise me. I can't imagine losing both my parents. I can see it still bothers you a lot, and I completely understand."

Khalil relaxed a bit, having recognized that his entire demeanor had changed in that instant. He took a deep breath, his chest heaving slightly as he regained his composure.

"It was a long time ago, in another land," Khalil stated, looking down at his plate.

"Hey, let's change the subject," Matt instructed. "You haven't finished dinner, and I'm afraid our conversation has ruined what's left."

"It's all right. Thinking about what happened, at least what I had been told had happened, brings back the pain that I thought I had outgrown. I believed that I had learned how to suppress it, make it disappear."

"Well, I know in my case, the pain never really goes away," said Matt. "But at least I know that my dad died while serving his country, trying to stop the evil that existed in the world back then. In fact, that evil still exists," he said. "Maybe it's *my* turn to deal with it, to eliminate it."

Intrigued by Matt's discussion about the circumstances of his father's death, Khalil pressed him for more information.

"Was he in combat, flying an American fighter jet when he was killed?"

"Yeah, he was flying a mission in the Middle East—in Syria, in fact. It's my understanding that the mission was to eliminate one of the world's most wanted terrorists at that time—someone affiliated with a particularly brutal group known then as Black Dawn."

Khalil sat straight up in his chair when he heard the name. At first he just tried to process in his brain what he just heard. *Can this be?*

Matt continued, "Khalil, my dad was an F-15E pilot flying out of RAF Lakenheath Air Base in England. He led a strike force that took out the terrorist and hopefully helped spare the lives of so many Syrian citizens who had lived in the horror that Black Dawn inflicted on them."

As Matt went on, Khalil stared intently at him.

"Unfortunately, the cost was pretty steep. A sadistic terrorist was removed from the earth"—his voice now grew a bit softer—"but my father was shot down and didn't survive."

As Matt looked down at his plate, he said, "I lost my best friend that day."

As he continued to focus on Matt's eyes, Khalil said, "I can see that your father's death affected you greatly as well. Even though it was a long time ago, the pain is still there. I can see it in your eyes. You said you were thirteen then, so it was 1993 or thereabout?"

"I'll never forget the date. It *was* 1993. June twenty-eighth, 1993!"

Khalil did his best not to react, but he knew the date quite well. That date was very personal to him—imprinted like a flaming-hot brand into his memory. The date was the day he and his sister memorialized the tragic death of their family each year as they grew up. It was the date when the Americans had taken his family from him—the date that his life and the life of his sister had changed forever. That date he would *never* forget, until he obtained some measure of retribution from the country that destroyed his life.

"I think I need to head back to the hangar and check up on my second shift," Khalil said abruptly.

He needed to quickly get away from this dinner conversation. Away from the son of the man who had ripped his life apart.

"Okay, Khalil. Sorry for the somber tone of the dinner conversation. I promise to make it a bit more upbeat the next time we get together," said Matt.

They shook hands as they left the restaurant before heading to their respective cars. As Khalil walked away, his face was contorted in rage, reflecting the same feelings he had felt in the restaurant. But now, besides hating the United States and everything it stood for, he had a very specific person on whom to focus his hatred— Captain Matt "Ace" Black!

As he drove from the parking lot, Khalil's mind was spinning wildly. A pleasant dinner had turned into an infusion of disjointed thoughts. He thought about his family—his father and mother, his brothers. He saw his sister's face as well, just as clearly as if she was sitting next to him. He saw the face of his uncle, his father, who had been a major influence on him, helping him grow into manhood, helping him achieve everything he had accomplished. He also saw the face of his imam, Sheikh Rahainee, his tutor and mentor, who had shaped his thinking, turning his seething resentment for those who had taken his family into a holy mission—a mission of destruction!

How could this possibly be? Allah has truly blessed me with this impossible unlikely encounter. Beyond all odds, I have met the man whose father destroyed my life. This is a holy message for me. It is clearly a divine signal from Allah that my destiny is tied to completing the most important task I have ever been given. I will ensure that all the Raptor aircraft get their deadly modifications. Epsilon will be silently sleeping, buried deep within the Raptors, until the time comes when it is activated—and then Islam will triumph! The American fleet of stealth fighters will be destroyed, along with Captain Matt Black! Allahu Akbar!

Khalil smiled as he drove away, imagining the expected joyfulness once he extracted his personal piece of revenge for his family's brutal death. All that remained was the completion of the Langley aircraft modifications, and then the modification of all the other F-22s scattered throughout the United States and the world. He expected Omega's additional teams would deploy to every Raptor base and begin the same upgrade—and compete them all within six months, per the USAF's plan.

He seethed as he recalled what he had been told by Matt Black, and the direct link to his family. While the young fighter pilot had lost a father, he had perished while attacking Khalil's country, the Syrian people.

He deserved to die. His father was responsible! The arrogant Americans cared nothing for the Syrian people. The infidels constantly stuck their noses into the Muslim world, and nothing good ever came of it—only destruction and death. As his anger continued to boil, Khalil wished he could personally inflict the most terrible pain imaginable on Matt. *Blood must pay with blood.*

He knew that at some point in the near future, he would have his revenge when the Raptors were shot out of the sky. The retribution he sought would come from the shocked look on the arrogant faces of the American pilots as Iranian missiles homed in on their stealthy jets. Epsilon would make their Raptors bloom for Iranian missiles to target—the jets no longer stealthy, no longer invulnerable. He would end their lives. Whether Matt Black would feel the pain of being struck from the sky, tumbling to the ground in flaming wreckage, was a question he couldn't yet answer. But he truly hoped Matt would be among the dead.

Chapter 53

In the morning, Khalil arrived at the hangar as his team was busy completing the final aircraft modification. With the last of the first squadron's jets done, Khalil had passed the responsibility to his on-site engineering manager to finish the remaining Langley jets. He planned to return to Omega and provide the full report on the first squadron's successful modifications. Before departing, he made a final call on the Fighter Wing leadership. He thanked them for the great support and assured them that he was leaving the remaining jets in good hands.

He also made a final visit to the 94th Fighter Squadron to say goodbye to the commander and to Matt Black. As he walked in the door, several of the pilots waved to him. A few came over to shake his hand and congratulate him on the great job he had done. As Khalil shook their hands, he couldn't help but look into their eyes and wonder if he would be looking at them for the last time.

Will they all be victims of the deadly code buried deep within the Raptor's software program?

"Hey, Khalil, great to see you," said Matt as he walked over and extended his hand to greet him. "Hope you got some sleep after our dinner last night. I know the conversation was a bit unnerving, but I enjoyed talking with you."

"Likewise," Khalil said. "I just wanted to say goodbye before I head back to Omega. My job's done here, but my team will press ahead with the remaining two fighter squadrons. We've got a good tempo going and I don't expect any problems. But I'll continue to monitor their progress."

"I can't thank you enough," replied Matt. "I look forward to seeing you again sometime."

Khalil would have liked to tell Matt the fate that would eventually come to him and his Air Force. He would have loved to explain to him the impending destruction of the Raptors and violent deaths that would happen to all the F-22 pilots if they decided to foolishly attack Iran. He would have enjoyed seeing the reaction on Matt's face if he could tell him his fate. It would be fitting for Matt to understand that, in a particularly personal way, he would pay for his father's savage actions in Syria many years before. Khalil could never forgive what the Americans had done.

But clearly, he could not say a word about what was to come. No, this would have to be a *great* surprise to the American pilots.

———•———

After six months of Omega's aggressive performance around the country at every Raptor base, the fleet modifications were complete. With the conclusion of the latest Department of Defense-funded upgrade, the F-22s now possessed more lethal capability than ever before. The entire Raptor fleet of 187 aircraft had received the expensive central computer upgrade, giving the aircraft the ability to use some of the latest, most advanced weapons available in the world. It also resolved many of the nuisance problems that cropped up over time during thousands of flying hours.

The Omega Company had delivered on its promise to design, develop, produce, and install the upgrade—and they had accomplished the extremely complex and difficult challenge ahead of schedule and under budget. The nature of their performance contract meant large bonuses for the company. Their success would hopefully guarantee many future projects from the Department of Defense.

Lieutenant Rebecca Casey was a hero in the hallways of the expansive Wright-Patterson AFB headquarters. She had successfully led an effort that many were skeptical could be completed without extensive cost and technical problems. Her performance in this important effort supported her upcoming promotion and advancement to the rank of captain.

Omega rewarded Khalil Ruffa handsomely for his performance. Beyond a fat cash bonus, he was offered a promotion to vice president of Omega's Advanced Projects Division. Khalil enjoyed the notoriety that came with all the praise and financial rewards. He believed he had more than earned it. The upgrade had been difficult. It delivered everything that the Air Force had wanted in improved capability. More importantly, as a direct result of Khalil's personal touch in the critical software development, the Air Force was getting a little something extra.

Chapter 54

The situation in the Middle East was beginning to boil over. The strength of radical elements seemed to increase over time, enhanced by their acquisition of advanced weaponry from countries willing to disregard international arms sales prohibitions. As their numbers increased exponentially, their influence across the Middle East spread like wildfire. Well-trained elements of the Caliphate, directed by Iran's Ayatollah Batani, led uprisings within key cities across the region. The numbers of violent religious zealots dedicated to the Caliphate swelled to the point that they threatened the ability of standing armies to control them—especially when the radical groups were supported by Iranian military power.

Iran had done its best to poison the region with their hegemonic aims, providing a holy alternative to the infidel presence that corrupted the Muslim culture and violated every principle of the Islamic faith. Most nations in the Persian Gulf region were eager to remove the finger of Western influence. In the past, they had believed they needed the Americans mainly for protection. But over the years, few had seen any real economic or political gain from US involvement. Some countries had been the recipient of aid in the form of used military hardware. Some received permission to acquire new American weapons and equipment. But the significance of the aid was outweighed by the widespread imprint of Western influence. That imprint was not viewed by most of the Islamic nations as a good thing.

Iran expected it would be difficult at first to assemble a precedent-setting coalition of diverse Muslim nations. Years of hatred between Sunnis and Shiites were going to be extremely tough to overcome. But the likelihood of eliminating American influence, and gaining the protection of an Islamic military power like Iran, was growing in its attractiveness. The promise of free and open commerce, the establishment of strict religious standards under Sharia law, and the protection provided by a new Islamic nuclear powerhouse was enough to coalesce the Gulf nations to form the Group of Seven. Iraq, Kuwait, Bahrain, UAE, Qatar, Syria, and Iran were to be "equal partners" according to the ink on the coalition agreement. But Iran would be the de facto chair of the Group of Seven. Saudi Arabia, at the time the coalition was being formed, was not interested in becoming part of it.

The unprecedented extremely covert meeting had taken place with the coalition state leaders under the guise of an economic forum. The presidents of Iraq, Syria, Qatar, and UAE, the king of Bahrain, the emir of Kuwait, and of course, the Supreme Leader of Iran all attended the meeting in Iran's Imperial Palace. The gathering in the large gilded conference room was the first time the rulers of these Gulf and Arabian nations had come together. Their purpose—to structure an agreement of mutual economic and military benefit, and to potentially unite in a common bond of faith—and a common bond of hate!

The leaders in attendance were divided—those of predominantly Sunni states clustered together, as did those with mostly Shiite populations. That was expected. After all, no matter what the agenda, it was unlikely to bridge the centuries of hate and distrust. It would take more, much more, to gain any truly common agreement.

"I ask your indulgence, some time for me to lay the groundwork for our discussion," the Ayatollah stated.

"I am well aware of our long-standing differences. But thousands of years of animosity toward each other doesn't necessarily portend the same for the next thousand." He let his words sink in.

"These are different times. The West is stronger than they have ever been, and they continue to corrupt our culture. The times call for change. The times demand change. But only the kind of change that can set the geopolitical balance as it should be—a true union of Islamic States!"

The two clusters of religiously disparate leaders cast spurious glances at each other, glances that conveyed the deep-seated hatred, the contempt, the mistrust each group had for the other.

"I know that mere words from me will never gain your trust. Actions are what convey the will and cooperation between any parties trying to reach a mutual agreement."

A few heads nodded, seeming to indicate concurrence, at least with the premise.

"I see infinite strength in our collective union. That strength comes from a common military defense of our holy lands—a common embrace of the true tenets of Islam and the holy Quran—a common set of economic policies related to trade. And, of course, oil."

The heads had stopped nodding. Now there were just silent stares focused on the Ayatollah. Some whispers between leaders. But not one of them was ready to say anything, yet.

"Before you consider rejecting my forthcoming proposal out-right, allow me to offer this. You are all well aware of the corrupting influence of the West. You fully understand the poison they spread on our sacred lands and in our culture. You have all become some-what dependent on the West over the years—due to either war or economic or political problems. But with that dependency came their corruption of our people, our religion, our land.

"You are also aware of the Western alliances with Israel, and the support provided to the Zionist regime. Israel's foothold on the Arabian Peninsula has, since its inception, posed an imminent threat to us all. They are unpredictable, as their past behavior has readily demonstrated. At any time, the Israelis have the capability to strike us all without warning. They have proven this in Syria and Iraq.

"Iran will soon possess the military might that is necessary to secure our collective defense against any aggressor. Our nuclear program is nearly complete, and our ballistic missiles will have the capability to reach any adversary, if our coalition is threatened."

The Ayatollah let his stunning declaration of Iran's nuclear capability spin in the minds.

"I know that you are thinking—how can this be? The West established an agreement to prevent this from happening. Believe me when I say the agreement was worthless and allowed Iran to proceed with the critical development of our much needed weapons."

There were now worried looks—the United States had to know what Iran was doing. Some of them whispered that the US would strike Iran soon. What then? All-out war in the Gulf?

The Ayatollah knew what they were thinking.

"We are taking measures to prevent the Americans from striking our country. Those measures will make certain that we complete our nuclear program before they decide to strike us. And we will make sure the Americans are well aware of the consequences of any attack, and the risk of starting a nuclear exchange. I can't go into detail on our plans at this point. The level of secrecy needed is paramount."

The nods began again, this time with nearly all of the heads of state concurring with the Ayatollah. For the next three hours, the details of what would become a landmark agreement were unfolded. At the heart was a bolstered common military defense program, including an Iranian nuclear arsenal, and supported by the establishment of deployed Iranian forces in each country to help them in the collective defense of the Group of Seven. But the real incentive to the agreement involved something much more onerous. It involved the one thing that there would be unanimous agreement upon by all the leaders—the elimination of the state of Israel.

"You can't be serious," the Iraqi president responded. "How can you think that the Zionists could be eliminated without a massive response by them or their sponsors?" He paused. "Any attack on their country would unleash hell on the attacker—that is if the Israeli spies don't discover what you are doing and attack Iran first."

"The militarization of our nations will present an imposing force," Batani responded. "That force will be coupled with the expulsion of the Americans and other Western forces from the region.

"For now, the Americans will keep Israel in check. They provide tremendous influence over any potential Zionist strike. Once we make our declaration to the world that our nuclear-tipped missiles are in place, Israel would not dare strike our country for fear of a retaliatory nuclear attack. The Israelis have a powerful military, but it is a small one. Our years of advanced fighter aircraft purchases, and the establishment of state-of-the-art air defenses, are formidable enough to stop an Israeli attack. The one ace in the hole they have is their nuclear capability. But we will counter that with our own nuclear weapons."

Again, silence from the potential leaders of the new coalition.

"When the time is right, we can move to defeat Israel. Their military will no longer have their allies, their Western forces, present in the Gulf. If we choose the right time, we can defeat them with a conventional attack. The Israelis don't have the forces to defeat a massive attack from all Gulf nations. And they would never use their nuclear weapons in response to a conventional attack. They would know that any nuclear launch by them would result in a corresponding nuclear launch on Israel and the certain annihilation of the Jewish State. Even if they survived, the fallout in their small country would make it uninhabitable. At the right time, we will decapitate the Israeli snake."

By the meeting's conclusion, the Supreme Leader of Iran had obtained pledges of allegiance from them all in return for protecting them from what many of them viewed as "imperialism" by the United States and most of the NATO nations that placed forces in the Gulf region. The pledges also ensured that Iran, under its soon-to-be "protective" nuclear umbrella, would help build the coalition defenses. This included allowing Iran to disperse their military forces, weapons and equipment around the Persian Gulf, extending the reach of Iran's military influence. It also included mutual training in their respective countries, joint exercises, troop movements, and installation of common air defense systems. The new agreement had some of the same core collective defense tenets the United States had implemented with South Korea to bolster that country's defense against a North Korean attack. As such, the Americans should find nothing out of the ordinary with the Group of Seven agreement.

Additionally, the pledge of allegiance was linked inextricably to unifying the Islamic faith among these states, and aligning themselves with a more radical interpretation of key Quran tenets. The primary message to all—rid the Gulf of the Western presence. In the eyes of the mullahs, there had been too many Gulf countries willing to open their sacred lands to the Western world. The American presence brought with it their corrupt, disgraceful behavior, contaminating the holy ground that had once been home to the Prophet Mohammad. Even one American on their holy ground was one too many.

Most of these countries had tolerated this presence, but secretly, they actually abhorred having Americans in the region. For years, they had hoped there would be an opportunity to remove them permanently.

The United States had used its influence to place bases and outposts in the region. America viewed a foothold in the Gulf, its forward basing of its forces, as absolutely essential to decreasing its reaction time in the event of a crisis there. Without this foothold, the military advantages of forward presence were lost.

Chapter 55

nside Iran, Ayatollah Batani was intensely focused on completing their nuclear testing. He knew the Chinese engineers were miniaturizing devices for the applications the Iranians desired most.

Iran did not seek a long-range ICBM capability—their leadership believed that long-range intercontinental ballistic missiles that could strike the United States would put them in a threat category that would prompt a preemptive strike by the Americans. On the other hand, Iran's neighbors in Pakistan, India, and Israel all had a nuclear capability that could strike at the heart of the Persian soil. The Supreme Leader and Iran's governing body believed that tactical nuclear weapons were the answer. They could fend off neighboring belligerents and any potential American incursion. The weapons would shore up their defense and provide the necessary nuclear umbrella to bring the Gulf states together in a holy Caliphate.

Meanwhile, the civilized world reeled with shock as Iran's declared Caliphate appeared to be effectively uniting both Sunni and Shiite Muslims in a common cause. As time progressed, they had to swallow the cold hard fact that the Group of Seven was rapidly moving forward to eliminate Western influence on their holy ground and in their culture. The principal terrorist state in the region had positioned itself now as the leader of the Caliphate.

———•———

In the desolate nuclear testing area in Southeast Xinjiang, China, it was a day to celebrate. The miniaturized warhead with the fissionable material worked precisely as the brilliant Chinese physicists and engineers had designed it. The resulting tactical nuclear explosion, occurring deep underground, proved the capability of the warhead the Iranians so desperately desired. Receiving word of the successful final test in China, Ayatollah Batani turned to his faithful staff.

He loudly proclaimed, *"Allahu Akbar!* We are now ready to accelerate our weapons production and secure the Caliphate's success."

"It will take us a short time to complete our first six ballistic missile warheads," replied the chief scientist. "Our production facility is ready for the arrival of the final key components from China. They verified that the devices worked as designed, and once we have them, we can have the warheads installed on our delivery vehicles within weeks."

The worried look on the Ayatollah's face surprised the chief scientist.

"We must proceed quickly. We can't trust the Americans—or the Israelis. They undoubtedly know what we have been doing, even though they may not be aware of how close we are to final production of a weapon."

The Ayatollah continued, "We must be prepared to take down any attacking American force. That means stopping the F-22s that will lead the attack."

"Holy one," the chief scientist replied, "the Epsilon trigger is orbiting above us as we speak. It has proven its power to defeat the stealth advantage. Any attack on our homeland will result in the destruction of their aircraft. Epsilon will allow our massive defenses to decimate the attackers before they can hit any of our critical nuclear facilities."

"Waste no time in getting our nuclear warhead production completed. Once we have them installed, the Americans would not dare attack our country for fear of a retaliatory strike of the *worst* kind."

The Ayatollah turned and left the room.

———————•———————

As things continued to heat up across the Middle East, even the Saudis were beginning to rethink their hard-line stance against everything Iran stood for. Most of the other Gulf states, now part of the Group of Seven, had already pledged their allegiance and had ordered Western non-Muslim personnel out of their areas. Although Qatar had reluctantly signed on to the Group of Seven's coalition, they questioned the advantages of aligning themselves with Iran as opposed to the United States. At risk to the Americans in Qatar was the use of the large military base in al-Udeid. That location was a key forward operating location for many of the US military fighter and bomber aircraft. Iran's order directing non-Muslim personnel to vacate the area set in motion a chain of events that would eventually strike at the heart of the US military capability.

Within the United States Department of Defense, the chairman of the Joint Chiefs of Staff met with an array of senior officers and government civilians.

"We're making plans to offset the clearly offensive tactics coming from Iran. It appears they have gotten backing from most of the Gulf states to kick our forces out of the region. If that weren't enough, Assad just unleashed another brutal attack on his own people. We're trying to verify if he used weapons of mass destruction—WMDs. It appears likely they used nerve agents and chlorine in barrel bombs.

"I'm recommending to the president that we move a large contingent of fighters and bombers into the region. We'll obviously avoid the Group of Seven. We'll make this a massive show of force. Our Raptors will be there to lead strikes on Assad and helping patrol the airspace.

"We're also getting some as-yet-unverified intel on developments by Iran on their nuke program. Nothing concrete yet. Their program could be progressing much faster than we anticipated. We'll know more once we can get more tangible information from our sources on the ground there."

Chapter 56

As expected, the Langley Raptors launched at the prescribed hour and headed across the star-studded sky above the cold, blue Atlantic water. They flew toward Central Europe and then turned southeast toward Turkey. They had been there many months before to shut down Assad's barrel bomb production. Clearly it had resurrected itself like a phoenix from the ashes.

The 94th Fighter Squadron and its sister squadron, the 27th Fighter Squadron, executed a perfect flight, using their air bridge of refueling tankers positioned in the skies across the Atlantic Ocean to provide them the gas they needed. The thirsty stealth fighter jets were refueled six times throughout the flight. After twelve hours airborne in the cramped cockpit, Matt was a happy camper when he stepped down on the tarmac. He shook hands with his crew chief, who had beaten him there to personally welcome him to Incirlik.

Over the course of seventy-two hours, the sky over Turkey had been filled with the sounds of arriving Raptors and airlift aircraft bringing in the rest of the supporting personnel and equipment. The F-22s were quickly repositioned into hardened aircraft shelters. These clamshell-shaped reinforced concrete buildings provided a measure of protection from a potential enemy attack, and some cover to shade the jets from the hot summer sun.

The aircraft maintenance mechanics got busy working on the assorted problems that some of the jets had arrived with after the long flight. Their goal was to get as many ready, as quickly as possible, for a combat tasking. The tired pilots knew that a launch order could come at any moment, and many of them tried to get some rest.

The Syrian situation had not improved in the time since Matt Black's father had given his life years before. In fact, it had gotten progressively worse as the United States withheld its forces, afraid of the possibility that they would again be embroiled in another bloody Middle East conflict. More than two decades of combat operations in Iraq and Afghanistan had decimated so many American military families that the public had grown wary of another engagement. But Americans had big hearts and couldn't sit idly by and tolerate Assad's slaughter of innocent people. What little support was provided had been in the form of aiding rebel forces opposed to Bashar al-Assad. Even that support had its limits—almost no military aid was provided directly to them for fear of the arms getting into the hands of Assad's army, already resourced with sufficient men and firepower to handle most rebel actions.

Most of the efforts to help the Syrian people escape Assad's carnage had little effect. As civilian casualty numbers grew, the American president agreed to up the ante to stop it. The forward positioning of a large contingent of Raptors and a substantial number of fighter and bomber aircraft was a major step. That, along with agreements by NATO forces to integrate their aircraft and support personnel into the American effort, was intended to send a strong signal to Assad. It was also intended to send a message to Iran and the Gulf states that the United States had a long and powerful reach. They would be told not to interfere with any US operation in Syria. If massing the potent array of forces was not enough to get Assad's attention, then a major air campaign against the Syrian Army and Air Force would be the next step.

It was already approaching midnight when Captain Matt Black headed to his temporary home away from home, his sleeping quarters, to get some shut-eye. Before turning in, he grabbed some chow at the dining hall, took a steamy shower to wash off the hours of sweat from the flight, and made one Skype call to his bride back at Langley.

"Hey, Julie, as you can see, I made it here okay. How's everything in the zoo?" he said, using his affectionate term for the house with three wild but lovable kids.

"They already miss their father, and I do too," she said, looking at his tired but smiling face on the screen of her iPad.

"Sorry to call so late, but I had to take care of some squadron stuff that couldn't wait. With the time difference, this is the first chance I got to break free. Where are my babies?"

"Let me put the iPad in front of them so you can say hi," she said.

As Matt looked at his children, he again realized how important each one of them was to him. They were his life. They were what gave his life *true* meaning. He fought back the swell of tears in his eyes and talked a couple of minutes to each of them. Julie then turned the screen back to her.

"I hope you're going to be careful over there. The news on TV is not very reassuring. Some people are saying an all-out war is going to break out."

"Hey, baby, I'm always careful when it comes to flying. You know that. Besides, the most important thing to me is finishing up whatever we're going to do here and getting back to you guys." He paused.

"And don't believe everything you hear on the tube. It's usually never as bad as they make it out to be."

"I just want you home, safe and sound," she said. "I hope this mess gets over quickly."

At this point, Julie was wiping tears from her eyes, trying not to show her emotion in front of the kids.

"I love you," she said.

"I love you too, baby. I'll call again when I can."

As he ended the call, he thought how lucky he was to have his family.

Chapter 57

Things were heating up pretty quickly at Incirlik Air Base, and not just from the blazing summer sun, as the next day of battle preparations progressed. Word had been received through the Combined Air Operations Center, or CAOC, that a combat tasking was imminent based on new reports of expanded Syrian atrocities. In spite of previous warnings on chemical weapons, Assad had chosen to use them on a troublesome rebel group outside Damascus. As a result, the US president had gained agreement from a few of his European partners to help stop the carnage. France, Germany, and Great Britain joined with the American military, presenting a potent force that would hopefully quell the Syrian bombing campaign.

The Saudis decided to stay out of this impending conflict, as did most of the Islamic countries in the area. While most of the Gulf countries were busy unifying themselves under the Iranian Caliphate, the Americans knew that they had to tread carefully. If push came to shove, they believed that Islamic countries would stick together if they saw the West applying too much force. The United States viewed them all as passively supporting Assad. None of them had taken any action to stop the Syrian tragedy.

The WMDs took their deadly toll. The Syrian Air Force unleashed a barrage of barrel bombs. Some contained conventional explosives, others had toxic chlorine gas, and a few contained deadly sarin nerve gas. The poison gas was nonpersistent, in that it didn't last long in the windy environment—just long enough to kill anyone in the immediate blast areas.

Prior to the attacks, the rebels had mixed in within the local population to avoid being targeted by Syrian aircraft. Assad's forces didn't care where they hid—and unfortunately, this was a death sentence to the civilians providing them shelter.

The attack had not fooled the international community, which kept a close watch on the dictator's activities. Photos taken by brave journalists again made their way out of the country in a desperate attempt to stir the world into action against the brutal regime. Combat action was soon to come.

The 94th Fighter Squadron got an early-morning call to report for an update on the evolving Syrian situation. As the mob of flight-suited fighter pilots assembled, the tone among them was serious. Each pilot had his own thoughts racing through his mind, mostly on the conflict ahead of them, but also on their families back in the States.

As "Ace" Black took his seat, he thought about the test his upgraded Raptor would get in combat. After all, his jet, along with all the deployed F-22s, was sporting the Omega upgrade. The major central computer improvements provided the Raptor with not only advanced weapons employment capabilities but some added ability to integrate communication messages and signals of NATO partnered aircraft. He also knew that his IFF interrogator system would now operate as intended while the jet flew with the coalition aircraft.

As the briefing progressed, it was evident to all that there would be a combat mission tasking within the next forty-eight hours. The upcoming engagement into Syria was drastically larger than the last time Raptors had been here. Ninety-six aircraft would be involved in missions to destroy the Syrian WMD storage areas and chemical production factories. If successful, the attack would eliminate the essence of Assad's capability to mount assaults on his own people.

The attacks would come from three separate entry points into Syrian air space. Happening nearly simultaneously with the assault by the coalition aircraft, Tomahawk cruise missiles fired from US

Navy submarines and ships in the Mediterranean would target every single Syrian air base. The massive preemptive cruise missile attack would hit the runways, taxiways and aircraft parking ramps. Hopefully it would eliminate the ability of these air bases to threaten aircraft, to launch counterattacks, or to continue the assault on the innocent Syrian population.

Every army installation suspected of either producing or storing weapons of mass destruction would be targeted. These sites would each be hit with a specially developed new weapon that produced the white-hot burning effects of thermite to contain the dispersion of the chemical agents. In theory, the weapons should almost instantaneously destroy the deadly chemicals and eliminate the likelihood of spreading the contaminants as a result of the blast.

But of course, the weapons would need to get to their targets first. The Navy intended to clear out the threat of surface-to-air missiles, targeting the air defense network that would be on the receiving end of the Growler's anti-radiation missiles.

The F-22 stealth fighters would lead all of the strike force cells. Matt would be responsible for a twenty-four aircraft cell across the northern Syrian border that included Strike Eagles, Fighting Falcons, French Mirage and Rafale aircraft, and German Tornado bombers. An E-3 AWACS would provide battle space awareness, with F-15C Eagles providing their protection. The US Navy would provide a carrier battle group in the Mediterranean, including Hornets and Growlers.

The incredible capability of the Raptor, constantly improved since it was first produced, meant that it was now the most dominant air warfare system in the world. The F-22's advanced radar, sensors and communication capabilities would help effectively coordinate the air battle among all aircraft. The attack was designed to proceed in the early-morning hours under the cover of darkness, to optimize what little concealment there might be from the Syrian air defense forces. Ace expected to rendezvous with his strike package at an assembly point in the sky one hundred miles from

Incirlik. The 94th FS was on tap to lead this first mission, with the 27th FS holding back in the event that another series of attacks was necessary.

Matt, sitting next to Flamer, elbowed him in the ribs.

"Excellent! We're leading the first attack. This couldn't be working out better for us."

"Yeah, I agree, Ace. First in, last out. That's the way we like it. I'm looking forward to seeing how our Raptors perform with the new upgrade—and I'm really liking the fact that the shitty IFF system is finally fixed."

"I am too," replied Matt while silently hoping he was right about the interrogator fix.

When the briefing concluded, Matt and the other cell leaders were summoned by their squadron commander for more detailed discussions about the mission. Matt smiled as he listened to his boss identify him as the first flight to launch. Flamer would be in Matt's cell as he had hoped, and Matt gave him a quick thumbs-up.

The launch would take place the next morning. As the commander's discussion concluded, the pilots immediately headed out to the flight line to check the status of their aircraft. The maintenance teams were working balls-to-the-wall, a phrase used by the troops to identify their maximum effort to make sure the first wave of jets were ready.

Satisfied that his flight of four aircraft was close to combat-ready, he thanked the maintainers for their efforts. He quickly checked that the two additional aircraft identified as "air spares" were also ready. This was important. If a ground or air abort of any of the primary aircraft in the first attacking cell occurred, it needed to be filled by one or more of the spare aircraft. Everything would be set for the early-morning launch.

The pilots were encouraged to get some sleep, even though it was daylight. With a long combat mission ahead, they would need their rest to make sure their bodies, and especially their brains, were at one hundred percent when engaging the Syrians. Mission planning would begin at 2200 hours that evening, followed by drawing their life support gear and a 9 mm Beretta sidearm, removing identifying patches from their flight suits, and finally taking a short crew van ride to their jets at 0100 hours.

"Flamer, our Raptors look like they're ready to take their talons out. These birds of prey are going to clear the skies of any Syrians foolish enough to get airborne. And we'll get our strike package safely to the targets."

"Roger that, Ace," replied Flamer. "Let's get some grub. My gut is growling at me. Then maybe a few hours of sack time before the fun starts."

Matt and Flamer grabbed some food from the chow hall, wolfed it down, and headed to their rooms to hopefully get some sleep. Matt blacked out the light blazing through his window, pulling the dark shade all the way down. After setting his alarm and stuffing foam plugs in his ears to shut out the jet noise from the busy airfield, he settled in for whatever sleep he could get. In a matter of moments, he was asleep, dreaming about his children and the last time he'd wrestled with them on the playroom rug.

Chapter 58

Captain Matt "Ace" Black slowly walked around his jet, enjoying the coolness of the Turkish night air.

A far cry from the heat of the day, he thought to himself.

From nearby Adana, just outside the base main gate, he could smell the flavorful odor coming from the sizzling grills of the local restaurants. The prevailing wind easily blew the sweet-smelling smoke from the marinated lamb and chicken toward the base. Matt licked his lips.

That smells a hell of a lot better than the crap we ate a few hours ago in the chow hall. What exactly is in our mystery meat? The strange blend of something that resembled spam on steroids was barely tolerable to him.

The tall airfield lights surrounding the aircraft parking ramp lit the upper fuselage of the light gray Raptors but created dark shadows underneath the jets as the large diagonal tails rudely interrupted the light beams. Portable lights near the aircraft helped to somewhat illuminate the undersides of the jets, but a trusty flashlight was always essential for a close-up look.

"Chief! Anything unusual in the forms that I need to be aware of?" he asked.

"We patched up a couple of dings in the right wing leading edge. You probably picked those up on your flight over the pond," Staff Sergeant Kyle Jacobson answered.

"Good catch."

"No problem, sir. The jet's coatings are good to go."

"Thanks, Kyle."

"Other than that, this baby is ready to kick ass and take names!" The crew chief was clearly proud of the jet's condition—ready for war!

Matt paged through the electronic forms.

"Looks like we're good to go."

He climbed the aircraft ladder, placed his helmet in the cockpit, and stepped back down onto the concrete ramp. He began to run his preflight checklist. Despite Kyle's assurances about the jet's condition, he looked closely for any obvious problems. Finding none, he continued to thoroughly inspect his fighter as his crew chief walked with him.

Matt smiled as he continued. He paid particular attention to his weapons load. For this first cell of aircraft, the Raptors would be in an air-to-air weapons configuration only. Although the jet could carry bombs in its weapons bay, the Raptors were fully prepared to knock out any enemy aircraft that might challenge the strike force. Their air-to-air munitions load was standard for the mission—AIM-9 Sidewinder heat-seeking missiles and AIM-120 AMRAAM radar-guided missiles. Matt checked that the safety pins were removed from his deadly cargo. He didn't want to find out that a missile was unable to leave the aircraft when he executed the launch command. Matt's crew chief showed him the array of safety pins—landing gear, arresting gear, and pitot covers. Matt nodded as Kyle stored them away on the Raptor.

"The jet looks good, Chief," he remarked.

Matt headed up the boarding ladder, stepped over the canopy rail, and settled into the Raptor's ejection seat. His crew chief grabbed the helmet from him while he strapped in and then handed it back. Matt continued to run his checklist, working his way methodically through one of the most advanced fighter cockpits on earth. When he had completed his checks, he looked at his watch. He also looked to his left and right at the three Raptors that would accompany him. Flamer and the two other pilots that comprised the aircraft four-ship cell looked back at their flight lead and indicated they were ready.

The crew chief headed to the side of the jet and connected his comm cord to the F-22.

Sergeant Jacobson spoke into his headset microphone. "Comm check."

"Loud and clear," replied Matt.

"Roger, sir, I read you four by four."

Checking his watch again, Matt looked across both sides of his jet and signaled for his cell to start engines.

"Starting number one," Matt said to his crew chief as his powerful airframe whined with the rapidly escalating sound of the turbine engine reaching idle speed. The sound of the Pratt and Whitney engines spooling up rudely broke the silence of the otherwise serene flight line. Everything looked good so far, as indicated by the solid instrument readings. He glanced over at the assistant crew chief, who was manning the red one-hundred-gallon fire bottle adjacent to his jet.

Hope I don't need that.

"Starting number two," he said. The second engine quickly came up to idle speed.

Matt continued to monitor the engine pressure and temperature. *Good so far.*

"Raptor One One, flight check." Matt waited for acknowledgement from the other pilots.

"Two...Three...Four...copy," came the crisp response from each member of his flight.

"Ground Control, Raptor One One, flight of four, request clearance to taxi."

"Raptor One One, cleared to taxi. Departure Runway Zero Five, winds southwest at five. Visibility ten miles."

Matt continued to stand on the brakes as he gave the signal to pull the chocks. The assistant crew chief pulled them to the side of the jet while Kyle Jacobson stood in front, signaling his pilot to hold his position.

On Kyle's direction, Matt released the brakes and moved forward out of the parking spot, following the taxi lines as they curved away. A sharp salute from Sergeant Jacobson was smartly returned by Matt. He looked over his shoulder at the remaining three jets in his flight. They had pulled out of their spots and aligned themselves behind him.

As the four Raptors turned onto the main taxiway, they left the glowing lights of the main parking ramp and moved into the blackness of the Turkish night toward the arming area. After his short ride, Matt watched the crews as they darted underneath his jet, being always mindful of the large engine intakes. If a person got too close, the powerful turbofans could quickly ingest a headset, or worse, an individual. It had happened before to a careless airman, and the consequences had been gruesome and deadly. Likewise, the powerful jet wash coming from the engines could ruin a good day.

The arming crews finished their final checks, and Matt checked his multifunction displays for any sign of an anomaly that would degrade or prevent his jet from optimum performance in combat. Looking out his canopy, he could see the rest of the pilots in his flight were busy doing the same thing. He was satisfied that all was in order. When the arming crews finished, he got the signal that all jets were ready for launch.

"Tower, Raptor One One, flight of four, ready for takeoff," he said.

Without any delay, the tower responded, "Raptor One One, you are cleared for departure."

Matt advanced his jet's throttles and slowly pulled away from the arming area. It was a short trip to the departure end of Runway 05. He made room on his left for his wingman, Flamer, who slid his Raptor into position behind him. Matt "Ace" Black switched his flight to departure control frequency and commanded his flight to run 'em up.

Matt slowly advanced the throttles, holding the jet in position until he reached the desired engine RPM. He enjoyed the feeling—the gradual increase in vibration and low-level rumble from his aircraft. At brake release, he pushed the throttles to full military power and was jerked back into his ejection seat as the big jet rocketed down the runway. At about 150 knots, he pulled the nose up and broke ground around 180 knots, accelerating into the clear, dry Turkish air. As his aircraft continued to accelerate in the climb toward the initial prescribed altitude, he noted Flamer closing into formation with him. Twenty-seconds behind the first two jets were the number three and four Raptors in his flight, each speeding down the runway and making a graceful liftoff from the safety of the mottled gray concrete strip.

They joined in a loose fingertip formation and headed to their rendezvous with the coalition aircraft. Along the route, they took on jet fuel from the pre-positioned refueling tankers. When the final jet in Matt's flight disconnected from the tanker, they continued their route to the assembly point.

The Raptor's advanced radar and sensors picked up the large concentration of aircraft they would lead into combat about eighty miles north of the Syrian border, near the Turkish town of Osmaniye. The CAOC had securely transmitted the air order of battle to all forces involved in the attack. All were aware of the defensive actions that would likely take place once the Syrians realized they were under attack. The Center would continue to pass critical encrypted information obtained from the myriad intelligence sources around the region throughout the strike, to help prevent enemy surprises. Mission success was paramount—including the goal to bring every combat warrior safely home.

Inside his dark cockpit, illuminated by the low glow of his multifunction instrument displays, Ace was getting his mojo up as the reality of the events unfolded. He thought briefly about the pressure on him to successfully carry out the mission and keep control of the coalition forces. He would have help from the NATO AWACS that constantly scanned the skies for any sign of hostile aircraft. Keeping an eye out for mobile SAMs and the movement of enemy ground forces, the Joint Surveillance Targeting Attack Radar System aircraft, JSTARS, orbited off the Mediterranean coast. Matt was always concerned about the mobile SAM threat. He was confident that the Growlers would take out the fixed SAM sites if they turned on their acquisition radar. Their locations were well known. Hopefully the mobile SAMs would be dealt with as well, before they launched their missiles!

Over the Raptor's secure comm, Flamer said, "Ace, this is what we've been waiting for. We're going to clean Assad's clock."

"Roger that, Flamer—just got to keep our wits about us with this band of coalition forces. They've got their targets, and we need to keep them out of harm's way as much as we can."

Ace went through his mental prep for combat. Two Raptors would split off to take half the strike force aircraft toward Assad's primary chemical production facilities. The other two Raptors would take the remaining force to hit the two primary chemical storage locations near Syrian air bases.

Ace knew that the air defenses near Damascus were going to be fierce, and he counted on the Growlers to do their job. Of course, danger was everywhere in Syria. The entire country was a powder keg.

He turned his force toward Damascus as he crossed the Syrian border at thirty-five thousand feet. He checked his Breitling aviators watch, a birthday gift from his mom a few years back. It was three o'clock in the morning. As Ace streaked across the border, the entire array of attacking aircraft was silent, with no further communication occurring between them. Raptors would be the first in and last out.

Chapter 59

J ust ahead of the attacking strike forces, the sleek Tomahawk cruise missiles were now reaching their targets. The missiles had flown low-level, hugging the terrain as they crossed the Syrian landscape. Their internal navigation systems, guided by GPS satellites, zeroed in on the coordinates of each airfield. The staccato of exploding missile warheads quickly roused Syrian military forces as their runways and taxiways were cratered. They had been caught by surprise!

As Syrian air defense radar around the target areas began scanning the sky, the Growlers quickly put them out of commission with their high-speed anti-radiation missiles. With the key SAM command-and-control nodes eliminated, the likelihood of avoiding a Syrian missile was greatly increased, improving the potential for the attacking force's success. However, the massive explosions taking out the radar sites also guaranteed that the Syrians were now well aware that they were under attack.

With the Raptors controlling the air space near the target areas, the F-15E Strike Eagles attacked the suspected chemical production and storage facilities, and reduced the buildings to rubble. The detonation of the bomb's white-hot explosive mixture burned nearly all the poisonous chemicals being dispersed in the expanding blast clouds.

Four Syrian Su-35s had managed to get off the ground before the Tomahawk cruise missiles, launched by the submarine USS *Gerald Ford*, cratered their runway. The four unlucky Syrians were vectored by their command-and-control center to intercept the Strike Eagles. They raced toward them, fully loaded with air-to-air missiles that the Syrian pilots hoped would bring down the American jets.

Matt's Raptor picked up the Su-35 Flankers almost immediately. The Syrian jets were not yet in range to hit the Strike Eagles that were now exiting the target areas. As the Syrians tried to close the gap and get within range of their intended victims, they never saw the Raptors on their radar. The F-22's advanced fire-control system quickly zeroed in on the Flankers, and Matt launched two AMRAAMs.

"Fox One," Matt said, indicating his missile launch.

Flamer, flying two miles abreast of Matt, did the same. The first indication the Syrian pilots had that they were under attack was the blaring sound of their Soviet-made missile warning system in their cockpits. As they attempted to take evasive maneuvers, the two aircraft were blasted from the sky by the incoming missiles.

"Splash two bogeys," Matt said to himself as his deadly missiles found their marks. His buddy Flamer had the same results with the other two Flankers.

The other two cells led by Raptors also quickly eliminated a host of Syrian fighter aircraft that had chosen to challenge the strike force.

The multipronged attack had caught the Syrians sleeping. The Syrians did not launch any other aircraft. It would have been difficult anyway, given that nearly every runway in the general target area had been heavily damaged. Most of the missile batteries were destroyed, but the surviving SAM batteries fired a few missiles toward the coalition force—none found their marks, thanks to the Growlers. The SAM acquisition radars had been destroyed, and once out of commission, their SAMs were blind, unable to find their intended targets.

Coalition forces had done well. They had hit their targets and taken no losses due to enemy fire. They headed home.

———— • ————

Back on the tarmac at Incirlik Air Base, Matt climbed down the ladder from his stealth fighter. After shaking hands with his crew chief, he headed for the debrief facility to close out the successful mission. The strikes on Syria could not have gone any better. He saw Flamer walking across the ramp and waved at him.

"Flamer, I've gotta tell you—the upgraded central computer worked superbly, and thankfully, with no IFF issues at all," he said. "Our Raptors were invincible."

"Roger that, Ace. You never really know until you're puckering a bit under enemy fire. But I agree. Our jets performed exactly as advertised."

"I'll have to shoot Khalil a note of thanks. I'd like to send him some premium whiskey, but it would obviously go to waste, given his cultural and religious prohibitions."

"Well, I don't want you to be disappointed, Ace. I'll drink your whiskey, as long as you're buying. I can assure you—I won't waste any of it!"

Matt just shook his head while laughing at Flamer's comment.

While continuing his walk from the flight line, Matt thought about what he had just done—leading a strike force of integrated fighter aircraft to take out targets that clearly needed eliminating.

Hopefully the blasts from the fighter bombers pulverized the chemical weapons production factories. I suspect that post-mission intel will confirm that. And knocking a few enemy aircraft out of the sky, aircraft that tried to threaten the strike aircraft, was especially sweet. The team did what needed to be done.

Before he headed to the debrief facility, his mind started to wander. He remembered what had happened many years ago when he was just a boy—the strike mission in Syria that had done what needed to be done—but at a terrible cost. That mission brought back memories of the day his father had died.

Matt Black believed that his father would have been proud of him on this day. He firmly believed his dad had been watching over him during the entire mission, perhaps even making sure, with a protective hand, that he would be safe while flying over the dangerous Syrian countryside. Matt also relished the opportunity to inflict his own small bit of pain, maybe even vengeance, on Assad and the Syrian military, especially given their propensity to slaughter their own people.

As a result of the successful air and ground attacks, there would be no more strikes on Syria associated with the current situation. A strong message had been sent to Assad. His military infrastructure had been hit hard. The weapons of mass destruction he had used on his own people were at least temporarily destroyed—hopefully permanently. The American forces would remain at their forward staging bases for a couple of weeks until there was no further evidence of continued attacks on Syrian citizens. The president of the United States provided the dictator a stern warning that any further attempt to use chemical weapons would likely be the catalyst to remove him from power by whatever means necessary.

Almost as soon as it had begun, it was over. The pilots of the 94th Fighter Squadron would have an opportunity to briefly throttle back—wait for the clock to spin ahead for another two weeks and then redeploy to the States.

———•———

Iran watched the newscasts of the US strikes in Syria. There had been no mention of problems with the Raptors, but then again, the US military would never divulge that information publicly. Covert Iranian sources on the ground in Turkey, embedded as workers at the large air base, kept a close ear for any loose talk, especially talk of interrogator system problems. There were no issues reported.

From every bit of information the Iranian intelligence sources could capture, the interrogator systems in the Raptors had functioned as designed, operating normally. Epsilon was still silently buried in the code, awaiting the proper time for activation and execution.

Ayatollah Batani was not surprised to get the telephone call from President Xi. Batani expected to get some encouragement to test the anti-stealth capability as soon as possible. At this point, it appeared that the plans were ready for the satellite to trigger the Epsilon code, when and if the Americans attacked. But Xi offered up yet another opportunity to Iran. China was willing to quickly deliver three Shengdau radar systems to Iran to provide a level of redundancy in defeating stealth. Batani quickly agreed. He saw this offer as an additional means to help protect his emerging nuclear capability. China saw it as a way to validate their new radar.

Within days, three large cargo aircraft arrived at dispersed locations in Iran. Chinese engineers and radar operators accompanied the cargo.

Chapter 60

The news had broken across the United States in the early morning following the strikes on Syria. Every major network preempted regular programming to cover the attack on Assad's army and air forces. Normally, the media had enough noses under the blanket to pick up the subtle and sometimes not-so-subtle details of military forces deploying around the world. *This* movement of military war planes had caught them flatfooted. The level of secrecy over the deployment and pre-positioning of forces had been unprecedented.

At Omega's expansive software lab, Khalil was grabbing some coffee in the lounge. The large-screen TV gave a crowd of employees quite a show, the video images of bright explosions lighting up the early-morning darkness in the country of his birth. As the film footage was made available, the Al Jazeera news network pushed images to as many networks as they could to garner sympathy and support from around the world. They claimed that atrocities had been committed by infidel American forces on the innocent, free Syrian people.

As was often the case when bombs were dropped from aircraft, some unfortunate collateral damage occurred. While it appeared the blasts had caused the destruction of the chemical storage facilities, some of the deadly agent caused civilian deaths. The bombs that should have obliterated the chemicals had been mostly, but not completely, effective. The outrage claimed by Al Jazeera did not, of course, address what Assad had brutally done to his people with those very same chemicals prior to the coalition force attacks.

Khalil stood transfixed as the BBC and US newscasters described what had happened. They reported that the international community apparently had had enough of Assad's genocidal activity and especially his continued use of chemicals—a banned munition across most of the world. A coalition of nations had been assembled to stop Assad. The involvement of America's most advanced fighter jet, the F-22, caught Khalil's attention in particular. While many other aircraft had been involved in the Syrian attacks, the Raptor was getting a lot of press. Khalil thought about Epsilon, thinking that it would have been wonderful if it had been activated during the attack. Then the Syrians might have had a chance. He wondered to himself whether Captain Matt Black had been involved in the attacks. He also wondered if Iran had even contemplated using Epsilon to help defeat the Raptors.

It surely would have helped prevent yet another attack on my homeland.

However, Khalil suspected that it was unlikely Epsilon would have been used in Syria. He had heard nothing about its potential near-term use from his contact, Dr. Katari, or his imam, Sheikh Rahainee. He knew that when it was used, it would likely only be to protect Iran's nuclear development program, and in the event of an American attack on Iran.

Nonetheless, Khalil was very curious as to what the actual plan was to be.

When was Epsilon going to bring the Americans to their knees? It had to be soon. Something like Epsilon couldn't wait forever to be activated. There was always a chance that the Americans would discover the corrupt code before it was ever used. What a waste of technology and money that would be.

He had to find out. After all, he had risked his life to make this deadly code a reality. He decided to visit the Abdallah Mosque at his first opportunity. There he hoped he would find answers to his questions.

That opportunity came the very next day. He had sent a message on his personal iPhone to Sheikh Rahainee, indicating that he would like to meet to discuss an urgent matter. Saturday morning, he drove out of the Dallas area and headed down the two-lane road that led to his gray-bearded mentor. He pulled into the parking lot at the Abdallah Mosque, locked his truck, and walked in. Khalil removed his shoes, stepped over to the area designated for prayer, knelt, and gave his thanks to Allah. When he finished, he stood up and looked around the quiet, ornately decorated prayer room. He admired the inscriptions on the tiles. Most were phrases from the Quran that were reminders to the Muslim faithful of their obligation to adhere to the tenets of Islam as they lived their daily lives.

The bespectacled imam appeared out of the shadows and beckoned Khalil with a wave to follow him down the darkened hallway. They entered a small room toward the back of the mosque, a special room that had been specifically designed to be impervious to external eavesdropping.

As Khalil stepped toward his sheikh, he remarked, "*As-salaamu alaikum.*"

"*Wa alaikum assalaam,*" responded Rahainee.

"My imam," Khalil began, "I was greatly disturbed by what I saw yesterday. The carnage in Syria, my home, caused by the Americans and their coconspirators. The death and destruction they caused surely could have been prevented if we had acted to help our Muslim brothers. Why wasn't Epsilon used?"

"My son, do not worry yourself. We have prepared the Islamic world to respond to the devils at the right time. That time is when we can cause the most pain and suffering to them. That time is when we will unite all our Muslim brothers in the holy Caliphate, to rid the Middle East of all the poison caused by the insidious Western influence." He paused. "There are other key factors in play."

"If I may be so bold to ask, what are the key factors? When is the time that Epsilon *will* be used?" Khalil said.

"Khalil, the Quran teaches us that patience is a virtue. You must trust that Allah will guide our sword at the right time, at a time of his choosing. The sword will cut off the head of the

American serpent—it will lead all Muslims to their rightful place in our lands."

"I understand. I saw evidence that the F-22s were performing with seeming impunity over Syria. I only hope that my past efforts with Epsilon will fulfill my holy pledge."

"The destiny of the Americans has already been determined. The time for the fulfillment of that destiny is near," Sheikh Rahainee said. "Put your trust in Allah."

Khalil left his mentor and headed back to his home, wrestling in his mind with how and when his efforts would finally pay off. He wondered what the Iranians were doing as a result of the attack on his homeland. He knew that Iran had heavily invested itself in Syria's survival. Surely Iran would not sit idly by and watch his country be attacked by the Americans. Maybe Syria was not important enough to the Caliphate. Maybe that was why they hadn't activated Epsilon.

The sheikh knew full well that the conflict in Syria was not going unnoticed in Iran. In fact, the Supreme Council of Iran's ruling party watched the Syrian assault with keen interest. As the battle unfolded, they had been in communication with Bashar al-Assad and assured him of Iran's support if it appeared his hold on the regime was being threatened. Any attempt to dislodge him from power would result in an immediate armed response from Iran. The Supreme Leader had also assured Assad of their willingness to support any subsequent military aid to reconstitute Syrian forces after the attack, including resurrecting the destroyed chemical weapons capability.

Within the top levels of leadership in Iran, things could not have been working out better. The attack on Assad was viewed as a vital test. It was an early look at how the Americans would employ the Raptors in striking key facilities like the Syrian chemical weapons plants. American military tactics had been studied for years, but only recently had the US employed the F-22s in combat. Now, Iran was getting a close-up look at the current methods the Raptors use in a military strike.

It was in Iran's best interest to keep Assad in power. Every ally that Iran could maintain within the region was crucial. The Iranians had previously supported arms sales to Assad. They were willing to up the ante to keep Syria aligned with them after the American assault, and to support the Caliphate's regional cleansing operations.

Iran received the reports from senior Syrian Air Force representatives that the fight against the Americans was no contest. The Syrian fighter aircraft had never known what hit them. Those that launched from their airfields before their runways were taken out had been quickly dispatched by the F-22s. Although the Syrians had some of the latest fighter aircraft acquired from both Russia and China, the Raptors were virtually invisible to them. As a result, their aircraft were quickly acquired on the F-22's powerful radar and targeted before the Syrian pilots even knew their enemy was there. If they had had the ability to detect the Raptors, their fighter aircraft might have had a chance to use the advanced air-to-air missiles provided by their Russian benefactors. A pilot has to *acquire* his enemy first before he can lock on, launch and destroy him.

This conflict, although brief, gave the Iranians valuable information about the likely strategy the United States would use in another future conflict in the region—a conflict the Iranians knew was coming very soon. It would be coming to *their* country and likely threaten their ability to achieve the nuclear capability they so desired.

The Supreme Leader of Iran believed the knowledge they had gained from the American strikes on Syria would play a key role in the execution of Epsilon. It would buy the time needed to complete Iran's nuclear destiny.

Chapter 61

Iran's strategy appeared to be executing perfectly. Epsilon was ready. Their nuclear program was nearly complete. Warheads were being produced, and in a short time, their ballistic missiles would be armed. The Supreme Leader was nonetheless worried that after all they had done, there was still some risk that the strategy would ultimately fail. He didn't believe in luck. He believed in his faith. He prayed to Allah for guidance. He waited for a sign, anything that would point him towards success for the Islamic Caliphate.

Ayatollah Batani claimed he received the message in a dream. He would achieve his goals—he would succeed—but he must delay any possible American attack, at least for a few months. In order to buy the time needed before the expected American strike on their nuclear facilities, Iran would need to divert the attention of the US military. His dreams told the Ayatollah to create a veritable firestorm that would require the US to divide its forces to address multiple crises across the world. When the Americans finally were able to catch their breath, Iran would be finished standing up a potent nuclear missile force.

In the aftermath of the coalition forces attack on Syria, the Middle East was in turmoil. Prompted by Iran, skirmishes broke out across the region, with many countries reacting in a largely whiplash response to what they viewed as a Western assault on the Muslim world. Countries that had allowed their airfields to be used by American aircraft were culpable in the eyes of the more radical Islamic community—now effectively stirred up by Batani.

In Israel, the Palestinians, with Iranian encouragement and sponsorship, reacted with violence. The Palestinian rage was widely publicized over the Al Jazeera network. While Israel didn't actively participate in the attack, their airfields were used to recover coalition jets that experienced in-flight emergencies and required an immediate divert to the nearest friendly runway.

Equipped with some of the latest long-range rockets obtained from Iran, a radical Hezbollah faction near the West Bank unleashed a massive barrage at Israeli settlements and towns. Israel's Iron Dome defensive system was able to destroy many of the incoming rockets, but enough got through to cause extensive damage and death of innocent Jewish citizens. Any hope for a continuation of the on-again, off-again Israeli-Palestinian peace talks was squelched, and the attack prompted an immediate bombing campaign on the suspected rocket sites.

A splinter group from the faction operating in Southern Gaza also launched rockets into Israel, striking nearby towns before taking their refuge into Egypt. As the attacks continued, Israel wasted no time in executing drastic steps to stem the carnage among their citizens. Israeli intelligence believed the Hezbollah faction was playing a cat-and-mouse game, firing rockets from Gaza and then seeking protection across the border in towns just inside Egypt.

The radical group hoped their hit-and-run strategy would spare their likely destruction. It was not to be, as Israel's response was rapid and violent. Strikes by F-15I and F-16 aircraft pounded the area pinpointed by airborne intelligence assets. They also hit the border towns in Egypt where they believed the radicals were hiding. In spite of the precision munitions used, significant collateral damage occurred, and some innocent Egyptians lost their lives.

As the action unfolded, Egypt reacted angrily. They believed Israel's actions were overly violent and inhumane, resulting in the indiscriminate killing of innocent villagers. A formal protest was sent to the Israeli government declaring a violation of sovereign

Egyptian airspace and the reckless slaughter of their people. Lacking any substantive apology from Israel, the Egyptian army began massing its forces along the Israeli border, and moved forward a mix of its most advanced surface-to-air missiles to help counter any subsequent Israeli strikes. The United States secretary of state called the Israeli prime minister to encourage restraint.

Elsewhere, in Saudi Arabia, the United Arab Emirates, Qatar, and Bahrain, riots broke out in every major city in the largest display of near-simultaneous civil unrest ever seen. While the forward staging bases in the Middle East were not used to launch attacks into Syria, the anger over the American bombings and killing of civilians had been further inflamed by a massive influx of anti-American propaganda. Iran's fingerprints were, of course, all over every piece of media, electronic and paper, that permeated down to the lowest levels of each country's population. Politically, these Middle Eastern states were already leaning toward eliminating Americans and their forward operating bases from their territories. The US attack on Syria, a member of the Group of Seven, sealed the deal.

Tehran's Supreme Council believed they had achieved their desired objectives. It looked to the rest of the world like a major Islamic backlash had begun against the Americans. More importantly, the Iranian subterfuge throughout the region was growing quickly, insidiously, within the totality of the Persian Gulf community. The linkage between Shiites and Sunnis had tightened, and there was still more to come to help permanently cement that linkage.

Iran had done its best to incentivize countries along the southern tip of the Arabian Peninsula to become an active participant in the Caliphate. Yemen had not yet agreed but was strongly considering it. The incentive for Yemen was the delivery of fast-attack boats and weapons to them. The new weaponry enabled the strategically located country on the Gulf of Aden to escalate the harassment of ships. In spite of efforts by the United States to keep the sea lanes clear, there were too many fast attack boats and too large an area to protect with the resources available. Major oil transports and cargo ships were taken over by heavily armed pirates, the captors demanding exorbitant payment for the ships' release. But these "pirates" were actually trained and led by Iranian military operatives. As Yemen expanded its seaborne reach eastward, off the coast of Oman, they benefited from Iranian freighters that provided fuel and other support essential for the pirates to extend their range close to the Persian Gulf entrance. Some of the commercial traffic was sunk in the Iranian-backed Yemeni efforts to disrupt sea traffic. In the Strait of Hormuz, two large container ships were captured and sunk in an attempt to block the entrance to key ports. While Yemen claimed responsibility in the name of Allah, the US knew that the actions had all the hallmarks of Iran's treacherous involvement.

In Tehran, the Ayatollah had a smile on his face. It appeared that the "perfect storm" of events was happening in the Middle East. The widespread meltdown of peace across the region offered him the opportunity to continue to germinate the deadly seeds of their holy Islamic Caliphate, and to buy the critical time he needed. But it would take more to ensure that all Muslims, Sunni and Shiite, would unite to permanently rid the region of the Western infidel presence.

Based on another dream that gave him his "holy" guidance, the Ayatollah's plan had been in the making for some time. While Tehran was gaining support from their western neighbors across the Persian Gulf, a final push was needed to draw all Muslims together, to cement their hatred of the Americans and all they represented. That push involved the destruction of holy mosques scattered around the Middle East. The blame, of course, would be placed squarely on the United States.

Iran infiltrated saboteurs into Saudi Arabia, Bahrain, Kuwait, UAE, Qatar, and Iraq and linked them up with sources aligned to the Caliphate's goal of a single Islamic power in the region. The explosives used in the mosque attacks had been relatively easy to acquire and bring into each of these countries. Their borders were mostly porous and unguarded, especially in the less inhabited areas. And the ports along the Gulf never turned back an Iranian ship doing commerce. While it seemed abhorrent for a Muslim to destroy a mosque, the Supreme Iranian Council rationalized this as the needs of the many outweighing the needs of the few. Some casualties were to be expected. In the greater good of radical Islam, it was acceptable in order to achieve their holy Caliphate.

As the violent mosque explosions occurred, the death toll of innocent Sunni and Shiite Muslim worshippers rose quickly. The reaction was as Ayatollah Batani had expected. Who would attack the deeply religious sites of the Islamic faith? The subsequent anger throughout the Gulf was fueled by the discovery of "evidence" that had been cleverly planted by the saboteurs. The *explosives* fingerprints of the mosque destruction traced directly back to the Americans.

Any doubt about ordering the United States forces out of the Gulf countries was eliminated by the widespread attacks on the holy sites. The United States government protested vehemently, denying any part in the destruction. They appealed to the leaders of the victimized Gulf nations—their previous allies and partners— but the well was now poisoned. The Group of Seven called for the immediate removal of all Western forces from their soil.

The expected loss of a major forward presence in this volatile part of the world was a significant blow to the United States and its overarching military strategy. While the order to vacate the region had given the US ninety days to extract its forces, it was logistically impossible to get it done. After all, American presence had grown over a number of years, with millions of tons of equipment, munitions stockpiles, and vehicles to remove or abandon.

The impact on the United States was devastating. The forward air bases and ports used by US military forces had effectively been shut down, and in fact, closed to any nation that had previously been part of the broad allied coalition. That would limit visible

American influence to the outer periphery of the Arabian continent. Israel and Jordan, staunch allies of the US, were willing to allow American forces into their countries. The powerful United States Navy was limited to areas outside the declared sovereign territory limits imposed by each Iranian-aligned country. There was also significant worry about security and control of the vast oil fields and reserves that serviced the entire world. The US depended on their Gulf allies to protect the freedom of oil flow to the world's consumers. With those allies disappearing, the available quantity of oil, and even the price, could be a pawn used to influence or even threaten the global market.

As the United States reviewed its options, they were still trying to reconstitute their forces used in the Syrian attacks. At this point, they were already stretched thin due to continuing tension in North Korea and the South China Sea. Additionally, they weren't sure if the two large nuclear powers in the region, India and Pakistan, would remain neutral and stay out of the escalating turmoil. The Americans also knew it was unlikely that they would be able to use either India or Pakistan to stage forces forward.

Turkey was still a basing option, although the deteriorating political situation and rapidly growing anti-American sentiment added some risk for even using Turkish bases at Incirlik and other classified locations. For now, those bases were still an option, but would they be there when needed?

There were few other viable alternatives for the United States. Outside the region, the likely options for basing were Italy, Greece, Bulgaria, Turkmenistan, and Uzbekistan, presuming the countries' respective leaders would allow that to happen. After watching years of allied coalition involvement in the Gulf area and in Afghanistan, there was waning interest in getting involved in yet another futile campaign.

Chapter 62

Matt was enjoying the pleasant fall weather. October in the Langley area was just awesome. The trees had begun to change from their summer green foliage into a plethora of color. It was football season, Matt's favorite time of the year, even with the kids occasionally disrupting his concentration while watching his favorite teams. As the husband of a former Florida Gator, Matt never missed catching a game with Julie, either on the television, when an SEC game was actually broadcast, or at the local Gator Bar in Newport News if they could arrange a babysitter and escape the house for a few hours. His favorite professional team was the Indianapolis Colts, and Matt believed they needed a lot of help on their ongoing offensive strategy.

"These guys are pitiful," he said to Flamer one Sunday afternoon as they watched them getting slaughtered by the New England Patriots. "They've got to overcome the lousy recruiting and get some talent. They also need to provide their quarterback some passing targets and some protection when he's in the pocket."

"I'm with you on that, but the Pats are a tough bunch." He paused a minute, looking over at Matt, and then continued. "The Colts aren't even in this game. Must have been out partying last night," he laughed.

"Hey, I don't need any crap about their performance. I can see it pretty plainly."

"Easy now, big boy," replied Flamer as he saw Matt's jaw clenching a bit.

"They'll get better—they just need a new coach! And some additional talent."

Matt had inherited his fondness for the Colts from his father. He could still remember his dad talking about the old Baltimore Colts and heroes like Johnny Unitas, a real leader who had spurred that team to victory.

"Where's the next Unitas?" he asked Flamer, who just stared back at him.

The clueless look on Flamer's face let Matt know that his friend had no idea who Johnny Unitas was. He shook his head. "You hungry?"

As if on cue, halftime began and the two of them headed to the kitchen to rustle up some nachos with plenty of cheese and jalapeños. The tasty treats were washed down with ice-cold Bitburger beer, a German brand that Matt's father used to drink. He'd developed a fondness over the years for the slightly bitter pilsner, still made in the single brewery in Bitburg, Germany since 1817.

"I'm not sure I can continue to watch this slaughter. At least the beer is tasty," Matt remarked.

"Ace, look at it this way. We're not working right now. We're just chilling out on a pleasant Sunday afternoon."

At that moment, Claire came running into the den, screeching happily at the top of her lungs. She was followed by the family's new puppy, a miniature schnauzer. The dog, named Zelda by Claire, raced after her, yapping loudly, almost in synchronization with her own shrieks.

"You get that mutt housebroken yet?" asked Flamer sarcastically.

"Just about. Only one little puddle in the last two days. We're making progress!"

As they shot the breeze while munching on their snacks, Flamer brought up the mess taking place in the Middle East.

"I was thinking about our next likely deployment, given the disaster going on in the Persian Gulf. You know, it's just a matter of time before we take on Iran. I keep reading the reports about their military strength levels. They're not going to be a pushover."

"Roger that, Flamer. But we're not going to be intimidated by Iran or anyone else. Besides, I think their nuke program is close to being completed. Every piece of intel we've gotten seems to point to that. Can't believe we haven't already done something to stop it."

"Well, we'll see. If we go, it'll raise *my* pucker factor to new levels, in spite of flying the best aircraft on earth." He paused. "Iran has built up some of the most formidable air defense systems in the region. They've picked up advanced fighter jets from our old friends China and Russia. It's going to make any conflict pretty challenging. Although, given the upgrades we have in our Raptors, I'm confident that we can carry the day," Matt said.

"On a different subject, are you and Julie interested in hauling our gang of kids to McDonald's for dinner after the game?" Flamer asked.

"Sounds good, Flamer. Julie didn't want to cook tonight anyway. Let's shoot for about five o'clock."

"Perfect. I'll head back across the street to my house and let Colene know. Besides, I don't want to see a grown man cry as his Colts get their ass whipped." Flamer was laughing loudly as he headed out the door.

As halftime ended, Matt couldn't help but think about what Flamer had said about Iran. He reviewed in his mind what had transpired in the Persian Gulf, and specifically in Iran, during the last couple of years. He wondered what was really going on inside the head of the Iran's Supreme Leader.

———————•———————

Matt and his fellow warriors had been briefed in detail about how the Middle East had changed in just a short time. The Americans knew that Iran was now a powerful and dangerous threat to the region. The past few years had been a new era in rebuilding Iran's military—their rearmament plans exceeding the ruling party's expectations. The massive buildup in offensive and defensive capability was a reassuring cloak of protection offered to the surrounding Islamic Gulf nations and would ultimately prove to be a key incentive in Iran's desire to unify the surrounding region's Muslim community.

Once sanctions had been lifted on Iran, oil revenue had once again soared and provided a nice injection of cash into the Ayatollah's coffers. Iran had used some of its wealth to expand and strengthen ties across both the Sunni and Shiite communities. Billions of dollars held hostage by the United States had been released back to Iran, opening the proverbial barn door for continued rearming of the country. It made Iran a prime customer for advanced Chinese and Russian fighter aircraft, and the supporting infrastructure and training to sustain lethal combat operations.

Iran had used its massive influx of new cash to assemble the third-largest fleet of advanced fighter aircraft in the world. The Iranian Air Force had wisely used the past few years to refine their flying skills. Intensive training programs using experienced Chinese and Russian military representatives gave Iranian fighter pilots a level of capability never before seen within their military forces. After receiving weapons and tactics training at locations in China and Russia, the fighter pilots brought their newly acquired skills back home, where they continued to train continuously throughout the country and into the Persian Gulf region.

State-of-the-art military airfields were built at strategically placed locations around the country. All had hardened aircraft shelters, including underground hangars and taxiways, which made the targeting of these locations more difficult for any belligerent trying to take them out.

The latest air defense systems were also acquired and installed around the country's strategic facilities, including weapons labs, command-and-control structures, missile launch centers, and fuel storage areas.

The Iranian Air Force was not the only beneficiary of the cash bonanza. Their navy had acquired the latest torpedo-equipped fast-attack boats from China, along with a couple of nuclear attack submarines, giving their blue-water fleet the teeth it needed to control the sea lanes along their western shore. Iran was already using swarming tactics with fast attack boats in the open Gulf waters to harass the US Navy, who up to now had been reluctant to engage unless there was a real threat of an offensive attack. Existing Iranian cruisers and minelayers had a key role in the defense of Iran—now the nuclear attack submarines put them in a new category of countries to be respected for their military might. Not since the days of the Shah of Iran, back in 1975, had the Iranians presented themselves as such a formidable force within the region.

Iran was not alone in reaping the benefits of loose restrictions on world arms sales. Many members of the Group of Seven had used the wealth from the escalating price of oil to rebuild their fleets of military aircraft and navy vessels as well. As a result, the region had now grown to be a powerhouse of military strength, and no longer needed the United States to support their defense interests. Rather, each state had established military and economic cooperation agreements with Iran, and together, their military muscle was a clear and potentially serious threat to the United States if conflict were to break out in the region. Ironically, many of these nations' pilots had received their training in the United States. It was incredible how, in just a few short years, the balance of power had shifted so significantly in the region.

While the United States and its allies had been vocal about the apparent rapid expansion of Iran's military strength, there had been no overt actions to limit its growth. After all, eight years of a US administration's belief in the power of passive negotiation, supplemented by a weak agreement to limit Iran's nuclear program's expansion, had done very little to actually stop most areas of military growth. As a result, Iran now had a powerful military force, one that was now the largest in the region.

———————•———————

At this point, Iran had garnered much support throughout the Muslim world for a regional uprising of all of their faithful to support the most important holy cause to come their way in decades. A union of all Islamic states, with Iran as the leader, was looking more and more likely. Iran believed it possessed all the tools needed to move the Caliphate forward through its final steps.

Chapter 63

T he United States was scrambling. The secretary of state had tried to open up diplomatic channels that slammed shut as a result of the widespread mosque destruction—but to no avail. There was no tolerance in the eyes of the Muslim community at this point for continued presence by the United States in their holy lands.

The ninety-day threat to remove the forward-based American military forces was now a unified directive by the Iranian-led Group of Seven. No further deployment of forces into these countries would be allowed. This raised major concerns in the United States. Airlift and seaborne support to extract troops and critical equipment did not have nearly enough time to complete the withdrawal. The bases and ports used to move outsized cargo would close at the end of the directed withdrawal time as well, limiting what could be removed. Outside of each military installation in the Gulf where Americans forces and civilians were located, angry mobs of citizens, radical groups, and even members of the country's armed forces had unofficially mobilized to further threaten the Americans, demanding their immediate departure.

Within the National Security Council, the president and his staff were searching for viable options. Aircraft and nearly all of their immediate support could be extracted within the short time line—but millions of dollars in equipment, vehicles, and even some of the munitions stockpiles would be left. There just was not sufficient time to do an about-face after countless years of prepositioning assets.

The president contemplated taking a hard line on the mandate as an unreasonable and impossible demand. The US certainly had the military power to protect itself at these locations, if it came down to actually doing it. But the apparent unified front by nearly all Islamic nations made the situation dicey.

If the US dragged its feet on their withdrawal, exceeding the ninety-day evacuation order, the consequences could be unacceptable. There was no desire to risk American lives over equipment. The critical assets would be removed. Much of what would remain was reaching the end of its useful service life anyway. Any munitions remaining had to be rendered unusable. The United States began to move forward at breakneck speed to remove their forces from the Gulf.

The military depended on open air and sea lanes to protect their forward-deployed units, if it came to that, and to safeguard the world's access to the oil reserves. As points of access disappeared, the obvious choice was to find other "friendly" countries that would accept them.

In short order, the vast negotiating power of the United States nailed down potential locations to reposition their forces. There were plenty of carrots to offer countries willing to help, including the promise of financial resources, military and economic support. Turkey had not wanted to be involved with expanded American presence but reluctantly agreed to short-term restaging of US forces. Jordan, Oman, and Israel were also sympathetic to the American predicament and had agreed to limited support at their bases. Saudi Arabia held firm in its desire to keep foreign troops from their territory, as had been their practice since the end of the second Gulf War.

After gaining these agreements, within a little more than two months, the majority of US military personnel were gone from the region, moved to their new temporary homes in the few countries that reluctantly welcomed them. The fighter aircraft came out first, followed by a massive effort using military and civilian cargo aircraft to pull out as many key assets as possible.

Politically, it didn't seem to matter that the decision to expel Americans would end any US support some members of the

Group of Seven enjoyed. Even the adamant assurance by the president of the United States that his nation was not responsible for the destruction of the holy mosques had not been believed. Most of the Islamic world thought the Americans would say anything, fabricate any story, and act in the arrogant fashion they had always done to get what they wanted. What they had to say really didn't matter now.

———•———

The Supreme Leader of Iran was pleased, and sharply focused on his ultimate objectives. Iran had made every effort to maintain the highest levels of secrecy in their nuclear weapons lab development and production facilities. Over the past eighteen months, their nuclear program had moved forward at high speed—all the while under the "supervision" of the six nations that were signatories to the 2015 JCPOA nuclear agreement, specifically designed to prevent exactly what Iran had accomplished. He laughed softly, a very uncharacteristic behavior for the Ayatollah.

Iran had declared that they were proceeding with the peaceful use of nuclear power. They had cleverly hidden their centrifuge capability, which wasn't difficult given the extremely generous ground rules of the nuclear agreement. While the "legal" levels of relatively impure enriched uranium headed to the nuclear power reactors, prohibited quantities of highly enriched uranium made its way to their underground weapons production facilities.

Their Chinese technological benefactor had been extremely careful when inserting its key people into Iran to support the nuclear program development. Their caution was understandable. They wanted no backlash from the Americans or anyone else as a result of their involvement. They didn't want the likely consequences of meddling on the world stage in this particular arena. After all, facilitating nuclear weapons development in a rogue nation would place China in the same category of villains as North Korea.

Chinese scientists and engineers helped Iran produce the desired results—the detailed nuclear warhead design and critical engineering. The end result was stunning. Tactical nuclear warheads with variable yields were produced to effectively mate with Iran's ballistic missiles. Of course, the designs bore a striking resemblance to many of the weapons in the Chinese inventory. Minor design changes would hopefully keep China's fingerprints off any subsequent investigation into their complicity. China had been somewhat hesitant at first to help move yet another country into the nuclear club. But the deal they got was sweet. Beyond the guarantee of current and future sales of Chinese military hardware to Iran, it included the use of Iran to forward-base its forces. China had also been offered exclusive economic incentives, including discounted oil.

The Americans never started a war that they didn't think they could win. They chose to overwhelm their enemy with firepower. But war was often like a game of chess, where just a few key strategic moves were all that was needed to halt an advance. The completion of the Iran's nuclear program was one key move. Like chess, your opponent had to see the board, had to see the moves, had to awaken to the developing strategy that might win the game.

Ayatollah Batani knew he would execute those key moves—provide evidence to the Americans, at precisely the right time, that nuclear capability had been achieved, before their adversary launched an attack. It was simply not enough to expect US satellite imagery to conclude that ballistic missiles were on fixed and mobile launchers. That alone would not be enough to convince the Americans. There had to be one more chess move—at just the right time—proof that Iran was now a nuclear power. That evidence would stop the United States from ever attacking Iran again. *Checkmate!*

The plan to make the final chess move was intricately formulated. Batani's staff reviewed the details with him and reassured him that it was a very viable, executable plan.

His chief scientist explained the approach.

"Most holy one," he began, "given the high confidence gained from the tests conducted in China on the miniaturized warhead design, we have begun producing them. While that is ongoing, we will conduct an underground nuclear test at our desert site. It will provide final proof to the world of our success.

"The warhead test will occur in the Kavir Desert, inside a cavern nearly five hundred feet beneath the barren surface. The warhead will be set in place, and at the right time, the detonation will occur. The sensors installed by our engineers and Chinese technicians will detect the blast and verify that the fissionable material has been triggered successfully. The test will demonstrate that the warheads planned for our launch sites will function as intended."

The scientist waited for a response from Ayatollah Batani. Not receiving any, he continued.

"While the nuclear yield will be less than what had been used in the World War II Hiroshima blast, it will verify the success of our production warhead's design. It will also assure the tactical warheads planned for our ballistic missiles will work as intended."

The Ayatollah nodded his understanding, and perhaps his concurrence that the plan was a good one. Iran also counted on the elaborate overhead sensors used by the United States and its allies to verify that a nuclear detonation occurred, and their country was indeed a new nuclear power. The gray-bearded Ayatollah was very sure the scheme would work. But the demonstration would need to be timed precisely—soon. When the production warheads were produced and at least one installed on a ballistic missile, the test should follow.

Once the detonation was accomplished, they would advise the world, and the United States in particular, that Iran's military possessed a number of nuclear-tipped ballistic missiles. They would further declare that those missiles would *only* be used in the defense of Iran or of their seven-nation agreement, united under the holy Islamic Caliphate. Batani hoped that the Americans and the Israelis would react by backing off any plans they might have to strike his country. If not, then he could always, as a last resort, use his nuclear arsenal in self-defense.

Batani ushered a stern warning to all those present.

"We are very close to achieving all that Allah has promised. Your underground tests better work as advertised," he said to General Baghdadi and the chief scientist. "There must be nothing that interferes with our destiny. Nothing!"

He focused on the eyes of his key staff. The cold, dead stare penetrated each of them, sending a chill of uneasiness through them all.

His generals and scientists nodded their agreement. All of them knew the risk of discovery by the Americans was extreme. It was highly likely that the discovery had already been made. If so, the consequences would be rapid, massive, violent, and deadly. They all knew that time was of the essence. Once warheads were installed, the Americans would never risk an attack for fear of a nuclear escalation and the spreading holocaust around the Persian Gulf—possibly even into Europe or America.

Although the test in the Kavir Desert was only days away, General Baghdadi believed a US attack was imminent—to eliminate what they must already know was an unacceptable emerging threat. He believed that the American satellites already could see the beginning stages of Iranian missiles being prepped for their nuclear warheads. The Americans would resolve the problem before it became unstoppable. *The Americans will strike soon*, he thought, *before Israel takes matters in their own hands. The United States is unlikely to try to negotiate any further with Iran and give Israel time for their own preemptive attack that could turn the region into a flaming quagmire.* Baghdadi was worried, as he should be.

General Baghdadi's hope was that his country's new defenses would help stop an American attack. Iran could stave off the destruction of their nuclear program for a short time. They could stop a stealth fighter attack—Epsilon would hopefully buy them days to complete the final warhead integration. Additionally, the

Shengdau radar with their Chinese operators was now in place, providing Iran another level of defense to stop a stealthy attack. Any non-stealth attack could already be stopped by the advanced air defense weapon systems acquired from China and Russia. Baghdadi was confident that even the cruise missiles could be intercepted before hitting their nuclear-tipped missiles.

It will all work, he thought, trying to reassure himself. *It has to!*

Chapter 64

General Baghdadi's confidence only went so far. He knew there was still a chance that Epsilon might not work. After all, Iran had never *really* tested Epsilon and the satellites' ability to morph the deadly code on an *actual* F-22. What if there was special shielding that prevented the satellite pulse from triggering the code buried deep in the Raptor's central computer? What if there were other special protections in the Raptor that could block Epsilon? Baghdadi couldn't risk failure. The survival of his country's nuclear program depended on it. His own survival depended on the success of the deadly code. He decided to take it upon himself to try triggering Epsilon on a Raptor as soon as possible.

Baghdadi knew the Americans were flying constantly up and down the western coast of the Persian Gulf. In spite of the departure of all US fighter aircraft from their previous forward-deployed locations in the Gulf region, the Raptor still retained a presence there. Supported by tanker aircraft, the F-22s loitered off the coast of Iran, the Raptors watching over the future potential battle space. Their missions were getting more and more predictable, and were tracked closely by Iran. But the Raptor missions, for some reason, had not yet been picked up by the Shengdau radar—the Chinese engineers were working to solve the problem. For now, Epsilon was the only means available to identify the stealthy Raptor. General Baghdadi pulled the small group of close confidants together privately and secretly to discuss a way to minimize the likelihood of failure.

"Is it possible to run a short test of Epsilon on an actual Raptor without revealing the capability we have? Could we activate the satellite briefly, broadcast a short pulse toward the Raptors, and determine if Epsilon was triggered?"

The group looked stunned as they listened to what some thought was a preposterous test that might risk everything.

"If we are successful in triggering Epsilon and the jet's interrogator system, we'll see the Raptor's radar signature. But is it likely the Americans would be tipped off to what had happened and allow them time to design a fix before attacking Iran's nuclear facilities?" Baghdadi waited for the group's reaction.

"General, what you suggest has much danger associated with it. But we agree, the time to find out that Epsilon doesn't work is not during a full-scale American attack on our country."

The general knew what he must do, mainly for his own survival. He would arrange to test Epsilon on a Raptor.

Unbeknownst to his Ayatollah, General Baghdadi secretly proceeded with his test. He had a few trusted engineers who also valued the ultimate success of Epsilon and agreed to help him test the Epsilon's effectiveness. The test would only last a few seconds. A short pulse by the satellite, and Epsilon would hopefully direct the Raptor transponder to transmit. Iranian acquisition radar would be looking intently for the bloom they trusted would come from the F-22.

———•———

The young F-22 pilot was on a routine patrol. No real threats were expected, or so he had been briefed. When the satellite pulse penetrated his jet's software and his IFF came to life on its own with no action by him, he was startled. After a few moments, it turned off.

Hmmm. Must still have problems with this system, he thought. *It was supposed to be fixed with the central computer and interrogator upgrades. I'll let my maintenance guys know about it when I get back to the base.*

When he landed at his forward operating base in Thumrait, Oman, he reported the issue. The Raptor maintenance team dug in to the problem. Not finding anything abnormal, they cleared the jet for its next flight. Meanwhile, the report of the spurious issue made its way back to Langley, and a young avionics specialist wondered about it. He reported it to the F-22 Program Office at Wright-Patterson.

General Baghdadi breathed a sigh of relief. A few Iranian fighters flying near the coast and the country's defensive radar array had clearly picked up the Raptor bloom. He was now confident that he would not be summarily executed for failure to ensure the Caliphate's success.

The past two years of highly covert intensive nuclear engineering and development had been successfully completed. The tactical dial-a-yield warheads had been produced in the top secret facility buried deep in the southwest side of the Elburz Mountains. As the warheads were completed, they made their trek in darkness, by the most secure means of transport, to the six different strategic locations around the country. The ballistic missile launch complexes in each location eagerly awaited warhead arrivals. As the first one was mounted atop the intermediate range ballistic missile, Ayatollah Batani actually smiled. His closest advisors had never seen the Supreme Leader express this much happiness.

Their underground test took place in accordance with the Ayatollah's direction, and proved to be a tremendous success, producing the desired nuclear yield that their scientists had anticipated. Iran provided proof to the world that they had entered the nuclear club.

When America's vast array of sensors picked up the clear evidence of the nuclear detonation, the president was stunned. The United States knew they were pretty late to the game, and it was time to act. The intelligence it had obtained about the current status of Iran's nuclear program had come as a shock. When key sensors picked up evidence of the nuclear detonation in the Kavir Desert, a flurry of activity had taken place to verify that it was, in fact, proof of Iran's progress in advancing their program. Between satellite, airborne, and ground intelligence-gathering sensors, there was no doubt what had occurred, and what was happening at the launch facilities. It foretold an ominous message about the historically rogue nation. What had previously been thought, that Iran was arming their missiles with conventional explosive warheads, now had a new wrinkle. Was there now clear evidence that Iran was in fact arming missiles with a nuclear warheads?

At an altitude of twenty-three thousand miles, high above the surface of the planet, one particular satellite in a geostationary orbit among the array of communication platforms kept its silent vigil. There was no broadcast or transmission from this satellite. It awaited the time when it would help fulfill Iran's destiny. To all outward appearances, it was just another in the large constellation of communication satellites that the US monitored. The American military continued to believe their purpose was peaceful.

Chapter 65

Within the world of spooks and spies, the United States had few if any equals. The nation's intelligence apparatus was second-to-none, in spite of a few media pundits who would criticize their own mothers. At the top of the political food chain, the president and the director of the National Security Agency controlled a budget that never saw the light of day in Congress. The "black" budget financed a world of super-secret gadgets and sensors designed to eavesdrop on virtually any person, any conversation, and any action taking place anywhere on the surface of the planet. Along with an intricate network of covert operatives in almost every country, the United States tried to keep up with every emerging threat, and there were plenty of new threats to go around.

Under the infamous period of pullback from America's historical leadership role in the world, the black budget had been the smallest in many decades. As such, crucial developments in a few countries that were not necessarily America's friends moved ahead unchecked, unwatched, and unchallenged. Iran's nuclear program had germinated its deadly seeds during that period. By the time the US woke up to the danger, it was nearly too late to do anything about it.

The rapid expansion of Iran's holy Caliphate was unifying most of the Islamic world, both inside and outside the Gulf region. Exacerbating the situation, it looked like Iran was moving large amounts of ship and vehicle traffic between many of the Gulf states. None of this was reassuring to the intelligence analysts buried deep in their cybersecure facilities in Washington, D.C. Iran was up to something more devious than providing economic support to their neighbors. The collection of intelligence data indicated otherwise. While not looking to engage in another conflict in the Middle East, the nuclear program threat, and now the movement of what had to be military forces from Iran, were prompting a decision to move US forces into a region they had just been thrown out of. They had to be prepared to answer any threat to Saudi Arabia and the control of the vast Persian Gulf oil reserves.

"There's little doubt about the Iran situation, is there?" the American president asked his National Security Agency Director.

"No, Mr. President. Between the blatant evidence we've collected on their underground test, and the overhead imagery we have of their ballistic missile launch facilities, Iran is now a clear and present danger to the Gulf region, and likely to the Western world." He paused. "We clearly have to respond strongly."

"I don't want to be the one to start up another war in that region, or anywhere else for that matter," replied the president.

He adjusted his glasses as he peered down at the top secret documents, including the photo imagery, that provided the proof of Iran's new capability. He shook his head in disgust, wondering how the situation had gotten this far. He thought again about the agreement that was supposed to keep Iran in check. It was intended to stop any possibility of that country ever getting close to developing a nuclear capability, and subsequently a nuclear weapon. He knew that it had been doomed, almost guaranteed to fail the moment the ink was dry on the document. The agreement ground rules had been as soft as warm Jell-O. So what came as a shock should have come as an expectation. All of that didn't matter much at this point.

"But at the same time, we can't sit idly on the sidelines and let Iran potentially threaten all of the Middle East and Europe. Maybe the United States as well."

"Mr. President, we do have some options, some forceful ones that can position us to carry out a variety of economic and military actions. Once we share the intel we have with our NATO counterparts, I don't believe there will be hesitation from any of them that immediate, direct actions must take place. We can likely also get support from Israel and Jordan, although they are not part of NATO. After all, the threat is pretty damn close to them."

The Director paused and then continued.

"A complete economic embargo of all products—agricultural, industrial, everything—should get plenty of support. We can effectively shut down all traffic coming in to the region, even air traffic. The economic actions may seem to many as cruel to the Iranian people, but I don't believe we have much choice at this point. We've got to hit the regime where it hurts—send a strong message to the country's leadership that the world is not going to tolerate weapons of mass destruction in their country or anywhere else in the Middle East."

"I don't see a way out of this with economic actions alone," said the president. "I presume you're also going to recommend a large prepositioning of our military forces in strategic locations around the Gulf region—at least in the few places we have left."

He thought about what he was going to say next.

"I've got to tell you, I really dread the thought of a military strike on Iran at this point. If they decide to overreact to a conventional attack by us and take a step that no other country has ever taken by launching nukes, God help us all."

"Sir, I needn't remind you that time is of the essence. Any hope we have to slow down this rogue regime requires immediate action," the NSA Director responded.

The chairman of the Joint Chiefs of Staff nodded his concurrence with what was just said. "Mr. President, we can have a large contingent of forces moved forward in forty-eight hours and ready to respond to any Iranian aggression."

"Let me be clear," replied the president. "I intend, at least for now, to rely on the *threat* of our military response to influence Batani. And of course the tough economic sanctions we will impose. If that doesn't work, then we'll take the next step."

The meeting continued for another two hours. Intelligence sources had provided enough credible information, including detailed photographs, that it was crystal clear that nuclear warheads were being installed on Iran's ballistic missiles.

Fortunately, the US had compiled enough overhead imagery, along with eighteen months of extremely sensitive and detailed signals and communications intelligence, to put together an integrated targeting plan. Included in the targeting plan were suspected underground centrifuge facilities, the heavily bunkered uranium enrichment centers, and the fixed ballistic missile launch sites. Any mobile sites equipped with nukes would be another challenge, since their specific locations could constantly change.

The real question to the US president and the American people would be whether they would choose to start yet another war in the Middle East and execute the targeting plan. Or would they, at the very least, rely on an economic blockade? Would putting a stranglehold on any economic or military traffic into Iran send a strong enough message? Would China and Russia honor the blockade, or would they continue to support their Iranian proxy? Could the US apply enough pressure to influence the two superpowers to stay out of the way? In the end, would economic starvation send a strong message to Iran and the other Gulf states that denuclearization was their only option?

The deployment order came quickly, directing Langley to send two squadrons to bases in Southern Europe, at initial staging locations for their forces and equipment. The F-22s were not the only aircraft directed to deploy. Four squadrons of Fighting Falcons would supplement the units already in Europe. Likewise, two squadrons of Strike Eagles out of Seymour Johnson AFB in Goldsboro, North Carolina would also be part of the action, supplementing RAF Lakenheath aircraft. The US Navy was planning to move their Middle Eastern carrier group into the Mediterranean to supply sufficient Growlers to suppress enemy air defense capability, as well as enough Hornets to support the air campaign.

Supplementing the Growlers was a squadron of Wild Weasels from Shaw AFB in South Carolina.

The 94th FS Raptor pilots all came to attention as the briefing in the Wing Conference Room came to a close. They had received all the latest information on the nuclear-tipped ballistic missiles in Iran and of the plans for moving forces forward to the European theater, then closer to the threat in the Middle East. The essence of the deployment was a show of force—in fact, one of the largest since the first Gulf War. If the leverage of an economic stranglehold wasn't enough to get Ayatollah Batani to stand down his nuclear efforts, then leverage of a different sort would be applied.

The pilots were told of the targeting plans developed to potentially take out the Iranian nuclear capability, something that for now may not be necessary. When the briefings were over, the pilots began funneling out of the room and picked up their cell phones outside the door of the secure area. Matt grabbed his and headed for the stairs. Flamer caught up to him as he was about halfway down the steps. They both looked at each other for a moment before either spoke.

"You've gotta be shitting me, Ace. We're actually thinking about an attack on nuclear ballistic missiles?"

"Well, it wouldn't be the first attack on another country's nuclear capability. Remember, Israel took out Iraq's nuclear reactor at Osirak back in 1981 and Syria's in 2007, before either one could become operational. Of course, this is a big difference, if it actually comes down to hitting launch facilities."

He looked intently into Flamer's eyes.

"These Iranian nutballs could actually launch a nuke if we don't take it out first. Then who knows what would happen? Where would they launch it at? Israel? Turkey? Paris? What happens next? A chain reaction of nukes flying through the region?"

"I just hope that if we're tasked to take them out, we can get to them *before* they launch. Maybe they'll think twice before doing it. Maybe they'll realize that if they do pop one off, it'll be the end of their country as they know it. Ace, can you imagine the reaction by the world, and *us*, if they send a nuke warhead downrange?"

"Gotta agree with you on that last point. Once cities are pulverized after Iranian nuclear warheads detonates over them, I think we'd use our own tactical nukes to completely decimate every militarily significant target in the country. There's no question that their leadership would be eliminated as well. It would be the end of Iran as we know it!

"Well, Flamer, looks like we're going to show the Iranians what we've got—hopefully, if we even get a chance to engage," he said to his best friend.

Fred "Flamer" Lightner had been with Matt the entire time at Langley. It was pretty unusual for pilots to remain at a base more than a few years without reassignment. Constricting federal budgets had put a real crimp on moves. That wasn't all bad, as most Air Force folks in the operational business got pretty sick of uprooting every couple years and longed to stay put and minimize the trauma on their families—and to build long-lasting friendships.

"Ace, you know we're ready. In fact, we're past ready," he said. "You can train until you think you're doing it in your sleep, but there's no substitute for kicking up a bit of fur with a real adversary. Like we did in Syria, but this time, it ain't no cakewalk. And the stakes are a lot higher!"

"I'm with you, buddy. Sounds like in forty-eight hours we'll be on our way across the pond. But you *do* know that right now, this is just being advertised as a major show of force. It's clearly one of the biggest I've ever seen, so my guess is there's more to it than just showing the Ayatollah that we're pissed off at what's going on and that they need to cut out that nuclear shit."

"I believe we're definitely going after them," Flamer responded. "We're going to give them a taste of good-old American kick-ass firepower and remind them that we have a boatload of forces ready to shut them down if need be."

"Hey, man," Matt said. "There's some real risk here. The president is betting that we can threaten Iran with economic and military force to remove their warheads. He's betting that, when faced with the potential destruction of their country, Iran will comply. He's betting also that they won't pop off a nuke or two in retaliation. I'm not so sure that last one is a safe bet. Iran's leadership is just crazy enough to roll the dice and do it."

———•———

The Iranian ambassador to the United States sat somberly in the mahogany-walled office in Washington. He had been summoned by the secretary of state to receive a forcefully blunt message. The most severe international sanctions ever placed on Iran were going to be implemented in forty-eight hours. The country's lifeline of commerce was going to be cut, and remain severed until Iran agreed to immediately dismantle its nuclear arsenal. The ambassador was shown the evidence—photographic and other secretly sourced information. If Iran refused to cooperate, the United States would not stand by and tolerate the nuclearization of their country and the Gulf region. Potential follow-on military action could be used to enforce the old nuclear agreement.

The ambassador vehemently denied the American claims being made. He insisted that any evidence was manufactured, fake, done so to bully the rapidly emerging nation that was garnering so much support by the regional Islamic community of nations. As he prepared to leave the meeting, he indicated he would discuss the American threats with President Batani.

Chapter 66

The Group of Seven had tightly bonded together to support the coming Caliphate in the Middle East. Saudi Arabia, while only somewhat sympathetic to some of their common goals, had taken a renewed course of cultural modernization under their king. When Prince Mohammad bin Salman had succeeded his aging father as the de facto ruler, he'd brought a mandate to move his country into a more pro-Western stance in virtually all areas of political and economic development. It was more of a business decision than a cultural one. He was definitely not turning his back on Islam. Instead, he believed his people could fully embrace their religion while exhibiting nearly all the freedoms and rights of powerhouses like the United States.

The growing turmoil in the region had now prompted the Saudi king to clearly see the Group of Seven as a major obstacle to his plans. In fact, he viewed them as a detriment to inculcating Saudi Muslims into modern society. He had opened his country to a more progressive stance, establishing economic and social reforms. Saudi women were given the right to drive a car, long since prohibited within their culture. He planned to remove many of the restrictions on both men and women that he believed hindered their path to modernization. As such, he resisted the move to unite Sunni and Shiite Muslims in a cause he believed would keep them in the Stone Age.

He did not believe his country was a subordinate military power to Iran, although they hadn't rebuilt their forces to the same degree as Tehran. They relied on their strong past relationship with the

United States for any added security needs that might arise. The Americans were more than willing to supply a steady stream of military hardware to a trusted ally. In fact, the Saudis still believed that even though the US wasn't present on their soil, their relationship with the superpower was so strong that if the Saudis were threatened, the United States would quickly come to their defense. Then again, it was likely that the security of their large oil reserves *might* be a primary reason for any rapid response.

———————•———————

The cargo vessel flying a United States flag arrived in the Dhahran port thirty-six hours earlier to offload cargo. Months before, Iran had completed their conversion of the Singapore-flagged cargo ship to its new identity as the *Crimson Rose*. From Singapore, it had sailed to Hawaii and donned its new US flag and registration. After being anchored off Maui for a month, it began a circuitous route that took it west across the Pacific. Near Okinawa, Japan, it turned off its transponder. It then made its way to the North Korean port of Nampo. Over the next few days, the freighter was loaded down with a deadly cargo of high explosives. Once loading was complete, the *Crimson Rose* headed toward the South China Sea, where it reactivated its transponder. The freighter continued its voyage and ended it in the Persian Gulf, where it waited its turn behind a line of other commercial flagged vessels to pull into the port, eventually docking at the most central location among the other freighters.

When the explosive-laden ship detonated in a violent blast, its billowing black-and-orange ball of flame expanded over fifty-seven hundred feet, taking out the primary cargo docks and destroying three additional ships anchored within the blast radius. The concussive force of the resulting pressure wave was felt much further into the surrounding port area, collapsing buildings and causing the loss of over twenty-five hundred lives.

The Iranians had planned this attack carefully. While they had not divulged their intent to the Group of Seven coalition, they knew that a radical move had to be made to ensure the Saudis would eventually capitulate to the Iranian Muslim reunification plan. The largely Sunni Muslim population of Saudi Arabia had just received a violent shove by the newest nuclear power.

The Saudis reacted with horror at the devastation. Their first reaction was to blame the Americans. Beyond the ship's registration that appeared to belong to their former ally, the US links to the widespread mosque attacks further supported the Saudi conclusions.

The president of the United States was briefed on the explosion and was assured that it was not a US flagged vessel, in spite of the Saudi claims. Efforts by the president to convince Mohammad bin Salman that this was surely a terrorist attack on their Saudi port were met initially with outright skepticism. The Saudi monarch knew that the Americans had not been pleased with the expulsion of foreign military forces from their soil years before.

Eventually, reason won out in the Saudi king's mind and, a bit reluctantly, he accepted America's denial of culpability. He also knew that Iran was not happy with the Saudi reluctance to join the Caliphate and might have been behind the attack. Tehran was a threat to the United States *and* the Gulf region. The Americans now desperately hoped the Saudis would open their country to stage their military aircraft for the battle that was sure to come. That hope never materialized.

In the months preceding the unprovoked attack on Saudi Arabia's main port, Iran had worked very closely with the Group of Seven to slowly position a massive number of Iranian Army personnel on the ground within the borders of each alliance nation. The gradual buildup, including the movement of armor and artillery, was done in a piecemeal fashion over many months so as to not draw undue attention by either the Saudis or the United States. Iranian ship traffic transited the Gulf to forward-position nearly a million men across the entire eastern land border of Saudi Arabia. This unprecedented move by Group of Seven countries to "host"

Iranian forces in their shared collective defense was a vital part of their commitment to execute the holy Caliphate. It was part of the guaranteed "protective nuclear umbrella" of the alliance. Iran's Army had also massed their forces in southern and western Iraq and in Kuwait, where they could move quickly to capture and isolate the oil fields, refineries, and ports.

Ayatollah Batani, Iran's Supreme Leader, had taken a big risk. His hope to blame the Americans for the Dhahran explosion had failed. He realized that now, Saudi Arabia was aligned more strongly than ever with the West.

Their kingdom will pay a heavy price, he thought to himself.

Chapter 67

Almost immediately after the Dhahran blast, the next phase began. The massive attack on Saudi Arabia's air force and army bases was devastating, and hit with little warning. It began when Iran launched the largest nonnuclear tactical ballistic missile strike ever seen in modern warfare, followed closely by an array of ground- and sea-launched cruise missiles. The strikes were so destructive that any exposed Saudi aircraft were damaged or destroyed. While much of the Saudi aircraft fleet were in heavily reinforced underground hangars, the missile attack cratered nearly every runway and taxiway, making any subsequent Saudi counterattack impossible in the short term. Army units were equally decimated, not expecting such an overt violent strike by Iran.

The leaders within the Group of Seven knew of the strikes before they happened. Despite their reluctance to support the Iranian attack, their desire to force the Saudi king to join the Caliphate overrode common sense. They all agreed to remain neutral during the conflict but permit unrestricted use of their territory by Iranian military ground and air forces. The follow-on large-scale Iranian bombing campaign was designed to cripple the Saudi Army's ability to defend the regime. Iran quickly moved their pre-positioned army forces inland in a blitzkrieg fashion and supplemented them with large-scale paratroop insertions and shoreline landings by Iranian marines. The forces moved quickly through the desolate landscape of the Empty Quarter, securing Saudi's oil fields, and establishing defensive perimeters around them all. The crude oil processing facility at Abqaiq was shut down. At this point, Iran controlled the spigot for a healthy part of the world's oil supply. Iranian forces also captured major Saudi coastal cities, including Dhahran and Al Jubayl.

The Saudis repaired a few runways as quickly as they could and used their sheltered fighter aircraft that survived the initial assault to attempt a counterattack. Unfortunately, their reluctance to upgrade their fighters in the past ten years was a tragic mistake. Iran's advanced aircraft, equipped with the latest weaponry purchased from China and Russia, effectively eliminated the Saudi jets while taking few losses. Within only thirty-six hours, the battle to control Saudi Arabia was over. With the exception of a few oil fields in Oman, Iran now had complete control of all the oil resources within the Persian Gulf.

Stroking his long gray beard, Ayatollah Batani was pleased. He considered his next steps.

The United States had been a bit surprised when the freighter had exploded in Dhahran. And they hadn't expected Iran to quickly follow it up with what came next. When they detected the large-scale missile attack on Saudi Arabia, they were stunned at both the size of the attack and Iran's aggression against a fellow Islamic nation. Overhead imagery by orbiting satellites had picked up the gradual movement of Iran's forces over the past months, moving carefully and strategically into the Gulf states. Within diplomatic circles, the movement appeared to be solid evidence of the shared military defense agreement that was a key part of the new alliance.

There had been indicators leading up to these hostilities, signs that the growing tension between Saudi Arabia and Iran might result in military action, but the United States had been slow to react. Additionally, the intel they had received about the Group of Seven's long-term goals of an Islamic Caliphate had not been taken seriously given the long-standing hatred between the Sunni and Shiite Muslim sects. Even with the extraction of US presence from the region, the obvious signs of an impending attack were not acted upon until the Dhahran port explosion and missile attacks.

Within twenty-four hours of the assault on Saudi Arabia, the deployed American forces in Europe and Turkey were placed on alert for potential receipt of air tasking orders to support the king. The Saudi monarch had urgently called the US president to solicit military assistance to protect the country and the royal family. He was effectively surrounded in Riyadh, protected by the only force keeping the Iranians out—his die-hard elite national guard. Unfortunately for the Saudis, the speed with which the Iranians carried out the follow-on attacks left the US forces behind the power curve and unable to slow the rapid Iranian advance.

As the Americans began to move the Fifth Fleet back toward the entrance of the Gulf, Iran executed the next phase of their plan. The attempted closure of the Strait of Hormuz came as another surprise. Even though they had overhead satellite assets closely watching activity in the Gulf, there had been no real expectation that Iran or anyone else would attempt something so drastic. In the past weeks, Iran had begun moving a number of their large freighters toward the narrow mouth of the Strait, anchoring them in strategic positions. The freighters were purportedly laden with agricultural products destined for their customers around the world. The ships were actually decommissioned vessels that were subsequently sunk to block all but a narrow waterway and significantly restrict freedom of navigation.

An extensive array of acoustic, contact and radar-proximity mines were placed in the Strait to restrict any traffic that might try to maneuver past the sunken vessels. To make entry to the Gulf even more difficult, Iran had installed an impressive number of antiaircraft and antiship missile and artillery batteries along the mountainous coastal area surrounding Bandar Abbas, near the narrowest opening of the Strait. Many of these batteries were in hardened structures within the mountain range, making them extremely difficult to destroy.

The strategic significance of closing the entrance to the Gulf was twofold. It would severely restrict the flow of oil, that at least for the moment, was now completely controlled by Iran. It would, at the very least, delay any American forces from operating inside the Gulf waters. The closure of the Strait was currently more about temporarily restricting US warships from entering the Gulf to prevent them from being able to quickly engage in operations against Iranian aggression. Iran knew the Strait of Hormuz likely couldn't stay closed for long but was betting it would remain closed long enough for them to refortify their forces around the Gulf states.

With the closure of the Strait of Hormuz, the Navy positioned their fleet assets outside the Persian Gulf across a wide expanse of ocean off the coast of Oman. It made any air support from their carrier battle group much more difficult, and more dependent on air-to-air refueling to reach the longer-range targets. The other Navy assets were in the Mediterranean, a long way from being able to reach out to touch the enemy. The United States was, for the first time, struggling with the major loss of presence in the Middle East and how they would now respond to Iran's aggression. Within the Pentagon, the Joint Chiefs of Staff ordered the additional forward deployment of long-range bombers into Europe and to Diego Garcia. Additionally, cruise missile warships and submarines were directed to sail toward the anticipated combat arena.

Ayatollah Batani had taken a big gamble with his daring strategy. But he was confident. He knew it was already too late for the Americans to attack—warheads were now being produced and installed at all six ballistic missile launch sites. *If the Americans choose to attack our nuclear facilities, Epsilon will work as designed. Our military can then eliminate the Raptors and the remaining attacking aircraft*, he thought to himself. *We also now have the Shengdau radar—further assurance of our ability to knock the Raptors out of the sky.* Besides, he believed no sane country would attack a nuclear-armed nation.

In Tehran, the military strategists plotted the likely locations where US forces would forward deploy. Iran had eliminated the option to stage in the Group of Seven countries. Turkey, Israel,

Jordan, and Oman were the only remaining locations that could reasonably be used for American strikes against Iran. Iran had made lucrative economic and military support agreements with Turkmenistan and Uzbekistan, which would hopefully prevent any likelihood of US forces being based there.

Iran prepared its air campaign plan, along with its integrated air defense plan, to help counter the American attack that might come. They knew that from each of these locations, the United States would move their top-of-the-line fighter, the Raptor, to lead the strike packages that would attack Iranian territory. After that occurred, Ayatollah Batani would strike a massive blow against the Americans, reducing their stealth fighters to burning hulks on the dusty Persian soil.

The Chinese military advisors present in Tehran were eager to see the war plans move forward. The elimination of the Raptors, America's most advanced stealth fighter, fit nicely into the expansionist strategy. Already, new military installations and outposts dotted the disputed islands and archipelagos in the critical sea lanes off China's coast. Some runways and air defense weapons had been built from almost nothing—islands built on reefs that before had been little more than a beautiful habitat for tropical fish. China believed their new stealth aircraft would dominate any air war once Epsilon and their Shengdau radar proved it could take the Raptors out of the equation. Their leadership was eager to prove their technology, clearing the way for them to firmly plant their flag across the South China Sea—and in Taiwan.

Iran's Supreme Leadership needed just a little more time to complete *all* the warhead installations. A three-pronged diversionary attack should be sufficient to split US forces enough to provide the critical time Batani needed to delay an attack by the Americans, even if only for a few days.

The first prong in Iran's strategy, already underway, was to get the US to direct their attacks on Iranian forces in Saudi Arabia, to focus on the Saudi occupation and the threat to the royal Saudi family. Batani cherished his army, but they were expendable—a useful tool if the end result was a nuclear Iran. His army would fight bravely, and help buy the time he needed. He knew that in the end, the army occupation of Saudi Arabia would fail. It was nothing more than a holding action, a delaying tactic. He could always rebuild his army.

The second prong was a deadly diversionary plot involving another cargo ship. In Sardinia, the *Kangi*, a two-hundred-ton freighter of Yemeni registry, had slowly pulled into the harbor. It was purportedly laden with olives, oranges, and goods manufactured throughout the Gulf region—products to be sold by vendors on the crowded tourist-filled streets of the area around the ship's berthing area. But it had actually been loaded with one hundred tons of ammonium nitrite and fuel oil, an explosive cocktail that would cause incredible blast damage when detonated.

When it exploded, the fireball from the massive explosion encompassed the immediate dock area and destroyed virtually every structure within two thousand yards. Key US Naval facilities were destroyed, and seventy-five Americans were among the dead. The death toll would have been much worse had the explosion happened during peak daylight hours. The United States' immediate outrage was held in check while they assessed who was behind the attack, but they strongly suspected Iran. The reaction by the world, and especially the United States, to another attack on a port city was exactly what Ayatollah Batani had predicted.

The final and third prong had been set in motion a month earlier. Two additional freighters of Middle Eastern registry, configured with high explosives, anchored themselves in US contiguous waters, lining up among the hundreds of freighters waiting for their opportunity to slowly enter the harbors of New York and Boston. The time for them to enter their target harbors was coming soon. The Supreme Leader did not believe that the United States was yet aware of the threat they posed, but he knew that once the detonation occurred in Sardinia, the two freighters would be suspect, and likely stopped. He expected the US Navy to disperse their assets around the United States coastline to look for and eliminate similar threats.

Ayatollah Batani believed that if the Americans focused on Saudi Arabia, the Mediterranean, and the threat to the American mainland, he would buy just a bit more time. Perhaps it would be enough to delay an all-out military attack on his country. In thoughtful prayer, he sought the advice of Allah to send him the message he needed to help carry out his twisted strategy.

Epsilon, for now, still remained a deadly secret to the Americans.

Chapter 68

Captain Matt "Ace" Black climbed out of the cockpit after the long flight over the Atlantic. The air base in central Jordan was new to him, although other American forces had deployed into that location in the past for joint training with their air force. Jordan had been a staunch ally of the United States for years. With the explosion of activity in the Gulf, the Jordanian king welcomed the Raptors.

The fuses had been lit initially by the attack on Saudi Arabia, and then by the Sardinia blast. Now, just days before his squadron landed, a major Turkish city was hit by cruise missiles launched from Iraq, likely from mobile launchers owned and operated by the Iranians. Hundreds of civilian casualties caused Turkey to threaten Tehran's destruction. The US president reacted immediately, desperately trying to keep Turkey from retaliating. Turkey agreed to hold back their forces and join the growing American coalition. Turkish bases were on the list of the few forward locations for American aircraft and were being counted upon to be available for strike force aircraft.

Five squadrons of the United States Air Force F-22 Raptors, over half of the entire Raptor fleet, deployed to the region in an attempt to gain control of the mess that was happening. More would have been sent, but fear of overcommitment of its forces kept that from occurring. After all, things were not well in other parts of the world, in places like the Korean peninsula, and *that* powder keg could be set off at any moment. Raptors needed to be held back to respond to other potential aggressors.

Along with the Raptors, key intelligence-gathering aircraft were positioned in the theater of operations. RC-135 aircraft, critical to the collection of electronic data, were based at classified locations just outside the Gulf region in an effort to limit any potential targeting of these crucial limited assets.

Ace glanced across the broad airfield parking ramp at the array of Royal Jordanian Air Force fighter aircraft. Since the uptick in hostilities, all the jets were fully armed and ready for combat. Next to Ace, his buddy Flamer was already doing his jet's postflight inspection.

"Bet you're glad to get out of that seat, Flamer. I'll never get used to the long hops over the pond. But it sure beats a stuffy airline seat crammed in between crying kids and dudes who brought their salami sandwich with them to stink up the air."

"You got that right, Ace. My ass cheeks feel like they're burning up about now. I gotta walk a bit to get the circulation back!"

Ace chuckled at the comment and then began his own postflight inspection. His jet performed superbly throughout the long flight. One thing he could always count on was his top-notch maintenance team.

All the 94th Fighter Squadron jets arrived in Jordan ready for combat. They flew in with the full complement of ordnance the Raptors needed to fly their first combat mission. The limited availability of airfield parking reduced the number of jets that could use the base, and only their eighteen F-22s had been sent there. The remainder of the tasked Raptors were sent to locations in Turkey and Oman. Israel, while having space to bed down some US aircraft, chose to remain neutral, at least for the time being. Their prime minister was concerned that they were too easy a target for Iran's intermediate range ballistic missiles, should the Ayatollah be given a reason to attack them—and letting the Americans stage war planes there was a great reason! This was the largest deployment of F-22s to date—and the message it sent to Iran was significant. The US was clearly signaling that the power and might of the world's greatest military was prepared to reset the geopolitical environment that Iran so violently upended.

The weary Langley fighter pilots headed into the Jordanian squadron operations facility. There would be time later for rest. Ace and Flamer grabbed some bottled water from the table inside the briefing room and took their seats. First, they would receive a series of briefings outlining the likelihood of combat operations beginning in the very near future.

Looking up at the large Middle East map, and the countries bordering the entire coastline of the Persian Gulf, they couldn't help but think about how many conflicts had happened in the past decades. What had really changed? Not much in their minds. A dictator removed here—a government change there—new partnerships made, and some broken. It was as if the entire region was content to be in a constant state of strife. It appeared the result of indecision about whether to move forward into the advanced technological world, to embrace some of what the developed world offered, or retreat back a thousand years or more and adopt the rigid structure that came with Sharia law.

"Flamer, I can just sense where all this is going. If we think Iran is going to just hand back the territory they've grabbed as if nothing had happened, then we're sadly mistaken. They aren't going to give up anything without a fight—and certainly not their nukes. They didn't just spend their cash on prayer rugs and misbaha beads. Now they can just about match us in firepower when it comes to the advanced fighters they got from Russia and China."

"Roger that, Ace. But it's been a while since we did a major-league ass kicking. I'm itching for another test of my awesome skill as the world's best fighter pilot," Flamer said with a wide grin on his face.

"I know you didn't slip a flask of whiskey into your cockpit—so the only thing I can think of is that you're suffering from oxygen deprivation from your flight. Even *you* know that nobody outdoes me when it comes to handling this jet," Ace said, laughing good-naturedly.

The room snapped to attention when the brigadier general from Central Command stepped through the doorway and onto the stage.

"Take your seats," he directed.

What followed was a sobering discussion on the state of Iran's military, including their formidable air defenses, air force assets, and advanced weaponry. The battle plan for a conflict with the Persian country had been in place for many years and was constantly updated as Tehran invested heavily in their military. New defensive systems in place along all of Iran's borders and around critical airfields and weapons depots were deadly accurate. The bountiful Iranian harvest purchased from Russia included an assortment of radar-directed antiaircraft guns ranging from 23 mm to 100 mm, all of which presented a direct threat to low-flying aircraft. In the surface-to-air missile category, the SAMs included the SA-6, SA-8, and SA-13 mobile missiles with ranges from six to fourteen miles. Long-range acquisition and targeting radar systems, now in place, guaranteed that there were virtually no areas of ingress that were without significant threats to any attacking force. Likewise, Iran's purchase of advanced fighters carrying long-range air-to-air missiles would force the US to use their stealth fighters to lead any attack into the heavily fortified country. Tehran also had hardened their command-and-control centers for survivability and networked them in an overlapping fashion. This minimized the likelihood of a one-strike decapitation of their ability to prosecute their fight. All of these factors were rolled into the American battle planning.

"As you all know from the press, the threat of economic sanctions didn't cause Iran to skip a beat. Their aggression in Saudi Arabia, Turkey, and the blasts in Sardinia and Dhahran, are graphic evidence that their country is out of control.

"Unfortunately, the global nature of all these attacks have caused quite a problem for us. Instead of focusing our military might singularly on Iran, we've had to split up our forces to counter the multiple threats across the globe. That doesn't mean we can't handle the job here in the Gulf, but it definitely has pulled some of the teeth from our bite."

The senior officer discussed the disruption of Iran's ship-borne threat to the US. He explained that America had been expecting an attack for some time, similar to what had happened in Dhahran and Sardinia. The softness of the world's ports was a tempting target and clearly present in the mind of any terrorist wanting to make a big-time statement. All indications from both blasts were that a dirty bomb had not been used, but the loss of life and widespread damage from the massive explosion was still tragic.

While comforted with the fact that no similar attack had happened in the US, the military, along with Customs and Border Protection, shifted their already-heightened intelligence apparatus into high gear. On any given day, there were hundreds of foreign-registered freighters arrayed off the east and west coasts of the continental United States. Each ship was carefully scrutinized for its intended port of call, the flag it was flying under, its originating port, and the cargo it was expected to deliver. Homeland Security, the Coast Guard, and the Navy were on high alert for similar attacks in America.

Two Middle Eastern–flagged vessels that drew the most scrutiny had transited a circuitous route over the past two months. Both had, at some point in their travels, stopped in the Persian Gulf. There were gaps where each freighter had stopped before arriving at their current position. While they did not show Iranian registry, intel analysts suspected that might be a ruse and that the ships could be a similar configuration to the Dhahran and Sardinian attacks, now set to explode in US ports.

"You have all heard the reports on the explosions in Dhahran and Sardinia—nasty attacks with quite a few lives lost. We've traced the ships that caused the destruction there to the true owner. That would be Iran, who did a pretty clever job of disguising ship used in the Dhahran attack to appear as an American-flagged vessel. The

Sardinia blast was also traced to Iran. Our intel guys back at NSA advised the president of the likely threat posed by two freighters off New York and Boston. Our commander-in-chief gave the order to interdict them and neutralize the threat. We've received reports already that our SEAL teams have taken care of the problem with no loss of American lives. Can't say the same for the freighters' crews. The Navy SEAL attacks came so fast and silently that the crews never knew what was happening until it was too late. The SEALs found no nuclear devices but did find massive quantities of explosives. If the ships had gotten into our ports, the death and damage caused by the blasts would have been severe. Both freighters were safely secured."

He paused for a moment.

"Sanctions haven't worked, with both China and Russia opposed to them altogether. Fortunately, they both indicated they had no real desire to engage in combat operations in Iran.

"The United States is not going to stand idly by while Iran flexes its newly found muscle. At the same time, nobody is interested in engaging in another long, drawn-out conflict like Iraq or Afghanistan. The objectives laid out by our military strategists and the National Command Authority are going to be very specific, and very limited. We know we need to hit multiple targets on the Arabian Peninsula, in countries where Iranian forces are launching attacks or holding key areas. Although the US believes it might further alienate countries that we have previously had good relations with, the threat in those countries has to be neutralized. Resetting the status quo will be the first order of battle in that area.

"The president has given our Joint Chiefs the go-ahead to begin combat ops against Iranian targets. Although we have no diplomatic relations with Iran, we're using an intermediary to pass information to Ayatollah Batani. We're letting him know that we are, for now, not attacking his nuclear weapons capability. We are only doing what we can to liberate our friends, the Saudis, from illegal Iranian aggression. We have demanded that Iran withdraw its forces from Saudi Arabia and dismantle all SAM batteries they've put in place along the western Persian Gulf territories.

"We've also demanded the removal of any offensive military forces from those areas. We intend to use our military power to encourage that to happen. Some of that power will be in Iranian air space, to limit counterstrikes by them as we take out the Iranian occupation forces along the Saudi coast. We are also letting Iran know that we unquestionably have the backing from our allies to enforce the eventual denuclearization of their country.

"This isn't going to be easy," the general said. "As you are all intimately aware, Iran has had years to build up military forces. We certainly have the technology and mass on our side, but they now possess powerful offensive and defensive forces.

"Additionally, the absence of our previous forward operating bases poses a real challenge. We'll make do with what we've got. We're going to rely on the Raptors to lead most of the strike forces, using their stealth and ability to control the battle space and execute attacks on the specific strike package targets. We've definitely got the edge over Iran's fighter aircraft, but with the advanced missiles they've acquired from China, we've got to be on our toes. Nobody here wants Iran to 'reach out and touch them' with their low-observable long-range air-to-air missiles. Our objective is to hit them first, hit them hard, and take out as many of their fighters as we can before they can do any real damage to us."

He went on to address how strike packages from Turkey would hit key Iranian targets in Saudi Arabia, essentially trying to limit any further action by them.

"The mission packages for the attack will be led by your Raptors and composed of the usual Strike Eagles, Falcons, and Eagles. You may be wondering about our B-2 Spirit stealth bombers and F-35 Lightning II stealth fighters. Unfortunately, our F-35s are still not yet suitable for combat due to major problems with the life support system and maintenance software. You remember that we had some early development issues with the Raptors and solved them. The F-35s are a different issue from the Raptors—engineers are wrestling with the nagging problems and should soon have them solved. Our B-2s are being held back as well until we have significantly degraded the advanced Iranian SAM network. Then, if needed, they'll be turned loose.

"The Navy will provide their Growlers to run interdiction of Iranian radar sites. Unfortunately, with the closure of the Gulf, they are competing with our limited refueling assets just to get to the targets and back. As usual, the E-3 AWACS will provide battlespace awareness and keep you informed of anything that might approach friendly aircraft. We've got significant NATO support as well—England, Germany, France, and Spain—but their strike packages will be separate from ours.

"Since the Iranians have shut down a number of the primary forward staging areas that we've used in the past, we are limited to Jordan, western Oman, and Turkey. We expected that Uzbekistan and Turkmenistan would open up for us, but for some reason, they have not yet given their approval to stage from there. We've got an air bridge for fighters coming from Mediterranean bases, but as you might guess, we have limits on tanker support to cover all the requirements. There is a possibility that we may have a couple of bases in Israel open up, but at the present time, they are holding back their approval to use their territory.

"The air tasking order will likely occur within the next seventy-two hours. So, take the time to get your jets ready for combat, and get some rest. Once we kick this thing off, there won't be much leisure time," he said. "Any questions?"

"Yes, sir, I have one," said Captain Black. "You mentioned we weren't striking targets on the Arabian Peninsula, but we understand Iran has moved quite a few of their fighter aircraft to those locations. Shouldn't we be hitting those bases to prevent them from trying to take out our strike packages?"

"Good question. We'll have our AWACS watching for anything that might try to move against us from those bases. Threats to our forces will be taken out, and the AWACS will direct which targets are to be killed. I want to be clear. We will not hit the bases. We're not trying to shut down their runways, or hit their facilities. Remember that those bases ultimately belong to countries that we used to have some pretty good relations with. We're not going to risk destroying those bases and eliminate any likelihood of resuming our previous relations when this mess is over. But we'll hit any SAM sites that try to target our aircraft, no matter where the sites are located. Iranian aircraft will be free game if they take to the air. We want to make sure that when this conflict is over, we convince these countries that this battle was against Iran's brand of radical Islam—not against them. We hope they'll let us back into their bases in the future."

"Sir, what about the nukes? Are we going to take them out?" Matt felt compelled to ask that question.

"Not at this time. We prefer to try to forcefully encourage Iran to dismantle them. If we get solid intel of their intent to launch one, we will likely get the order to take it out. No one really likes that option, as you might imagine. Any decision on that will come straight from our president—he being the single point to authorize a strike against Iran's nuclear forces. He did not want a military leader, either in Washington or in the combat theater, to be making that critical decision. He and he alone would decide to attack another country's nuclear arsenal.

"If we do hit a nuke launch site, we could get plenty of radiation from the tactical nuclear warheads. We'd expect radioactive debris to be dispersed around the area. DoD has some ideas, though, that would *almost* eliminate that possibility. I'm not at liberty to go into that with you at this time.

"If they launch before we hit them first, who knows what our National Command Authority will direct regarding our own nuclear response. It could likely end up as the first nuclear exchange in history."

In Washington, D.C., the president actually believed that to fundamentally reset the status quo, he must eventually strike at the heart of the expanding radical Islamic power base. He must essentially decapitate the leadership, remove Iran's ability to sustain operations around the Gulf, and thus encourage the reestablishment of the previous norm, if one could call it that.

The briefing concluded, and the weary pilots exited the room. Most were deep in thought as they tried to imagine exactly what they would face once they received the launch order. Ace and Flamer headed back to the portable air-conditioned buildings set up for the aircrews. The Jordanians had done the best they could with the limited space they had and at least provided the aircrews hard-sided buildings instead of tents. The maintenance and support folks had to deal with living in tents—not unusual when at a base with limited accommodations. At least they had wooden floors and air-conditioning units.

"I need a shower to wash this grime off me. Then maybe grab some grub before I turn in. Sound reasonable to you, Flamer?"

"Good idea. Meet you at the chow hall in thirty minutes."

"I'd like to make a call back home, but the general said we're in a comm shutdown condition until after we kick things off against the Iranians," Matt commented.

"I know what you mean. But I believe the network back at Langley has gotten in touch with our families to let them know we got here in one piece."

A few hours later, his stomach no longer growling from lack of food, Matt Black's head hit the pillow. He was asleep within minutes.

Chapter 69

"This is a great day for Islam," Batani remarked to his closest advisors. He turned and looked directly into General Baghdadi's eyes. The general nodded his acknowledgement.

Baghdadi knew the meaning of the Ayatollah's dark stare. The onus was on him to ensure the remaining parts of the Caliphate's plan were successfully executed. He had created the diversions for the Americans—the plan to divide their forces. The attacks on Saudi Arabia, Sardinia, and the freighters off America's coast, their deployment of forces throughout the Group of Seven—it had to work!

"The Americans have already begun moving their forces forward. They are dispersing exactly where we expected. Our alliances appear to be holding firm in their desire to keep the Americans out of their countries. Our military strength is present in force across the Gulf." Baghdadi was a bit proud of his profound statement.

The Ayatollah pronounced, "Iran is now the true leader of Islam in the Persian Gulf. *Inshallah!*"

———•———

It was rapidly becoming obvious to the Iranians that they had underestimated the breadth and reach of the United States armed forces. America had always prided itself on being able to handle any contingency, even multiple contingencies at the same time. It was seldom easy, but American willpower and the nation's expansive resources always managed to get it done.

Within hours of the Saudi royal family's request, a large contingent of US forces, led by members of the 82nd Airborne, were on their way. They were inserted in blocking positions around Riyadh, bolstering Saudi Arabia's national guard forces. Additionally, batteries of advanced Patriot missiles were airlifted into Riyadh to supplement those already in place and to defend against any subsequent Iranian air strike. For now, the Saudi Royals were secure.

The United States now prioritized their target list. In spite of what the Iranian leadership had hoped about delaying actions, the US had other ideas about their top priority targets, and some of those were in the heart of Iran. The Americans weren't ignoring Iranian targets outside of Iran either. They would attack them all.

Ayatollah Batani remarked, "General, I expect that you have done as I have asked. I presume our jet fighters are prepared for launch and our missile defenses are ready for the assault that we know is coming?" His question to Baghdadi was more of a veiled threat.

"Our antiaircraft missile batteries are on high alert, and our radar sites and control centers are prepared to take out the infidels when they are in range."

The general smiled with confidence. In spite of the test he had run earlier on the lone Raptor, he silently hoped that the means to defeat the F-22s' stealth capability would work as planned. If not, then the destruction of key Iranian facilities and their nuclear capability was virtually assured. His own tenure in the military, and even his ability to *keep on living*, were also at great risk.

Iran had done its homework. The reports from Syria verified that Raptors led the strike forces into battle—and would assuredly lead the attack in the Iranian sky as well.

"Our fighter aircraft are ready to kill anything that gets by our missile batteries," the general said.

"The long-range low-observable air-to-air missiles provided by our Chinese friends will take a heavy toll once Epsilon highlights the Raptor's position."

He thought about the expected bloom in the stealthy Raptor's radar signature once the embedded Epsilon code was triggered by the satellite. This was, after all, the key to success, and even more so, the key to survivability for Iran's fighter aircraft, and the defense of their critical military and technological facilities. Once the Raptors were out of the way, the rest of the attacking American force would be easy pickings for Iran's formidable military.

"Proceed with Epsilon when we know the American fighters have launched and are approaching our border," the Ayatollah declared, his bony finger pointed toward the sky. "Allah will guide our sword to strike at the heart of evil in this world."

General Baghdadi nodded, turned abruptly, and headed out of the gilded conference room. Ayatollah Batani watched his general depart. He knew so much was relying on his underling to carry out his plan, and equally on his scientists and their ability to release the satellite burst at precisely the right time, when the majority of Raptors were most vulnerable. From twenty-three thousand miles up, the satellite had the capability of broadcasting the signal to every part of Iran's land mass and the air space above it. If done at the right time, Iranian fighter jets, equipped with their long-range stealth missiles, and upgraded SAMs with the latest Russian technology would easily pick off the Raptors leading the mission cells.

———•———

Back at Omega, Khalil intently watched the newscasts. He knew that the fruits of his labor were about to be harvested. He fully expected to see US forces engaged in a battle with Iran at any moment. He wondered about how effective the deadly defense strategy would be. Would the Americans be stopped in their tracks? Would the plan to defeat the stealth capability actually *work*, allowing Iran to strike a monumental blow in the name of Islam? He wished he was not on the sidelines back in the United States. He longed to be part of the plan, part of the action, part of Epsilon's execution. He didn't know it yet, but he would get his wish.

Two weeks earlier, as Ayatollah Batani had planned for what he hoped would be Iran's biggest victory ever, he had insisted that he be surrounded by his best scientists and engineers. He wanted them to be present with him in the hardened underground command center so that any strategy changes could be done quickly. The chief engineer mentioned that Khalil Ruffa was an integral part of the Epsilon strategy and that he should be considered among the key technical staff in the command post. After all, he knew more about the F-22 and Epsilon than anyone. Word was quickly passed to Sheikh Rahainee in Texas, and simultaneously to Dr. Katari. As soon as the messages were received, Katari contacted Khalil.

The Ayatollah knew that once Khalil left the United States, it was unlikely that he would ever return to Omega. Even the best-kept secrets are eventually revealed. Once that happened, Khalil would be a marked man, wanted by the American authorities for his treasonous actions. It was time for Khalil to sever his ties to his adopted country and join Ayatollah Batani's inner circle.

Khalil's travel to Tehran had to happen quickly. It could not draw any attention from a country on hyperalert for any unusual signals of radical activity. There was no reason that Khalil would be the subject of federal agent scrutiny, but his handlers were taking no chances. A reasonable alibi had been formulated. Katari arranged his travel to Buenos Aires, Argentina—another flight would eventually get him into Tehran. The Argentina stop was billed as an opportunity for Khalil to represent Omega at a leading technical academy and discuss opportunities in science, technology, engineering and math—to help advance the company's stature on the world stage. Tehran worked with their South American contacts to create this subterfuge.

Khalil was more than excited about the opportunity in front of him.

"Allah be praised," he remarked aloud to himself. "I have been granted the opportunity of a lifetime—to be present when the

American military is punished, and hopefully destroyed by my own hand, by my work on Epsilon. It is the revenge I have been waiting for."

Khalil hoped with all his heart that the long-standing blood debt would be paid very soon. He prayed that Matt "Ace" Black, the son of the man who had killed his family, would pay the ultimate price with his life while trapped in his Raptor's flaming wreckage.

Nonetheless, Khalil was concerned. It had to appear to Omega that his travel was routine, for a professional purpose. There could be no suspicion raised that his purpose was other than to represent his company in a technical briefing. Fortunately, the CEO readily agreed to Khalil's travel—Omega's best engineer was the right choice for this event.

———————•———————

The upcoming conflict between Iran and the United States was about to explode on the world stage. Time was now of the essence for Khalil to get to Tehran as fast as possible.

Khalil caught the flight to Buenos Aires out of the Dallas–Fort Worth International Airport and landed in Argentina late in the evening. Per his instructions, he checked in to the Buenos Aires Plaza Hotel and awaited the call he knew was coming. Dr. Katari told him to report to the airport early the next morning to begin his travel to Iran. His first-class ticket would be waiting for him at check-in.

Once he arrived in Tehran, he was met by the chief engineer and whisked away to the hardened command center near Rostamabad. Khalil was surprised at the innocuous appearance of the terrain that hid the heart of Iran's ability to prosecute the upcoming conflict with the Americans. He was amazed at the elaborate security, the blast doors that provided entry, the elevators that took him and his escorts to the integrated command center deep underground. He was met by a few of the engineers and scientists, who praised his critical contributions to the Islamic Caliphate.

Dr. Katari met Khalil there and escorted him for a brief meeting with Ayatollah Batani, a rare opportunity for anyone not tied to the Supreme Leader's inner circle. Khalil entered the small secure chamber within the expansive facility and saw the Ayatollah sitting by an ornate gold-inlaid table. He was flanked by two very large, very serious-looking bodyguards. Batani motioned for Khalil to approach and pointed toward one of the two brown calf-leather chairs across from him. Before Khalil could speak, the Ayatollah began.

"My son, you have done a great thing in the name of Allah. You have risked much to ensure the success of our holy Caliphate."

He paused a moment, his dark stare focused on Khalil's eyes.

"A great deal is dependent upon your work, *and* the success of Epsilon. I trust that it will strike the Americans from our sky. Our destiny is in your hands."

Khalil was stunned and wide-eyed on hearing that Iran's destiny, its future, was riding on *his* efforts.

"There are no second chances with Epsilon," Batani said. "It must work as intended, the first time we use it. The Americans will not hesitate to destroy us if it fails."

"Your holiness, I understand. Epsilon will work—I assure you. I have done all that you have asked. I want to see the Raptors fall from the sky. Iran will have its victory, and its destiny will be assured."

Batani nodded and with his bony fingers waved Khalil away from his chamber. The meeting was over. As Khalil exited the small room, he couldn't control the rising tide of bile surging up through his throat. He choked it down and tried not to display the fear he felt—the fear of failure, and the consequences.

Why does the responsibility for success or failure rest on me? I did my part. Epsilon is perfectly embedded in the Raptor's software. Whether it works when the satellite pulse triggers it is another thing. I had nothing to do with that testing. But it will work. It must work!

He wandered through the facility, clearly impressed with the level of technology Iran had installed to manage their military forces. He stopped at a large electronic screen that displayed the anticipated location of American and coalition forces. When Khalil saw that the 94th Fighter Squadron was present, his heart soared.

Chapter 70

Royal Jordanian Air Base

T he pilots were restless—red-blooded warriors didn't like to wait. They were Type A, full-throttle people. All of them were eager for the order to begin combat operations. They were told that the war room in the Pentagon had been running around the clock for the past week. The myriad worldwide intelligence assets were streaming their critical bits of information into the cells of analysts intent on deciphering each fragment, trying to make sense of the information.

After two days of tense waiting, everyone at the eastern Jordanian base was getting pretty antsy. Captain Matt "Ace" Black received the message to join the pilots in the main briefing room to get the latest update on the rapidly degrading situation in the Gulf and off the coast of the United States.

Ace looked over at the briefer who had just stepped to the podium.

"Gentlemen and ladies, take your seats and let's get right to it," Colonel Rafe Armstrong directed.

"Our forces have already moved forward from the US and Europe to every potential friendly location that we can use to stage our aircraft. As you know, our previous forward base locations have been shut down, so combat sorties will be pretty long, and require plenty of tanker support. The Navy is moving a carrier battle group off the coast of Oman and Pakistan. That's as close as we can get since the entrance to the Gulf is shut down.

"Within the next twenty-four hours, expect to get the order to go. The remaining forces from the States and Europe are ready to integrate with a combined set of strike packages—all led by Raptors. Besides your unit, you're probably aware of the other four Raptor squadrons dispersed at other bases in Jordan, Turkey, and Oman. Israel hasn't given the clearance yet. Our NATO partners stepped up to the plate, but in a limited fashion. As you know, years of open borders have significantly increased the Muslim representation within most of their countries. As a result, their governments have reacted in a bit of a whipsaw fashion to any engagement in a war against any Islamic country. You and I know it's not about a war on Islam, but eliminating the radical element that seems to want to impose its twisted, ideological ideals on the entire Gulf region, and eventually, the rest of the world.

"Of course we'll have AWACS and our RC-135 assets to help where they can. We'll do the join-up of our tactical mission cells at our specified orbits over nonthreatening territory. Our tanker orbits will be in strategic locations to keep your jets with as much fuel as possible before engaging the enemy. Our Eagles will have the job of keeping the tankers out of harm's way.

"An initial strike by our Navy assets from off the coast of Oman—four SSBns, Ohio-class ballistic missile subs—will launch Tomahawk Land Attack Missiles, or TLAMs. They'll go after the command-and-control nodes in order to disrupt their ability to effectively control their air defense missile sites and coordinate air strikes from their airfields.

"If the TLAMs are successful, ingress into our key targets will be a bit less hairy. We should be able to pick up enough intel from the strikes to give us a good indication on mission success. That info will get to you ASAP. But the real evidence of success will hopefully be the absence of SAMs as you head for your targets."

He continued, "If you take battle damage and need to eject, you'll have to make it to feet wet—the Gulf—or to friendly airspace. As you might guess, there are no search-and-recovery assets going into Iran at this point. We'll reassess that once we establish control of the battle.

"Some of you have asked about information that has come from our European sources about a new counterstealth radar. Supposedly, a Chinese-developed system is purported to be capable of accurately targeting a fifth-generation stealth aircraft. There were some rumors that Iran may have acquired it from China, but we have no real evidence that they received it—or that it even works.

"Diplomatic efforts are ongoing, as best they can, to persuade Iran to dismantle their missiles immediately—but at this point, it's unlikely to happen." He paused.

"If Batani expects to keep his country from being decimated, he'll need to stop the aggression and get into discussion on eliminating the nukes. If the worst happens and we get intel of an impending or actual nuclear missile launch, then all bets are off. The full power of the United States will be used to eliminate the threat. That could include our own use of tactical nuclear weapons. That, of course, will be the president's decision."

The silence in the briefing room was deafening.

"Holy shit," whispered Flamer to Ace. "We're actually planning a nuclear strike of our own?"

"But," continued the colonel, "we hope it doesn't come to that. Instead we'll move to essentially shut down their leadership once and for all. That is the ultimate center of gravity in Iran. It's the one thing that will make them quit the fight. We'll also do our best to reduce their military to their pre-growth levels and get them back to the relative equilibrium that existed in the Gulf ten years ago."

He continued, "Of course, if there is an impending launch, we'll also hit every target linked to their nuclear capability—command-and-control, labs, centrifuge facilities, warhead production centers, launch sites."

He paused. "We just need to stay vigilant for any new threats. If there are no questions, make sure the support teams have your aircraft ready to go."

Before Colonel Armstrong walked off, he turned to the solemn aircrews.

"This is going to be a tough one. Without a doubt, we're going to face an adversary like we haven't faced before. Iran has the firepower to make us pay dearly if we're not careful. We've got the edge, I'm sure, but there's no room for error. Good luck and Godspeed."

The apprehensive group of warriors snapped to attention as the colonel left the stage. The thoughts flying through their heads ranged from eagerness to take the fight to the enemy to concern over their ability to survive the toughest battle they had ever engaged in. There were, of course, thoughts of their families, and thoughts about how many of the aircrews in the room might not see their families again. They had thoughts about bailing out over enemy territory and about the slim margin between life and death.

As Ace and Flamer headed out of the building, the beauty of the Jordanian sunset stunned them. The golden hue from the rapidly disappearing solar orb seemed to bounce off the concrete parking ramp, making the F-22s a beautiful silhouette against the darkening sky. As they looked across the ramp at their squadron of war birds, a surreal feeling came over them both. What appeared to them as objects of beauty, would, in a few hours, be objects of war, objects of death.

"This shit is getting real," Flamer exclaimed to Ace. "When you get these crazies threatening our homeland, you've really got my attention. And I'm pissed, to say the least."

"We've been pretty fortunate since 9/11 to have stopped anything major from hitting our soil. Guess it was just a matter of time."

Ace headed out to the flight line, taking a good look at the Raptors. His maintenance team, the most hardworking, dedicated bunch of men and women he had ever seen, were busy inspecting, repairing, fueling and arming the aircraft. The Raptors would be ready when the air tasking order came, directing the beginning of the Iranian strikes.

"Sir, great to see you out here mingling with the riffraff." Senior Master Sergeant Joseph Osgood was one of the best aircraft production superintendents Ace had on his team.

Ace always enjoyed the good-natured sparring he had with the folks he trusted most, and those who saw in him one of the best pilots on earth.

"Osgood, I'm surprised you aren't already in the rack. After all, you're getting up in your years and desperately need your beauty sleep," replied Ace, laughing as he said it.

The tall, lanky senior noncommissioned officer extended his grease-stained hand, expecting the young captain to pull back from the offered hand shake. Ace grabbed his hand and, with an unusually firm grip, shook it hard. Sergeant Osgood winced just a bit but recovered quickly from the viselike compression Ace offered him. He wouldn't let an officer think he couldn't take a challenge. Osgood squeezed back, looking straight into Ace's eyes for any sign of pain. He saw none.

"The fleet is just about ready. Just a few more maintenance actions needed. Don't want you guys to light up the sky for enemy radar." Osgood was dead serious with the conversation now.

"I know you'll take good care of us, Joe," replied Ace. "All I ask is for good, solid Code One jets, with no issues that prevent us from taking out these radicals."

"No problem, sir." He continued, "All *I* ask is that *you* bring yourself and our pilots back in one piece. I heard scuttlebutt about the type of threat we'll be going up against. It sounds like it's going to be pretty dangerous. Almost like going up against a major superpower, from a military capability standpoint."

Ace nodded almost imperceptibly.

"We can handle it. Nothing tops the F-22 Raptor. We'll be leading the strike forces in and out of harm's way. I may not get a chance tonight to thank all the folks for getting our jets combat-ready. Please make sure you pass it on to all of them."

"Will do, sir. Kick some ass for us!"

THOMAS BELISLE

Chapter 71

The launch order was disseminated the following day at 1700 hours, local Jordanian time. All aircraft from the 94th Fighter Squadron were armed and ready. Matt met with the other pilots in his flight prior to mission planning the separate strike packages that would attack key sites in Iran.

"I want you all to know that we're as ready as we'll ever be to conduct combat operations against this radical regime. Our training has been world-class, and our aircraft have received the latest modifications, including threat data updates for the areas we are attacking. We have four flights of four Raptors launching to join with the strike packages that we'll lead into Iran. Other strike packages are hitting targets in Saudi Arabia, eliminating the occupying forces. Our launch times vary with the distance to the orbits for each package. At the prescribed time, we will simultaneously ingress Iran to overwhelm their command-and-control capability—it should be significantly degraded by the TLAMs that will hit their critical nodes and air defenses thirty minutes prior to us crossing the border."

"All aircraft within our individual strike packages have secure communication with our F-22s. But, to that point, keep the dialogue to an absolute minimum to avoid compromising our locations to enemy eavesdropping. Although we should be okay with minimum comm, there's no telling what added capabilities Iran has procured during their buying spree."

"Finally, be careful. Watch your six. Hit the targets hard. Kill any fighters before they know we're there—and bring all our teammates home."

Ace made it a point to shake hands with all of the pilots. He knew that there was always a possibility that somebody would not make it back. The heavy feeling within the pit of his stomach was an automatic reflex, the result of his concern and love for all combat warriors.

The launches began at 0200 the following morning. Each flight of four Raptors roared off the long dark runway and climbed slowly into the starlit Jordanian sky. Across the entire Gulf region, similar launches were taking place, joining Raptors with their respective strike packages.

The largest collection of tanker assets ever assembled in one theater of war was in position, bridging the long flight times for aircraft orbiting outside Iran—from its northern border, along its western flank, and down to its southernmost tip. Every in-commission tanker was engaged outside the threat areas, providing fuel to the thirsty fighter aircraft before they began their attacks into the heart of Iran. The trusty Eagles, armed with AMRAAMs and Sidewinders, watched for any sign of Iranian fighters that might threaten the tankers.

———————•———————

In the command-and-control bunker near Rostamabad, Ayatollah Batani received reports of the TLAM attacks. They had done some damage, but Iran's military had fully expected the cruise missile assault. As the TLAMs were inbound, Iran's advanced fighters took to the air, armed with stealthy long-range air-to-air missiles. The fighter aircraft fleet dispersed their forces across the countryside, using every available commercial airfield to help limit the impact of the expected air base damage.

Their advanced missile defense network was able to destroy most of the attacking TLAMs, and as a result, the command-and-control network survived with only minimal degradation.

"Excellent," Batani exclaimed. "We are still on track to execute the trap on the Raptor aircraft. Keep to our plan, General. Our intelligence cells embedded across the region have been providing data on all enemy aircraft launches, including the F-22s. The fools in Jordan, western Oman and Turkey don't even know we're tracking their activities. The information has painted a clear picture of their attack timing. The Raptors will be arriving at our borders soon, since the TLAMs have already hit us. You must be sure that our satellite signal is transmitted at the right time."

"We are ready to engage our satellite, and broadcast the signal that will reveal the Raptor's position in our sky," Baghdadi responded. "Our Chinese radar operators insist that the Shengdau system is set to engage as well. Our fighter pilots are ready with our long-range missiles to destroy these infidels while they foolishly believe they are invisible! Allah is by our side, Supreme Leader, and will guide our swords. The Caliphate will strike a mighty blow for the glory of Islam."

———————•———————

Orbit Crisco, the assembly point thirty-five thousand feet in the sky near northern Saudi Arabia, was getting pretty busy. As Ace approached it with his two four-ship flights of eight Raptors, his radio was alive with coded chatter from each group of fighter aircraft. All aircraft had topped off their gas from the string of refueling tankers. Ace was now assembled with his force of Strike Eagles, Fighting Falcons, Growlers and Wild Weasels. On cue, he turned the nose of his stealthy aircraft, followed by the remaining three Raptors in his flight, toward the coast of Iran. His strike force split into their prescribed attack formations. It was 0400 in the predawn hours.

At the same time, nearly identical activities were taking place from seven other orbits bracketing the perimeter of the Iranian territory. F-22 crews began leading their respective combat forces toward targets in Iran. The massive power of the Raptors' sensors and radar scanned the sky for bogeys. They also looked for any SAM radar signals trying to identify their position.

The Growlers and Wild Weasels knew their targets, at least the fixed SAM sites identified from satellite imagery. Those would be their primary tasks to take out ahead of the non-stealthy strike aircraft. The mobile SAM sites were another matter. They were well-camouflaged, moved constantly, and were just as deadly as the fixed sites. The pilots had to stay on their toes to avoid ambush by the mobile missile batteries while they focused on the fixed sites.

The Raptors began their run across Iran's border. As the Raptors detected SAM radar signals well out of range of the strike force, they securely passed the locations to the Growlers and Wild Weasels. Across Iran, high-speed anti-radiation missiles, HARMs, streaked across the sky and zeroed in on the command-and-control radar units. Bright yellow explosions lit the dark countryside as the radar sites disappeared into unrecognizable rubble.

Ace proceeded with his flight of four Raptors through the maze of surface-to-air missile threat areas, using their stealth to move forward ahead of the strike force. He passed encrypted critical targeting information through secure communication links to his force and was surprised that his long-range systems had not picked up any threatening enemy aircraft yet.

Deep in the underground command center near Rostamabad, Ayatollah Batani was getting nervous. Reports were coming in from all corners of his country about the assault from attacking forces. He turned to his general with a look of rage.

"General Baghdadi, activate our satellite signal before our country is destroyed. Our fighters must bring down the Raptors now!"

Iranian squadrons of Flankers and Fulcrums were already airborne, armed with the most advanced stealthy air-to-air missiles that China provided. They were ready to knock out the Raptors leading the strike forces to their intended targets. All they needed was Epsilon to highlight the attacking forces.

The order to trigger the satellite pulse came almost instantaneously. In less than ten seconds, the geostationary satellite began transmitting the signal that penetrated the Raptor's central computer. The signal was immediately recognized by the Epsilon code buried deeply within the software. The code, a unique mix of ones and zeroes once intended to respond to the Raptor's pilot, now morphed within itself as the Chinese scientists had designed it. It changed, repurposing itself, directing the IFF system to broadcast a deadly signal—a transmission that would immediately be picked up by Iranian Air Force fighters.

As the eight cells of strike aircraft streaked through the Persian sky, the unwanted transmissions were generated deep within each Raptor. The pilots reacted with confusion at first, and then with some controlled panic at the signals emanating from their jets. Their interrogator systems were supposed to be silent, not giving their enemy any indication of their presence in the sky. But now their systems were squawking loudly, broadcasting a noise that could be easily picked up by Iranian aircraft and ground-based SAM radar systems. In spite of their stealthy coatings, their Raptors were now blooms on the enemy's radar, soon to be targets for destruction. The highly trained pilots had never expected something like this to happen, especially while moving inbound toward targets in one of the most heavily defended countries in the region. They tried to shut down their interrogator systems, but the deadly signals kept emanating from their jets.

Ace knew immediately that he was now plainly visible to his enemy. Whatever was causing his interrogator system to transmit, it made his ability to remain stealthy disappear. His aircraft, along with every other Raptor flying over the Iranian countryside, was blooming, creating a visible position indicator to the enemy. If they had his position, he knew it was just a matter of seconds before enemy missiles would be streaking inbound toward him and every other F-22 leading a strike force.

His radar warning receiver screeched to life, indicating incoming missiles. The other Raptors had similar signals. What had looked like a relatively moderate-risk target attack scenario had become a disaster in just seconds. Not only were the Raptors getting targeted, but all attacking fighters were being lit up on Iran's missile radar systems. Ace ordered his trailing force of aircraft to abort the mission and head back to their bases. In the next few seconds, he concentrated on evading the incoming missile threat. Airborne Iranian fighters had waited for the Raptors to bloom. They locked on and launched their missiles. Ace now had both SAMs and air-to-air missiles to contend with. He was determined to protect his strike force and punched off AMRAAMs toward two enemy aircraft.

Stealthy Chinese long-range radar-homing missiles fired by the Iranian fighters traveled at Mach 4, or four times the speed of sound. In spite of the Raptors tactical maneuvering across the early dawn sky, several missiles found their mark. For the first time in US history, F-22s were being hit by enemy fire. In the first missile salvo across Iranian airspace, twenty-three Raptors from the five participating squadrons were either damaged or lost—Epsilon had worked!

Iran took losses as well. The highly trained Raptor pilots managed to eliminate thirty-two Flankers and Fulcrums from Iran's Air Force inventory. Unfortunately, the kill-loss ratio was like nothing the United States Air Force had ever experienced. The disaster happening in the sky over Iran might eliminate any advantage the stealthy aircraft could pose in future conflicts.

Ace had been fortunate and managed to evade the first incoming missiles through a series of high-g evasive tactical maneuvers and countermeasures. One Raptor within his flight was not so lucky and lost its right wing from a missile explosion. The pilot managed to bail out over the coastline before his jet tumbled from the sky in flames. Ace was relieved that his buddy Flamer was not hit. As his strike force began their exit from Iranian airspace, Ace could only wonder what had gone wrong with the central computer and interrogator system. Within several minutes of the IFF's spurious activation, it had gone silent. The transponder was no longer squawking—performing precisely as the Chinese had designed Epsilon to perform.

Shortly before crossing the Iranian border, Matt's radar warning receiver loudly came to life. He was being targeted by an incoming missile. He executed evasive maneuvers and popped off countermeasures. He believed he could escape the missile headed toward him. It was not to be. The missile warhead detonated within thirty feet of his jet. Ace struggled to keep control of the flailing jet as it began a twisting inverted descent toward the Gulf.

Flamer screamed into his radio for Matt to eject. He lost sight of his buddy as he too tried to avoid an incoming missile. When he successfully evaded the missile, he again tried to see where his buddy was—there was nothing to see as he stared down toward the dark Gulf waters.

———————•———————

In Tehran, Ayatollah Batani and his Supreme Council were elated with the results of the battle. While they had lost some of their fighter aircraft fleet, they had taken out the equivalent of one squadron of America's top-of-the-line stealth fighters. As a result of the Raptor losses, the American attacks had been stopped, at least for the moment. Batani and his military staff knew that this was unprecedented. The world would now know the power of the Caliphate. Iran was a new world power, with the strength not just to challenge the United States but to bring it to its knees in battle.

Batani's senior military staff was jubilant. Epsilon had worked as intended. Unfortunately, the Chinese had not had the same success with the Shengdau radar. While it had easily picked up most of the non-stealthy attacking aircraft, the Shengdau's purported capability to acquire the Raptor had not been conclusively proven. The advanced Chinese radar system had not seen the Raptor before it began transponding, as it had been designed to do. At this point, the Shengdau radar was still unproven in defeating stealth—a key point that was kept from the Ayatollah and his staff.

In the days that followed, Iran believed that it would not take long for the United States to react to its losses. The Ayatollah knew that Americans didn't like to lose and would seek retribution for the loss of their pilots and precious F-22s. He expected the American reaction to be scaled up significantly from the first strike.

A massive effort was undertaken to quickly reestablish Iran's SAM radar command-and-control network that was damaged in the first few hours of the American strikes. Within twenty-four hours, they were back to seventy-five percent of their strength and ready to handle another impending attack.

Iran's Supreme Council knew they could not sustain a long-term fight with the United States. What they sought was to strike a strong blow that would signal their place among world powers and safeguard their nuclear arsenal. They had never intended to keep the Saudi territory they now occupied. The other Gulf states were firmly aligned with them economically, and now militarily. Iran *could* control the Gulf under the Caliphate and establish unity under a single Islamic cause.

Batani wanted a cessation of hostilities as soon as possible. He would offer up their withdrawal from the Saudi oil fields and what was left of Dhahran. The Supreme Council believed the US might go for this, since the Americans now clearly knew that Iran had established a nuclear weapons capability and could defeat stealth.

Khalil was nearly euphoric. He had seen the reports of the F-22 losses. Epsilon had worked perfectly—just as he had expected. He believed that he now had a bright future in Iran. He was a hero to the Caliphate. He also thought about Captain Matt "Ace" Black— and prayed that he had finally met his fate.

"*Allahu akbar,*" he said softly.

Chapter 72

O utside the threat area, the RC-135 continued its orbit while keeping a close watch on the US withdrawal from the evolving air war. Fortunately, the United States had not committed ground forces, at least not yet. It had not been a pretty picture in the air. The expected unchallenged air domination by the Raptors turned out to be a surprise blow by the Iranian fighters. Somehow, Iran had been able to acquire the Raptors, in spite of their stealth, and unleash their SAMs and advanced air-to-air missiles, with tragic consequences on the American side. What had happened in the skies over Iran was disastrous and completely dumbfounding to the Air Force leadership—the entire campaign rested on the Raptor's stealth.

Within the reconnaissance aircraft's nerve center, the battle commander had his sensor operators closely monitoring the unique signals they picked up during the conflict. The signals had not come from the ground or from the attacking Iranian fighters. They also had a unique signature. While the primary sensor operator had never seen it before, the battle commander had seen it many months ago, when this very same aircraft was monitoring signals traffic in the region.

"That's the same electronic signature we picked up some time ago in Iran's airspace, shortly after their satellite launch. I remember it specifically as pretty strange—it wasn't coming from our usual tracking locations." The commander leaned over the console to take a closer look at the replay of the signal.

"It's definitely the same signal, but generated from a space-based asset. We characterized it before, and it was verified by the NSA boys. We need to get the exact transmission point nailed down. If we can pinpoint it, maybe NSA can figure out exactly what's happening, and what effect, if any, it's having on our air battle."

"Roger that, sir," replied the sensor operator. "I've securely passed everything we picked up to the CAOC. From there, I guess it will move pretty quickly up the chain."

Meanwhile, the coalition forces had returned to their forward operating bases outside Iran, knowing that they had to reconstitute their strike packages with a strategy that befit the new threat. The atypical actions from the F-22's central computer and IFF had to be solved. The F-22 was too important to any combat operation.

———————•———————

Ryan Woods was one of the shining stars at the Air Force Research Lab, AFRL, across the base from the F-22 Program Office. He had been writing complex code, programming, and building computers since he was eight years old. He was a child prodigy and truly gifted. He had first proven himself in a high school apprenticeship and subsequently worked summers in government labs during his college days. AFRL knew he was a genius and had hired him at the first opportunity.

Weeks ago, the world-class research facilities had been notified by Air Combat Command about the suspected interrogator system problem encountered by the lone Raptor pilot patrolling the Saudi coastline. At that time, Ryan was asked to take a crack at the Raptor's new central computer and IFF code to find out if anything had been missed in the final software acceptance many months before.

The talented software programmer had run the Raptor's program in the lab over and over again, looking for any anomaly. If there was a problem, he was convinced he would find it. Even though the software engineering team had certified the program's integrity before it was installed in the Raptor fleet, they were more than willing to have the brightest engineer at AFRL take a closer look. As word came from the Middle East that Raptors had been lost in the latest attack on Iran, he heard the reports that the IFF was believed to have been the primary cause.

His weeks of grueling, detailed analysis had produced no real answers—but Ryan continued to dissect the string of complex code.

Interesting, he thought. *This software patch seems redundant. Why are there so many backups to the interrogator execution function?*

He continued to look closely at the patch. He found nothing out of the ordinary anywhere else in the massive strings of code—nothing that would draw his attention. But one area continued to intrigue him. He saw the clever algorithm in the midst of myriad combinations of ones and zeroes. He knew that what he was looking at wasn't a necessary function of the interrogator system.

I've seen this before, in some of the advanced studies I've done. This is like a morphing code that's based on AI. Sandia Labs was working on this type of capability during my internship there. They were designing it for defensive purposes, to protect critical systems from being hacked. The Sandia code could morph within itself when it was penetrated by a cyberattack and then bridge back to its original function. This is a bit different, though. It looks like it works the other way—some kind of trigger changes its function. I think this is what might have caused the IFF to transmit. I wonder what the trigger was.

AFRL was on to something. They were stunned at first, then grateful that the young software engineer had found a possible anomaly in the code. How could the best government coders have missed it as they'd reviewed the final product from Omega? At this point, what mattered most was figuring out the cause of the Raptor's issue and fixing it! The patch in the code appeared to map to the interrogator function, but at this point it was only speculation. It would have to be tested and proven to be the likely cause of the disaster.

Omega was contacted immediately to help to fix the problem, even though many government folks believed the company was ultimately responsible for the disaster. After all, it was *their* contract, *their* work that supposedly *improved* the central computer and interrogator functions. But time was of the essence. Omega's best, Khalil Ruffa, was requested to join Ryan in the Ohio lab.

"He's actually not available," replied the CEO to the F-22 program director. "Khalil was sent to Buenos Aires to participate in a discussion at their leading engineering university. But we've gotten reports that he never showed up. We've been trying to contact him, but his phone seems to be dead."

Fortunately, the CEO couldn't see the dark purple hue on the face of the program director on the other end of the secure telephone line between Fairborn and Omega. The face was contorted in rage. The colonel now began thinking the worst.

Meanwhile, on his own at AFRL, Woods was already working nonstop to try to build a fix to the problem. He removed the redundant string of code, presuming it was the likely cause of the dubious IFF transmission. He ran an integration analysis to confirm the removal didn't cause any unintended consequences. After several runs of the revised programs, he was confident his fix allowed the Raptor code to function as originally intended. But the large, complex software program would need final testing before it would be allowed to replace the corrupted code in the F-22s.

The revised programs were sent immediately to the Lockheed plant in Fort Worth, Texas. The large integrated software facility would run the revised program and verify it for final testing in the Raptor. At this point, it was still unknown what specifically had triggered the code to morph and subsequently caused the IFF to transmit. But the RC-135 crew's intercept of the signal from space gave the engineering team at Lockheed a pretty good idea that a satellite signal likely triggered the code to repurpose itself into its insidious new form.

In the Lockheed lab, the consolidated team of Omega's engineers, Air Force and Lockheed software specialists worked around the clock. They focused themselves on reviewing the program that Ryan Woods revised. Rebecca Casey was on site as well, along with her boss, Colonel Fredericks. Their presence was a clear statement about the level of importance the United States Air Force, the Department of Defense, and even the president placed on getting a national asset like the F-22 back into the fight.

The lead Air Force engineer tried to contain his growing anger as he turned to the Omega engineers.

"I can't believe what I'm seeing here. Your people's incompetence caused one of the biggest disasters I've ever seen. Where's the guy responsible for this, your so-called brilliant program manager who directed this design?"

The Omega representative's face was a mottled blend of beet red and white splotches.

"Sir, he's not here. He's on travel out of the country. But let us build the fix for this. We can do it pretty quickly."

"Are you shitting me?" the lead engineer replied rather loudly. "I don't want you *or* your software engineers anywhere near this! You've done enough, and there'll be dire consequences for your company."

The reaction by the Air Force was not entirely unexpected, but it became evident that in order to validate Wood's fix to the program, Omega would be needed. But they would have plenty of on-site help from the Air Force and Lockheed to observe every action.

Rebecca pulled the Omega engineer aside to question him about Khalil. She had fully expected to see him at Lockheed's lab as part of the consolidated team. She began to think that there was a reason for his absence. Khalil had led the complete development of the central computer upgrade—all those extra hours spent in the lab, the assurances he had constantly provided her on the excellence of the software build—and the intimacy she'd shared with him might have been designed to cloud her judgement, to make her focus less on the technical aspects of the software build and to get her to completely trust him. The thoughts were flying around in her head. She felt sick to her stomach—she had been duped by Khalil. She had let her emotions take over her brain. As a result, the Raptor fleet, an American national asset, was completely vulnerable.

Rebecca was able to get enough information from Omega to at least learn where Khalil had gone. While she wasn't surprised that he had reportedly gone to South America to join a technical discussion for Omega, she was surprised at the timing. Why now, at a time when the Middle East was boiling over and the Raptor fleet, with *his* modifications, were flying combat missions in the Persian sky? Had he known all this would happen while he was in Argentina, or wherever he was?

He's a traitor to our country, she thought. *And he'll get what all traitors deserve. I'll follow this recovery project through to completion. We'll get the fix done, get it tested and loaded onto the Raptor fleet as fast as humanly possible. I swear I'll get even with that bastard for what he's done.*

As one would expect, any actions, conclusions and recommendations by Omega were watched, reviewed, and then double-checked.

There was no room for error, and no time to waste in verifying the answer to the problem. They had Ryan Wood's proposed solution. A thorough but expedited integration and test process would take the final fix through every possible check, ensuring that the new software could completely replace the specific lines of code that had caused the disaster in Iran's skies. Within forty-eight hours from the time the team had begun, they had certified the replacement code. It took the Lockheed team no time to run the revised program a final time and approve it. At least in the lab, everything looked good.

———•———

In the high desert air eighteen miles east of Rosamond, the lights were burning especially bright in the secure hangar adjacent to the large aircraft parking ramp. A mix of the best engineers and scientists available had converged on the Edwards test facility to resolve one of the most significant challenges to ever face the F-22 fleet.

The revised software update had been flown from Texas directly to Edwards AFB, where system engineers pushed the code into the Raptor test aircraft. Americans are patriots, and when called upon, defense contractors like Lockheed, Boeing, and Omega came willingly to help. One man was noticeably absent from the Omega team—Khalil Ruffa.

On the government side of the house, AFRL and, of course, the F-22 Program Office were represented. Beyond the core of engineering and scientific talent, Captain Rebecca Casey had convinced her boss that she needed to be there. The central computer upgrade had been her baby. She felt personally responsible that it hadn't performed as designed.

While there had been some reluctance to send her to Edwards to participate in the final certification, her boss felt that she might learn something from the brain-trust gathered there. He knew that she was extremely bright, and in spite of the problems that the Raptor encountered, Rebecca still had promise as an Air Force acquisition officer. After all, even the Air Force software testers who had witnessed the development had given the approval on virtually every phase of the upgrade. One mistake is sometimes recoverable for an officer. Maybe that would be true for Rebecca Casey.

After a couple of hours running the code, with experts wringing out the system for any possible hiccup, it was functioning as originally intended. Lockheed was confident that from every possible means of analysis, short of having the triggering signal, the revised code should ensure the proper IFF function. With the morphing line of code now removed, the software should not be susceptible to an external trigger.

Chapter 73

The Pentagon had monitored all Middle East activity as the disaster had unfolded. Experts were trying desperately to come up with a solution that could be applied to the new Iranian threat. While they were reasonably confident the Raptor's software patch would work, they needed to take out the means that had triggered the IFF, just to be sure. While they were unsure what had triggered the software to change, they were pretty sure they knew where the signal had come from. The NSA had been working nonstop since receiving the tapes of the mysterious signals that appeared to be somehow linked to the Raptor losses.

They recreated each minute of the air battle, every missile fired, every enemy aircraft destroyed, and every Raptor damaged or lost in combat. Every move by the strike force was modeled, and a simulation built to the most finite detail. On this model was overlaid the exact timing of the intercepted signals from the RC-135. The timing of the Raptor losses had a direct correlation to the signal generation and the launch of the Iranian air-to-air missiles. Somehow, there had to be a relationship between the signal and the burst of noise from the Raptor's interrogator systems. There was no other answer, as all other ground- and air-based signal-generating assets had been ruled out.

The vast resources of the United States Space Command were tapped to help zero in on the likely source of the deadly signals. It didn't take them long to determine that a satellite in Iran's constellation was the likely source. Somehow, a satellite's signal had prompted a function within the Raptor's central computer code, and specifically the interrogator system, to operate in a way that had never been intended—and had produced deadly consequences.

"Mr. President, we have space-based assets that can take out that Iranian satellite in their constellation," the secretary of defense reported across the broad mahogany conference table.

The director of the National Security Agency nodded in agreement at the comment as the president of the United States thought about setting the first-ever precedent of a nation taking out an enemy space asset. This would be the first time in history that a country would deliberately destroy another country's satellite. Additionally, the action could generate literally thousands of pieces of space junk in the process. The Chinese had produced large quantities of space debris years before in their own test of an antisatellite missile. The result of that test put hundreds of the world's satellites and the International Space Station at risk.

The director of the NSA said, "Mr. President, I think we have a plan that will minimize the likelihood of any significant amount of space debris and keep us from being labeled a pariah in the eyes of most of the world. As you know, the X-40B has been in orbit for a few months. I believe it is the solution we are looking for.

"We need to do two things: quickly kill that satellite, and then understand the nature of its triggering signal for future reference. We may see it again." The director continued, "If they have managed to build a signal transmitter that can actually cause an aircraft's software to do what it's not originally designed to do, then we need to know everything we can about it."

He went on, "We have our best and brightest engineers at Edwards AFB running an array of tests on one of our Raptors. They're confident that the code fix will prevent the trigger response when the Raptors go back into combat. The reprogramming of the F-22s will follow shortly. But to be absolutely certain our Raptors are good to go, we need to get that satellite and eliminate the signal source. The X-40B is the answer."

"Please go on," the president replied. "I'm interested in how you plan to do what you say. Are you talking about somehow capturing the satellite?"

"Mr. President, we leveraged the success of the top secret X-37B Orbital Test Vehicle, which stayed aloft for over two years. You were briefed on the success of the X-37B, kind of a mini–space shuttle that we had doing some pretty highly classified stuff. It successfully landed back at the Cape after its mission. Well, the X-40B is a much larger version of the X-37B, with a bigger payload bay, and some of the same hardware our shuttles had for positioning or capturing our satellites."

He continued, "We can also disable a satellite before we try to grab it. We have in place a purely defensive system in the X-40B. We don't refer to it as a weapon due to the international ban on weapons in space. The defensive system is used to protect the interests of the United States. It was originally designed to help us disable our own satellites that wouldn't respond to our direction from the ground. But, in this case, it can essentially send a pulse at a rogue satellite and neutralize it. Once that's done, I believe our Raptors can proceed with near certainty that their IFF systems won't create the bloom that got them shot out of the sky. Then we'll grab the dead satellite and quickly return it to Edwards. Hopefully our neutralization efforts on the satellite won't prevent us from seeing how Iran actually used it to trigger our IFF systems."

"So, you're talking about using the X-40B to essentially disable the Iranian satellite, grab it, and then bring it back to earth?" said the president. "Can we actually do that, successfully? Without damaging it?"

"Yes, Mr. President, we can. But we might create some very minor space junk in the process. We think we can minimize it, though."

"How do you know which satellite was the problem within the Iranian constellation?"

"Our advanced modeling and simulation capabilities synched up every piece of data our sensors captured during the air battle. We were able to precisely pinpoint the one satellite among the six in the constellation. There's no question that it's the one, Mr. President."

The leader of the most powerful nation in the world was well-briefed on the many "black" programs the average American and the rest of the world were not aware of. As he thought about the suggestion, he asked for a detailed brief immediately on how the United States could quickly get this done before the next planned attack on Iran.

The key, beyond capturing a satellite in orbit and returning it to the earth without damaging it, was ensuring that the artificial intelligence systems in the X-40B functioned perfectly. The defensive system on the spacecraft would fire a tightly focused electromagnetic pulse at the rogue satellite, permanently disabling it.

The AI system within the unmanned mini-shuttle would activate a scanner from the payload bay that would determine the precise means to capture the satellite by its robotic arms. Fortunately, the United States had enough intel on the satellite's size already, based on the configuration of the launch vehicle used by the Iranians, and knew that it would very likely fit in the payload bay. At the conclusion of the briefing, it was clear to the president that the X-40B could pull off the capture.

Within thirty minutes, the briefing to the president was completed. "Mr. President, we just need your go-ahead to proceed. We can do this in a way that will be a complete surprise to Iran. The X-40B can quickly move from its current orbit to align with Iran's satellite constellation. We're ready to execute and have it done within twenty-four hours, then bring it back to Edwards shortly thereafter."

This was not a difficult decision for the president. For all intents and purposes, the US was in an undeclared at war with Iran, one of many Middle East conflicts his country had engaged in throughout the region over many years. He wouldn't advise his NATO allies about what he was planning to do. This was a national security issue, and the utility and effectiveness of one of its chief weapons, stealth technology, was at stake.

"You have my authority to execute the plan," the president replied. "Make it happen as quickly as possible. We're going to get our Raptor fleet back into the fight and shut down any thinking around the world that our fleet is vulnerable. God knows what the Russians and Chinese are already thinking if they believe our stealth technology could be compromised."

With that decision made, the wheels of the most powerful nation in the world moved quickly. The X-40B quickly began to position itself to carry out its mission to kill a satellite and then snatch it out of its twenty-three-thousand-mile-high orbit.

Chapter 74

Following an exhausting debriefing and reconstruction of the mission, Flamer stood on the tarmac at the forward operating base where his Raptor had landed. They had just received a disastrous and unacceptable shellacking at the hands of what he viewed as a third-rate air force. Most of his squadron was intact, but six aircraft had been heavily damaged or lost. That number—in fact, *any number*—was unacceptable in the stealthy world in which he operated. Worse yet, they had lost one pilot in the battle fray. Almost two! Captain Matt Black was not one of those killed.

While Flamer had thought the worst about his buddy when he'd lost sight of the tumbling aircraft, Ace had managed to eject over the Persian Gulf. He had been quickly picked up by a US Navy rescue helicopter and flown to a carrier sitting just outside the Strait of Hormuz.

A guardian angel, his father, had made his survival possible— Matt was certain of that. After being quickly flown back to Jordan and receiving a thorough medical checkup, he was cleared for duty within seventy-two hours from the time he had been shot from the sky.

"Flamer, how could this have possibly happened? We're too good to have the shit kicked out of us like this. Our F-22s were screaming to the enemy, *see me—kill me.*"

"It looks like they accommodated us. You know, it hurt bad to see our buds get shot out of the sky. All but one managed to get to the coastline, and a couple, like you, bailed out over water. They were also recovered by rescue teams that at least could operate safely off the coast of Iran. But one ejection was unsuccessful, likely due to cockpit damage caused by the SAM. He never got out of his jet. His wingman watched the Raptor tumble, on fire, all the way to the ground and explode on impact. Our teammate rode it in. I heard that the CAOC made a decision to not even try a search-and-rescue effort due to the location deep in Iran, and the extremely unlikely possibility that he survived the impact."

The final verification of the pilot's unfortunate death had been confirmed by a stealthy RQ-180 drone flown over the site. It verified the destruction of the Raptor and there was no sign of life from its pilot.

Matt just hung his head, thinking about the tragic situation—and of the pilot's family that would soon be getting notified, receiving the one message they hoped would never come.

"I heard that cruise missile strikes have already hit the Raptor's impact coordinates to demolish any pieces left of the jet. No way were we going to let Iran get intel on the Raptor's stealth properties," Flamer remarked.

"We took out a lot of the stinking enemy aircraft, but the odds definitely shifted away from us, and the price was too high. We can't reengage with them if our stealth is working when it's not. Our tactics have got to change until we figure out what's causing the squawk from our IFF," Matt replied.

"Do you think that's the problem?"

"That's the only anomaly I saw, and the same thing the rest reported."

"But what the hell triggered it to squawk?"

"Don't know, Flamer, but we'd better have some serious reckoning going on at the Program Office to get this figured out quickly. We need something, a software reboot, an emergency update, *something* to get us back in the fight."

"I hear they're already working on reprogramming our jets."

"I'm also pissed at the damn advanced aircraft the Iranians are putting up against us. We can thank our Russian and Chinese friends for that. We basically opened the spigot for the Ayatollah to rearm his air force, and most of the other aspects of what used to be a pretty pathetic military. This never would have happened if our country hadn't had its head up its ass, looking for how to make peace with terrorists. Now we're living with the result," Matt said disgustedly.

Matt continued. "Something had to trigger the IFF, I guess. Not sure what or how. Maybe the Iranians bought that technology, too. And maybe that Shengdau radar actually was up and running, identifying our location for a kill by Iranian missiles."

"You know, Ace, we've been flying around with our upgraded systems for months. We never had any problems like this. In fact, the IFF worked great since the upgrade was finished, with none of the old problems. Why now?"

"I don't know what to tell you. But I know one thing. That damn Omega engineer, Khalil Ruffa, assured us all that the problem was gone forever. To think that I actually admired him for his talent, his skill, and his commitment to our Air Force. Now I've got a dead buddy as a result of his failed assurances." Ace thought about it for a moment. "I'd like to have a very close and personal face-to-face conversation with that dude."

He looked across the ramp, his squadron short six jets and, more importantly, one pilot. "The commander asked me to help put a letter together," he said. "I've appointed one of our flight leads to gather the personal stuff from our lost pilot—we'll get it secured and wait for guidance on what to do with it."

His head hung down, his chin almost touching his chest as he started to think about his lost friend, and of course the dead pilot's family. Matt did his best to keep from tearing up in front of Flamer and had to turn away to avoid being seen.

He headed back to his temporary quarters and sat on his bed. He could only think of his wife and three precious kids. He realized he might not have survived from being shot down. Someone else might have had to gather up *his* things, write the dreaded letter.

He was a good pilot—in fact, a great one—but when a missile had your name on it, it was over. He checked the Breitling on his wrist and realized that it was the middle of the night back in the States. He couldn't even call his bride, no matter what time it was—not with the security restrictions in the combat zone. And he knew she would be freaking out on hearing that Raptors had been shot down—including him!

———————•———————

The next two weeks involved a temporary pause in combat operations as the United States grappled with getting its premier fighter aircraft ready to employ its stealth again—this time the right way. The revised central computer program was now ready, with the repaired IFF system software. The experts at Lockheed transferred the final product into a program that would serve as the emergency software update for every Raptor worldwide. Priority airlift was provided by the Air Force to gain rapid access to some very remote F-22 locations. A team of engineers landed at Matt's base with the new operational flight program, the upload taking only a few hours per jet. Matt and the rest of the team of warriors were briefed on how their interrogator system had been corrupted, and how the fix had been made.

Within a matter of ninety-six hours from the time the consolidated team had received Ryan Wood's solution, every F-22 worldwide had the new update. When the United States pulled its resources together to focus on a critical problem, there was no other country in the world that had the capability to accomplish what it had done. The Raptors were ready to reengage the enemy. All aircraft had been successfully reprogrammed, and the warbirds were ready for combat. The only thing missing was the order to turn the F-22 Raptor loose to hunt, and confidence that the IFF transponders would work as originally intended.

Happening nearly simultaneously with the reprogramming effort, the final step was the elimination of the Iranian "communications" satellite. In the bitter cold, stark darkness of the twenty-three-thousand-mile orbit, the X-40B maneuvered close to the deadly Iranian satellite.

For the past year, the public had been unaware of the true mission of this unmanned space vehicle. The NSA hadn't acknowledged that a payload bay existed, including the bay's contents and capabilities. This was one of the most highly classified projects ever undertaken in a joint venture by the Department of Defense and the NSA. The project was one of the many space-based contingency missions envisioned for this one-of-a-kind space plane.

Up to this point, the American military had never seriously considered using a weapon from space. In fact, the US and other civilized nations had signed an agreement pledging *never* to position weapons in space. The operative words were *civilized nations*. There were plenty of rogue states that were not in that particular category. The "defensive" system in the X-40B was a hedge against being caught flatfooted with no rapid executable strategy to handle those rogue elements that might threaten the American national interests from space. Up to now, a snatch-and-grab of a satellite had only been simulated on the ground in the large test facility at Cape Canaveral Air Force Station. The NSA knew it could work. They just needed a bit of luck to securely capture it on the first attempt. There was some very minor risk. An overly hard impact by the capture arm when grabbing the satellite could send it out of its geostationary position and quite likely cause it to depart from its orbit and eventually burn up on reentering the atmosphere.

The task at hand was no easy feat. The US had the best engineers on the planet. They were able to expertly position the large spacecraft where the robotic EMP probe within the "defensive system" could carry out its mission. When the bay doors opened, the AI system acquired the suspect satellite and activated the probe. Within a few seconds, a pulse penetrated the recesses of Iran's deadly satellite. The result was a complete and permanent shutdown of the satellite's capacity to function in any way. The

NSA was hopeful that the satellite's internal computer and software would be intact—it was needed to understand how it could have triggered the corrupt code.

Next, the scanner in the open cargo bay generated a 3-D image of the satellite that was quickly assessed within the AI-driven "brain" of the X-40B. It rapidly calculated the precise approach for the robotic arm and its mechanical "hands" to capture the satellite. The robotic arm was then directed to extend out and down toward the satellite.

The NSA engineer passed the encrypted commands to the advanced spacecraft. Over the course of forty-five minutes, the satellite was secured firmly in the robotic fingers extending from the X-40B's arm. The satellite was lowered into the payload bay, the robotic fingers firmly closing on the bright, metallic sides of Iran's precious asset. It remained firmly secured for the spacecraft's descent through the earth's atmosphere and back to a safe landing at Edwards AFB. Eager engineers waited for their prize.

The satellite was quickly taken under the highest level of protective security to a specialized software laboratory for analysis. Engineers wasted little time disassembling the hardware and accessing the software program in the satellite's computer. They were relieved that the electromagnetic pulse had not destroyed the program.

During disassembly, there was some concern that antitamper devices might have been built into the satellite. Fortunately, there were none. It had never occurred to the Iranians that the technology in their satellite would ever be compromised by an adversary. They believed, along with their Chinese cohorts, that the worst case would likely be its destruction by an antisatellite weapon, or that it would degrade from orbit and burn up on reentry into the earth's atmosphere.

The Edwards engineers also paid particular attention to the satellite's distinctive signal probe. They believed this was the likely means used to generate and transmit the signal into Iranian airspace, and trigger the IFF within the F-22's central computer. Creativity was one of the major facets of America's intellectual talent. After an expedited but detailed analysis, the team was able to replicate the satellite's signal and apply it to the old corrupted Raptor software. They were able to see the specific messaging that directed the interrogator to function. More detailed analysis stunned the engineers, who discovered that the code actually morphed within itself to trigger the interrogator's activation. The Edwards team quickly communicated their success to the National Command Authority in Washington, D.C.

Convinced they now knew the trigger, they applied the same signal to the emergency software update that was being installed in the Raptor fleet. As they had hoped, the signal did not trigger any change, nor any IFF function. There was now high confidence that the F-22s would be able to retain their stealth in combat. The Raptor was once again the most powerful stealth fighter on earth.

———————•———————

In Tehran, the chief scientist was astonished at what had happened. Somehow, within their "communications" satellite constellation, the Epsilon triggering vehicle was not talking to the bank of technicians in their control room. It had essentially gone dead and was not responding to any signal from the ground. On top of that, the sensors that Iran used to monitor their constellation now showed one fewer satellite in the collection. There had been a cluster of six, and now there were only five. The satellite that had enabled Iran's military to bring down the Raptor fleet and stop the American attack had vanished.

Chapter 75

The power of the United States military was unmatched anywhere in the world. Every nation on the planet knew it, including those that spent as much as they could afford to build up their own offensive and defensive military forces. Few had the economic and industrial might to even try to match American technological superiority. Even after having been dealt a setback in their ability to use their stealth technology as part of their offensive strategy, the United States could still overpower virtually any adversary.

Americans had little tolerance for their premier fighter, the Raptor, getting blown out of the sky. With the new operational flight program containing the emergency software update loaded in the entire fleet of F-22 stealth fighters, the US was ready to pick up where it had left off two weeks earlier.

Captain Matt "Ace" Black was ready to take the fight back to the Iranians. But this time, he knew that he would have the advantage of all the capability his Raptor had been designed to provide him. As he walked the flight line at the Jordanian air base, he ducked under the low-hanging wing of his jet and leaned in close to examine a load of AMRAAMs in the center weapons bay. These lethal missiles would bring down some bogeys the next time his Raptor got into it with Iranian fighters.

The Combined Air Operations Center received the top secret notification that there would be no threat to the Raptors on this next strike. The previously corrupted software and the satellite that had triggered the bloom from their jets had been eliminated. The team of scientists at Edwards AFB had also run a series of tests on the other stealth assets that might be affected by the previous triggering signals of the now-defunct Iranian satellite. The B-2 Spirit stealth bombers, and the newest stealth fighter, the F-35, had different software configurations than the Raptor, as well as completely different central computer systems. They were all found to be free of any vulnerability to the Iranian triggering signal. That was just an extra measure of assurance if Iran had more than one of the deadly satellites in orbit. The United States Air Force was ready to unleash its full force of advanced capability if needed to quickly shut down the rogue Iranian regime. The current battle strategy counted on a quick, massive counterstrike.

The follow-on attack against Ayatollah Batani's rogue regime came with little warning. Similar to the first strike on Iran, the US military unleashed a massive attack, but this time on a day that nobody would expect—the first day of the Muslim holy period of Ramadan. The American president, in concert with his allies, believed that the timing of this surprise offensive would provide some advantage to get to the heart of the Iranian leadership. If the strike was successful, the snake's head would be cut off, and the relative geopolitical balance would hopefully be restored.

The size of the attacking coalition force was unprecedented. NATO allies had been reluctantly persuaded to fully engage their combat forces, even though Raptors had been previously lost in combat. Iran had to be stopped at all costs. But now, the United States knew they had solved the problem that had caused the Raptor bloom. Now, the imminent threat of nuclear-tipped ballistic missiles had become *the* major incentive for NATO and other coalition forces to come together in one unified combat team. The subsequent battle over the Iranian countryside would be heavily one-sided now. Joining the already potent force were the F-35 Lightning II stealth aircraft, now released to engage the enemy. The attacking forces led by Raptors would attack their targets with impunity. The Raptor's full stealth capability was now restored.

The United States, at this point, was unwilling to allow Iran even the possibility of a retaliatory nuclear launch. There was a way to take out the deadly ballistic missiles without warning, thanks to the Raytheon Company. In the dark recesses of one of the most secret counternuclear missile development efforts, the Pulsar Six weapon had been born. The stealthy missile had the ability to fly at hypersonic speed, at only fifty feet above the earth's surface, and navigate its way precisely to its target. The ground-hugging weapon was guided by the latest in advanced secure GPS technology. The warhead of the Pulsar Six produced a massive pulse that fried even the most hardened, shielded electronics.

The American president firmly believed that Iran would never suspect an attack on their nuclear missiles for fear of starting a nuclear exchange. Surprise was of the essence. The fog of war—the confusion about what strategy your enemy might use—and the belief that they were invulnerable to a stealth attack was just heavy enough in the minds of the Ayatollah and his generals to give the Americans the edge needed to take out their nukes. Fortunately, the precise locations of all sites armed with tactical nuclear weapons were known to the Americans. A midlevel general in Iran's Islamic Revolutionary Guard Corps could not bear to see his native land turned into dust should the Ayatollah actually order a nuclear missile launch. He had provided the GPS positions of each site to covert operatives whose goal was to extricate the country from the Ayatollah's radical Caliphate and hopefully move the Iranian people toward a more peaceful society.

It was going to be a *really* bad day for Iran—and so it began.

Chapter 76

The American counterattack on Iran slaughtered their military forces. Unbeknownst to the Supreme Leader, he had lost any benefit he believed he had with Epsilon or the Shengdau radar. Iran's top-of-the-line fighter aircraft were decimated by the Raptor's deadly missiles in the very first wave of the attack, being struck before they could figure out where the incoming missiles were coming from. They had never picked up the Raptors on their radar, nor had their missile defense networks. The F-22's AMRAAMs quickly cleared the sky of every enemy aircraft. The once-formidable SAM sites were wiped out as fast as their control center's acquisition radar transmitted. For Captain Matt "Ace" Black and his 94th FS buddies, it was almost like a turkey shoot. Without Epsilon, and with the failure of the Shengdau radar system, the Americans were able to easily strike every key Iranian target.

Deep underground in their hardened secure command center, the Ayatollah and his key staff were not at all pleased with the way the current battle had unfolded. As his general provided the disheartening news of the disastrous losses to his once state-of-the-art advanced fighter aircraft, the Ayatollah hung his head, shaking it from side to side in despair.

"How can this be happening? We have the advantage over the American stealth fighters. Why have we lost so many of our best attacking aircraft? Why haven't our air defense systems been able to knock the Raptors out of the sky?"

The chief of Iran's general staff had not broken the news about the satellite and Epsilon. When Baghdadi had received the report that they had lost contact with the satellite, he was sure it was just an intermittent problem that would correct itself quickly. He was assured that the satellite had redundant power sources, and the receiver should be coming back online shortly. However, it soon became apparent that the reason there was no contact was because there *was* no satellite. Somehow, it had disappeared from its orbit. Iran's space agency had seen multiple objects near the constellation, including a fairly large contact that they could not readily identify. The large contact had been in the area for only an hour and then departed the constellation. As it moved away, their space agency tracking system noted the loss of their satellite's signal. They reported it quickly to Baghdadi—but not to the Ayatollah.

The Ayatollah looked across the faces staring at him in the small command bunker.

"How are the Raptors getting through? Epsilon helped destroy them during the previous attack. Why is it not working?"

He looked at the frightened stares around him.

"What about the Shengdau radar?"

He tried to find Dr. Yu, but the Chinese scientist had disappeared.

"President Xi assured me that the radar would acquire and target the Raptors. He assured me that the radar would help eliminate the attacking American aircraft, along with our Epsilon code."

Ayatollah Batani was scrambling, looking for someone, anyone to blame for the disaster.

"Find Yu. He has lied to us—nothing is working!"

Good news was always welcome when dealing with the Ayatollah, especially during a pitched battle against their hated enemy, the Americans. Bad news was not something anyone wanted to share with the elderly leader of this Islamic nation. Bad news had the tendency to guarantee some pretty negative consequences that affected the health of whomever shared it.

"Most holy one," replied General Baghdadi. "The satellite is operating, but for some reason, the Americans are not being affected," he lied. "Perhaps our engineers have not done the job we demanded of them. The satellite was key to our success, and it appears they have failed to make it operate as we had directed."

Khalil was standing a few feet behind the Ayatollah, listening to every word from the general's lying mouth. He had managed to see the report from the space agency technicians. He had discovered the information on the disappearing satellite too late to tell the Ayatollah of the disaster that was likely to happen. He was horrified at the massive losses of Iran's prized advanced fighter fleet.

Before the Ayatollah could react, Khalil approached him and asked if he could talk with him privately. The Ayatollah respected the young engineer. He nodded and waved a bony finger at him to follow. The general cast a harsh stare at Khalil, but what Khalil saw in his eyes was fear.

"What is it?" asked the Ayatollah, clearly impatient to get back to the command center and hopefully stop the horrendous losses from his entire military establishment.

Khalil thought carefully about how he would tell the Supreme Leader of Iran that his military was being completely obliterated and that it could likely have been salvaged if the information on the satellite had been shared by the general. As Khalil explained what he knew, the Ayatollah's eyes sharpened, the deepness of the stare rattling Khalil to his core.

"Are you just making an excuse for your own failure and the failure of your engineers?" demanded Batani, angrier than he had ever been.

"No, most holy one. Epsilon worked, as did the satellite. You saw it demonstrated when we destroyed the F-22s in the previous battle. The Americans must be behind the loss of our satellite. I believe that somehow, they intercepted the signal that activated Epsilon."

Khalil's mind raced. He continued, "There is no chance that the Americans could have figured this out so quickly without knowing about Epsilon before the first battle. Someone had to have activated the satellite weeks ago to test its effectiveness on the Epsilon code. Perhaps General Baghdadi?"

Khalil was guessing, but since things were already going to shit, what did he have to lose?

"After all, he had much at stake if the satellite failed to activate Epsilon in the attacking Raptors." He paused.

"If the general did in fact do this, the Americans surely picked up the signal—and any pilot seeing the IFF anomaly repeat itself after Omega's upgrade of their central computer would have reported it immediately. That would have given them time to trace the problem, discover the Epsilon code, and immediately begin trying to fix it."

Khalil also knew, from his one remaining source at Omega, that changes were being made to the Raptor code. While almost all of the Omega staff viewed him as a traitor, one software technician sympathetic to the Islamic cause had managed to contact him with that information. Now was not the time to divulge *that* to the Ayatollah.

"Of course, the advanced American sensors could have readily tracked the pulse signal to the satellite. The United States has ways of disabling space systems, especially if they were tipped off as to its purpose…by your general."

Ayatollah Batani stared at Khalil throughout the preposterous-sounding explanation. Maybe it was not so preposterous. He knew his general staff feared him—in fact, everyone feared him. This was a very plausible explanation, he began to believe.

"You are a smart man, Khalil. But General Baghdadi is my trusted advisor and has been close to me throughout the rebuilding of our military forces, including our nuclear program. I am not sure you are correct about him. He has, on the other hand, appeared very nervous."

Khalil continued. "General Baghdadi was also aware that the satellite had stopped transmitting during the attack." He saw the change in the Ayatollah's face. "The real treason here is within your general staff. By withholding the information on the loss of the satellite, they willingly allowed the Raptors to target and kill Iran's true patriots, our pilots. The treasonous actions of your generals are the cause of this disaster."

The Ayatollah's stare was unrelenting, peering deeply into Khalil, searching for the truth.

"We still have the Shengdau radar to help target the Raptors," the Ayatollah said. That, perhaps, was his last hope to salvage the disaster that was unfolding.

"Holy one," Khalil said, "Baghdadi has known all along that Shengdau was not working as the Chinese had advertised. We are very vulnerable to an American attack, and especially an assault by the F-22 Raptors."

The Supreme Leader thought about how things could have been done differently if only his staff had given him the proper information. "We would likely have limited our engagement with the enemy before the battle even started. We could have used the nuclear ballistic missiles as a warning to the Americans of the consequences of an attack. We could have lived to fight another day."

Batani abruptly turned and walked back to the command center. General Baghdadi was standing near one of the consoles, reviewing what was left of the obliterated defense infrastructure. As the Ayatollah approached, the general turned, his face a mix of arrogance and fear.

Before he could say a word, the Ayatollah raised his arm from beneath his robe, a chrome-plated Russian Serdyukov SPS semiautomatic pistol in his hand. Before the general could utter a word, a loud pop sounded and a single hollow-point round entered General Baghdadi's forehead, splattering bone and blood onto the display console. As the general collapsed to the floor, Khalil reeled backwards, fearing he was next.

As the Ayatollah holstered the pistol under his robe, he asked the general's shocked assistant what assets were left to fight off the Americans. The news was not good, but at least the Ayatollah now had the truth about his diminished, nearly nonexistent military capability. There was only one thing left to do. Only one way to respond before he lost everything.

"We must launch our nuclear missiles. Now! Our preplanned targets in Europe and Israel will teach the Americans and their allies that Iran will leave a lasting mark on the world."

The Ayatollah looked across the room, the stunned faces of his staff reflected the insanity of his demands.

"We can at least destroy Tel Aviv and the Zionists," he said.

The silence was deafening. The remaining general staff was reluctant to tell their Supreme Leader about the status of their nuclear launch facilities, now fearful for their own lives. The ballistic missile launch pads had already been hit by the Pulsar Six missiles, eliminating any possibility of their use. The stealthy missiles had never been detected. The first indication that Iran's weapons of mass destruction were under attack was the massive electronic pulse over each nuclear launch site, which had stopped any near-term use of the nukes.

"Execute the order," the Ayatollah shouted.

"Holy one, our missiles are destroyed," responded a very reluctant assistant. "The Americans have hit them all with a secret weapon. Our defenses never saw them coming. We cannot launch our missiles. Our air force is destroyed. Our army weapons have been neutralized. At this point, we need to consider the unthinkable. Surrender."

The words hung for a few moments in the surrounding silence, amidst the deadly stare coming from Ayatollah Batani's eyes. Khalil thought he saw movement of the Ayatollah's hand toward the pistol under his robe. But the Supreme Leader of Iran turned his back on them all and began pacing toward his chamber.

Chapter 77

n the air over Iran, the sounds of battle raging were from American bombs impacting every military target, including those that could support any offensive or defensive operation. The United States attempted to be careful not to punish innocent civilians in the strikes. Revered historical sites, mosques, hospitals and schools were deliberately avoided. But the Iranian Air Force had been destroyed, as had their entire SAM defense capability. Since Iranian Army units had not engaged in the battle, their personnel were spared death from the sky. But their armor and artillery had specifically been targeted to ensure it could not be used if the army foolishly changed its mind. Every known munitions stockpile was also hit.

There was one other particular mission underway. The B-2 Spirit stealth bombers had been held back until Iran's air threats, along with their air defense systems, had been eliminated. Launched on a nonstop mission from Whiteman AFB, the two aircraft, the *Spirit of Kansas* and the *Spirit of Missouri,* carried a very special cargo. Within their huge bomb bays were two of the largest conventional weapons in the US arsenal. The GBU-57 Massive Ordnance Penetrator, or MOP, was in fact massive, weighing in at thirty thousand pounds. It was specifically designed to penetrate over two hundred feet of earth and over sixty feet of hardened reinforced concrete to deliver its fifty-three-hundred-pound explosive punch. It had been used in combat only once before.

"We're ten minutes to target," said the copilot.

"Roger, all systems are go for weapons delivery," replied the pilot.

The B-2 stealth bombers flew unopposed as they approached their targets, just south of Tehran. The "secret" underground command post was not so secret, as it turned out. The US had intel from assets on the ground in Iran, and the location of this prized facility was well known. It had been pinpointed as a target by the American intelligence analysts.

Deep in the command post, the Ayatollah called his remaining staff together, frantically trying to determine how to get out of the conflict with their lives and hopefully keep control of the shattered country. Could they immediately transmit a message to the American president that Iran would cease all military offensive operations? Then again, little was left of their military capability, other than their army. Batani thought it was useless to pursue peace at this point. It would be an admission of the holy Caliphate's failure, and that of his own personal leadership. Perhaps the Americans would stop bombing Iran when nobody was shooting back at them. When that happened, perhaps he could negotiate with them for a way to keep control of his country. He would offer strong concessions to the United States—declare that Iran would give up its radical path and immediately stop its nuclear ambitions.

At least for now, Ayatollah Hamid Batani felt that this reinforced underground bunker was the safest place amidst the carnage going on two hundred feet above him. The facility was designed to survive any type of attack, possibly even a small nuclear hit, and *that* gave the Ayatollah some degree of comfort that he wasn't in immediate danger.

Khalil had breathed a sigh of relief when the Ayatollah had put his pistol away. He had no doubt that with the disaster taking place on Persian soil, *his* usefulness might be in question—likely *was* in question. There was no longer an air force to contend with, and the satellite and his Epsilon code were now defunct. He worried that in his immediate future, there was quite possibly a quick bullet to the head. Khalil began thinking about how he could get away.

———————•———————

THOMAS BELISLE

Within the cockpit of the *Spirit of Missouri,* the pilots were all business.

"Three, two, one, bombs away," said the pilot. The large black flying wing pitched up slightly as the heavy load left the aircraft. "Let's get the hell out of here," he added to his copilot.

As the black-skinned stealth bomber banked to the north, the two MOPs hurtled down toward their target. Inside the Ayatollah's command post, the only remaining advanced radar systems not targeted by the Americans never picked up the B-2s. Even if they had, it would have been a bit late for any lifesaving reactions from the Ayatollah, his remaining general staff, and the system operators managing the consoles.

As the two MOPs penetrated the rocky soil outside Rostamabad, they burrowed deep into the earth, reached the reinforced concrete command post, and easily breached it. The warheads functioned perfectly, their triggering devices delayed until the deadly bombs broke through the inside wall of the target. The violent explosion two hundred feet underground obliterated the leader of the Islamic Caliphate and everyone remaining in the facility. The force of the blast, contained by the surrounding concrete and earth, was almost unnoticeable on the surface, aside from an extremely large diameter, slightly raised mound in the soil.

The second B-2 dropped its load on the underground laboratory site and the extensive tunnel complex used to test Iran's satellite triggering capability. The destruction would prevent any future use of these facilities for a long time to come. After bomb release, the *Spirit of Kansas* followed a flight path similar to the other stealth bomber, quickly heading toward friendlier territory.

Chapter 78

K halil had paid close attention to the layout of the command center and remembered the reference to the escape tunnel and its approximate location. With an air battle raging overhead, most of the Iranian leadership's attention had at first been focused on winning a war, or at least keeping as much of their military forces as possible intact to fight another day. When their situation had rapidly deteriorated, they had begun to instead focus on ultimately surviving in their underground bunker.

Somehow, he had not drawn any undue attention from the security personnel when he'd slipped away from the Ayatollah after Baghdadi's execution and headed down the long hallway toward the rear of the facility.

Before the B-2s dropped their deadly ordnance load, Khalil had made his escape. He quickly climbed a steel ladder angled toward the surface, above and away from the command center. The ladder had been installed in a tunnel attached to the underground command center, designed to facilitate a rapid means of escape for Iran's leadership if the need arose. While the tunnel was intended to be used principally in the event of a nuclear strike by an enemy of their state, it now had a very different purpose. As Khalil unlatched the mechanism securing the hatch, he hoped there was nothing obstructing it. He pushed the hatch open and breathed in the warm air, but choked from the intense smoke and dust caused by the earlier bombing runs. He considered himself extremely fortunate that he had made his way out of the main command center when he did.

The MOPs had exploded deep in the earth seconds after he reached the surface-level escape hatch. It was pure luck that Khalil was not crushed by the underground concussive wave that rippled through the soil toward the surface, collapsing much of the tunnel beneath him.

Khalil surveyed the destruction around him. Mounds of rock and dirt surrounded the bomb's entry holes. The surrounding area showed the obvious signs of the American's bombing campaign, which had effectively taken out any structure near the military operation command center. As he wandered through the rubble toward the outskirts of Rostamabad, his mind raced with thoughts about how he could safely and quickly extract himself from the area, and the country.

Khalil knew that he was now a wanted man. He was convinced that the Iranians, those still alive who might be left in the Ayatollah's allegiance, would see him as a primary cause of the disaster. He had been the catalyst in getting the critical technology onto the American aircraft. While it had worked initially, it had ultimately failed through no fault of his. Also, he was sure that by now, the United States had his face plastered on their list of most wanted terrorists. He knew that the US had a history of remembering their enemies. More often than not, they eventually got the target they were after.

As he continued down the debris-strewn road, Khalil found a sympathetic villager who was willing to shelter him after he shared a very convincing story—how he had survived the attack on their homeland. He planned to lay low for a day or two to plan his escape from Iran, likely up the coastline of the Caspian Sea to the border with Azerbaijan. From there, he believed he could make his way to Turkey and eventually out of the immediate area of turmoil in Iran. The network of radical Islamists was broad enough that Khalil believed he would quickly link up with groups sympathetic to the Caliphate.

Khalil was able to secure transportation and spent the next day traveling without incident toward Tabriz in a small truck hauling vegetables. While en route, he stopped in a small village, where he encountered two senior Iranian Air Force officers also trying to make their way north. As they shared a relatively meager meal of flatbread and bean curd, their conversation was subdued, even guarded. Khalil did not want to identify himself as a member of the Ayatollah's inner circle and give himself away as a coward, fleeing the country while Iran was in a war for its survival.

He noticed that the air force officers had removed their rank and tried to make their uniforms look less conspicuous. They noticed Khalil's eyes on them and responded with some angry remarks.

"Why do you stare at us, at our uniforms? Who are you to look at us like we are something to be despised?" one of them snapped.

The second officer began to move toward Khalil in a threatening manner that Khalil sensed was motivated by fear.

Khalil held up both hands and said, "Please, I am no threat to you, and I was just curious about your uniforms. I have worked closely with the air force and respect them for who they are, for what they represent, for their selfless role in this glorious battle."

"Who are you?" one of them asked Khalil, eyeing him critically.

Khalil sensed that these two officers were fleeing the country as he was. That would explain their efforts to disguise their uniforms.

"I am Khalil Ruffa, an engineer who helped enable your air force to develop special weapons to strike a mighty blow against the Americans."

"One victorious battle was not enough. We were overwhelmed in the American counterattack. The air force has been reduced to rubble—we're now a toothless animal," replied the officer.

"We are no longer the power we were in past years. The Americans have seen to that. There is little left, and the regime believes that we are the reason for the great defeat. We left Hamedan air base as the Ayatollah's henchmen began executing those of us still alive after the massive losses incurred in the air battle. There is not much safety in this country for senior officers after such a disaster."

"Where are you going?" replied Khalil, now becoming a bit bolder given his understanding that these officers were also escaping the country.

"Our contacts at Tabriz air base have told us of a safe way out. We are headed there to meet others like us, who fear for their lives."

Now understanding who Khalil was, he continued, "You were a member of the Ayatollah's staff. You are the one who made our victories over the American stealth aircraft happen. At least for a short time, anyway. You should come with us. Your experience and knowledge has great value. It can be useful in the future when Iran gets back on its feet, at a time when we can return."

"I thought our bases and aircraft had been destroyed?" asked Khalil.

"That is true for the most part, but the west area of the base at Tabriz was not hit. An aircraft awaits there to get us out of this country."

Khalil thought about what he was being offered—a way out, possibly a quick flight from Tabriz to some location, any location that was outside Iran. It sounded better than his trek to the border and hopefully finding some refuge in Azerbaijan.

"I would be honored to accept your invitation," he replied.

———•———

With the bombing campaign over and their nuclear-tipped ballistic missiles neutralized, the president saw no real threat from Iran, at least for the near term. Overhead, the Americans had begun a steady stream of missions across the Iranian countryside to keep a close eye on any possible resurgence of military activity. American satellites and certain classified reconnaissance aircraft kept a close watch on the neutralized nuclear launch sites. Iran was told to evacuate all personnel from those locations, a measure of security the United States insisted on to ensure no effort would be made to put them back in commission.

They imposed a strict no-fly order to the Iranians, giving any remaining pilots from their now-defunct air force a chance to stay alive. Iran's military, and for certain its air force, were no longer a threat, but the no-fly order would also ensure that no more offensive actions would be taken against the Americans without severe consequences. Unbeknownst to the two senior air force officers and Khalil, anything that took to the air would be quickly shot down.

Chapter 79

aptain Matt "Ace" Black had six enemy aircraft kills as a result of the air war. The only disappointment he had was that the small painted symbols of Iran's flag, representing each kill, couldn't be painted on the fuselage of his aircraft. The Raptor's stealthy skin could not be doctored in any way that might risk it becoming another possible bloom.

One bloom is enough, he thought, shaking his head about what could have been the end for the Raptor fleet.

That problem had been fixed, and now his F-22s performed in the way they were designed. The mission over the skies of Iran was now mostly a policing effort, to fly top cover for Strike Eagles and Fighting Falcons and be on alert to eliminate any potential resurgence in Iranian military actions.

The F-22s were widely dispersed in fighter escort flights that covered the entire country. There were plenty of partially operating military installations to monitor the nineteen air bases that were attacked across Iran. In addition, there were sixteen army installations that would be watched for any threatening troop movements. The Raptors were not too worried about ground threats from SAMs at this point. Iran's air defense network had been effectively neutralized by the extremely accurate targeting, and the Growlers and Wild Weasels had eliminated every acquisition radar command node that had threatened the attacking aircraft. While there was no expectation on the part of the United States that Iran would try to mount a counteroffensive, there would be no chances taken at this point. Anything that moved was going to be destroyed. Any radar that had survived, if it foolishly came online, would be quickly eliminated by a tactical strike.

The flight Ace planned for today was going to be another routine sortie. He would be burning holes in the sky, patrolling his designated area, monitoring for anything unusual, and then returning to his base. This wasn't real combat anymore, but even though the emotional rush was now gone, the policing missions were still important.

The big AWACS aircraft with the large rotating dome on top was like a "big brother" during the battle over Iran. Now, it was also helping to monitor the sky for anything that moved in any part of the Iranian air space.

"Ajax One, this is King Nine, we just picked up a contact coming off the ground at Tabriz. Turn to 020 degrees and I will vector you to the target," said the AWACS controller.

Matt's senses immediately sharpened. "King Nine, Ajax One. Roger, I'll follow your lead. Turning 020."

As Matt pushed the throttles forward, he double-checked his radar display, tuning his acquisition radar toward Tabriz air base. He had a full load of ordnance—his AMRAAMs and Sidewinders ready if needed for another encounter.

———•———

The two senior officers from Iran's now-defunct air force had carefully planned their escape and arranged a rendezvous with their contacts at Tabriz. A few hangars at what used to be a vibrant Iranian fighter aircraft base were undamaged, but exposed aircraft on the parking ramp had not been so lucky and had become victims of the American bombing and strafing campaign. These aircraft had never made it off the ground to engage with the US forces. In spite of the airfield damage, the runway was clear enough to allow the business-sized jet enough intact concrete to get airborne.

Hours before, the small eight-passenger military executive jet had been pulled from an inconspicuously small undamaged hangar at Tabriz. It had been waiting for precisely this time, late in the day as dusk was approaching, for its important passengers to quickly board the jet. The manifest for this flight was not published anywhere. The mission plan was never filed. In fact, there was virtually no communication about this flight to anyone outside a very small, close-knit group of people. It had one pilot on board.

The officers had paid a hefty sum of cash to make this mission possible, the cash taken from the coffers of the Iranian Air Force headquarters. After all, nobody would notice the theft at this point. They had agreed to take Khalil with them for one reason—Khalil might be a bargaining chip for them to use at a future date. They had no real intention of letting him out of their sight when they reached their destination outside Iran. Although Khalil didn't know it, his days of freedom were over. He would be kept in a secure location by powerful allies of these senior officers.

As soon as they boarded the aircraft, the pilot of the small jet taxied out and streaked down the runway. As it lifted off, the sun was already well below the horizon. The jet headed northeast toward Azerbaijan. The flight out of Iran would be a short one. The jet climbed only to one thousand feet above the terrain, hoping to avoid being picked up by Americans patrolling the sky. If they could get to Azerbaijan, they were home free.

Ace transmitted, "King Nine, Ajax One. I have the bogey, proceeding on heading of 020."

"Ajax One, King Nine, you are cleared to engage."

"Copy," replied Ace.

The advanced medium-range weapon wouldn't take long to close on the escaping jet. It would reach its intended target seconds before the senior officers and Khalil reached the Azerbaijan border.

The three passengers in the Iranian jet breathed a sigh of relief as their ticket out of Iran sped toward safety. Darkness surrounded them outside the small windows at each of the comfortable leather passenger seats. Stars were becoming visible, and the snowcapped peaks of the mountain range seemed to zip by the windows as the jet kept as low as it could while making its escape.

Khalil smiled. He had done it. He would live to fight another day for the glory of the radical brand of Islam represented by the failed Caliphate. He thought about the Ayatollah in the destroyed command center. He would have perished as well if he had not made his escape before the bombs hit the underground facility. How fortunate he was. Allah had truly guided him, kept a hand on his shoulder, spoken to him to channel his destiny as a soldier of a future Caliphate. He wondered about Matt Black. Had he been killed in the first attack on Iran? He hoped with all his heart that the son of the man who had killed his family was dead. He began to believe that it was so.

He stared out the small jet's window at the twinkling stars above. How truly beautiful they were, he thought. He closed his eyes and allowed himself to think of his father and mother, his brothers and his sister. He had a scrambled vision of having dinner in the small earthen block house he had lived in when he was a small child in Syria. He smiled almost imperceptibly as he heard his older brother taunt him to eat his meal of goat meat and flatbread. He heard his mother's voice clearly, scolding his brothers for their behavior. His father's gruff voice was also clear to him, bringing order back to their meal. His father reminded the children of all they had to be thankful for, and for all the things that Allah had provided to them. The daydream was good, and Khalil felt he was really back home. It was a feeling that he had not experienced in a very long time.

"Fox one," said Matt as the missile left his Raptor, heading for the small jet. In the darkness, the bright plume of the lethal AMRAAM lit up the sky in front of his Raptor, quickly accelerating away until it was nothing more than a pinprick of light in Matt's eyes.

The sleek missile streaked toward its target. It was guided by its active homing radar and traveled at four times the speed of sound. There was no way the small jet would escape. As it approached the jet, the proximity fuse triggered the high-explosive blast-fragmentation warhead. Khalil's dream was violently interrupted by the explosion. The massive blast tore the left wing and part of the tail off the business jet. It sent the small aircraft into a flat death spiral toward the snow-covered ground below. Khalil somehow survived the initial blast. He was unlucky enough to witness with wide, terrified eyes the thousand-foot plunge to the ground in what was left of the aircraft with him in it. The jet impacted the Azerbaijan landscape a few miles from the border.

"King Nine, Ajax One. Splash one bogey," said Ace.

Matt wasn't quite sure why any sane person would enter the sky under a no-fly order.

They had to know it was likely they would die, he thought. *Too bad, another senseless loss.*

Of course, he had no idea that the traitor to America known as Khalil Ruffa had been on the receiving end of his deadly missile.

As Matt "Ace" Black turned his Raptor southwest to rejoin the force that was on patrol with him, he thought about the past few weeks. His engagement with enemy aircraft was a true test of his combat abilities. He thought about his good fortune, being able to rid the sky of a few Iranian fighters while avoiding being a fatal target from one of their missiles. He thought about when he would be able to return home to see his wife and kids, and he thought about his dad.

I think he would have been proud of me, Matt thought to himself, a smile on his face.

———•———

The wreckage of the small military jet was discovered by the Azerbaijani military. It was largely confined to a five-hundred-yard radius of burnt, scattered debris in the flatlands several miles west of Salyan. The Azerbaijani Army's response to the crash had occurred quickly, the military not certain if hostilities might be flaring up near their border. What they found amidst the wreckage were three mangled remains, all wearing what appeared to be what was left of their burnt Iranian Air Force uniforms. They had no idea that a fourth passenger had been on the jet. Khalil's body was not one of those found.

Epilogue

In the aftermath of the battle that ended Iran's nuclear ambitions, it would take many months, even years, to reestablish any sense of peace and trust in the region. While every known aspect of Iran's nuclear infrastructure had been destroyed, the message to the world was straightforward. If Iran could surreptitiously build weapons of mass destruction right under the eyes of a world that believed it had done everything necessary to prevent it, how many other countries were doing the same? The international community came together after Iran's blatant disregard for the previous nuclear agreement. The first order of business would be to certify the removal and destruction of anything tied to Iran's nuclear development program—but this time, it would be done right. The previous shell game used by the radical Iranian regime to hide key elements of their nuclear weapons program was replaced by open access to any facility, anywhere, at any time by the international inspectors. All tactical nuclear warheads were secured and sent to the United States for disposal.

New leadership emerged in Iran after the dust settled. A more moderate government sought to bury the anti-Western hatred that had been the core of Iran's radical Caliphate. With their air forces and defense systems essentially destroyed, Iran was offered the protection of its defenseless territory by the United States, in exchange for a number of concessions—most aimed to keep the previous radical regime from ever establishing a foothold there again. Their current standing army was sufficient to handle low-end skirmishes if required, along with domestic policing. If the country's sovereignty was threatened in the future, the Americans would step in.

The Group of Seven alliance quickly dissolved, the paper the agreement had been written on worthless now that their expected benefactor was no longer capable of fulfilling its previous role. The Americans had provided the alliance convincing evidence that Iran had been behind the attacks on their holy mosques. This alone was enough to turn even the most strident Muslims away from Iran and their radical views. The Gulf states quickly began reconsidering the use of their territories to again host Western forces and the reestablishment of economic and military relations.

China's guarantee of Iranian basing rights and port access dissolved quickly. The Shengdau radar had failed to work as advertised. More important, given the quick fix the United States had made to the Raptors software, the long-term value of Epsilon was now seriously in question. It had not been linked back to China. The United States had been unable to trace the footprints of Iran's nuclear weapons development back to China as well. President Xi vociferously denied any collusion. Since China had now hit a roadblock in their desire to use software corruption and their breakthrough Shengdau radar technology to defeat stealth, it slowed any plan it had to expand their already large footprint in the South China Sea.

Saudi Arabia began to rebuild their cities after Iran's ground forces left the country. Repairing the destruction in Dhahran was the most difficult task, given the blast from the Iranian cargo vessel. The oil fields, shut down during the conflict while occupied by Iranian armed forces, had survived intact. They quickly ramped up production to record levels. The king vowed to reopen his country to limited US military presence, an effort to insulate their homeland from future attacks. In addition, contracts were signed with the United States to purchase the most advanced stealth fighter available on the open market—the F-35 Lightning II.

Sheikh Rahainee was arrested by the United States Federal Bureau of Investigation within weeks after the final battle in the skies of Iran. He had been quickly singled out following a rapid investigation into Khalil Ruffa's twisted path into the world of terrorism. Enough evidence had been assembled against the sheikh to award him first class passage to Guantanamo Bay, where he now resides in a small cell.

The Federal Bureau of Investigation took a hard look at the Omega Company. Fortunately for the CEO, there was no real evidence that the company had any idea about what Khalil Ruffa had been up to. The one insider who had collaborated with Khalil had left the company, and the country. While the United States government was pretty unhappy with Omega, other military programs being managed by the company were assured they would not be shut down—but they would be watched much more closely.

Captain Rebecca Casey survived her disastrous ordeal as a program manager. She was selected for Squadron Officers' School at Maxwell Air Force Base, Montgomery, Alabama, an assignment that would hopefully build the leadership skills that she sorely lacked. Upon graduating from the school, she was selected to a career-broadening assignment outside her primary career field. Even though she had been trained as an acquisition officer, she was being cross-trained into aircraft maintenance—a fitting place for her to learn more about what it took to manage the care and feeding of aircraft. The assignment would help her in future jobs within the Air Force.

In Azerbaijan, near the small town of Salyan, the wreckage of an Iranian military business jet had been cleaned up and the area around the impact zone now looked like nothing had happened. American intel sources obtained information from pro-Western Iranian operatives that revealed Khalil Ruffa had tried to flee the country. The world now believed that the one man who had nearly brought America's stealth program to its knees was dead, killed in the destruction of the escaping Iranian military executive jet. When Captain Matt "Ace" Black heard the news, he had mixed feelings. He didn't like the fact that he had killed a man with whom he had developed an initial friendly acquaintance.

But that same man was the reason for the death of one of his squadron pilots, and almost his own. While Khalil's body had not been found, there was a general consensus that no one could have survived that crash.

Ace arrived home at Langley following the intense battles over the Middle Eastern skies. He and his comrades-in-arms were greeted by cheering crowds on the Langley aircraft parking ramp. In spite of the long flight across the Atlantic Ocean, Matt had plenty of energy stored up. As he climbed down the boarding ladder from his Raptor's cockpit, he saw Julie standing thirty feet away, arms full with two squirming boys, and of course Claire holding on tightly to her mother's leg in the light breeze. When Claire recognized her daddy, she ran to him and jumped into his arms. Matt teared up as his daughter wrapped her arms around his neck. Julie and the boys were quickly reacquainted with their war hero. It was a very sweet reunion. Matt was also greeted with military orders directing his next move. He was headed to Air Command and Staff College at Maxwell AFB, Alabama. There he would spend a year away from the demands of the cockpit, refreshing and strengthening his knowledge of the profession of arms, leadership, joint operations, and the employment of airpower—the last subject one that he already had plenty of experience with. He already knew his follow-on assignment to another Raptor squadron.

Interestingly, within minutes of the Iranian jet's destruction, a goat herder had found a battered body and taken it to his ramshackle hut. He was surprised that anyone could be alive in the surrounding wreckage. Perhaps the person had been an innocent bystander on the ground, unlucky enough to have been in the wrong place at the wrong time when the flaming, disintegrating aircraft had hit the ground. Yet there was life in the shattered frame. The goat herder had detected shallow breathing from the man, who had multiple bone fractures, massive contusions, and had lost much blood. He didn't know if the man would live. He didn't know that the man was one of the most wanted terrorists in the world. But it was his duty as a devout Muslim to provide any assistance that he could. He would do his best, true to his Islamic faith, to try to save this life.

Acknowledgements

My sincere gratitude goes out to a cast of folks that helped transform an idea into a story of action and intrigue. This novel was a challenge that came together piece by piece, with some significant changes along the path to finishing the manuscript. I owe much of my success in completing it to the encouragement, technical support, and feedback from family and friends.

First, my initial encouragement came from my cousin, Dr. Alexander Belisle, Ph.D., Professor Emeritus of English and Philosophy. An author in his own right, he helped guide me through the many phases and aspects of constructing a good story. My golf buddy, Ernie Dorling, himself a published author, helped advise me on structure and on what it takes to get a novel published.

My personal thanks for the technical support I received in the military arena. A distinguished group helped keep my story grounded in some semblance of realism and accuracy. They are, Sam Angelella, Lieutenant General, USAF (retired), my brother, Ken Belisle, Vice Admiral, USNR (retired), Paul Bielowicz, Major General, USAF (retired), Richard Mather, Colonel, USAF (retired), Mark (Buzz) Masters, Colonel, USAF (retired), Steve Newbold, Colonel, USAF (retired), Brett Haswell, Colonel, USAF (retired), Barney Clary, Colonel, USAF (retired), my son, Matthew Belisle, Lieutenant Colonel, USMCR (retired), and Joe Aylsworth, Senior Master Sergeant, USAF (retired).

My technical help wading into the world of software coding, programming, hacking, and computer systems was supported by Pat Reilly, Vincent Simone, and my grandson, Ryan Birchfield. All of you helped open the door to the possibilities and potential threats that are facing the world in this rapidly evolving area.

My cover art concept was done by a terrific graphic artist, Matthew Wisniewski, who captured the essence of the Raptor Bloom story.

It was tough work editing and keeping my story on track. Thanks to Eliza Dee, Karen Dibbern, my daughter, Colene Birchfield, and my sister-in-law, Ginger Belisle. Your help was invaluable, and I owe you all my sincere thanks.

Finally, I owe much love to my wife, Cathy, who tolerated plenty of time by herself over the past couple of years. Writing a novel is hard work, and I isolated myself in my office for countless hours to get this story right. Any of my success certainly goes to her. Additionally, I'm sure my children didn't get their fair share of time with me during this period. I was often distracted with an intense focus to get this novel done. A special thanks goes to all of them—Matt, Colene and Kelly—whose patience and encouragement along the way was deeply appreciated.

THE END

Made in the USA
Middletown, DE
05 May 2020